Keepers of the Light

The Broken Prophecies Book One

SA McClure

What if your destiny is not your own and the prophecy about you has been broken?

Keepers of the Light

The Broken Prophecies Book One

By SA McClure

Copyrighted September 2016. All Rights Reserved.

Indianapolis, Indiana

ISBN: 978-0692767016

Edited by Andrew Young

Cover Art by Katelin Kinney

For my mother, who inspired my love of reading and curiosity in the world. Thank you.

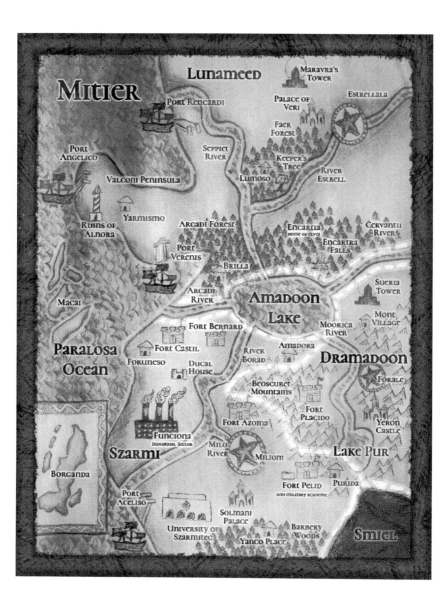

The First Prophecy

What do men know of the future or the past? We understand nothing. We know nothing. The world shifts like the waves of our oceans, ever changing, ever transforming. For eons, we have been the keepers of prophecy, the Keepers of the Light, or so we call ourselves. We have lived for ages, passing down the knowledge, the power, the Light. And still, the prophecy we hold dearest to us does not come true. We toil in our path to understand. But the Light does not bring answers.

And so we continue to wait.

Throughout the ages, the prophecies have been broken. The Wars of Darkness showed us that our prophecies were not what we believed them to be. The wars revealed to us that whosoever speaks of the prophecies outside of our Council, whatever the reason, destroys the Light's commands. So many of our brethren were lost in the battles. They were young and naïve. They perished in the name of our oldest prophecies. The only consolation is that they died before they could realize just how broken they were. Our brethren used the prophecies to inspire the courage of mortal men; they were the ones who sought to prove the validity of the Light and proclaim magic as the key. They believed that they would be redeemed through the fulfillment of the prophecies.

They were not.

And so our people perished.

We are all that remain. We, the Keepers of the Light, the custodians of the past, and the guardians of the future. We have sacrificed our lives in the hope that the First Prophecy—the one that few understand—will come true. We prepare for this day. We wait for this day. We know that this day will come.

***

There will come a day,

> *when the rivers have changed course and the land is laid barren,*
>
> *when the sun and the stars and the depths of the ocean become one,*
>
> *when the world has ended and a new begun.*

There will come a day,

> *when the Keepers of the Light unite as one to protect,*
>
> *and the realm is quieted by a single breath,*
>
> *when the Harbinger gives birth to new life.*

There will come a day,

> *when the Light has been extinguished from the world and Darkness invades,*
>
> *and the Harbinger's sacrifice ignites the flame of rebirth.*

There will come a day,

when suffering abounds and hope is lost.

There will come a day,

when the Harbinger will return to restore what has been lost,

when what has been broken is made whole,

and the Light will begin anew.

There will come a day.

Chapter One

The Battle of Alnora, the Third Darkness

Blood dripped from Kilian's double-headed war axe as he swung it through the man's head the way a butcher slides a cleaver through a slab of meat. Sweat made his once-pristine linen shirt cling to his muscular body as he twisted around to slice in half a man who was charging him from behind. The man's top half slid off of his legs in one smooth motion. The roar of clanging swords against shields and horses' hooves crunching men's skulls was deafening. As the soldier's body sunk to the blood-sodden ground, Kilian took the moment of reprieve to search the mass of bodies around him. He was relieved when he didn't see hers. Grunting, he hoisted his axe up once more and charged into a throng of men standing a few paces in front of him.

The shock of his attack barely registered on their faces as he cut through the first soldier. An arrow grazed his cheek as he turned to slam his axe down on the head of another soldier standing behind him. His jaw clenching, Kilian jerked his head up and glanced around again the beach where the battle was taking place. Blood trailed down his neck from where the arrow had nicked his flesh, but he didn't feel the pain. The salty sea air mixed with the coppery scent of blood and a hint of decay as more bodies covered the sandy beach.

A ball of fire came flying at him from his left side, missing him by scant inches. It was close enough for him to feel its heat. Turning, Kilian saw a group of hooded figures standing together in a circle, flanked by a few armed guards. He couldn't see their faces, but he knew their lips would be moving in recitation of ancient incantations. The ones she had taught them. The ones they were going to use to kill him. Gripping his axe firmly in his hand, Kilian slammed it into his iron breastplate several times, taunting them. What the initiates didn't know was that he couldn't be killed. She had seen to that. Still, that didn't stop their bodyguards from loosing their arrows at him.

Letting a cry escape his lips, he ran towards the group. Kilian wondered, not for the first time, why he had been chosen above all others to fight the Light Council's battles for them. His wondering was purely rhetorical; he knew why, of course. She had desired him, and he had succumbed. It was his blessing and his curse.

Arrows buried themselves deep into Kilian's breastplate and through the leather jerkin he wore for protection. Ignoring them, Kilian lifted his axe high above his head. His muscles strained as he cut through the bodyguard closest to him and then slammed the handle of his axe into another's head with a sickening crunch. Only one bodyguard remained.

The remaining guard swung his sword at Kilian so quickly that Kilian barely had enough time to evade the attack. Indeed, the blade cut through the fringe of his jerkin, causing the leather to fall to the ground.

"Oh, you'll pay for that one, my good fellow," Kilian said as he winked at the bodyguard.

In response, the man swung at him again. This time, Kilian used his axe to parry the assault. Leaping forward, Kilian expertly pulled a long, thin knife from his belt and jammed it into the guard's throat. Warm blood spurted onto his face as Kilian wrenched his blade free. The man fell to ground in front of the initiates.

They did not shy away from Kilian as he snarled at them and raised his axe to attack. Instead, they turned their faces towards him in one collective motion. A dark mist emanated from their bodies and swirled around them. As Kilian stood motionless before them, the mist slowly encased him within its folds. Gooseflesh covered his arms as the temperature dropped and the sun was blotted from the sky. The initiates were chanting before him; their voices sounded like the hiss of water as it is dripped upon a hot surface. Their eyes glowed green in the darkness that surrounded them. Kilian paused. This was not something he had ever seen her teach them.

Suddenly, all six of the figures raised their hands in unison. Each of their young, slender hands shriveled and turned to an ashen grey as they stood shoulder to shoulder, creating a wall of black robes and glowing green eyes. Lightning crackled in the sky. Kilian didn't break eye contact with the initiates. Their eyes narrowed on him as he raised his axe.

Too late.

Bright light filled the darkened air around them. What felt like a burning fist slammed into Kilian's chest, melting the iron breastplate and burning through the jerkin protecting him. He smelled singed hair as his body shot through the air from the force of the blast. His grip on his axe slipped as he was thrown high into the air. He had a momentary sensation of weightlessness, and then he heard his bones crack as he fell into a heap upon the packed sand. The flesh on his chest was seared; he could smell his own skin melting as he landed heavily on the ground outside the walls of Alnora. Kilian lay crumpled in the sand for several moments as he felt his skin stretch and tighten against his destroyed chest. The healing process only took a few moments, but it felt like thousands of ants crawling across his skin without him being able to wipe them away. He knew he didn't have time to wait for the healing process to complete itself. The council needed him. She needed him.

He tried lifting his arm, but the muscles around his bones hadn't mended yet. Ocean water lapped against his body, soaking his cotton breeches and undershirt. His open wounds stung as the water seeped into them. He heard his bones snap as they pushed back into place. Kilian wasn't sure how much time had passed since he'd been struck by the initiates, but he knew he couldn't wait any longer.

Gritting his teeth, Kilian pushed himself up from the ground. He stumbled a bit as he took his first step, but was able to keep himself upright. *Today will not be my last,* he told himself as he pulled his long sword out of its sheath, but today would be the last of the battles against the Szarmian and Smielian soldiers.

Arrows rained down upon him as he clambered towards the tower's walls. Several of the arrows exploded as they hit the ground. Smoke billowed up from the broken tips and suffocated him as he continued pushing forward. Bodies, laden with arrows or burned to the point of being unrecognizable, covered the ground. In some places they were piled so high that one would have to climb over them in order to get past. Kilian gagged each time he used the walls of bodies as a shield as he made his way towards the breach in the wall.

The breach made Kilian grimace as he stared at it. The wall had been breached during the night; one minute, he'd been sleeping, the next minute, he'd felt the earth quake and the sky was alight with a bright white glow. The Szarmians had dug a trench beneath the wall and then used liquid fire to rip a hole into the wall that was wide enough for their soldiers to march into the tower's courtyard five at a time. They had been fighting ever since.

Now, as he stared at the breach in the wall that was mostly filled with the dead bodies of his men and the Szarmian swine, he wanted nothing more than to kill every last one of the Szarmians who had dared to join forces with the traitorous initiates. He wanted nothing more than to cut down the initiates and watch their pain and their fear as they took their last breaths.

Taking a deep breath, Kilian plunged into the mound of dead bodies blocking the breach. Arrows plummeted into his body from above, but he ignored the pain. The scent of excrement and death filled his nostrils as he began climbing over the dead bodies towards the breach.

Reaching the top, Kilian slid down the mound of bodies and landed feet first inside the tower's courtyard. Kilian looked around the war zone. The initiates had disappeared from the courtyard. Kilian's stomach tightened as he realized where they were: the tower. Lunameedian soldiers fought alongside magical beings as they grappled with the iron-clad soldiers from the south. His men were fighting a losing battle. Looking towards the tower, Kilian saw a group of Szarmian soldiers racing towards it. He heard their cries as they slammed into the tower's last ring of defense. His heart pounded in his chest. She was in the tower. He couldn't let them reach her. Without assessing the battlefield before him, Kilian rushed into the fray.

A pike rammed through his shoulder from behind and Kilian felt himself being lifted from the ground. He squirmed, trying to free himself, but couldn't get the muscles of his shoulder and chest to slide off of the scalloped metal. He growled in pain and anger as he was once again sent airborne.

The ground shook when he hit the earth a few feet away. Not from his weight but from a force coming from the tower. The binding had begun, and he was helpless to stop it.

Panting, Kilian tried to sit up, but a boot slammed into his face and then his wounded shoulder.

"Kilian Clearwater, the greatest warrior Mitier has ever seen," a voice said softly by his ear. "They say you cannot die. Is that true?"

Kilian's eyes watered as the boot pressed into his wound, stopping the healing. By focusing on his breathing, Kilian was able to stop himself from passing out from the pain.

"No answer? I'll take that as a no then. There must be some way to destroy you," the man's voice was deep and smooth. It carried the lilt of the eastern territory of Lunameed. Kilian had the strange sensation that he knew that voice, but he couldn't quite grasp from where. He tried to see the man's face, but his long, dark, hooded robe shrouded his face in darkness.

Sweat trickled down Kilian's forehead as he watched the man pull out a long, thin blade from inside his jacket. Kilian squirmed but was unable to move.

"Let's see just how much of this you can take," the man said as he dangled the dagger in front of Kilian's face.

He slid the blade between the skin and the muscle of Kilian's forearm. At first, Kilian felt nothing as the sharp blade pierced his skin. Then, as the air hit his exposed muscle, the pain felt like a year's worth of wounds happening at once. Kilian couldn't control the scream that came from deep inside him. He barely recognized the howl that bellowed out; he sounded so much like a wounded animal.

"Tsk, tsk, Kilian. I expected more from you," the man sneered.

He cut Kilian again.

"Aren't you supposed to be stronger than this? Braver than this? Come now, where has your strength gone?"

The man cut off a piece of Kilian's skin for a third time and again he screamed. He tried thinking about her. Tried remembering the promise he'd made to her when she'd bestowed upon him the gift of life. Despite his strength, he could still feel pain.

"You think you can save them, Kilian? The binding has already begun."

"No!" Kilian shouted. "No," he said more softly. Tears leaked from his eyes and ran down his cheeks. He could feel their wetness mingling with his blood-soaked shirt. He knew the man was right. He knew there was nothing he could do.

The man in a black robe just laughed.

Chapter Two

*The city of Estrellala in the kingdom of Lunameed,
three hundred years later*

"You cannot be serious!" Amaleah shouted as she
bolted from her father's private quarters. The royal
councilors tried following her through the hidden passages,
but she baffled them when she took a passageway that she
had only just discovered the day before. Closing the
painting door behind her, Amaleah sprinted down a dusty
and spider-infested stairwell before reaching her
destination: an underground cavern. She guessed the
kitchen and banquet hall were both above the cavern
because she could hear servants' feet sliding over the
stones of the banquet hall floor and feel the heat from the
cast iron ovens that stretched against the back wall of the
kitchens. A small ring of stone and sand circled around a
pool of deep water that smelled of fish and something close
to cinnamon. Amaleah still hadn't decided what was
causing that smell to linger within the cave; it seemed so
out of place.

Although the cavern was so dark that Amaleah
couldn't see more than a hand's length into its depths, she
felt safe. Flinging herself into the cushions she'd placed in
the cave the night before, Amaleah lit the lantern she'd
hidden next to the cushions. Instantly, the cavern came
alight with a soft, warm glow. Then, and only then, did she
let the tears pour down her face as she tried to come up
with a plan of escape.

What am I doing? she thought. Breathing deeply and wiping away the tears, she reexamined her father's proposal. She was seventeen now. She could be married off to anyone, at any time, for any reason—so long as it benefited her kingdom. Many of the knights and nobles of Lunameed had courted her since her return to the capital, but Amaleah had been uninterested in all of them. She wanted more. She wanted to experience the world, to see where she could take herself before settling for someone. She'd been a prisoner within her own kingdom for the past five years, and now she wanted to be free.

She remembered the day her father had exiled her from Estrellala. Rain had pattered on the stone and metal roof covering the loading area for the carriage that was to transport her to Maravra's Tower. It had sounded like millions of tiny rocks falling on her head. The sky was the greyish-purple color that storms turn before they erupt into a torrent of fury. Although it had been the middle of summer, Amaleah's skin had prickled with a chill she couldn't control. Tears had streamed down her face when her father had turned away from her without saying goodbye.

Now she had returned.

During her time at Maravra's Tower, the only people she'd interacted with had been her nursemaid and her tutor. Both of them were old, greying, highly unamusing—if not outright boring—and wise. Every day Amaleah had woken up to some new phrase or proverb such as, "The early bird gets the worm," or "Magic here, magic there, the only magic anyway," or better still, "Work, and you receive your reward." Her tutor had spent hours searching for new sayings that he could present to her in the mornings when she woke. He said it was part of her common sense training, since this was the one necessary attribute many of the kings and queens of Lunameed had been lacking for the past three hundred years.

Unfortunately, despite all of her tutor's planning, she still felt unprepared for the proposition her father had presented to her. She hadn't made any friends during her month back at court. Her tutor hadn't been allowed to return to Estrellala with her, and she couldn't trust her nursemaid to protect her. She was alone.

He wanted to marry her. Him… her father. The thought made her skin crawl. To think that her father wanted her, his daughter, over all the other women who had tried to capture his attention made her stomach twist into knots. Of course, even at twelve years of age she had begun to suspect that her father's mind had started to slip. He had demanded that she be sent away to one of the houses far enough away from Estrellala that he needn't look upon her every day, yet close enough so that she could be returned to court within a matter of days. She had thought, when he'd finally called her home a month ago, that this madness had finally left him. She had been wrong.

Water splashed behind her, sending sprinkles cascading down upon her face. Startled from her unhappy memories, Amaleah jerked up from the pillows. Black water soaked through the train of her gown. Gripping the smooth satin within her hands, Amaleah deftly pulled the train away from the water's edge. Slowly, she lifted her head to peer around the cavern.

Everything seemed to be the way she remembered it—dark, dank, and a little scary. As she continued scanning the room, she noticed a greenish-silver light flickering on the stone wall at the furthest point of the cavern. Narrowing her eyes, Amaleah tried to see what was causing the light. It was faint—as faint as the highest star in the sky. Amaleah moved closer to the water's edge. Damp ground squished beneath her feet as she inched closer. The cinnamon scent grew stronger the closer she got to the pool of water. Without realizing what she was doing, Amaleah leaned her body out over the water's edge. Suddenly, the light winked out.

Amaleah didn't have time to move away from the water before she was once again splashed by the cold, fish-smelling water. She fell back on her rump in surprise as a fin slapped the water with a loud smack just a few feet in front of her. She scooted back from the pool and pulled her legs in tight to her chest. Her heart beating quickly, she pressed her back against the damp wall of the cavern. The lantern's light flickered; Amaleah could smell the tendrils of smoke puffing out from the lantern's fire as it struggled to stay alight. The hard, icy stone of the cavern wall pressed uncomfortably into her back, but Amaleah couldn't force herself to move.

"Amaleah," a voice echoed, musical and lofty. It was impossible to tell which part of the pool the sound had originated from. Amaleah squeezed her eyes shut and tried to let her mind go blank as she waited for the voice to speak again. The silence of the cavern felt heavy, as if it were trying to suffocate her. A soft cry escaped her lips as she tried to think of a way to escape. It reverberated around the cavern, transforming into the faintest of whispers.

She waited and she listened, but still the voice didn't speak again. Creeping along the wall, Amaleah inched her way towards the stairwell. Sweat dripped down her back as she moved as quietly and as slowly as she could. She didn't understand how a place that had felt so comfortable, so safe, could turn into one of the most horrifying places she'd ever been.

Her foot slipped on the wet stone and loose rock of the cavern floor sending tiny pebbles of stone cascading into the water. *Plop. Plop. Plop.* Amaleah instantly stopped moving. Her heart beat so loudly in her chest that she was sure whoever—or whatever—was in the water would be able to hear it.

Amaleah tried to remember what her tutor had said about the magical creatures who lived in the many rivers and lakes covering Lunameed. His crackling voice filled her mind, "You must be careful how close you get to the water's edge, Princess. Sea dragons, the merfolk, and the vodyanoy all reside within the water's depths. The vodyanoy are the worst, My Lady. They are big, rotund creatures who look like giant frogs. They lie in wait for beautiful young maidens to come close to the water's edge and then they steal them away to their underwater kingdoms. None survive the journey."

Why didn't I listen to him? Cursing beneath her breath, Amaleah stood up and peered into the darkness of the cavern. The lantern's light cast shadows on the water's surface, but it was enough for her to see the ripples of something moving below.

"Amaleah, come to the water's edge." The voice was so clear, so compelling, that Amaleah could hardly resist the temptation to search for the creature calling her name.

"Amaleah, do not be afraid, for I am of you and you of me. I will not harm you." The voice was musical and Amaleah could feel her body relaxing. Her mind raced with thoughts that seemed to go nowhere. Each anxious idea about what was to come next dissipated as soon as it had arisen. The voice kept calling to her, and with every note, Amaleah felt her fears slip away from her.

Taking a delicate step towards the water's edge, Amaleah tried to see who was talking in such a beautiful voice. Still, all she saw were the ripples. The voice called her name one last time and Amaleah felt the last of her reservations melt away. She walked confidently towards the water's edge and knelt upon the cold, wet rock. Now that the lantern cast its light directly onto the water, Amaleah realized that she could see dark shadows constantly moving beneath its surface. Memories of fear floated through her mind, but were replaced with the beauty of the darkness. The water was so beautiful. It called to her. The creature called to her. The water no longer smelled fishy, but was filled with the sweet and slightly spicy scent of cinnamon. Instinctively, Amaleah reached out with one finger towards the water's surface.

A silver and blue fin shot out of the water and fanned itself out in front of her face. The shock of the water droplets cascading upon her face broke the spell of the water. Amaleah once again shoved herself away from the water's edge—from the tail—and took several steps backwards. Her feet hit the bottom step of the stairs and she began to lift her foot to start the climb when she heard the voice speak to her once more.

"Amaleah," the voice whispered. "I will not harm you. Please, do not be afraid." The voice was certainly lyrical, yet there was a note of timidity in it that sparked Amaleah's curiosity. The longer the voice spoke, the more her fears dissipated. She set her foot back down on the cavern floor.

"Who are you?" she asked in a trembling voice.

"I am of you just as you are of me, just as all creatures of the Light are of each other, connected."

Amaleah tried to remember all of the lessons her tutor had given her on the magical creatures of the realm. Not once had he mentioned 'creatures of the light.' She was certain that if she were one of them that she would know, wouldn't she?

"What do you mean that all the creatures of the Light are connected?" Amaleah shook slightly as she waited for the creature to respond. She added, "You're not a vodyanoy are you?"

Still, the creature did not respond to her questions. The prickling of fear crept into her as she continued to wait for the creature to speak to her. Her mind began to race and Amaleah felt her entire body shiver with a rising heat.

Finally, Amaleah spoke again, just to break the silence, "I'm a human. A princess, if you must know. *The* princess. I'm not some creature. I'm not like you. I don't even possess magic. None of the Lunameedian rulers do. Not since the Wars of Darkness concluded and we formed the Peace Accordance with Szarmi."

Amaleah had begun rambling now, but she couldn't seem to make herself stop. "Listen, if you're here to steal me away to your magical, underwater kingdom, save yourself the trouble and just don't. I promise I don't taste good anyway."

She tried to lift her foot again—to climb the stairs— but, her foot seemed to be rooted to the cavern floor. Her muscles strained as she continued to try lifting her legs. She sent up a soft cry of frustration as once again her foot remained cemented to the floor.

"Why are you so afraid, Amaleah?" The voice was soft and held a tremor of remorse to it, but it did not sound unkind. This time, as the voice spoke, Amaleah did not feel the comfort she had previously experienced. *What kind of magic does this creature possess?*

"Afraid? I'm not afraid." Her words sounded unsteady, even to her own ears. She laughed nervously as she continued, "I just want to go upstairs is all."

The fin slapped the water and Amaleah felt a wave of agitation hit her. Biting her lip until she could taste the coppery liquid of her blood, Amaleah tried to still the emotions roiling inside of her, but was unable to do so.

"Amaleah, if you are not afraid, then I am no longer capable of reading human emotions."

Ignoring the creature's comment, Amaleah asked, "What are you doing to me?" Her voice pitched at the end of the question into a high shrill. As she spoke, Amaleah felt an icy chill pass through her. She wrapped her arms tight around her chest and gripped her elbows with her hands.

She heard movement within the water followed by a deep sigh, "I am sorry, Princess. My power is stronger here than I am accustomed to."

"What do you mean?"

The creature did not answer Amaleah's question, instead it responded with, "I have been watching over you for many days now. I have seen the troubles you have faced in your father's court since your return to Estrellala. I have felt the internal struggle you feel to be yourself when you do not yet know yourself."

The voice paused and Amaleah felt something tug on her emotions as she waited for the voice to continue in silence. It was just a gentle tug, but it felt so unnatural that Amaleah let out a little yelp of surprise. As soon as the sound escaped her lips, she felt the tug loosen its hold and disappear.

"There!" the voice exclaimed, "You see? You can feel me playing with your emotions. This should be enough evidence for you to know that I feel what you feel."

The chill left her and a sense of warmth flooded through her body, starting at her toes and rising up until her entire body felt warm. "I'm sorry, I just-"

"Listen to me, Princess Amaleah Bluefischer," the voice said, cutting her off, "you are so much more important to this world, to the Light, than anyone could ever imagine. The reason you can sense..."

"I think you-" Amaleah started to say as she cut the voice off.

"Perhaps it was foolish of me," the voice muttered, "Perhaps I was not meant to speak to you today. And yet, I cannot help but feel that I must." Water splashed at the edge of the pool. "Amaleah, please tell me so that I can hear from your own lips, why were you weeping?"

Thoughts tumbled through Amaleah's mind the way her father's jester tumbled on the hard marble floor of the throne room. She wasn't exactly sure where she would land, but she hoped it would be a place that she could hold her ground.

Finally, she said, "I will answer your question, but first you must answer one of mine."

"I will answer what I can, My Princess."

Amaleah lips quirked at the creature's response. She remembered what her tutor had told her about magical creatures playing tricks on humans and using plays on words to control them. Even if the voice didn't belong to a vodyanoy, there was still a chance it would try to harm her.

"You mentioned that you had been watching me for several days." Amaleah paused before continuing, "I want to know why. Why have you been watching me?"

"That is an easy question to answer, dear one. I was sent here to protect you."

Amaleah rocked on her toes as she waited for the creature to continue. When it didn't, Amaleah asked, "By whom? And from what?"

When the voice didn't respond to her additional questions, Amaleah nearly shouted, "Please tell me. I promise-"

"There will be time enough for me to answer this line of questioning in the future, My Lady. For now, I must hear why you shed so many tears earlier. It is of the utmost importance that I know what is troubling you."

Amaleah stared at the water, her face warped into an angry scowl, "My father, the king, as I am sure you know if you've been watching me, once married the most beautiful woman he had ever seen. It is said that her hair was the color of the deepest chocolate mixed with hues of raspberry. Many say that it was her hair that the king could not resist on the day of their meeting. He had saved her from some terrible plight. I'm not sure what plight... just a plight. But my father became obsessed with her from their very first meeting." Amaleah paused, letting her words sink in. "They were in love. At least, I think they were; they must have been." She paused again, searching for the words she needed to finish her tale.

"They waited for a child for many years and had many losses. Until, finally, my mother became heavy with child. With me. It was a difficult birth. I was difficult. And I ripped my mother's life away from her just as I had been ripped away from her womb. In her dying breaths, she made my father promise to only marry someone as beautiful as she was. To only marry one with the same color hair." Amaleah sat back against one of the cushions. The story of her birth was not one she had to tell often. "As the years passed, my father searched the entire kingdom to find a suitable new bride. He wanted me to have a mother. But as each new maiden arrived to our palace, my father was only met with disappointment. His advisors warned that if he didn't choose a new bride soon and conceive a male heir that the kingdom's succession would be in peril."

Amaleah laughed at that, a cold, dull laugh. She wanted to inherit the throne when her father passed. She wanted to leave her kingdom better than it was now. Shaking her head in the darkening cavern, she continued, "One day, as my father and I were walking in my mother's garden, as we often did, he told me how much I reminded him of my mother. At first, it made me happy to think that I could resemble someone who had been so admired that she was sought after, even in death. But then he told me he needed to send me away so as to fight the demons that haunted him."

Tears fell, unbidden, from Amaleah's eyes. She did not wipe them away but let them slide down her cheeks and fall to the ground beneath her feet.

"I have been gone for five years. I was not allowed back at court. I was not allowed to have interactions with anyone except for my tutor, my nurse, and small number of servants and guards stationed at Maravra's Tower." Amaleah hadn't realized how angry she was about her situation until she began recounting it. "Now that I am fully grown, my father... well... my father's mind is not what it used to be. A madness has taken him. And... against the laws of our land, he wishes to marry me, his own daughter." Her voice fell as she whispered the last of her words. Bowing her head, she let the tears soak into her dress.

"I am afraid he cannot be reasoned with." Amaleah said this last line almost as an afterthought, but as she said it, she realized that she knew it was true.

She let her voice fade into the darkness. The lamp's light had dimmed significantly while she had been talking and now was nothing more than a whisper of light. Not for the first time, Amaleah wished that she had the ability to create fire from the darkness. As she waited in silence, she began to wonder if the voice, the creature, in the water had disappeared. *Was it even here at all?*

Suddenly, she saw the shadow of the tail rise above the water's edge and smack its once peaceful surface. Water sprayed Amaleah in the face.

"Amaleah, my sister, you must not allow this to happen." The voice was urgent now, with little of the alluring music in it that had originally compelled Amaleah to come closer to the water's edge.

"I know, but there is no one who can help me. No one who can save me from my fate. Remember, I have been alone for these past five years. Even my closest confidants are spies for my father."

"I hear the fear in your voice, My Princess, but fear not. This is not your fate, for I have heard of what shall come to pass. Listen to me. I will help you, but you must be willing to do what I tell you to do."

Amaleah felt the hair on her arms rise as the voice spoke. *What does this creature want me to do? Has it really seen the future?* It didn't matter.

"I'll do anything," Amaleah spoke firmly. No quaver entered her voice as she continued, "I will do anything to escape marrying my father and to save my kingdom from ruin."

"What I most desire," the voice said clearly, "is for you to come to the water's edge before you leave, so that I might look upon your face."

Such a strange request. Everything within Amaleah warned her of danger. All of her training, all of the stories her tutor had told her left a residual fear forming a pit in her stomach.

"Why?"

The sound of water splashing caused gooseflesh to pebble on her arms.

Suddenly, the voice rang through the darkness, "My dearest Amaleah, there are things that cannot be explained here. There are too many ears and eyes within these hallowed walls, perhaps, even here in this cavern. All I can tell you is that I will not cause you harm." The voice took on a musical quality again, and Amaleah felt its presence pressing upon her mind once more. She was ready for the creature's intrusion this time and forced the sensation out.

She weighed her options. *Should I trust a voice in the dark or trust my training to be wary of the magical world, even though I was born to rule it?* Taking a deep breath, Amaleah forced herself to focus on the sound of her heartbeat. Closing her eyes, she let the sounds of the cavern flow over her—through her. She heard the thumping of her heart. She heard the rippling sounds of water as the creature shifted beneath its surface. She heard the sound of muffled feet on the floor above the cavern. Her heartbeat was in rhythm with it all. She was a part of this place, her kingdom, the land of Lunameed. She took a deep breath.

Her instincts told her that there was no danger for her here. Whoever—whatever—this creature was, it had to be better than her father. Opening her eyes, Amaleah made her choice.

She crept warily to the water's edge. Tiny ripples disturbed the dark surface. Once more, she knelt beside the surface and dipped her fingers into the pool. The water was icy cold and smelled so strongly of cinnamon that she was sure it was burning the hair in her nose. Wiggling her fingers, Amaleah waited for the creature to react to her demonstration of trust.

"You can show yourself to me. I'm not afraid of you anymore," she said.

"Are you sure, my dearest?"

"Yes."

A head popped up from beneath the depths of the water. Amaleah didn't understand how anyone could be afraid of such a face. Her skin was a mixture of the blue-black of the water and the white of freshly fallen snow. Water slid over the woman's skin, glistening in the faint light of the lamp. Her skin cast rainbows along the water's surface and Amaleah gasped. Although damp, her hair fell in long, silver-blue curls. Amaleah forced herself to stop looking at the woman's skin and stared straight into the woman's eyes. They seemed to swim, like the waves of the ocean.

A mermaid.

Stunned, Amaleah exclaimed, "You're... gorgeous! How- why did you not show me your face before?"

Turning her back on Amaleah, the mermaid asked, "Do you promise not to scream?"

"Why would I ever scream?"

Amaleah had read about mermaids in the deepest recesses of her father's library many years ago, before her exile. They were described as being dangerous when they felt threatened, but typically harmless. A memory of herself tugging at her tutor's robe came to Amaleah's mind. She had maybe been six or seven years of age and had just discovered a story about the merfolk. Her tutor had explained that they had been extinct since the end of the Wars of Darkness. When Amaleah had heard this news she'd cried for over an hour. She had always wanted to meet a mermaid.

"Do you promise, Amaleah?"

"Yes, I promise," she nearly screamed in anticipation.

The mermaid slowly turned to face her again. Her ice blue lips curled into a smile, revealing a row of sharp, pointed teeth, with jagged edges for ripping and tearing flesh. For killing.

Amaleah gasped as she watched the mermaid's jaw snap. She ripped her hand out of the water and clutched it to her chest, but she didn't move away from the water's edge. She didn't feel afraid. Closing her eyes, Amaleah tried to determine if the mermaid was once again controlling her emotions, but she felt as if she were in total control.

None of the texts she'd found about the merfolk had mentioned their massive maw and rows of teeth.

She shivered but then forced herself to say, "It's n-not so b-bad." Her words came out in a stutter.

"You are braver than I thought, my dearest."

Amaleah nodded in acknowledgement of the mermaid's words. She was brave. Or, at least, she tried to be. Questions swam through Amaleah's mind. *Why is she here? How did she come to be so far inland?* The words came tumbling out of a Amaleah's mouth rapidly, "What should I call you? Where have you been hiding? I thought all mermaids had been killed during the Third Darkness."

The mermaid remained silent for several heartbeats. She dipped her lips beneath the pool and peered up at

Amaleah. The cinnamon scent had subsided slightly. Now, the fishy scent of the water permeated the air once more. Amaleah reached her hand out and gently touched the mermaid's cheek. It was scaly and surprisingly dry. Amaleah pulled her hand back in surprise.

Without responding to Amaleah's touch, the mermaid said, "No one has asked me that question in over a hundred years." Her voice was low and sounded as if she were trying to hold back tears. "You may call me Cordelia."

"Cordelia." Amaleah let name roll over her tongue as she memorized it. They sat in silence for several moments.

"Now, I promised that I would help you escape your father."

"Yes." Anticipation filled Amaleah. *Perhaps there is a way to escape.*

"You must give him a challenge," Cordelia said matter-of-factly, "something that he would never be able to do in a lifetime, something so hard that it is inconceivable."

Amaleah stood in silence. *What in the Light is Cordelia talking about?* She had absolutely no idea what kind of a challenge she could issue to her father that would stop him from achieving his goal of marrying her. She didn't even know how she would be able to convince him to attempt such a challenge.

"I don't know what to ask him to do. Do you have any suggestions?"

Cordelia's eyes rolled back into her head until her eye sockets were filled with the black of her eyes. The scent of sulfur filled the room, erasing all traces of fish and cinnamon from the air. Amaleah once again felt cold. Only this time, the chill did not seem to be emanating from her own body. She watched as the water surrounding Cordelia began to crystalize. The mermaid's breath came out in visible puffs as she breathed hard. The little remaining lamp light flickered with the icy breeze that seemed to come from nowhere.

Amaleah took a step back but then stopped when she heard Cordelia speaking softly into the dark cavern air. Her voice came out raspy and low. Each word was stilted, as if it were coming from a place beyond the cavern. They echoed through the stone corridors leading away from Amaleah and Cordelia.

"To defeat the king's desire. There will be three. Three dresses. One of the stars, one of the sun, and one of the ocean's depths. And a coat of a thousand furs. An escape. A destiny."

Cordelia's eyes unrolled from the back of her skull and returned to their normal silver-blue color. Her body shook rapidly as the ice around her melted away and her breath returned to normal. Her skin looked paler than it had before, but it was difficult to tell in the dim light.

Amaleah's fingers twitched. *Is this what a prophecy looks and sounds like? A destiny?* She leaned over the water's edge and cupped the mermaid's cheek in her hand. Cordelia leaned into her hand as if Amaleah's warmth were the only thing keeping the mermaid afloat.

"What was that?" Amaleah asked.

Cordelia ducked her head under the water for a moment and then popped back up just out of arm's reach of Amaleah. Her sharp teeth glimmered in the soft lamp light, casting shadows around her.

"The merfolk were blessed by the Creators with the gift of foresight."

Creators? Amaleah tried to remember a time when her tutor had discussed a group of magical beings called the creators.

Cordelia continued, almost as if reading Amaleah's thoughts, "You would know them as the Ancient Ones. They were the first of the magical beings to inhabit Mitier. Some say they existed before men. Some say they created everything and everyone who lives."

Her voice trailed off and Amaleah hugged herself tightly. The Ancient Ones had disappeared during the Third Darkness. None knew where they had gone. Since then, the magical folk of Mitier had been diminishing. Despite the fact that Lunameed was the clear victor of the wars, her ancestors had been unable to stop the weakening of magic in the world.

"I've heard the rumors. It all seems so fantastical to me. I mean, how could they have granted anyone magical abilities? Only the Light can do that."

Cordelia laughed like a tinkling bell.

"Oh, my poor, sweet child. Whatever did your tutors teach you of the magical world?"

Amaleah scowled, "Quite a bit, actually."

Cordelia regarded her with a look of pity that Amaleah did not appreciate.

"I mean, I've read all the books and I've learned the histories…"

"Yes, and who wrote those histories? Do not take your formal training and education as the ultimate truth. The winners oftentimes distort the facts to align more closely with their interpretation of the world. Be careful how much of your histories you take at face value."

Amaleah opened her mouth to argue and then closed it abruptly. Fighting with Cordelia about their interpretations of history would do nothing to aid Amaleah in her pursuit of a solution to her problem. When she opened her mouth again, she asked, "This… challenge you spoke of. Do you think this will work?"

Cordelia stared Amaleah straight in the eyes and whispered, "Yes, my dearest Amaleah, I believe it will work."

Amaleah let the mermaid's words sink in. She tried memorizing the cadence of the mermaid's speech. She needed to convince her father that she needed three dresses and a coat made of a thousand furs. *Will this really stop him from marrying me?* Somehow Amaleah doubted it. She peered at the mermaid. She still didn't know who had sent her, why she had been watching Amaleah, or if she could honestly trust her.

Understanding motives is the life bread of being a strong leader. Her tutor's voice rang in her head. Doubt seeped into her bones. She did not understand what motivated Cordelia into aiding her in her escape from her father.

"Why are you helping me?"

Her voice shook as she spoke and she could hear the sharpness each word took on. She couldn't believe how quickly she had leapt at the chance to believe someone she had only just met. She was more desperate than she thought.

Cordelia sighed, "Because of who your mother was. Because of who you are. Because of who you will be."

"That's not really an answer, just another riddle!" Amaleah shouted. Her voice reverberated around the cavern. She hoped those above her in the kitchens couldn't hear what was below them. "How do you know who I will be? Did you know my mother? Tell me what you know."

The mermaid sighed heavily. "That I cannot say. It is not your time to know. But know this, my dearest Amaleah, you serve a purpose much greater than even you or I can conceive." Her voice was soft and melodic. Amaleah felt the tendrils of magic seeping into her body. She took a step back.

"All I know is that you must escape this place with the dresses and cloak," Cordelia continued, "You must not succumb to your father. You must find your way to the place where it all began. You must break the bonds of binding. You must promise me this."

Bonds of binding? Amaleah's thoughts raced through her head. She had so many questions.

"But if he makes the gowns and the coat, then I shall be bound to marry him. I have never broken a covenant before. You don't know my father the way I do. If he achieves his goal, he will force me to sign away my life to him. He will stop at nothing to ensure that he gets what he wants."

"No, my beloved, you will not become trapped by him. I have seen much and know much. You must have faith in the things you do not understand and cannot see. You must trust what I have said, what I have foreseen."

Amaleah chewed on her lower lip. Her father was a powerful man who would stop at nothing to ensure that he got what he wanted. She shuddered as thoughts of what that would entail poured into her mind.

"And if I cannot escape?" she asked, her voice thick.

Cordelia pushed herself to the edge of the pool and lifted herself out of the water. Her chest and abdomen were completely nude and Amaleah blushed as the mermaid's breasts became visible in the dim light. She stared at the place where Cordelia's human torso met the scaly fish tail. The cavern was now too dark to tell, but she thought Cordelia's fin was jet black.

"I shall bless you," Cordelia said, ignoring Amaleah's reaction to her body.

"What good is a blessing?" Amaleah scoffed.

"Have you never been taught the benefits of a mermaid's blessing?" Cordelia pulled herself further onto the rocky ledge of the cavern floor. Her tail was long and slender. "A mermaid's blessing contains the power to protect those it has been bestowed upon. It will help you when the time comes."

"How will I know when the time has come? How will I know when to escape or when to stay? How will-"

"You will know."

Amaleah closed her eyes and tried to stop the tears of frustration from leaking from her eyes. She had cried enough for one night.

Cordelia wiggled her fingers at Amaleah as if to say, 'come closer.' With only a moment's hesitation, Amaleah stepped forward.

"Kneel before me," Cordelia commanded.

Amaleah did as she was told. She felt Cordelia lay her cold, strangely slimy hand upon the crown of her head. Her hands felt so much different than the rest of the mermaid's body that Amaleah gasped at Cordelia's touch. Sparkling water streamed down Amaleah's face as Cordelia brushed her hair from her face.

Cordelia leaned in and pressed her cold lips to Amaleah's forehead. Her breath smelled of seaweed, brine, and fish. Amaleah's blood turned cold as the mermaid's lips pressed against her skin, felt her veins close in upon the freezing liquid coursing through them. Something heavy and cold fell between Amaleah's breasts.

Looking down, Amaleah saw a tiny silver and pink conch shell hung by a delicate silver chain hanging from her neck. The body of the shell contained faint silver etchings. Amaleah tried to distinguish them in the dim light but couldn't make what the etchings were of.

"What is this?"

"The blessing." Cordelia moved away from Amaleah in one swift motion. "Wear it always as a reminder of my people." She glanced up towards the stairs as if she could hear something high above them. Her eyes glazed over like they had before, turning completely black.

Cordelia shook vehemently within the water, causing tiny waves to lap against the water's edge. Amaleah was about to call out to the mermaid, but the shaking stopped as suddenly as it had begun and Cordelia's eyes returned to normal.

"It is time for me to leave," the mermaid whispered. "But know this, whenever you are in need, all you must do is trust that the shell will bring you luck."

Amaleah glanced around the cavern nervously. She still didn't know why Cordelia was going through all of this trouble to save her. "I'm not sure I understand. Why are you here? Why are you helping me? Why was it so important for you to be watching me? What's going to happen?"

Cordelia inclined her head towards Amaleah. "All good questions. But not ones that I can answer. You must find your own path. I fear that I have said and done too much already."

"But-"

"No buts, my dear. This is as it should be. I feel that I was fated to be with you today in your time of need. I am honored that I was able to bestow one of the sacred blessings of my people upon you. All this you shall come to understand in time. You are more important to our world than any before you."

Amaleah waited for Cordelia to say more, but she didn't. Sighing, she asked, "Will I at least see you again?"

"It is unlikely."

"Why is that unlikely?"

"My time is up, my dearest. We of the magical realm are not always immortal, although we live for hundreds of years." Cordelia's gaze shifted and the blackness returned. She remained silent for several moments. Amaleah thought about speaking, but felt uneasy breaking the silence. Suddenly, Cordelia began speaking again, "If we do meet again, then it will be in even graver circumstances than those of the present."

Amaleah let that sink in. "But… are you ill? Why is your time up?"

"Every creature on this earth must face his or her end at some point, Amaleah. Mine has been slowly creeping towards me for some time now. I am the last of my kind, and so it is only just that I now rejoin my brothers and sisters in the shadowy cavern of death."

"Why are you the last of the merfolk? I mean, I know I had read that your people perished during the Third Darkness, but nothing I have ever read explained why."

A sad smile spread across Cordelia's face. "This is a tale for another time, I think, to be told by someone else. The histories you were taught were not the histories of all people. Remember who wrote the texts, who bound the books, who distributed the stories to the masses. Not all is as it was described." Cordelia paused before coming to the rim of the pool again. She moved so quickly in the water that Amaleah barely registered the movement. Reaching a hand up, Cordelia stroked Amaleah's face gently.

"How little you know. How much you must learn, must experience. I am sorry for what the future may hold for you. I can only hope that my words will be of some small comfort to you in the coming of days and that my people's blessing with aid you."

Amaleah drew back. "You make it seem as if the world is ending."

"The tidings of the future are not set in stone, dearest one, nor are they unbreakable. I catch glimpses of what may come, but nothing is guaranteed. A choice now may change the entirety of the future."

Well, that's not comforting, Amaleah thought as she broke away from Cordelia's touch.

The mermaid's face fell as Amaleah moved away from her, but Amaleah kept her distance.

Cordelia spoke softly, "We may yet see one another when the time is right. Do not be afraid of what the future holds. You are stronger than you yet know."

Amaleah touched the shell at her neck gently. "Thank you for helping me."

"Do not thank me for something I would have done without you asking. You are the chosen one. When the time comes, do not forget the magic of the sea."

With that Cordelia did not wait for a response but flipped her tail in goodbye and disappeared within the deep abyss of the pool's dark water.

"I promise," Amaleah whispered. Tucking the small shell beneath the layers of her gown, Amaleah felt grief wash over her. *Will I truly never see her again?* Tears pooled in Amaleah's eyes as she watched the mermaid disappear into the darkness. *I can't believe that she's gone.*

Chapter Three

Wiping the mud off of her gown, Amaleah crept up the stairs. They creaked beneath her feet. The sound sent shivers down her spine. The heavy conch shell lay firmly pressed between her breasts. She could feel its cold, hard spikes poking into her flesh. She didn't look back as she climbed, but the shell was a reminder to never forget that even in her darkest hour, there was always someone watching over her.

When she finally crested the top of the stairs, Amaleah took a deep breath of air. The lingering scent of cinnamon was so faint that she thought she was just imagining it into being. Cordelia had left, she reminded herself. Delicately, Amaleah unlatched the metal trap at the top of the door and pushed it ajar. Peeping around the painting that served as the entrance to the hidden stairwell, Amaleah made sure that no one was in the hallway before sliding through the smallest crack she could make while still fitting through it. She stumbled slightly as she heard the rustle of fabric behind her.

"Princess Amaleah," the voice was cold and sharp. Although Amaleah knew she wasn't close enough to be able to smell him, she felt her stomach tighten as she imagined the smell of him. Despite wearing too much of a musk and elderberry cologne, he always maintained the slight scent of death. It made Amaleah gag each time she encountered him.

"Where have you been? Your father was becoming quite worried about you."

Amaleah spun around as she slid the painting back into place. Her father's high councilor, Namadus, took quick strides around the bend at the end of the hall. He was a tall man with a long, thin body. His pointed nose stuck straight into the air as he came towards her. His heavily drawn-on eyebrows rose as he scanned her dress. Looking down, Amaleah realized that the hem of her gown was still covered in mud up to her knees. She blushed a crimson red.

"We have been searching for you everywhere," he sneered, and Amaleah felt her stomach plummet as his eyes flicked towards the painting she had just climbed through. "Where have you been?"

Did he see me walk through the painting?

"I- I was just walking around the palace. It's been so long since I've a taken a tour of my home that I wanted to see all that there was to see." She bowed her head to him in a sign of respect. "I am sorry if I have caused you or my father any trouble, Namadus. I beg that you will forgive me," she struggled to keep her voice steady as she spoke. Her head was pounding and her knees felt weak. The conch shell turned to ice.

She snuck a glance at his face as she waited for him to respond. He was staring at her with his calculating eyes. She quickly looked away from him and began twisting her fingers in front of her. As expected he stomped his foot and said, "Stop that at once, Your Highness." He placed his

49

clammy hand on top of her hers. "Once you are ruler you will not want to show any sign of weakness. Twisting your fingers is a telltale sign that you are uncomfortable." He sighed loudly as he released his grip on her hands and continued.

"I suppose we shall have to change your attire in order for you to be presentable."

He spun on his heel and began heading back the way he'd come—towards her bedchamber. Without glancing over his shoulder, he asked, "Are you coming or are you going to make me search for you again?"

His voice held the answer. Amaleah followed him as quickly as she could without running. After a few paces of them walking side-by-side, Namadus began sniffing at the air. Every few seconds he would look over at Amaleah, sniff and then turn away. As they approached the end of their current hallway, he suddenly turned upon Amaleah, exclaiming, "What is that atrocious stench?"

Amaleah sniffed at the air but couldn't identify anything out of the ordinary. "What are you talking about?"

"You!" Namadus shouted. He gripped her shoulders firmly in his hands and scowled at her, "You smell like a dead fish!" He stared straight into her eyes, "I am going to give you one chance to explain to me exactly where you've been."

Amaleah lifted her hands to her face and sniffed at her fingers. They had the slight odor of the lake on them.

Pulling away from him, she smelled her clothes as well. They contained the faint scent of sweat but that was all. In her mind, there was no possibility of Namadus being able to smell the faint scent of the water on her hands.

She batted her eyes once and smiled up at him, "I told you, Namadus, I have simply been exploring the castle. Am I not allowed to explore my own home?"

She lowered her eyes and then said, "I'm sure that whatever you're smelling is not me. I am a princess of the blooded line of Lunameedian rulers. I do not smell."

Namadus scanned her from head to toe. Amaleah self-consciously patted her unruly hair down where it had come loose from its pins.

"How is it that you, an unyielding, buffoon of a girl, is set to be the next ruler of our people? You know your father shored up your succession to the throne? The Light knows why he's so hell-bent on you becoming the next ruler of our kingdom."

Namadus stared at her, his eyes assessing her. Amaleah blushed.

"Stop blushing, Your Highness. If you are ever going to be a great ruler, you will need to learn to control your emotions. Especially as a woman."

He said the last word as if it were as unsavory as spoiled meat. Amaleah felt her face flush again and turned away from Namadus.

"I'm sorry, Namadus."

He nodded at her once and then said, "Your father is expecting you. I'll ring for your nursemaid." He patted her on the shoulder in a patronizing way. "I know all of this must be very confusing to you. It's been a very long day and you have not been trained for this kind of intrigue at court." He squeezed her shoulders and Amaleah forced herself not to flinch. His voice was too close and too loud in her ears. His breath smelled too much like something rotting. She wanted nothing more than to be away from him. "But, you have nothing to fear. I and my council will take care of you. No matter what happens, you can count on us."

Likely chance.

"Of course, Namadus," she smiled sweetly up at him. "I never doubted that."

She felt bile rise up in her throat as she spoke. The acid burned as she forced it down again. Even his gesture of comradery to her felt like a trick.

He smiled back at her. His pearly white teeth glistened in the light streaming in from the open windows at the end of the hall. With the shadows cast about him, he looked like a feral animal about to attack its prey.

Amaleah subconsciously took a step back.

Shaking his head, Namadus clapped his hands twice. "Come now, Your Highness, we'd best be getting you ready." With that, Namadus turned and strode away from her, towards her father's private study.

Clenching her fist, Amaleah made a split decision to yell down the hall at her father's councilor, "And what would the great councilor of my father like for me to wear to the privy council chamber?" Even to her own ears, her voice sounded mocking and little. She instantly wished she hadn't said anything.

Whipping around to face her, Namadus replied, "Whatever is befitting of a royal princess of the court of Bluefischer. You are the crown princess of Lunameed and daughter of the king."

"Then what I am wearing will suit me just fine."

Her entire body felt numb as she spoke and she couldn't seem to piece together the words she was speaking. "My father doesn't deserve the show of reverence after what he's proclaimed today."

Throwing his hands into the air, Namadus nearly shouted at her, "You truly are impossible. How did such a noble leader as your father end up with such a self-centered, irrational child as you?"

His words cut through Amaleah, but she forced herself to listen, "And, you're the heir!" he snorted. Namadus strode down the hallway towards her. "If you think I'm going to let some pig-headed seventeen-year-old girl ruin the kingdom I have worked so hard to create, then you are mistaken."

He paused momentarily, as if realizing what he'd just said. His face paled, and Amaleah thought she could hear his heart pounding in his chest even from the distance between them. His breath came out is gusts of hot air. "Just put on one of your best dresses, redo your hair, and for goodness sake, make yourself look like a princess."

Amaleah took a step towards him and leaned in until their noses were nearly touching.

"You forget who you are speaking to, High Councilor," she whispered.

Namadus threw his head back and laughed a great, bellowing laugh. Amaleah leaned away from him and began twisting her hands again. She watched as his whole demeanor changed and the veneer of his court face faded into a look of complete condemnation.

"You stupid girl," he finally said as he struggled to regain composure, "It is you who forgets who you're speaking to. I have the king's ear, unlike you. I have the support of the people, unlike you. And I have the power to do anything I desire, unlike you." He smirked. "Now, go to your room, put on one of your best dresses and proceed to the privy council chambers. Do not make me say this again, Amaleah."

He turned on his heel to leave her but paused before walking down the hall. "Oh, and Amaleah," his voice felt like a knife piercing her skin as he spoke, "it would be best if you remembered this conversation in the future. I wouldn't want to have to explain to your father why it would be safer for you to be at Maravra's Tower again. Now that you're back after such a long... reprieve from court." He left her then, his robe floating around his ankles as he made his way to her father.

She shivered as she watched him.

After a few moments of standing in silence, Amaleah stomped her foot and snorted loudly inside the deserted hallway. No one was there to witness her acting in such an unladylike fashion, which was good because she did not want to have to have to confront Namadus again. Whispering a quick prayer to the Light for guidance, Amaleah finished the short walk back to her chambers.

They were not the same ones she'd had as a child living in the palace. Despite being out of favor with her father for the past five years, he'd given her a complete set of rooms from which to live. They consisted of three separate spaces. The front room was designed to be a comfortable receiving room. Chairs and couches were grouped together in little pods so that people could have intimate conversations within the same room. A doorway at the back of this room led to a private study. Books of every shape and size lined the walls and a small fireplace was nested into the room. Originally the space had been intended as a dressing room but once her father had discovered that she still loved to read he had the room converted into a library for her. The room smelled of old books and freshly brewed tea.

Amaleah quickly walked through these two rooms and entered her slumber chamber. The deep-red hardwood floors were covered with an ornate rug that was so soft to the touch that Amaleah had thought it must have been made out of the furs of kittens. It wasn't, or at least that's what her father had told her when she'd asked.

Her father had spared no expense in this room. Along with the plush carpet, he had a custom-made wardrobe constructed for her. The finest wood worker had etched in tiny designs from Amaleah's favorite history stories. The Lady Alnora was prominently featured along with Kilian Clearwater. The canopy bed was decorated with silken sheets and beaded tapestry. Wall sconces for candles had been nailed all around the room so that she was never without light. A big, claw-footed tub nested against the wardrobe. There was a closet just for shoes and accessories that her father had filled to the brim with supplies prior to her arrival. The room constantly smelled like vanilla and orchids.

Amaleah shrugged out of her muddied gown and pulled a long, lavender robe out of the wardrobe. Tiny flowers and birds had been embroidered into the silky fabric. The silk was smooth against Amaleah's skin as she settled atop her bed. As she waited for her nursemaid, Sylvia, to arrive, Amaleah examined the tiny conch that hung from a long silver chain about her neck. It was small and the shell was almost entirely white. Speckles of pink and purple covered the otherwise pristine shell. Parts of the shell had been worn smooth while other parts were rough to the touch.

As she nestled back into the overstuffed pillows, she went over the day's events in her mind. Everything seemed so rushed now: her breakfast with Sylvia, her meeting with her father and his councilors, her encounter with Cordelia, and her argument with Namadus. Had all of this really happened in a single day? Before she realized what she was doing, hot tears were streaming down her face and she was gasping for air against the globs of mucus building in her chest.

She needed more time. Her father wanted to marry her within the year, which left her with little time to form alliances with any of the noble families within the realm. She wasn't even sure if any of them would support her instead of her father anyway. He had been a good ruler for the majority of his reign. He had been kind and fair. Even in the years following her mother's death, King Magnus had been a caring ruler to the Lunameedian people. As the years progressed, he had become more and more withdrawn from reality. At times, Amaleah had believed that he would snap out of his destructive patterns, but he hadn't. And the kingdom had suffered because of it.

When Amaleah was eleven, he'd placed an embargo on the trade industry between the island nations of Borganda and Macai with Lunameed. The cost of much-needed imported goods became too expensive for the common people to purchase. They were able to eat because of the abundance of crops in Lunameed, but many began going without clothing or shoes.

The action that caused the most damage occurred when Amaleah had been thirteen. It was the year after he'd sent her away, and Amaleah had snuck into her tutor's office to read his letters from court. Her father had made the executive decision to stop all communication with the Szarmian royalty. Of course, the royal family and the military leaders of Szarmi had taken this action as a direct declaration of an impending war. Murders broke out en masse along the border between Szarmi and Lunameed. Countless magical beings had been slaughtered during their journeys between the two kingdoms.

Her father had sat on his throne in silence as even children were murdered by the Szarmians.

Relations between the two countries had never been particularly good. It was Szarmi who had led the charge against Lunameed and all things of the Light during the Wars of Darkness over three hundred years before. Lunameed had never forgiven Szarmi for the destruction they had caused to the land, and Szarmi had never forgiven Lunameed for protecting the magical creatures of Mitier.

To make matters worse, her father had actively supplied anti-magic organizations within Szarmi in exchange for contraband items from the island nations. Needless to say, the Lunameedian throne hung by a fraying thread. Amaleah did not want to see that thread snap.

Amaleah feared the worst.

With her father's proposal to her, he had the power to rip what remained of the Lunameedian's culture to shreds. The foundation of her kingdom was crumbling, and Amaleah intended to see it restored. Unfortunately, she wasn't sure the Lunameedian people would rally around her. Her father had done enough damage to the psyche of her people that she doubted they would have the courage to stand against him. Those who had defied him in the past had been brutally beaten and hung in public view of her people. She didn't know if she could succeed.

But she needed to try.

The future of her people depended on her. She just needed more time.

Amaleah wrung her hands in frustration. She didn't know how to stop the marriage from happening other than to escape. She had learned enough about Lunameed's ecosystem and way of life from her teachings that she believed she could survive on her own. Perhaps in the wilderness. But she would need to form contacts, make arrangements, and pack away food and other supplies in the cavern.

She needed a plan.

Amaleah peered about the ornate room and stroked the smooth covers on her bed. She would have to give up the splendor of being a princess if she was to be successful in escaping. Even when she'd been exiled, she'd been afforded the luxuries of being a princess. She wasn't sure if she would be able to survive without them.

As she looked about her room, a small leather-bound book laying on top of her dressing table caught her eye. It had been her mother's as a child and was one of the few things Amaleah had that belonged to her mother. Amaleah had cherished it from the moment her father had given it to her as a little girl.

Its gilded pages contained fantasized history stories of the magical creatures that used to live all throughout Mitier—before the Wars of Darkness. Tiny, hand-drawn pictures depicting the interactions between the magical creatures and the heroes from the past covered the margins of the pages. What Amaleah assumed was her mother's handwriting sprawled across the page everywhere there wasn't text or a picture drawn. In some places, her mother had stuck additional pieces of paper into the book's folds to continue annotating the stories.

Amaleah had spent hours poring over the book's contents. There was one story in particular that Queen Orianna had annotated extensively. The story told of a pig farmer who had, by all accounts, become the best in the country region in which he lived. One day, a poor, wandering woman found her way onto his farm and saw all of the fat pigs wallowing in the mud pits. Driven mad by her hunger, the woman slaughtered all but one of the pigs, causing the pig farmer to lose all of the business he had so diligently worked to build.

The farmer, not stopped by this setback, went about creating a new business. Selling the last pig he had, the farmer went into the textile business. He designed beautiful fabrics and sold them to the most prestigious stores in the land. One day, while the businessman was out discovering new patterns to weave into his cloths, the same wandering woman happened upon his shop. She was just as poor as she had been before, and her clothes were disintegrating on her body.

Seeing all of the beautiful fabrics displayed in the shop's storefront, the woman decided that she wanted some of the fabric for herself. As she was trying to break into the shop through a window at the back, she knocked over a candle, setting fire to the whole store and destroying all of the fabrics the farmer-turned-textile-man had created.

At this point in the story, Amaleah had always wanted to quit reading. She despised how the man's hard work and success were disrupted by the woman. He had lost his fortune, his home, and his businesses. Amaleah couldn't imagine being so thwarted by a single person and still having the strength to continue on. Her mother had shared Amaleah's thoughts on this tale and had written a tiny note across the bottom of one of the story's pages:

'This story is absolutely terrible. I cannot fathom losing all that I have and still pushing forward. There should be a lesson learned in here: never give up. Let's see what happens next.'

Wither her mother's words in her mind, Amaleah always continued reading.

The man, now having lost two businesses in horrific ways, began pondering what to do next. With his previous experience of losing everything he owned and held dear, the man had made the wise decision to invest a small portion of his fortune into the town. Over the years, the town thrived and grew into a major city on the southern border of the kingdom. It had grown so large, in fact, that a bank had been built and multiplied his money tenfold. Taking his money out of the bank, the man used his sum of gold to purchase a fishing boat and a small house on the rocky sea shore.

He continued to work hard and discover the best fish available. The man would leave so early in the morning that the sun was not yet in the sky and return only after the sister moons filled the darkness just so that he could catch the best fish in the sea. Over time, the man became famous for his fresh fish. People traveled from all over Mitier to purchase the various types that he was able to catch in the briny sea. Instead of using the income generated by the fishing business to purchase a new home, the man bought more boats and hired people to tend to them and take them out on fishing excursions. His business grew and he became very prosperous.

Well, one day the poor woman, hungry from her travels but without enough money to purchase even the hardest loaf of bread, made her way towards the man's primary fishing boat. Her eyes were milky with hunger.

Unlike all times before, he saw her approaching.

He intercepted her and began talking to her. He asked her about her ailments and why she traveled so much with so little. She said she needed a job so that she could provide for herself. The man, having built his third business around the principle of hiring the downtrodden, offered her a spot on his newest ship. She accepted immediately. Over time, they fell in love and married. And, they had lived happily ever after.

Amaleah's eyes trailed over the page to where her mother had written an annotation under the story.

'Wait, what? Is that truly how the story ends? 'They lived happily ever after.' This is certainly NOT how real life ends. Why is it that stories end in this way? It is better, I think, to use fae tales to teach our children morals about life and how to be strategic and forward-thinking. Besides, why does the man have to always lose that which he has worked so hard to achieve? If I had been in that situation, I think that I would have told the woman that she needed to complete three tasks for me prior to letting her on my newest ship. That way, I would have enough time to decide whether or she was worthy of my forgiveness and trust.'

Amaleah reread those words again "I would have told the woman that she needed to complete three tasks." Amaleah instantly thought of the three dresses and the coat Cordelia had spoken of. Her mind worked, and what felt like pieces of an unmapped puzzle fit solidly together. She knew what she needed to do.

It was customary within Lunameedian culture for a suitor to grant boons to their beloved. Amaleah had never thought much of this tradition because she believed that it placed the person being pursued in a state of gratitude. It gave power to the suitor that Amaleah didn't think was appropriate. Now, she wasn't so sure. If she asked her father to make the dresses and the coat, then there was a chance that he wouldn't be able to accomplish the tasks. It would, at the very minimum, provide her with more time.

Glancing at the clock on her mantel, Amaleah realized that too much time had passed since Namadus had left her to change. Her nursemaid, Sylvia, still hadn't arrived, but Amaleah couldn't wait for her any longer. She doubted that Namadus had actually rung the bell for her nursemaid at all. Sighing heavily, Amaleah pulled the rope cord attached to the servants' bells. And she waited.

The clock chimed a dreary six times as the minute hand met the hour hand. Not wanting to waste another moment, Amaleah went to her wardrobe and pulled out a lavender gown with deep violet embroidery around the hem and cuffs. The purple of the dress made her emerald eyes seem a deeper, lovelier shade of green. Her father loved this dress and she hoped that it would make the impression on him that she wanted.

As Amaleah was pulling the pins out of her long auburn hair, she heard the familiar footsteps of her nursemaid in the outer chambers of her room. Within minutes the wizened old woman hobbled into Amaleah's slumber chamber.

She was a hump-backed creature with straggly grey hair and big, blue eyes. She was short and wrinkled and smelled like moldy paper. To some people, the little old woman was endearing. Amaleah despised her.

"Princess Amaleah, what did you do to your dress?" Sylvia asked as she stooped to pick up the discarded gown. She made tsking noises as examined the brownish-red stains that ran from the hem up to the knee. "Child, how is it that you always ruin your best gowns? Do you know how much washing this will take to fix the damage you've done?" The older woman rubbed at the mud on the hem of Amaleah's dress. Her lips sagged into a downward slope as she realized the mud was dug deep into the fabric. Folds of wrinkles smooshed together as Sylvia continued to frown and Amaleah couldn't help but smirk at the woman's face.

"Sylvia," Amaleah began impatiently, "I don't have time for this right now. I've been summoned to the privy chamber and I need you to help me change. That's all."

Sylvia nearly dropped Amaleah's ruined gown as she listened to Amaleah speak. Her face turned a pale white color and sheen broke out on her brow.

"The p-privy chamber." Sylvia stuttered. "Are you sure you didn't mishear, My Lady? Surely your father doesn't want..." her voice quivered to a stop.

Amaleah waited for Sylvia to continue. She waited for Sylvia to acknowledge that she knew of her father's plan to marry her. For the past four years, Amaleah had suspected that Sylvia was one of her father's spies and she waited with bated breath for Sylvia to reveal this to be the case. There was no doubt in her mind that Sylvia knew exactly what her father wanted her for.

Slowly, Sylvia restarted, "My Lady, does this mean that you have consented to marry your own father?" The old woman's voice sounded strained as if she were struggling within herself to say just the right words in order to convey what she thought about this notion. "I'm sorry, My Lady, I don't mean to be impertinent, it's just that your father is not a suitable consort."

Amaleah sucked in a breath through her teeth. She had never, in all her seventeen years, heard the old woman speak ill of her father. Even when Sylvia had been separated from her family so that she could serve the royal line by caring for Amaleah in exile, Sylvia had always spoken highly of King Magnus. Sylvia hadn't seen her grandchildren during the five years they had been in exile and, when they had finally returned to Estrellala, her family had declined to visit with her. Even then, Sylvia had praised King Magnus as a noble and worthy leader.

Amaleah looked deep into Sylvia's eyes. Sylvia did not blink or look away from Amaleah. Instead, she said, "Child, please tell me this isn't so." The words reverberated in the air as Sylvia's voice shook. The older woman's eyes were blue and wet. Amaleah had to look away.

Instead of looking into her nursemaid's eyes, Amaleah looked at the tapestry hanging above Sylvia's head. It depicted a hunt. Three dogs surrounded a wounded unicorn. Blood streamed from the wounds on the animal's hind quarters and neck. Whoever had stitched the unicorn's face had spent quite a bit of time dedicated to showing the despair on the wounded animal's face. The eyes were wild with fear. Every time Amaleah looked at it, it made her want to cry. King Magnus had placed the tapestry—a gift from his long-lost friend, Baron Blodruth—in Amaleah's room when she was six years old, following his reconciliation with the baron.

Amaleah's mind wandered to the memories she had of the baron. He had been a jovial man, rotund in size with a booming voice. Amaleah had loved the baron fiercely. She loved how he had stormed through the castle talking about the stag that he had chased on a hunt or the rabbit he had hanging in the castle smokehouse. He used to sit her on his lap and tell her stories about the battles he'd fought during the Island Nations' civil unrest. He was always sweaty and smelled like a mixture of smoke and peppermint, but Amaleah had felt safe in his company. She wished she could talk to him now.

Unfortunately, the friendship her father had rekindled with Baron Blodruth had not lasted long. Shortly after the baron set up a home within the walls of Estrellala, he had brought his twenty-year-old daughter to court. Although Amaleah had been young, she remembered the sense of excitement she'd felt the first time she'd heard the servants discussing the upcoming wedding between her father and the Lady Nicolette Blodruth. Nicolette had been kind to Amaleah. She had tried teaching her how to embroider. She'd snuck into the kitchen and brought little pastries for the two of them to eat as they explored the gardens in the late afternoon. They had gone swimming in the rivers surrounding Estrellala. They had been happy.

Amaleah had wanted Nicolette to be her new mother. Really, the only mother she had ever known.

But then, her father had heard the servants' whispers and in a fit of rage had set fire to the Blodruth's chambers in the castle. Amaleah remembered the bloodcurdling screams of the servants who weren't able to get out of the chambers before the doors were covered in flames. Thankfully, Baron Blodruth and Nicolette had been away or else they would have perished along with their servants. The scent of burning flesh still lingered in Amaleah's memories. They seeped into her dreams at night and made her shake and cry.

The day after the fire, the Blodruths left Estrellala and never returned. It had snowed the day they left. Amaleah remembered how her father's fingers had dug into her skin as they stood on the highest balcony of the castle to watch them leave. Amaleah's breath had popped out of her in mists and her cheeks were red from the cold. When her father had noticed that she was crying, he had slapped her hard on the face. The bite of his gnarled fingers on her cheek made her face swell and a purple bruise spread across her skin. He barely looked at her as he did it. His eyes were transfixed on the group of people leaving the castle.

When he finally spoke to her, his words came out rough and low. In a hushed whisper, he had said, "Once you make a promise to someone, you can never break it, Amaleah. Always remember that. I promised your mother that I would only marry someone who was as beautiful as she was. The ambition that family demonstrated was unfathomable. To think that they actually *believed* that their daughter was worthy to replace your mother."

He had shaken his head as his own tears streamed down his grizzled face. "No, Amaleah, I won't let that happen. I won't break that promise. May the Light break my bones and spirit: I will only marry someone as beautiful as Orianna."

For years, her father's words had haunted her. Now, as she stood looking at the tapestry that had been the last gift the baron had given her before leaving the castle, Amaleah wondered if her father would be as cruel to her as he had been to the Blodruths. The look in the unicorn's face reminded Amaleah that, although she was a princess, she was still subject to the whims of men and kings. She was but a stag being chased through the woods, afraid of the dogs and hunters gaining on her. Her father had forgotten what it meant to be a king. Amaleah vowed to herself that if she ever got the chance to rule Lunameed that she would never make the same mistakes as her father. She would be strong but also kind and fair. She would take back the Light that had been dampened by the Wars of Darkness and lead her people into an era of justice and prosperity.

Never make a promise you can't keep, she reminded herself. If nothing else, this was the one lesson her father had taught her.

"My Lady?"

Sylvia's soft voice ripped Amaleah from her memories. Blinking her eyes, Amaleah peered at her nursemaid from where she sat. It took her a moment to realize that her nursemaid was still waiting for Amaleah to respond to her question. *Did I consent to marry my own father?*

Amaleah shook her head slowly. The old woman let out a trembling breath and Amaleah could see tears filling her eyes. *What is her game?* In all her time as Sylvia's charge, she had never felt like the older woman had cared about her at all. Of course, Sylvia had tended her injuries, taught her how to speak and act like a princess, and provided her with information from the courts, but Sylvia had never comforted her, spoken loving words to her, or embraced her as a mother would. When Amaleah had been younger, especially after Nicolette had left, she had craved Sylvia's affection. Every time she felt alone or scared she had silently begged Sylvia to comfort her. She never had. Now, Amaleah didn't want that from her nursemaid. Now she just wanted loyalty.

For as long as she could remember, Sylvia's loyalty had resided with her father. Over time, Amaleah had come to realize the distinction between servant and master. There had been times that Sylvia had been caring and kind, but she had only doted on Amaleah because she was being paid to do so. She couldn't be trusted.

And yet, she had seemed so concerned about Amaleah's betrothal to her father.

Sylvia's reluctance to support the marriage gave Amaleah hope.

Without warning, Sylvia placed a small, wrinkled hand on Amaleah's shoulder. Her touch was cold and her closeness allowed Amaleah to smell the vinegar and lemon scent Sylvia always seemed to carry with her.

"I know you might not believe me, and, when I think about how I have treated you these past seventeen years, you have no reason to, but this time your father has gone too far."

Spittle flew from Sylvia's mouth as she spoke, sprinkling Amaleah in a light mist. Amaleah cringed as the wet droplets landed on her face. They felt slimy as they slid down her cheeks. Despite her disgust, she leaned closer to her nursemaid.

"You're right; I have no reason to trust you," Amaleah interjected before Sylvia could say more. She held up her hands as she spoke and gently removed herself from Sylvia's grip. Her eyes flicked to the unicorn's face and the fear that resided there as it was brutally attacked by the dogs. Pausing for a split of a second as she glanced at the tapestry, Amaleah knew she only had two choices. She could accept her father's proposal, or she could try to rally as much support as possible for her escape. She might still fail, but at least she would have tried. "Unfortunately, I think that I do not have any other choice but to trust you."

Sylvia nodded once, visibly relieved at Amaleah's change of mind. "Well then, My Lady, I think we should start planning."

Amaleah wandered about her room before sitting down in front of her mirror. Sylvia hobbled to stand behind her. Looking down so that she didn't meet her nursemaid's eyes, Amaleah thought about what she should say to the woman. She opened her mouth to speak when a hard knock drew her attention to the door. She could hear metal clanking against metal coming from the hallway. Only guards wore enough metal to make a sound like that. If there was one thing she did not have time for right now, it was dealing with her father's guards.

"Yes?" she called out loudly.

"Your Highness, I'm here to escort you to the privy council. Your presence is required by the king." The guard coughed, uncomfortably, "Are you decent, My Lady? I was told that I was to watch you from the moment I found you."

Amaleah scoffed. This was most certainly the work of Namadus. Despite her father's poor health and growing uncertainty of the real world, she was sure he wouldn't have sent a guard to watch her every move. She was a grown princess, heir to the Lunameedian throne. A common guard would not have the privilege of seeing her change.

"I'm being dressed now," Amaleah's voice cracked as she spoke and another bout of tears came tumbling out. *Why am I crying?* Her cheeks flushed a deep red even though Sylvia was the only one who could see her. "Do not come into my room. I'll be out shortly."

The guard was silent for several beats before finally muttering his acquiescence to Amaleah's command through the door. She smiled into the mirror and Sylvia momentarily stared back at her in the reflection. They didn't say anything, but Amaleah could tell what her nursemaid was thinking: Amaleah had just controlled the guard. The moment passed quickly, but it left Amaleah feeling as if she could trust Sylvia. It was a weak, translucent trust, but it was there.

Sylvia quickly chose a small silver tiara embedded with sapphires and pearls, matched it with a pair of earrings and a necklace with the same jewels and turned back to face Amaleah. The finery matched the dress Amaleah had picked out perfectly. She smiled at Sylvia in the mirror and then rose so that Sylvia could lace up her corset. After the stays had been pulled tight against Amaleah's body, Sylvia helped her step into the fluffy, sky blue petticoat. Amaleah slid the velvety fabric of the dress over her shoulder. Following this, Sylvia tugged a custom-made sapphire blue bodice covered in birds and flowers over Amaleah's waist. It was heavily laden with pearls. Amaleah began to sweat profusely and the soft fabric of her dress clung to her body under the weight of the corset and the bodice.

Once the bodice was in place and Sylvia had finished tugging at Amaleah's dress until it lay exactly how she wanted it, she stood back to admire her work. A frown passed over her nursemaid's face.

"What is it?" Amaleah asked. "What's wrong?"

"Well, for starters, and I mean no offence, you stink. I mean, you really smell like dead fish and old water," Sylvia wrinkled her nose as she spoke. "I didn't notice it at first, but the closer I got to you, the stronger the smell became."

"Oh," was the only thing Amaleah could say to this.

"But it ain't just the smell of you," Sylvia licked her lips nervously before continuing, "it's your hair too. It's in shambles. I wouldn't feel right sending you in this state to see the king."

"We don't have time," Amaleah began.

"They've waited for you this long," Sylvia clucked. "They can wait until you're presentable."

Amaleah glanced at the door, but didn't hear anything coming from the other side of the door.

"Fine. Do whatever you like, but be quick. I don't want to keep him waiting so long that he's in a foul mood upon my arrival. Have you seen his reactions lately, Sylvia? He's not the man that he used to be." Amaleah once again sat in front of her mirror. Thoughts about how life had been when her father had reformed his friendship with Baron Blodruth. Not for the first time, Amaleah wondered whether or not life would have been different for them all if her father had chosen to accept the baron's daughter as his wife.

"She was beautiful!" Amaleah blurted out loudly. She immediately clutched her hands to her mouth as she realized she'd spoken out loud. Sylvia caught Amaleah's glance in the mirror and gave her a quizzical look.

"Nicolette Blodruth," Amaleah explained. "I remember her and the baron."

Sylvia nodded and then said, "She was beautiful. But, unfortunately, not beautiful enough to tempt your father."

"Do you think things would be different now if my father had chosen to marry her?"

Sylvia didn't meet Amaleah's eyes in the mirror. "No," she whispered softly. And then, "My Lady, you are more beautiful than you realize."

She pulled Amaleah's hair up into a knot of curls. "Just like your mother, no man can keep his eyes off of you. I have seen this with my own eyes."

It took all of Amaleah's willpower not to laugh. She was far from being a conventional beauty of the kingdom. Stocky in build and with a round, pale face, Amaleah didn't believe that she looked anything like what a princess should. She was not refined. Nor was she as elegant as even some of the ladies of the court. In fact, the only thing she had that the others did not was the beautiful, chocolate brown and auburn locks she had inherited from her mother.

It had been her hair that had caused her father's attention to be drawn to her. When Amaleah was a young child, she'd had blonde ringlets. Then, when Amaleah had been eight years old, all of her hair had fallen out. Sylvia told her that she had been granted a gift, the royal physicians were mystified, and her father grew even more cold and distant. When her hair grew back, it was the same color as her mother's. That's when her father's obsession began.

She knew the real reason he'd sent her away when she'd hit puberty; it wasn't to protect her or to train her, as he so often claimed to his noblemen. She looked too much like Orianna. For the first year she'd been exiled, he'd refused to visit her or allow her to visit at court. For the next three years, he'd only visited her twice a year: once on her name day and once on the anniversary of Lunameed's victory during the Third Darkness. Then, during the last year of her exile, he'd spent time with her every week. At first, she had cherished the time he spent with her. But then she had realized that he was paying too much attention to her. A couple of times he had called her Orianna. She hadn't thought about it too much. That is, until he tried to kiss her in the garden. By then, it was too late.

Looking at Sylvia, Amaleah said, "No, Sylvia, I am not beautiful. Cursed, maybe." She paused before continuing, "The only reason the younger men of the court stare at me is because they consider my worth in terms of wealth, nobility, and the ability to rule. Older men look at me to determine how they can leverage their sons into my path. If I were a pauper instead of a princess, they would not pay me the same attention."

"I believe that you have more charms than you know. You are too harsh on yourself, dear one."

Amaleah burst into laughter so loudly that it flooded the whole room with noise. The guard standing watch outside her room rapped on the door sharply.

"If you have time to laugh, My Lady, you have time to let me in," his voice was stern, but there was an edge to it that caused Amaleah to take note. "Please," he pleaded through the closed door, "the council is waiting on you and I am responsible for ensuring that you arrive."

There was a tinge of fear to the man's voice that Amaleah found compelling. She shushed her nursemaid before calling out, "Sylvia is just finishing up my hair. Please wait and I will be out in just one moment."

Sylvia began speaking again, as if Amaleah had not burst into laughter and the guard had not interrupted them.

"Princess Amaleah, your mother was considered the loveliest woman in the whole of Mitier. Your father was so enchanted by her that he promised to never marry someone unless they were as beautiful as she was." Sylvia squeezed Amaleah's shoulders gently before continuing, "Why do you think he sent you away, child?"

Sylvia tugged on Amaleah's hair as she pulled it into an ornate design at the back of her head. It was a little too tight and Amaleah jerked her head slightly.

"It wasn't because he was fearful for your safety. I think he knew even then that he wouldn't be able to fulfil his promise to your mother unless he married you," Sylvia continued.

The sapphire necklace that Sylvia had chosen glimmered slightly as the candlelight caught the facets of the gem; the flashes of light distracted her as Sylvia placed the tiara atop her head. The silver and sapphire headpiece was so heavy Amaleah felt like her neck might break by the end of the night. Gathering her skirts, Amaleah looked at herself in the mirror. She gasped when she saw Sylvia's finished work.

She looked like the pictures of her mother. Everything about her resembled the paintings she'd seen of Queen Orianna. Except for her eyes. Her mother's eyes had been violet, but Amaleah's eyes were emerald green. She took a deep breath, letting the air flow into her body until she could feel the pressure in her gut before slowly releasing her breath. She had to do this.

As Amaleah moved towards her chamber's door, Sylvia grasped Amaleah's arm tightly. Her fingers dug into Amaleah's arms but not enough to bruise her. Leaning in close, Sylvia whispered, "We will talk later," into Amaleah's ear.

Amaleah nodded but didn't speak. She was so close to the door that she was afraid the guard would be able to hear her voice. Tears filled her eyes as she opened the door and the guard took hold of her arm. Unlike Sylvia's touch, which had been almost gentle, the guard's grasp felt like thorns scraping against her skin. She wanted to scream out in pain.

Amaleah's silk-covered-high-heeled shoes clacked on the marble floor of the palace as she swiftly walked to the council room. Her lips trembled as she kept pace with the guard. He didn't seem to notice.

As they rounded the last turn on their way to the council room, Amaleah saw a squat man with a long mustache that reached past the man's round face standing in front of the room's doors. He paled and then turned a deep shade of red as Amaleah approached. The guard didn't acknowledge the herald as he deposited Amaleah in front of the doors and turned to face her. He stood at attention, clearly waiting for her to make the next move.

Sighing, Amaleah turned towards the herald. He looked at the floor, at the ceiling, even at the guard, but would not meet her eyes.

"I'm here to see my father, the king."

The man's eyes watered. "I'm so sorry, Your Highness." He stammered as he swung the doors open.

Amaleah strode into the room with her head as high as she could hold it with the heavy tiara weighing her down. Her father rose as the herald introduced her. His face was slack, but he smiled a crooked smile when he caught her gaze. He used a golden cane studded with rubies and diamonds to prop up his fat, sagging body.

He was a tall man with a wide girth and squat legs. His beard, once a fiery red, had started to turn grey and dull; Amaleah wasn't sure when the transition had started. His eyes were intelligent and thoughtful in his moments of lucidity. When the madness, as Amaleah had started to call it, took him, those same eyes would become glazed over and blank. Today, they were clear.

He clapped his hands several times and motioned towards Amaleah, "Ah, it is my bride to be. My Amaleah." He smiled gleefully at her.

"Hello, Father." Her voice faltered as she realized that none of the privy council members were looking at her. None of them had stood for her when she entered the room. Instead, they remained seated in their plush chairs.

There were ten privy council members in total. Each of them oversaw a different segment of Lunameed. They represented the greatest houses in the land. Many of them possessed the power of the Light that was so heavily sought after by those who had not been so gifted.

Amaleah had no reason to trust them. Although Lunameedian law did not prohibit a woman from inheriting the throne, all of the council members had worked diligently to ensure that her father would produce a male heir. They had thrown parties and balls. They had thrust countless women from the forgotten regions of the realm at her father. They had spent enormous amounts of money from the royal treasury in search of a suitable replacement to the beloved, but undeniably dead, queen.

Despite all of their attempts to find a suitable bride, none of them had stood for her when her father had declared that he would wed her before the year was complete. They had looked away from her, just as they were doing now. *The cowards.* If they wouldn't deny her father, then it would be up to her. Now, as she looked around the room, she couldn't identify a single person who she thought would support her cause.

"Are you not happy to see me, my dear?" His voice was calm, but there was an edge to it that made Amaleah's skin crawl.

"It's not that," she paused, trying to catch the eye of one of the privy council members. They continued looking away from her. "It's just that… well… I am barely back at court. Barely home. And now it is your pleasure that we be married."

Her father harrumphed at this.

Not letting his sign of warning deter her, Amaleah continued, "It's just that I have always dreamed about being courted and given lovely things from my suitors. I want to be romanced." Amaleah breathed in deeply as she stared at her father right in the eyes. Trying not to blink, she continued, "And so, I have a proposition for you, Father."

King Magnus looked questioningly at his daughter. He twirled a piece of long, reddish-grey beard between his fingers considering what Amaleah could possibly ask for.

"I'm listening," he said in a bemused tone.

Amaleah looked around the room. Where only moments before the privy councilors had tried to ignore her, they were now staring at her with rapt attention.

"My King, before I make my offer, I want you to swear on your rights as the king of Lunameed that you shall either complete my request or give up your pursuit of our marriage."

The king regarded her coldly. His jaw muscles clenched and she saw the knuckles clutching the golden cane turn white. Gooseflesh formed on Amaleah's skin as she waited for her father to reply. She could feel the tension from the privy council washing over her as they too anticipated the king's response.

Finally, and without warning, the king began to speak. His voice came out in a low rasp that was barely audible. Amaleah leaned forward slightly to hear his words. "Lovely lady, I swear on the Fountain of Prosperity that resides within the sacred land near Amadoon Lake that I shall grant you whatever it is you wish. You know that it is only you, has only ever been you." He took a step forward and his councilors leaned away from him. It was as if they were collectively disturbed by his presence.

"You have stolen my heart a thousand times over, and I know that you will continue to steal it for a thousand more."

Amaleah's heart pounded in her chest. Every nerve in her body cringed at his words. She felt the words, "no, Father, please," bubble up into her mouth. She forced them down even though it made her stomach clench and her face flush to do so.

Taking a step forward, she said in the loudest, clearest voice that she could muster, "You must swear on your rights as king that you will either complete my boon or not marry me." Her voice shook near the end, leaving the final word inaudible over the sudden intake of breath from the privy council.

The king laughed. Loudly.

He took several steps forward until he was directly in front of her. Kneeling, he exclaimed boisterously, "I, fair maiden, am king. And I swear by my rights as ruler of Lunameed, by my honor as king, and by my heart as your suitor that I will either complete your boon within a year or release you from your promise."

With King Magnus's final words, the entire room released its pent-up breath. He had accepted her terms. Collectively, all of the councilors turned towards Amaleah.

Squaring her shoulders, Amaleah stated in a calm, clear voice, "Well, then. What I most desire are three dresses: one made from cloth as bright and glorious as the sun; a second made from cloth as dark and flowing as the ocean's depths; and a third made from fabric that sparkles like the stars in the skies." The councilors turned back to face the king as Amaleah spoke. His face turned a dark shade of pink as he regarded her.

Amaleah continued, "Along with these dresses, I require a coat made from the pelts of all of the animals native to our kingdom. They must be sewn together in such a way as to make them appear to create a new animal once the hood has been pulled up and the length tied around the waist." Amaleah looked her father in the eyes as she finished her request. "Complete these tasks and I will consent to being your bride."

The room fell silent. The councilors, not knowing who to look at kept flipping their heads back and forth so as to the see the reactions on both Amaleah's and the king's faces. The now purple complexion on the king's face had faded and a menacing smile spread across his face.

"Done," he said in a cold, clear voice.

With that one word, Amaleah felt the muscles of her shoulders relax. She hadn't realized that she had tensed while waiting for him to speak.

Gaining courage, she looked around the room and cried out to the surrounding councilors, "Hear now, you have all seen and heard that my father, king of Lunameed, has promised to make the gowns and the coat within a year or forfeit his claim to my hand in marriage. Remember this day and bear witness to my oath that I shall marry the man I love when he has properly won my hand."

The room erupted in chatter. The councilors immediately began talking amongst themselves. Amaleah didn't notice as Namadus whispered to the man sitting next to him, Zaphiniro. She also didn't notice when Namadus exited the room through a small, hidden door made to look like a fireplace at the back of the room. Nor did she notice as Zaphiniro scribbled a note that he passed along to Miccilous and Matheus as he followed Namadus out the door.

All Amaleah saw was her father's features go slack and his eyes roll back, revealing the whites of his eyes.

Chapter Four

Fort Pelid, Szarmi

Colin Sammial Stormbearer fell to the ground in a heap of yellow-stained linen and mud. He could feel the bruise blossom over his face even as he lay crumpled on the ground. The soldiers in the training field laughed, their sounds filling the yard like a pack of wild dogs. His cheeks flushed as he tried to push himself up from the ground but fell again. He promised himself he wouldn't cry. He couldn't.

A big, meaty hand stretched out in front of his face. It was coated with dirt, and scars crisscrossed the leathery, dark skin. It smelled of sweat and metal and hard work. Colin took it and the man attached to the hand pulled him up from the ground.

"Thank you, Captain Conrad," Colin forced his voice not to tremble as he spoke.

"It is nothing, Your Highness."

Colin only shook his head at that. Despite Colin's years at Fort Pelid as a student of the military academy, he still had not mastered the art of hand-to-hand combat. He had spent every spring and summer at the academy since he was just six years old. When he was a child, his lack of fighting abilities had been endearing to the commanding officers of the military.

Now his lack of ability was a liability.

"Let's go again," Colin said, wiping the sweat from his brow.

"Do you think that's wise, Your Highness?" the captain looked at the scowling faces of his men. In a quieter voice, he said just loud enough for Colin to hear, "It doesn't do the men good to see their future commander struggling to defeat even the most ill-trained youngster in camp."

Colin sighed heavily. *No, I suppose it doesn't*, he thought bitterly as he took a quick glance around the training field. For the ones who weren't engaged in their own training, they stood watching their prince be beaten time and time again. They sneered at him openly and Colin could hear the muffled sounds of their voices fill the yard. He could only imagine what they were saying about their future commander.

"If I don't continue trying, Captain Conrad, then I will never get better."

The captain looked uncomfortable for the span of only a moment before he said, "I didn't mean that you should stop training, son." He gripped the hilt of his sword and clapped an arm around Colin's shoulders.

To the men, Captain Conrad exclaimed, "Soldiers of Fort Pelid, who among you believes that you can best our dear prince?"

Without pause, several—really all—the hands shot into the air. Colin's stomach squirmed. He needed their loyalty and respect if he was going to be their ruler. To do that, he needed to be a better fighter. They valued grit and determination. Colin had those. What he lacked was physical dominance and this is what they valued even more.

"Alright. And who among you would follow our prince into battle and trust your lives in his hands?"

All of the hands remained up.

Captain Conrad continued, "Tell me why, men. Tell me why."

In unison, the men said the words of their oath to the kingdom of Szarmi:

"We are the soldiers of Szarmi, keepers of the land and watchers of the people. We will fight for home and country. We will protect our sovereign and the royal line with our dying breaths. To this, we pledge our lives and our bodies."

Once the men had recited their oath, they went back to sparring with one another as if their training had not been interrupted. Only a few who were not engaged in combat continued to look on as the captain and their prince continued to talk.

Colin had heard the words recited his entire life. Young soldiers learned the oath during their first month at Fort Pelid. Despite Colin's place within the royal line, he had learned the words and sought to find meaning within them. The soldiers fought because it was their duty to do so, not because they held any loyalty to him.

Captain Conrad let go of Colin's shoulders and turned to face him.

"Your men will fight for you regardless of whether they believe that you can beat them in hand-to-hand combat."

"I know that, Captain. But, it is not just their duty that I want. It is their respect and their loyalty."

Captain Conrad nodded at this, as if he expected nothing less from Colin. The captain gripped Colin's arm and led him from the yard to his office near the center of the training field. Once inside the office, Colin looked out of the tall windows covering one side of the room. The view spanned the entire training field. All of the soldiers who had been watching Colin fail miserably at his sparring practice had dispersed or started their own hand-to-hand combats. Colin watched them with envy from the captain's office.

The sparsely decorated office was as familiar to Colin as his own quarters were at the fort. He glanced around the room. Nothing had changed since his very first meeting with Conrad fourteen years before. Only a plain-faced clock hung from the wall across from Captain Conrad's desk. On the same wall, a wash basin had been installed with running water that had been piped into the fort from the Moorica River. Windmill farms covered vast regions of Szarmi to ensure that the rivers' water was accessible to all who dwelled in the land. Despite this, Colin had always been surprised that the captain had requested for the water to be pumped to his office when only one of the barracks had running water. The rest of the academy had to retrieve their water from one of the three wells located on the grounds. Captain Conrad always said that lugging water across the academy's grounds built muscle as well as character.

The book shelves lining the back of the office were orderly. No papers rested on the captain's large wooden desk. Even the trash bin appeared organized. Unlike the hot, sweaty scent of the yard, the captain's office smelled fresh, like lemons and strawberries on a hot summer day. And, no matter how sweltering it was outside, the office always remained cool. Colin still wasn't sure how the captain had achieved that feat.

Captain Conrad motioned for Colin to sit in one of the two wooden chairs in front of his desk. The chairs were hard and uncomfortable, just like a soldier's life. Colin hated sitting in those chairs, but he did as the captain asked.

The captain handed Colin a cold, wet rag. Nodding thankfully, Colin swiped the rag across his hot, dirty skin. The white linen came back brown.

"Colin, how long have you been coming to my academy?" Conrad asked.

"For fourteen years, sir."

"And during those fourteen years, have you ever won a battle in hand-to-hand combat?"

"No, sir," Colin looked down at the rag in his hands as he spoke.

"Have you ever won an archery tournament?"

"No, sir."

"Have you ever bested one of your peers in the joust?"

Colin dropped the rag to the floor in frustration, "Is there a point to this, Captain?" His voice was loud and gruff and his heart hammered in his chest as he spoke.

"Sit down, Cadet," Conrad said in a quiet, firm voice.

Colin stared Captain Conrad in the eyes. His breathing increased and he felt his cheeks flush. Blinking, he sat down.

The captain continued, "Tell me, Colin, have you ever beaten an opponent during a joust?"

Colin almost said yes, but then realized that the one time he had actually won a jousting tournament, it had been because his opponent's squire hadn't fastened the saddle on properly and it had slid off the horse's back, toppling the rider to the ground and giving Colin the win.

"Not really," Colin murmured.

"You're telling me that you've been a student of this academy for fourteen years and you've never won a match or beaten an opponent?"

"Not when I was the one doing the fighting."

"Ahh," the captain exclaimed. "Explain that to me, Colin."

Colin looked up at the captain. His eyes were red from containing the hot tears threatening to spill out.

"You already know this, Captain."

"Tell me anyway."

"I may not have won a single battle in hand-to-hand combat, but I have won all but a few of the battles as the commander."

Captain Conrad stood in front of Colin with his hands on his hips and waited for Colin to continue. Sighing, Colin did, "I have successfully led my team to victory during every battle training game for the past ten years."

Colin blushed as he spoke. He didn't enjoy counting off his accomplishments like that, especially when he knew that if someone else had been leading him, he would not have been able to perform as well as his men had.

"Go on," Captain Conrad commanded.

Colin blinked at the captain. "I'm not sure what you mean, sir."

In a gruff voice, the captain said, "Every time I asked you to plan out a new strategy to capture your opponent's idol, you were able to map out tactical maneuvers that not only kept your team's men safe, but also capture the idol quickly and efficiently."

The captain held up a hand and began counting off Colin's accomplishments on it, "For the past ten years, you have never once lost a single battle. Even after I had you stop leading teams of men against your peers and start leading your peers against full-rank soldiers within the armies, you were able to out-strategize and out-maneuver them. In total, you have only lost three battles."

The captain stopped speaking and stared at Colin until he looked down.

"Tell me, Colin, how many of your men 'died' during these exercises?"

"To date, sir, I have only lost four," Colin mumbled.

"So you're telling me that in the past fourteen years that you have been my student you have only lost four men in battle training?"

"Yes, sir."

Captain Conrad just stared at Colin. He didn't say anything, but Colin felt like he could hear the captain's voice through his body language. Colin's hands went dry as he lifted his chin and said, "But-"

"There are no buts, Your Highness. Those are your accomplishments. There's not a single soldier out there who thinks you can best them in hand-to-hand combat. However, all of them trust you to make sure they return home alive from battle. That has earned you their highest respect and loyalty."

Colin fumbled with his hands and didn't look at the captain. He knew Conrad was right, but that didn't change the fact that the men constantly belittled him for not being a more powerful soldier. His mother told him that he would never survive as king unless he learned to instill fear in his people through sheer brute force. Colin didn't want to be that kind of leader, but he did want to be able to fight his own battles with his own hands.

"At this point, Your Highness, I think it's time that you admit that you won't ever be a strong fighter on your own. Instead, I think it's time that we dedicate more time to your strategic and commanding skills."

"I still need to train physically, Captain. If I don't, the men-"

"The men will think that you're finally doing what you're best at and will follow you anyway," Conrad stated firmly, cutting Colin off.

"But-"

"If you are so insistent that you continue your physical training, then I will have to make a compromise with you."

"Ok," Colin said warily. "What do you have in mind?"

"Each day you will spend an hour with me in my private training yard."

"What!" Colin exclaimed before he could stop himself. Only the best soldiers were invited to train one-on-one with the captain.

"You heard me. I think it would be better for the men if they didn't see how unskilled you are on the field. It is better for them to remember your greatness as a strategic war leader."

Colin sat in silence for several moments, contemplating the captain's offer.

"You know this is my last summer here, right? In just over eight months, I will return to Miliom and be crowned king. My official training here at Fort Pelid will conclude before then," Colin licked his dry, bruised lips. Once he was king, he would be on his own. Sure, he would have advisors, but he would be expected to be able to make decisions quickly and accurately. Even after all of his time preparing for the duties of the king, he wasn't sure he was ready.

At least, he thought to himself, *when I return home, I will be reunited with Vanessa.* Vanessa Wilhelm had been sent to Szarmi during the Island Nations' Civil War for protection by her father when she was only three years old. Unfortunately, her family had fallen during the war; she had been a ward of his family ever since. Over the past two years, Colin had grown to love the vibrant young woman. Once Colin was crowned king, he would be able to marry her with or without his mother's consent. A smile began to creep across Colin's face as he contemplated being in her arms once more.

"I know this, Your Highness," Conrad spoke, cutting into Colin's thoughts, "That doesn't mean you can't learn a few new skills in the meantime."

Colin nodded. "You really think this will stop the soldiers from harassing me?"

"Colin, they harass you because you react. If you would just learn to control your emotions, they would stop."

Colin picked at a stray thread on his trousers as he thought about Conrad's words.

"Son, there is much you still need to learn, but perhaps the most important is this: not all leaders are great warriors. And not all warriors are great leaders. You are a great leader, and you will do great things for Szarmi."

They spoke for several more moments about what the remainder of Colin's training would look like. They agreed that every morning before sunrise Colin would train with a staff and a bow before heading off to the masters to continue learning battle maneuvers and strategic warfare.

As Colin was leaving Conrad's office, he turned to back to face him.

"Thank you for believing in me, sir."

"It's not a matter of belief, Your Highness. It is a matter of duty."

With that, the Captain shut his office door and Colin was left to stand alone.

Chapter Five

Estrellala, Lunameed

Amaleah stood frozen in place as King Magnus crossed the space between them and grabbed her arm in a tight grasp. She could feel his fingernails cutting into her skin. She knew bruises were blossoming on her wrists and forearms. His grasp on her arm was so tight that her fingers lost sensation. She whimpered softly as she felt the heat of her blood dribble down her arm from where his fingernails had finally cut her. The councilors grew silent, but none moved to help her. Gritting her teeth, Amaleah forced herself to look her father in the face.

Only a moment ago his eyes had rolled back into his head and his face had slackened, but now his eyes were dark again, his features hard. Then, he smiled deeply at her as he leaned into her. His hot, lumpy body pressed into her. She could feel his sweat even through all the layers of clothing separating them. His breath tickled her neck as he whispered in her ear. It carried the scent of mulled ale and cheese. Her stomach wrenched at the smell of him.

He began reciting a poem about the Lady Marianna and her lover, Knight Patrik. As a child, Amaleah had loved Marianna's story. There was an abundance of ballads sung by the tavern bards about Lady Marianna. Amaleah remembered how her father had invited them to attend court and share their songs with Lady Nicolette Blodruth when she'd been at court. After the Blodruths left the castle, the bards had never been invited to return.

This particular poem told of Lady Marianna's immense powers as a sorceress during the First Darkness. She was a trained warrior on top of her magical prowess and easily defeated many of Lunameed's foes through the long war. Then, during the siege of the Szarmian defense line at Fort Castil, Patrik became injured in a bloody battle with the Obsidian Knight. Marianna, deeply in love with Patrik, had attempted to nurse him back to health. Forsaking her duties to King Erik the Second of Lunameed, Lady Marianna refused to leave Patrik's bedside. She used all of her magical knowledge to try to save him, but depleted her magical reserves in the process. Unable to help the Lunameedian army, they lost many battles during the First Darkness.

In anger, King Erik banished Lady Marianna to the farthest region of his domain: The Tower of Alnora. Sick and dying from the still-festering wound he had obtained during his battle with the Szarmians, Patrik abandoned his post as a guardian of the Silver Knight in order to reunite with his love. Upon seeing Patrik, Marianna used her last morsel of magic to finally cure him from the decaying sickness he had been poisoned with. As she passed her magic onto him, her light extinguished. The two lovers kissed as the lady took her last breath. Sir Patrik, overcome by his sorrow at the passing of his lover, had used his newfound life to fight for Lunameed and all magical creatures. During the Third Darkness, he suffered another severe wound. Lunameed had finally won and so he had refused medical care. He died whispering Marianna's name.

Their love story has been passed down for the three hundred and fifteen years since the First Darkness had ended.

Amaleah shivered as her father finished reciting the epic love ballad. He began relating their love to the love shared between the two warriors of old. She wanted to vomit. She wanted to scream. She wanted to escape. She began to pull away but his hand gripped her like a vice. He pulled her closer to him as he whispered one final line, "I cannot wait to make you my bride, Orianna."

Her mother's name.

Has my father gone completely insane? Amaleah took a small step back. He released her willingly and turned to go back to his seat.

Amaleah stood in shock as she tried to decipher what had just happened. He had called her by her mother's name. It could have been a slip of the tongue, but Amaleah wasn't convinced. Perhaps there was more to her father's obsession with marrying her than she had originally thought. *After all this time, he can't still be in love with my mother, can he?*

A coldness spread through Amaleah's body and the conch shell tucked between her breasts began to emit a burning heat. Images of her mother passed through her mind in rapid succession. They were the only ones Amaleah had: the paintings her father had commissioned of his wife to commemorate their courtship and marriage. Amaleah knew them well; they had been hung in every room in the castle. Even a small collection of sculptures had been created and installed within the palace walls.

From these examples, she knew their appearances were similar. They both had long, auburn and chocolate brown hair that fell in waving curls around their round faces. Amaleah had golden strands threaded throughout her thick hair that shimmered whenever she stepped into the sunlight; she suspected that her mother's hair did the same. They both had straight, lightly defined noses and lightly freckled skin. Unlike the other women of court, both Amaleah and her mother were broad shouldered and thick with voluptuous curves.

There had been multiple occasions of people mistaking one of Orianna's paintings for one of Amaleah. It was an easy thing to do if one did not look closely at the eyes. Amaleah had deep emerald eyes that seemed to change color based on her mood between green and grey. Her mother, at least in all of the paintings Amaleah had seen, had violet eyes. Since returning to court, people had constantly told Amaleah that she was the spitting image of her mother. Yet, whenever Amaleah looked at one of her mother's images, she never felt as beautiful as she thought her mother had been. Rumor had it that Queen Orianna had been blessed by the fae at birth; Amaleah wasn't sure if this was true or not, but she thought her mother was more beautiful than anyone she had ever seen. In Amaleah's mind, there was no way for her to compete. After all, all Amaleah had received was a quick thump on the rump to ensure that the queen had not died in vain at her birth, not a blessing from a magical creature.

Now, as Amaleah stood staring at her father in a room full of men staring at her, she felt as if she had been cursed at birth. Her father sat in his chair and played with his cane. He was no longer looking at her. The conch shell still burned into her skin, like a warning. *What did Cordelia call it? My blessing?* Amaleah wanted to take hold of the tiny shell and feel its warmth spread through her cold body, but she couldn't do that in the privy council room with so many of her father's spies sitting all around her.

She turned and walked quickly from the room without interruption. Her breath came in choppy, shallow bursts as she fled down the hallway. The stays in her dress pressed against her like the iron bars of a prison cell. She felt as if eyes were trained upon her, watching her every move. Instead of returning to her rooms, where she knew Sylvia would be waiting for her, Amaleah turned left at the fork in the hallway and sprinted to the library at the end of the hall.

A fire roared in the tall, stone fireplace. It crackled as Amaleah opened the door to the library. Instantly, the musty, familiar scent of old books washed over her. Her muscles relaxed and the tension that had been building in her lungs subsided. Sighing deeply, Amaleah ambled along the seemingly endless stacks of books. Many of the books were leather bound with gilded titles gleaming out from the light of the fire. Amaleah ran her fingers over the leather as she walked down one of the rows of books. Randomly selecting a book from the shelf, Amaleah sank into an overstuffed cloth chair close to the fire.

Unlike most of the books in the library, this one had a wooden cover that had been carved to depict Lunameedian history. Amaleah traced the designs with the tip of her finger. The wood was smooth to the touch. She smiled when she saw that the book was a first edition of *Lunameed: A History of the Wars of Darkness and their Consequences*. Flipping to the first page of the text, Amaleah began to read the familiar words:

"In the tenth year of our sovereign, King Erik the Second of Lunameed, the kingdom of Szarmi murdered the great hero of the Light, the Lady Alnora, at the Lighthouse of Verenis's Guide. Although her body was never found, the events following her disappearance and apparent murder led to the greatest devastation that Mitier has ever experienced. Twenty years of war, famine, murder, and civil unrest followed. The time now known as the Wars of Darkness—separately known as the First, Second, and Third Darknesses—was truly a period of fear and despair. Entire species of magical creatures were wiped from the land. Rivers changed course. The Ancient Ones left us in our time of greatest need and have not since been seen or heard from. These wars left the kingdoms of Szarmi and Lunameed bereft of an entire generation of men and women. Recognizing their imminent decline should the wars continue, the two kingdoms successfully came to an agreement and the fighting ceased. Although many in Lunameed observe the holiday of our victory over Szarmi

during these wars, the true victor of the war on magic is yet to be determined..."

Amaleah read the entirety of the first chapter. The words of her kingdom's history were as familiar to her as her own hand was. These words defined the past. She knew that if her ancestors could live through the horrors of the Wars of Darkness, then surely she could survive her father's madness. Yet, Cordelia's words echoed in her mind. Amaleah had always assumed that this book—and the other history texts she had read—were true to the actual events of history. Now, as she reread the words she had so often read as a child, doubt filled her mind. So much of the book lacked details about what had truly happened to the magical creatures following the wars. *Why did I never ask more questions?*

She sat in silence for several moments as she hugged the text to her chest. Sniffling a little, Amaleah wiped away the tears that had seeped from her eyes for what felt like the millionth time that day.

She breathed in the scent of the fire and books. Curling her feet in beneath her, Amaleah let herself enjoy the solitude of the library just a little bit longer. For as long as she could remember, Amaleah had loved being in libraries. In books, she had been able to explore the realms beyond the small estate her father had exiled her to. In books, she could be whoever she wanted to be. It was books that had set her free all those times she felt trapped as a child and now as a young woman. She had spent hours poring over old history texts and learning new languages.

During her time in exile, she had taught herself to speak the language of the fae and the elves. She'd learned the dialects of the mountain people from Dramadoon. She had even learned a small amount of Smielian, although not many books contained information about that kingdom's language.

Her tutor, who had attended school at the University of Szarmitec taught her Szarmian as well. Although the language had been banned from use in Lunameed for the past three hundred years, her tutor believed—and Amaleah agreed—that she needed to have a firm understanding of their enemy's language if she was to be a successful ruler once her father passed. Despite her abilities, her father and his court continued to treat her like a delicate little child. At least in exile she had been allowed to roam freely throughout the tower's lands. In the castle, except for when she escaped her guards, she was constantly watched.

Shaking her head, Amaleah set the book down on the side table next to the chair. She couldn't hide away anymore. She needed to face the facts. And the fact was that her father was going to force her to bend to his will if she didn't do something to stop it. Without another moment's hesitation, Amaleah left the library and proceeded to her chambers.

Thoughts of her mother consumed her as she walked back to her rooms. She'd never met her. Never heard her talk except in her dreams. Yet, Amaleah felt as if she knew her. She'd heard so many stories about her, seen so many images of her, looked too much like her, for

Amaleah to believe differently. She was so lost in her own thoughts that she began turning down corridors at random instead of taking the direct path to her rooms.

Turning a corner, Amaleah stumbled into a section of the castle she didn't recognize. It was a passageway that ended in a dead end. Dust covered the paintings lining the walls and the air smelled stale, as if this place hadn't been disturbed in a very long time. Both doors at the end of the hallway were charred with black stains spreading out of the frame. Taking in a sharp breath, Amaleah realized where she was. These rooms used to belong to the Blodruths.

Taking tentative steps down the long hallway, Amaleah peered up at the paintings that lined the hallway. They depicted images of the royal line all the way back to King Erik the First of His Name from over four hundred years prior. On the wall marking the dead end, Amaleah saw a picture of her mother holding a very pregnant belly. Her lips had been painted in an upward slope, as if she were about to laugh at a joke from someone standing in the room with her. Her belly extended far beyond her body. Whoever the artist had been, they had captured the heaviness of that belly in the way her mother's shoulders sagged slightly and the folds of the dress fell tightly against her stomach. Out of all the images she'd seen of her mother, this was the first one of her mother pregnant. With her.

It was the only painting she'd seen of the two of them together.

Tears threatened to sting her eyes once more, but Amaleah forced herself to continue looking at the image. Amaleah wondered what her mother's life had been like before marrying her father. There were so many differing stories about how her parents had met that Amaleah had long since stopped trying to figure out which story was true. Some said that her mother had been raised in the forest by creatures of the Light. Some said that she had been blessed by the fae but cursed by the black-hearted queen of the fae, Jessa. Some said she was a half-breed who had entered court to control her father. Others said that she had been a princess in disguise.

There were more, but it was hard for Amaleah to keep track of all of the stories she'd been told.

What Amaleah knew for a fact was that her mother and father had been deeply in love. Every bard, minstrel, and jester who had ever created tales about her mother and father all agreed on one thing: it only took one chance encounter for King Magnus to fall madly in love with the late queen, Orianna. The bards' songs described how the king had thought of nothing else except for her mother. Now, as Amaleah remembered those tales, she wondered if her mother had felt love towards her father or if she felt as trapped as Amaleah did now.

Chapter Six

The Battle of Alnora, the Third Darkness

A resounding boom filled the space between where Kilian lay and where the tower stood. The robed man sneered at him as screams could be heard from the depths of the tower. Kilian tried to sit up, but the boot pressed more firmly into his chest.

"I am going to thoroughly enjoy this, Kilian Clearwater."

The man wrenched a spiked club from the hands of a dead soldier on his left. He raised the club high, and Kilian could already feel the impact of the metal against his face. He closed his eyes as he waited for it, anticipated its fury.

There was nothing.

Cracking one eye, he saw that the robed figure was turned away from him, staring at the tower in awe. Light shot out of every window and doorway.

Seizing his moment, Kilian used what little strength that had been restored to him through the healing and shoved the man's boot off of his chest. Bolting upright, Kilian pushed his shoulder into the man's body until they were both laying in the bloody, soggy ground. The club fell from the man's fingers as Kilian slammed his fist into the man's face.

He could feel the mending of his shoulder and chest as he continued to pummel the man's face. He heard bones crack and felt his fist push into soft flesh, but still he kept hitting the man. He only stopped when his squire, Richard, pulled him away from the man. *How is Richard still alive?* Kilian thought as he stared at his young squire. The boy wasn't even fully trained.

Kilian stared down at the broken body beneath him and felt no remorse. The sorcerer deserved what he'd gotten for betraying the Light Council.

Turning towards the tower, Kilian left Richard behind as he sprinted toward the light and the screams that still rang out from the tower.

Dead bodies were strewn across the tower steps. Kilian stepped on them in his haste to reach the top. He nearly slipped on the wet stone as he raced up the stairs. His heart pounded as the screaming rang in his ears.

Finally reaching the top, Kilian steadied himself as he carefully pushed open the door to the main level.

Chapter Seven

Estrellala, Lunameed, three hundred years later

Sylvia paced around Amaleah's suite of rooms, waiting for her young charge to return. She wrung her hands as she listened for the familiar footsteps of the princess. It had been hours since the guard had taken the princess away and still she had not returned. Anxiety churned inside Sylvia's stomach as she continued walking across the same stretch of flooring over and over again.

Worse than her anxiety over how the princess's meeting with the king had gone, Sylvia dreaded the conversation she knew she needed to have with the princess upon her return. She knew that she needed to tell Amaleah all that she knew about King Magnus's condition and the Keepers, but felt unsure about how the young woman would react. Over the course of Amaleah's life, Sylvia had played her role as a spy for King Magnus too well. The princess despised her, mistrusted her. Although it had been her duty to make the princess distrust her so, now that it was time to reveal the princess's destiny and the story of Sylvia's past to her, Sylvia wasn't quite sure how to go about doing this. She didn't think the princess would believe her.

She had waited so long for Amaleah to return that the candles had melted down to nothing more than stubs in their holders. One of them extinguished itself in a flutter of smoke. Sylvia was just replacing the candle with a fresh one when Amaleah came storming back into her sleeping chamber. Her face was flushed and her curly hair fell in a knotted mess from the pins Sylvia had so carefully placed early that evening. Crusty streaks covered her cheeks and Sylvia instantly knew that the princess had been crying.

Sylvia watched as the princess strode into the room and came to stand directly in front of a large portrait of the dead queen. She stood across the room from Amaleah and watched as the princess's lips trembled and her eyes roamed over the painting. She was twirling a lock of her tangled hair between her index finger and thumb the way she had seen the princess do when she was contemplating a difficult problem. Sylvia opened her mouth to speak, but then closed it as the princess finally turned to face her.

"Will you tell me about my mother, please?" Her voice cracked as she spoke, and Sylvia wanted nothing more than to rush over to her young princess and scoop her into her arms.

She stopped herself, as she had done so many times before.

Instead, she searched Amaleah's face for clues as to why the princess was so interested in her mother on the day her father had declared that they would be wed. Somewhere deep inside herself, Sylvia knew it made perfect sense that Amaleah would want to know about the woman who had so captured King Magnus's heart and mind, but she hadn't thought that this would be the first thing Amaleah would ask about. There were too many other questions to be answered.

Smiling at Amaleah, Sylvia said, "Well, child, I suppose it depends on which woman you want to know about: the queen or the woman behind the crown."

Amaleah frowned. "Aren't they one and the same?"

Sylvia chuckled at this and hobbled her way over to where Amaleah stood. Her old bones ached as she moved and she wished that she hadn't exerted all of her energy pacing.

"No, my dear. They most certainly were not the same." Sylvia reached over to take Amaleah's hand in her own. Her wrinkled skin looked so much more wrinkled when compared to the princess's smooth hands.

"I knew your mother for several years before she married your father. After becoming the queen, she... changed."

Amaleah leaned towards Sylvia. Although the princess was several inches taller that she was, their foreheads rested against one another as Amaleah whispered, "What do you mean she changed?"

Sylvia leaned away from Amaleah and said, "I mean she changed. She became more aloof, less excited about the world around her. She was still as kind as she had ever been and as loyal to her friends, but she was less full of joy for the world around her."

They remained silent for several moments as Sylvia let her words sink in.

"Tell me about my mother as the woman," the princess finally said. Her voice was so quiet and small that Sylvia nearly missed Amaleah's words.

Leading Amaleah over to the bed, Sylvia settled onto the soft mattress before continuing. Amaleah pulled her knees in tight against her chest and leaned against the wall. Sylvia knew she was waiting for her to continue.

"Well, your mother was incredibly intelligent. She read more books in a week than I think most royalty do their entire lives. She used to say that books were the key to knowing the world and that the stories she read revealed more about life than any conversation she could have."

Sylvia licked her lips as she contemplated her next statement. Deciding it would be a good segue way into the conversation she knew she needed to have, Sylvia said, "Your mother had memorized nearly all of the Book of Prophecy before she became pregnant with you."

Amaleah sat up and looked Sylvia in the eyes, "I've never heard of the Book of Prophecy," she paused. "Why would my mother have memorized it? It can't be that important."

Sylvia patted Amaleah's hand absently as she explained, "The Book of Prophecy is the most important text ever created. Did you know that there have been prophecies about the magical world since before the beginning of the world as we know it?"

Amaleah shook her head, as Sylvia had expected. She continued, "They were a prominent part of the Wars of Darkness that have been forgotten over time. Your mother used to pour over the many prophecies that had been written into record."

Amaleah gripped Sylvia's papery skin tightly. Sylvia knew the young princess's fingers would leave bruise marks on her skin, but she didn't mind. At least the princess was willingly touching her.

"What does that mean, Sylvia? Was there something about her in the book?" Amaleah asked—then almost as if she were afraid to broach the topic—Amaleah continued, "was there something about me?"

Her voice sounded so pleading that Sylvia felt as if her heart would shatter.

Instead of answering Amaleah's question, Sylvia continued describing the queen she had once loved, "She used to journal all the time. There were times when she would run back to her room before an important meeting just so that she could have her journal to write notes to herself in. Your father used to love reading her journal entries. That is, he loved reading the ones she allowed him to see. She had this way of influencing him that was a great benefit to our kingdom. Everyone who knew her loved her."

"Sylvia, I need you to tell me more about the Book of Prophecy. Why have I never read it before—or even heard of it—when I've read so many other things?"

Sighing, Sylvia felt her shoulders sag. *The princess has a right to know her history and her destiny, doesn't she?*

"You will not have heard the things I am about to tell you," Sylvia whispered.

Amaleah's eyes widened and Sylvia knew the princess's attention was solely on her.

"The Book of Prophecy contained all of the destinies foreseen by the Ancient Ones and the Keepers. For thousands of years, creatures of the Light would read its passages in search of their destiny. Over time, the Keepers began writing the destinies of men, in addition to those of creatures of the Light."

Sylvia coughed as she realized she needed something to drink. Her throat was dry and scratchy. She could feel Amaleah's eyes on her as she moved to the water basin and drew a long sip of water from its ladle.

By the time Sylvia had hobbled her way back to the bed Amaleah was perched on the edge of the bed, waiting for her.

"Go on," the princess whispered.

And so Sylvia did.

"During the Wars of Darkness, these prophecies were broken. No one is sure what happened, but the destinies described in its texts never occurred. Countless creatures of the Light and men perished in pursuit of what they believed were their destinies. The reason you have never heard of this book is because the Keepers decided that the book was too dangerous. They believed that the prophecies should be kept secret from the world so as to ensure that no tampering could occur with their resolution."

"Your mother believed that she had been written about and that she could find some meaning within the text to help her understand what she was supposed to do. I'm not sure who gave her a copy of the book, but she died before she found her answers."

They sat in silence for several moments. Sylvia remembered Orianna as she had been before King Magnus had found her. She remembered how the young princess before her now had been before King Magnus declared his intentions. It always came back to King Magnus.

Clearing her throat, Sylvia said, "My Princess, I have something important that I wish to discuss with you."

To Sylvia's relief, Amaleah inclined her head towards her and nodded.

"It is about what we discussed earlier today." As she spoke, Sylvia gathered the candles from about the room, "I think that I may have a way to protect you in your time of need. But now that the time has come, I need you to promise me that you will never reveal what I am about to show you to anyone, no matter the cost."

Sylvia held her breath as she waited for the princess to respond. Amaleah had such a strange look on her face that it was impossible for Sylvia to tell what the young woman was thinking. She hoped it was that she could trust her, despite everything.

Although Amaleah hadn't responded, Sylvia scooped a fistful of fae dust from a pouch looped around her corded belt. Instantly, the dust burst into a colorful array of sparks before filling the room with a sickly sweet scent. Sylvia breathed in deeply. She had missed this smell.

Amaleah approached Sylvia, her eyes wide and her cheeks flushed. Sylvia knew she was taking a risk by using the fae dust before Amaleah had promised, but she wanted to be able to place a shadow of doubt on the princess about her loyalty to the king.

"Sylvia, what are you doing!" Amaleah voice was high-pitched in Sylvia's ear. "You know my father decreed that fae dust wasn't allowed to be used in the kingdom. He strictly forbids it."

Sylvia laughed loudly. "Your father thinks that he can deny the right that belongs to all who belong to the fae, but he is mistaken. He believes that just because he is the king of Lunameed—the birthplace of the Light—that he, above all others, has dominion over its creatures."

She struck another match and lit another candle. Staring Amaleah right in the eyes, Sylvia cast another handful of the dust onto its flame. The candle burst with pink and purple sparks. Smoke billowed out from the candle in a way that was unnatural for such a small flame. Sylvia heard Amaleah gasp.

"Little does he know that he is but a pawn in a much bigger plan, just as all men are pawns in the threads that bind all creatures of the Light together."

"What are you talking about?" Amaleah's voice cut through the wall of smoke filling her room.

Sylvia didn't respond but continued to light candles and throw fae dust until the entire room was filled with the scent. It had a sweet scent of strawberries and roses with a hint of cherry wood, yet it also contained an undertone of decay. Sylvia breathed as deeply as her weakened lungs would allow her to. Her shoulders rose and fell with her breaths. She closed her eyes as she drew in a long, deep breath. She could feel the magic of the fae fill her; it felt like warmth and lust and joy all rolled into one.

"Do you know why your father chose to ban the use of fae dust?" Sylvia peered at Amaleah over the light of the candles in front of her.

"Because Witches of Midnight were using the magic contained in its ingredients to summon innocent fae in order to steal their immortality for a bit of youth." Amaleah paused before continuing, "You're not a witch are you?"

Sylvia burst out in laughter until her lungs heaved and her chest hurt.

"No, child, I am not a witch. But your father did not tell the kingdom the whole truth about why he chose to ban this incense."

"What do you mean?"

"He banned this incense not because of the Witches of Midnight, but because he knew that the fae had integrated themselves into his court and he was afraid of what they would reveal to their queen if he continued to allow them easy access to correspond with their people."

"But if members of the fae have infiltrated court, wouldn't we be able to tell? I mean... they have always been depicted as looking so different from humans," Amaleah said.

"Not all fae look the way they have been described in the books. Amaleah, have you never wondered why your tales never talk about the tiefs?"

Sylvia waited for Amaleah to respond. When she didn't, Sylvia began to explain, "Tiefs are the offspring of two different species of magical creatures. Since the end of the Third Darkness, tiefs have been ostracized from society because they represent the destruction that was wrought during the wars. Recently, King Magnus has allowed them to be publically shamed by being placed in the Box."

Sylvia shuddered and her heart hammered in her chest. She had heard too many tales from her sisters for the telling of this tale to not affect her.

Continuing, Sylvia explained, "I know you have not yet been to town since your return to court, but the Box is a contraption in the middle of a street's square where the lowest creatures and criminals are sent for punishment."

Sylvia paused and took a deep breath of the smoke to fortify her. When she opened her eyes to look at Amaleah, she knew she needed to continue before the princess grew too impatient with her story, "Once inside the Box, crowds are allowed to throw stones, rotten food, and magic powders to cause all types of ailments to their occupants. To be a tief in Lunameed is to be considered less than nothing. Our kingdom does not have slaves the way that the Island Nations do, but if it did, tiefs would fall even below the slaves."

"Sylvia, how can you say all of these things? There's no proof that different magical creatures can even reproduce. How can you know that my father is targeting tiefs when they're not recorded in our kingdom's records?"

Tears welled in Sylvia's eyes. *What will this child think of me when she knows the truth?* "But they do exist, Amaleah. And they all have stories and lives and things to live for. Tiefs have been an integral part of the Light's history since its beginning. It was only after the wars that they were regarded as a detriment to society. Our stories are some of the most integral to Lunameedian history." Sylvia's voice quivered as she spoke.

"What do you mean by *our* stories?" Amaleah's voice shook as much as Sylvia's.

"I come from a long line of tiefs. My mother and her grandmother before her were all of the fae and human races. Although this makes my magical abilities weak among my kind, I hold a place of honor within the fae kingdom."

Amaleah's eyes widened. Sylvia reached out and cupped her cheek in her hand. The girl's face was warm and soothing. When Amaleah didn't pull away from her, Sylvia opened her mouth to continue. As she did, Amaleah burst out, "But how? How did you become a royal servant? How did you hide the fact that you were a tief for so long? Why did you take the risk?"

Sylvia held up her hands to stop Amaleah from continuing.

"Slow down, child. I will answer all that you have to ask, but later. Fae dust is hard to come by and we must call my sisterhood to our aid before its magic has run out."

The smoke in the room had already begun to dissipate and Sylvia feared that her small reserve of magic wouldn't be enough to reach her sisters. Raising her hands high above her head, Sylvia clapped her hands once.

Instantly all the candles in the room extinguished as one. The room was dark and smoky. Sylvia could no longer see Amaleah, but she prayed to the Light that the princess wasn't afraid of her. Sylvia's senses heightened. She could sense everything around her, hear her heartbeat, feel the roughness of her linen dress against her thin skin. She was getting old.

Whispering the incantation her mother had taught her, Sylvia called to her sisters. Just when she felt the barrier between them about to break, she said, in a much deeper and raspier voice than was usual, "Amaleah, close your eyes and only open them when I tell you to. My sisters of the forest will be upon us soon."

In the darkness, Sylvia couldn't tell if Amaleah had done as she was asked, but it didn't matter. She continued to chant the calling to her sisterhood. When the last word of the incantation had been spoken, three orbs of light zoomed out of the stick of incense: one pink, one blue, and one as white as the snow falling from the sky. Sylvia smiled as the orbs of light hovered near her face. A sense of calm washed over her as the lights danced about the room. Mirth bubbled inside of her and Sylvia laughed.

"Open your eyes, Amaleah, and meet my sisters."

Chapter Eight

Amaleah opened her eyes just as an orb of light came to sit right on the bridge of her nose. The blinding white light pierced her eyes as her eyelids fluttered open. Gasping, Amaleah tried to brush the light away. As she did, the brilliance of the light dissipated, leaving a strange little creature resting on Amaleah's nose. She crossed her eyes and tried to see the creature more clearly, but the creature only became blurrier.

The creature emitted dust from her body and laughed at Amaleah's expression. Wrinkling her nose, Amaleah tried to keep from sneezing, but couldn't control it. The creature shot into the air and hovered mere inches from Amaleah's face.

Unlike the stories Amaleah had read about the fae, the creature did not appear human. She was more catlike. Despite having the torso and head of a human, she had ears that pointed upwards, long nails that were curved like claws, and a long tail that swished in the breeze created by her flapping wings. Pink and gold lines mixed together to form intricate patterns all over her wings and body. When the fae smiled, her grin stretched wide across her face. There was something distinctly feminine about the fae; Amaleah just couldn't quite put her finger on it.

"Princess Amaleah, I am Madriala, princess of what you humans would call Faer Forest, but which we call Draxaflor," the catlike fae said in a high-pitched voice. "I am sister to Maribella, Mariposa, and the tief, Sylvia." She flapped her wings delicately and Amaleah felt a light breeze graze her cheek. "It is a great pleasure to finally meet you."

Amaleah stared at Madriala without blinking. The fae smiled at her blithely.

Suddenly, the blue light whizzed around her head, causing Amaleah to look away from Madriala. The light landed on her dressing table and transformed into a fish-tailed fairy. Seashells and seaweed clung to her hair. Her wings were short and slightly furry; they fluttered quickly behind the fae's body.

In a high-pitched shrill, the fae began speaking. It took Amaleah a moment to realize that the creature was speaking in Lunameedian. "Princess Amaleah, I am Maribella, and I am here to help you realize the great power and potential which you possess."

Amaleah blinked slowly and sank into a plush chair. *What great power could I possibly possess?* She thought as she continued staring at the blue fairy. The fae gave no further hints as to what she was talking about.

The third and final orb of light, whom Amaleah assumed was Mariposa, zipped past Amaleah's head as she made her way to the dresser upon which Maribella rested. Instead of instantly turning into her more human form, the fae hovered in the air above her sister.

In a deep, melodic voice, the third fae sang, "Sisters, be careful. We are not allowed to reveal what will come to pass. It is not yet time." Amaleah watched as the light bounced in the air several times, as if she were wagging a finger at the other fae in the room. Without warning, the orb of light suddenly began shaking and quickly shifted into the stereotypical fae form: human-shaped, with long graceful wings extending far on either side of the body. Like the fae's name, she looked like a butterfly as she fluttered near her sister. Amaleah gasped silently.

The tief, the three fae, and Amaleah stared at each other in silence for one long moment.

Sylvia was the first to speak, her voice coming out in a grumble, "Sister Mariposa, do not presume to think that we have forgotten our promise." Sylvia glared at the fae but continued talking, "Do you not feel the disturbance in the magical world? I fear that it is how our ancestors described it in the age of the Wars of Darkness. Perhaps it is time for a Gathering."

Amaleah looked between Sylvia and her sister. They glared at each other in silence. The other two fae erupted in a whir of whining notes as they argued amongst themselves. Sylvia and Mariposa responded in quiet, harsh tones. Amaleah tried to understand what they were saying but the fae spoke so quickly that she couldn't translate Fae—the language they were speaking—quickly enough to make sense of their speech. Sylvia kept gesturing at her as if she were some sort of show animal to be displayed at one of the merchants' fairs. Amaleah sunk deeper into her chair. She wished she could become invisible.

Finally, Mariposa spoke in a clear, deep voice that cut through the whir of her sisters.

"Sister Sylvia, why have you called upon us? You, who know better than most, the dangers of revealing that which has not come to pass. I thought that you would be better than this. Your actions could cost us all that we have worked for. You alone were chosen with the task of watching over her, protecting her, and teaching her. Why is it now that you have breached our trust and forced us into breaking our vows?"

Amaleah perked up at Mariposa's words. Leaning forward in her chair, she saw that the three fae were now glaring at Sylvia. For Sylvia's part, she stood firmly in place with her hands on her hips. To Amaleah, Sylvia looked like a much younger, braver version of the woman who had raised her. *Do I know this woman at all?*

With slow, deliberate words Sylvia responded, "Your arrogance has risen since the last time we met, Sister. Are you so blinded by ritual that you fail to see that which is right before you? How can the prophecy come to pass if she does not believe in herself? How am I to set her on the right path if she cannot see that I work for her best interests?"

Sylvia's face paled as she spoke, and Amaleah was afraid her nursemaid would collapse right in front of them. She watched as Sylvia steadied herself by leaning on one of Amaleah's sitting chairs.

Sylvia continued, "She believes I am a pawn of her father, the one who would enslave her through marriage."

The fae began chirping at these words, but Sylvia held up her hand to stop them. Amaleah was amazed at her nursemaid's ability to control her sisters.

"No, sisters, the time has come. We can no longer live in fear of the repercussions of using our knowledge. It is time that we take destiny into our own hands and send her on the path to right the wrongs which have come to pass. For she is of the Light, just as you and I are."

The three fae exchanged glances and silently formed a circle around her. Their movements were so quick that Amaleah barely had time to register the blur of lights before the three of them had surrounded her.

Amaleah shifted closer to Sylvia and whispered, "Uh, Sylvia, what are they doing?"

Although Amaleah saw Sylvia's ears twitch, her nursemaid did not respond to her. Amaleah repeated herself in a slightly louder voice. Still, the woman ignored her. Feeling ill at ease with the fae hovering in a triad around her, Amaleah moved as if to leave the circle.

Sylvia huffed loudly and pointed Amaleah back into the center of the fae's triad. Stiffly, the older woman joined the fae to form a circle around Amaleah. The hair on the back of Amaleah's neck rose and she felt the conch shell heat again. *A warning.* Amaleah wrapped her fingers around the shell and closed her eyes tightly. The shell began vibrating in her hand as the fae's wings began to beat in unison. All sound dampened and her body felt as weightless as it did when she was in a hot bath. Her body shivered as she realized that the fae were about to perform magic. On her.

Amaleah reached out her hands as if to stop them, but before she could say a word all four women around her began speaking in unison.

"We have heard the proposal of your father, King Magnus of Lunameed. Your plight has been much spoken of across our land, Amaleah of the bloodline Tiekgar, princess of Lunameed. The Harbinger of the Light."

The voices paused.

Amaleah's heart beat quickly in her chest. *Harbinger of the Light.* Amaleah let the words sink in. She had read stories, really just children's tales, of a savior named the Harbinger of the Light. She had always assumed that the title was just a formality bestowed upon the famous heroes from across the ages. She did not understand why they were calling her the Harbinger of the Light, when, clearly, she was not. She was about to say so when Madriala began speaking in her high-pitched voice.

"Our sister, Sylvia, is telling you the truth. She is bound to serve our father, king over all fae near and far. She was sent to your father's court to protect you."

"You are her charge," a voice to Amaleah's left said.

"You must leave this place."

She couldn't tell who was speaking now.

"Do not succumb to your father."

"You must leave."

"Do not despair at the trouble darkening your heart."

"For you are of us, just as we are of you."

"As are all creatures that contain the Light."

"You must trust Sylvia."

"For she shall not betray you."

"Believe our words and let this blessing pour upon you."

The voices spoke so quickly that Amaleah couldn't tell who was saying what. She felt as if she were in a tunnel being surrounded by the echoes of a thousand voices, and yet there were only four of them.

Suddenly, the voices became one again. Amaleah felt a shiver slide up her spine. The conch shell was shaking so violently now that Amaleah was afraid it would shatter in her hand.

"To you, dear Amaleah, protector of us all, we give the breath of the fae, of earth and air and water, so that you shall not perish when all seems lost and the darkness of the world swells around you. This blessing shall be a light within your world."

There was a blinding light as the fae stopped speaking. Amaleah felt a force push against her, shoving her backwards. A coldness followed that seemed to swallow her whole. It felt as if a blade made from ice were slowing sinking down her body, through her flesh, and into her very being. A wave of heat followed the coldness, causing sweat to bead on Amaleah's neck. She felt a prickling on her ankle as if she were being stung by bees.

The conch shell had stopped shaking.

Amaleah looked down at her ankle, expecting to see the blisters of a thousand attacks. Instead, she saw an intricate design of flowers, the sea, and the sun mixed together and wrapped around her ankle. The design glimmered as silvery ink sank into Amaleah's skin. She had never seen anything so beautiful. Or felt something so painful. Her skin burned where the ink resided. Amaleah let out the tiniest of moans as her skin flared red and then returned to its usual olive color.

The room was completely silent. Twirling around, Amaleah noted that all of the women's eyes were closed tightly. Their faces were smooth and blank of all emotion. She opened her mouth to speak but then quickly shut it. The fae joined hands as they moved inwards, closing in on her.

The tattoo throbbed.

"Remember this omen always." *Is that one voice or many?* Amaleah couldn't tell anymore. Closing her eyes tightly, she breathed in deeply as she let the voices encompass her.

"Be peaceful in the darkness, for your light is brighter than the sun or the stars. It is brighter than us all."

"Remember us. Remember the prophecy. Remember who you are."

The pressure Amaleah had been feeling subsided as the denseness of the air disappeared. Amaleah breathed out a sigh of relief.

She waited for the fae to speak again. They did not. A cool breeze caressed her cheek as it zipped through the room. Cracking her eyes to see if the fae were still there, Amaleah saw only the sharp, bright light of several lit candles. The sister moons shone through the open window. The fae had disappeared.

Except for Sylvia. She, of course, was still there.

Amaleah stood for several more moments as she waited for Sylvia to explain what had just happened to her. The older woman busied herself with extinguishing the candles and cleaning up the room. Impatiently, Amaleah began tapping her foot. Loudly.

Still, the older woman paid her no heed. Instead, she pulled out a duster from within the cleaning closet and began dusting the room. Quickly sweeping the remains of the candles and fae dust into a burlap satchel, Sylvia waddled over to the door leading to her room.

"Wait."

Amaleah said the word softly, but in a commanding voice. Sylvia hunched her shoulders and slowly turned to face her.

Amaleah hesitated as she remembered what her life had been like growing up.

The older woman had berated her and made her feel worthless, even when they were in exile together. There had been innumerable times that Sylvia had an opportunity to explain her real purpose in the Lunameedian court. She never had. Instead, she had let Amaleah believe that she was entirely alone.

When Amaleah was thirteen she had contracted the Sleeping Death. Not many children who took ill with the virus ever regained consciousness and would, eventually, waste away into nothing more than a starved corpse. Amaleah remembered hearing concerned voices around her. Her father had sent envoys from the Island Nations with the newest medicines to treat the illness. Yet, even when Amaleah had laid in what could have been her death bed, Sylvia had not offered her words of comfort.

Now she wanted Amaleah to believe that she had only ever done those things to ensure Amaleah's safety and happiness. Now she wanted Amaleah to believe that she was a tief who had the power to save her. Sylvia wanted Amaleah to trust her. Amaleah wasn't sure that she could.

In her earlier days, Amaleah believed that she had been loved. She remembered snuggling under the covers with a tiny kitten her father had given her. And listening to her father read to her by the fire during the deepest parts of winter. She remembered a girl, a friend, who had played with her. Sylvia's granddaughter, Naomi. She had been Amaleah's first and only friend.

Amaleah shook herself out of her jarring memories. Sylvia still stood before her. Her hands hung stiffly on either side of her body and she kept her back as straight as possible. Somehow her nursemaid did not look as formidable as Amaleah had always perceived her.

"How is Naomi?" Amaleah asked in huff.

Sylvia blinked at her. "Naomi?"

"Yes, Sylvia, Naomi. How is she?" Amaleah pursed her lips as she crossed her arms over her body.

"She's fine," Sylvia said curtly. "What do you really want to talk about, Your Highness?"

So formal.

"I remember her, Sylvia. I remember playing games with her in the garden. And sharing secrets with her as we cuddled in bed. I remember the day she was removed from court." Amaleah peered at Sylvia's face, "Do you remember that day, Sylvia? How we cried and clung to each other. How, even after days had passed I still asked for her? Do you remember what you said to me? Do you?" Amaleah's voice quivered as she spoke.

"Yes. I remember." Sylvia's voice did not quiver. It stood strong, stern, as it always had been.

"You told me that we will always lose the people we love."

Without saying a word, Sylvia crossed the distance between them in a single movement. Grasping Amaleah roughly by the arms, Sylvia leaned in close. Close enough that, even though Sylvia only spoke in the softest of whispers, Amaleah could hear her.

"What I said then is still true. If you live long enough, you will always lose the people you love. Or they'll lose you. That's just how life works."

As Sylvia pulled back, Amaleah noticed tears in the woman's eyes.

"I remember hating you." She didn't know why she said it, but she knew it was true. After everything that had happened today, she wasn't sure if it still was.

Sighing, Sylvia responded, "Then I accomplished what I was sent to do."

Amaleah closed her eyes. *So it was all an act.* Sylvia had made her feel alone as an act.

"And, My Princess, let's not forget that you weren't the only one who lost someone you loved when Naomi was taken away. Your pain was that of a child losing her first friend. My pain was that of losing a child I loved more than life itself."

Amaleah opened her eyes. Sylvia stepped towards Amaleah and gripped her arms firmly.

"Everything I've done, I've done to protect you."

Amaleah scoffed. "It's never felt that way. All I've ever wanted was for you to love me. To take care of me." She looked up into Sylvia's eyes. "Was there ever a time that you ever wanted to hold me? To make me feel comforted? To tell me the truth?"

Sylvia's reply came quickly. "No."

Amaleah's heart sunk, yet she also felt vindicated.

Sylvia continued, "I never wanted to tell you the truth. I knew that it would place you in too precarious a situation. But I always wanted to provide you with comfort." She moved her hand up to Amaleah's cheek.

"Do you remember when you contracted the Sleeping Death? I spent every day and night by your side. I used all of my magical reserves to keep you from dying. You, Amaleah, are the reason I have done everything that I have. All I ever wanted to do was protect you. I am entirely loyal to you."

Amaleah shook her face out of Sylvia's grasp. "Duty and protection are not the same thing as love."

"No. They're not. They're stronger."

Once again, Amaleah felt numb to Sylvia's words. She knew one thing for certain: she did not want to continue discussing the matter.

Ripping away from Sylvia, Amaleah crossed her bedroom and threw herself atop the bed. She fiddled with the fringe of her blanket. She could feel the tears building behind her eyes, causing a deep pressure within her head. Pressing her eyes tightly together, Amaleah forced the tears to stay hidden. Her head pounded.

How did all of this happen? Amaleah couldn't seem to make her thoughts run coherently together. Each time she had the segment of an idea it became jumbled with the next. *Is there any hope for me?* Amaleah was no longer sure.

She'd been successfully able to convince her father to make three dresses: one of the sun, one of the stars, and one of the ocean's depths. Nothing like what she had described had been made before. Add to them the coat made from a pelt of every type of animal in their land and she didn't know how her father could ever be successful in his quest. Amaleah smiled to herself as she covered up with the blanket. Exhaustion washed over her. Despite the pounding in her head, Amaleah felt her eyes drooping.

"You may leave, Sylvia."

Amaleah did not open her eyes to see if Sylvia had left. She heard the door creak open and close. Sylvia didn't say a word as she left the room. Amaleah wasn't sure if she felt elated or empty. The emotions were too similar in her memories for there to be a difference.

Amaleah sighed. She didn't want to try to figure everything out. Her entire life seemed like a lie. Not for the first time, Amaleah pondered whether or not her mother had been a part of the magical world. She doubted it. But, then again, she had never thought that Sylvia was part of that world either. None of the royals had had magic since the Wars of Darkness. Many claimed it was because the bloodline had been broken and that the true ruler was out there but was not part of the Bluefischer clan. Amaleah had certainly never demonstrated any magical abilities and she had never seen her father wield magic either.

Snuggling deeper into her bed, Amaleah let the weariness of the day encompass her. She had barely closed her eyes before sleep overtook her.

Chapter Nine

Sunlight poured into Amaleah's room through the high windows facing the east. Groaning, Amaleah tried turning over and covering her head with her covers. She had barely covered her head when a soft knock on the door preceded Sylvia bustling into the room. She hummed to herself as she pulled out Amaleah's outfit for the day.

Amaleah rolled over to face her nursemaid. The old woman smiled at her warmly. She hobbled over to the bed and sat primly on the edge. Patting Amaleah on the hand, Sylvia whispered, "How are you feeling this morning, my dear?"

Amaleah grunted as Sylvia brushed her hair out of her face. Amaleah grunted but didn't pull away.

"Are you going to say anything about me being a tief, My Lady?" Sylvia asked.

Stunned, Amaleah just stared at Sylvia.

"You know, I did a lot of thinking about our conversation last night. I think... I think it would be best if we continued talking about your mother. And my role in your life these past seventeen years."

Amaleah rolled away from her. "I don't want to hear anything you have to say."

"I believe you." A sad smile crept across Sylvia's face as she spoke, "But I also think that you will continue wanting answers until you get them. I can help you, Amaleah, if you let me."

Amaleah swatted away Sylvia's hand as the old woman tried to caress her cheek again.

"I don't want you to treat me kindly. Not now, after all these years." Tears threatened to spill from her eyes.

Amaleah wiggled out from beneath the covers and slid out of bed on the opposite side from Sylvia. It was then that she realized that she was still wearing her gown from the night before. It felt stiff against her skin. Amaleah cringed as she made her way towards her wardrobe.

Instead of picking up the gown Sylvia had laid out for her to wear, Amaleah selected a deep purple one from the depths of her wardrobe.

"I've been thinking too, Sylvia. I think it's time that I had a proper set of ladies' maids instead of a nursemaid. I'm seventeen now. I am not sure that your services are still required."

Sylvia's shoulders visibly slumped. "Of course, My Lady. If that is what you truly desire, I will arrange it."

She stood behind Amaleah and helped her slip out of yesterday's clothing. She retightened the corset. Amaleah sucked in her breath as the stays bit into her skin.

Sylvia pulled the laces taut and straightened the shift, chemise, and stays of Amaleah's undergarments. Amaleah could feel Sylvia's gnarled hands trembling on her skin as she ensured every part of her dress lay perfectly upon her body. Amaleah shivered against her nursemaid's touch.

Amaleah shifted slightly and asked in a raspy voice, "Why did they give me a blessing?"

"My sisters? That I cannot answer, for that was not actually part of the reason I called upon them. But I assume that the blessing will aid you in some aspect of the obstacles you must face in the future."

"You keep talking about challenges as if I haven't faced enough struggles in my seventeen years. What else could there be for me to face?"

Sylvia gave her a knowing smile in the mirror. "Oh, child, if only we could see the future in detail. Alas, all we see are phantoms of what could be should the pieces fall together."

"Do you always speak in such vague terms when you don't wish to speak of something? It would be better to just say nothing at all, I think."

"It is better to give answers when one can and to explain why you cannot in all other instances. Just because something is vague does not mean that it is unhelpful. You would be well served to remember this."

Amaleah's head jerked as Sylvia pulled a thick brush through her hair. "You know I have feelings, right? I am a real person. Not just some doll, some pawn that you and the other fae can use to do your bidding." Amaleah lifted her head high and looked at Sylvia in the mirror.

"Yes, My Lady. I know you're a real person. As do my sisters of the Light. You are a very special person to us."

Amaleah scoffed at that. "I wish I were not so special. Maybe then my own father wouldn't covet me and force me to marry him."

Sylvia reached out her hand as if to touch Amaleah's face, but Amaleah jerked away from her. "I think I can manage getting ready by myself from here." She closed her eyes. "That is all, Sylvia. Please go." She flicked her hand towards the door and waited until she heard the door close behind Sylvia before opening her eyes.

Once she was sure Sylvia was gone, Amaleah regretted being so harsh with her. She hadn't wanted to be so cruel to the older woman, but she couldn't change the fact that every time she saw her, felt her touch, she realized that she couldn't forget how Sylvia had made her feel all those years they had been exiled together. She had felt alone. Staring at herself in the mirror, Amaleah forced herself to smile before slipping out of the room to follow Sylvia down the hall.

Chapter Ten

Six months later

Amaleah paced around her receiving room, waiting for her father's favorite pastry chef to arrive for their meeting. Wedding preparations had become an everyday chore for Amaleah and the ladies of the court. For the past six months, High Councilor Namadus had sent a servant to Amaleah's room with a list of the things she needed to complete for the day. Despite Amaleah's grumblings, she knew that in order for her plan to work that she needed to comply with the demands of the councilors and the king.

She attended parties, court hearings, and parliament meetings. She had tea with the most influential women of Lunameed. She had meetings with dressmakers, floral arrangers, and pastry chefs. She took dance and riding lessons every evening. After her evening meal, her new tutor, Christophe, would give her lessons on court etiquette and manners, the history of Lunameed, and the tactics of war. During Amaleah's confinement at Maravra's Tower, she had read countless books on Lunameedian history. But the way that Christophe helped her understand politics and war through his stories made the history of not just Lunameed, but all of Mitier, come alive.

Amaleah wondered why Namadus was putting so much of his time and effort into giving her every opportunity to become the ideal queen of Lunameed. Each time they met in the corridors of the palace, he would smile at her warmly and ask how the wedding planning was going. Ever since her father had accepted her terms for the engagement, Namadus had become more and more cordial towards her. Yet, Amaleah couldn't shake the feeling that, if given the chance, Namadus would betray her.

Over the course of the six months since she'd made the agreement with her father, the royal councilors had sent her countless gifts. Hats, sets of gloves, new ball gowns that were more beautiful than any she had ever imagined. All of them arrived by servant with notes from the councilors. Namadus and his crew of supporters had been the most loyal to the cause. It seemed like every day she would receive something new from one of them. It was overwhelming.

Then, about a month ago, her face had started appearing on tea cups and wax seals. At that point, Namadus had requested that in addition to her lessons and the wedding planning that Amaleah needed to start giving public speeches to the people. Every week for the past five weeks, she had made an appearance at Estrellala's town center. He always had a speech prepared for her. And a new dress. To Amaleah, it felt like just another way for the high councilor to exert his control over her.

"The people need to see their princess and future queen, My Lady." Namadus had said at the first forum.

The minute Amaleah stepped out onto the podium to welcome all who were in attendance to the afternoon's speeches, she had been booed by several members of the gathering. A group of young children had even thrown tattered, smelly shoes at her. Amaleah had run off stage in embarrassment. None of the people had ever attempted to harm or humiliate her before. Christophe told her later that taxes had been raised on the people in order to support the king's obsession with sewing her desired dresses and coat. They thought it was an abomination that she had agreed to marry her own father should he be able to complete the request for the dresses and coat. Rumors had swept through the city that the magical creatures would rebel against the Lunameedians should the king force Amaleah into the union. Amaleah knew her people were afraid and simply rebelling in the only way they knew how. Knowing this did not stop the ache from building within Amaleah's heart.

Namadus claimed that by standing before the people, she would be able to gain their trust. So far, all he had succeeded in doing was subjecting her to ridicule and blame. The fancier the dresses were, the more the people cried out. The nobles, on the other hand, loved everything about her. Women at court had started following her fashion. The commoners hated her and the nobles had come to revere her. Amaleah hated it all.

Worse, everything Namadus did well had his name attached to it. When things did not go well, Amaleah was at fault. She felt like a pawn being moved around against her will. Despite having many acquaintances at court now, she felt as if all of her new connections were part of a facade. She was sure Namadus was using them as spies to determine his next steps. She knew he suspected her of plotting an escape plan. And he wasn't off the mark. But she didn't want him to know that.

He had made her life comfortable. More comfortable than it had ever been, even during the happy days before she had been exiled. She knew that, with the support of the nobles in his pocket and his economic standing, he could take away that comfort in an instant if he ever gained proof that she was planning on leaving. He assumed that because she had grown up away from court that she would be enthralled by all the pretty things and would stop fighting him. Amaleah was determined to prove his assumptions wrong. In fact, all that he was doing was teaching her how to become better at the game.

At times, she missed the freedom of her exile. The constant stream of social functions and duplicitous interactions bored her. She sometimes wished that she could still be the girl locked away in the tower. At least then she still had a chance at being rescued. The only rescuing that would be achieved now would have to be of her own doing. None of the nobles, Lunameedian subjects, or neighboring kingdoms would dare to defy her father. At least, not openly.

On occasion, Sylvia would tell Amaleah stories about the late queen, Orianna. Amaleah's mother had been well loved by all the realm. The commoners believed that she had grown up on the streets before marrying King Magnus, and the nobles believed that she had been a princess in disguise. In her way, Queen Orianna had been an inspiration to every single person in the realm.

Sylvia told her that the nobles had disliked her at first. They thought her quaint. However, after a few years at court, they had come to appreciate her genuine care for the Lunameedian people. She had been kind and fair and trustworthy to all who came to her. She was known for hearing people out, no matter the crimes they had committed or the debts that they owed. Her mother had been known for giving second chances. Amaleah wondered what she herself would be known for in the coming days.

A light tap on the door startled Amaleah out of her thoughts. The pastry chef had arrived. One of the many ladies assigned to Amaleah's entourage opened the door. Short, heavyset, and middle-aged, the pastry chef waddled into the room with his arms overladen with tarts and pies and cakes of such aroma that Amaleah was sure she should faint from the sweet scents scourging her nose. A light sheen of sweat covered his brow as he wheezed from the weight of his cargo.

"Oh my!" he exclaimed. "It is such a pleasure to finally meet you. Your Grace. Your Beauty. Ummm, Your Highest Majesty." His mouth kept moving and Amaleah knew he was going to continue exalting her if she didn't stop him.

"You poor dear," she said as she rushed forward to take one of the parcels from his arms. She could feel the heat wafting up from the freshly baked delight inside the box. "Couldn't any of the servants be prevailed upon to help you carry all of these things?" Amaleah smiled at him as she led him into her sitting room.

"Alas, they were all busy with other tasks." He huffed.

Amaleah watched in dismay as the boxes pinched beneath his arm slipped from their position and dropped to the floor. The top of one of the boxes exploded as it hit the ground, sending an array of brightly colored sweet cakes into the air. Time seemed to slow as Amaleah watched them arc through the sky and then land with a loud squishing noise upon the rug. Icing and fruit filling splattered across the room. A stray dollop of what tasted like lemon crème landed on Amaleah's cheek and rolled into her mouth.

The chef stared at her dumbfounded for several heart beats. Amaleah stared back and then burst into a fit of laughter. Wiping what remained of the crème off of her face, Amaleah rushed forward to help the pastry chef clean up with mess.

"Here, let me help you," she said as she wiped chocolate sauce from his boots.

"Thank you." His voice sounded surprised and Amaleah looked up at him with a quizzical expression.

The man blushed a deep cherry red. "I'm sorry, My Lady, it's just that… well, not many of the nobles in the court have ever offered to help me much less get on their hands and knees to scrub my messes up off the floor." He cleared his throat, "You are going to make a fine queen one day, My Lady."

It was Amaleah's turn to blush.

"It is nothing," she said, her voice tight. Once the bulk of the mess had been attended to, Amaleah led him to a collection of tables she had had set up special for the occasion. He dumped what remained of his parcels onto the tables alongside the bundle Amaleah had been carrying.

"There now, see. We've got them all right here."

"Well, except for the twenty more trays in the kitchen." He winked at her as he spoke. His plump cheeks dimpled in a happy, pleasant way.

"Heavens. That's so many!" She exclaimed as she motioned for three of her ladies to go to the kitchen to retrieve the rest of the trays.

"When one is planning the sweets for one's ruler, one must prepare the best and the most," he said solemnly.

"Well, if you're going to take such good care of me, then I believe that we should be properly introduced."

She stuck out her hand. "You may call me Amaleah instead of 'Your Majesty' or 'Your Highness' or any other such name. I quite believe that we will be splendid friends."

He stared at her with a shocked expression. Amaleah saw the color rise up on his cheeks. "I… well… I…was not expecting that," he finally mumbled.

Taking her hand in his, he introduced himself as well, "Most of the nobility know me as Mr. Danishly since that is my merchant name. But my real name is Mr. Charles Sweets."

Amaleah laughed. "With a name like Mr. Sweets why would you ever need a merchant name like 'Mr. Danishly?' You know you sell pastries and cakes for a living, yes?"

He grinned sheepishly. "I thought people wouldn't believe that Mr. Sweets was my real name."

They stood in silence for the barest of moments before they both burst out laughing. They only stopped when Amaleah's ladies burst into the room laden with the remaining trays.

Every pastry was more ornate and grander than the last. Mr. Sweets had created an array of cakes and pies decorated to depict both Amaleah and her father. He had used sugar cubes and icing as well as carved fruit to duplicate the palace, its gardens, and the animals in the nearby Faer Forest. Everything smelled so warm and sweet and fresh that Amaleah's mouth watered as she looked upon them. He had created delicate sugar work to cover many of the cakes. Amaleah was afraid to touch them for fear that they would crumble if disturbed.

Mr. Sweets had even gone as far as to create a replica of the coat design her father's tailor had produced for when the furs were supplied. Of course, Amaleah doubted that the tailor would actually be able to sew that many pelts together without the help of the fae. The perfectly sculpted icing was so realistic that it made

Amaleah shudder to look at it. She did not appreciate the reminder of her bargain with her father.

Amaleah and Mr. Sweets discussed which treats would be required for the twenty balls her father's advisors had convinced him to throw in honor of the impending marriage. It had taken six months for the balls to be planned. And now they were entering the final stages of progress. Still, none of the three dresses or the fur coat had been produced.

"I was planning on designing a series of ice sculptures to depict the gowns your father is supposed to be making. They will be the most splendid things ever seen in the kingdom." He stared at her as if she would be pleased by this plan.

"Ice sculptures? Do you not think that a bit extravagant, Mr. Sweets?"

"Extravagant? Why, my dearest Princess, everything I do is a bit extravagant. That is the very reason why so many of the nobility procure my services for their balls, parties, and weddings. I may be just a pastry chef, My Lady, but I know how to plan events to remember." He spoke so enthusiastically that Amaleah was sure that he meant what he said.

"Your passion speaks highly of you, Mr. Sweets." She tapped her fingers delicately on the table. "Yet, I think that it would be better to show a degree of economy in these times. Or to use the funds we don't spend on our desserts to help the poor in our cities who are starving."

She knew the minutes the minute her breath passed from her lips that she had misspoken. The Lunameedian court expected the best out of the king, even if the poorest in the cities starved. And, as the princess and bride-to-be, Amaleah was expected to follow suit. No matter how much she disliked the idea.

"Economy?" Mr. Sweets' face paled as he strode over to one of the more extravagant pieces he had designed for her to inspect. "My dear Princess, your father has commanded that these balls and your wedding be the most spectacular events the realm has seen in decades."

He scooped up a small cake that depicted one of the gardens within the Palace of Veri. The blues and greens of the fountain seemed to be moving, even though the water was only icing. He had even sculpted tiny red apples hanging from the tree in the exact spot it was planted in the garden. Squirrels and birds scuttled about the treetops and played in the fountain.

Mr. Sweets placed the cake on the table in front of Amaleah. His eyes darted between her and her ladies.

"Forgive me for saying so, Your Highness, but going the economic route is simply not possible."

Amaleah searched his eyes. They bored into her, and she could see the fear pinned beneath his relaxed demeanor.

"Of course, Mr. Sweets. I'm so sorry. Of course, you know best."

Noticing that her ladies were leaning towards where Mr. Sweets and she sat, Amaleah felt the fae's tattoo on her ankle turn to ice as she regarded them. *A warning.*

Clapping her hands loudly, Amaleah turned towards them, "Ladies, there is a secret present I wish to present to my father during the upcoming balls." She glanced at Mr. Sweets, but his back was turned towards her. "Come now and leave us be. I want to keep my plan as secret as possible."

She motioned for them to leave her room. There were some backward glances and hushed conversation between her ladies as they exited the room, but none of them disputed her.

Sighing, Amaleah turned back to Mr. Sweets. His shoulders were hunched up and, from the back, he appeared to be in great distress. Rushing forward, Amaleah positioned herself in front of him.

His hands were covering his face, but Amaleah could tell that the man had been crying. Snot covered his hands and there were wet splotches on his shirt.

"Why! Mr. Sweets, whatever is the matter?" she reached over and patted him on his arm as she spoke.

He only cried the harder.

Pulling a chair up behind him, Amaleah helped him sink into the plush carpet chair.

"You need to tell me what has happened," she tried to make her voice as soothing as possible, but left no room for him to interpret her command as a request."

He turned his face away from her, shaking slightly. "I…do not like to speak ill of your father, My Lady. But…" His voice cracked. "High Councilor Namadus made it very clear that if the desserts for the balls and the wedding weren't perfect that my family would be punished for my inadequacy."

He turned to face her, his eyes wet, "My daughter is but seven. My family depends upon me and the money I make as a royal pastry chef and merchant. Surely you can see how important it is that I follow through with your father's commands."

Amaleah remained silent as she contemplated the chef's explanation. *When did my father turn into such a tyrant? When did the madness consume him?* Amaleah had barely seen him since the day he had accepted her bargain. She hadn't noticed slips in his lucidity during the time that they had spent together, but she was concerned about how he would react in the future.

Just as Amaleah was about to respond to the pastry chef, Mr. Sweets slipped a knife into one of the pies, from which sprung two doves.

"I thought you would be particularly pleased with the white doves, My Lady."

Amaleah laughed delightedly as the doves flew to the vaulted beams of the ceiling. When she looked back at his face, he had wiped away the tears and the snot.

"I see I was correct." He smiled warmly, all remnants of the tears Amaleah had seen just moments before disappeared. "How many of the upcoming balls would you like these pies to appear?"

"The theme for the balls is metamorphosis and love. I suppose… that we should have at least one of these for each of the balls. What are your thoughts, Mr. Sweets?"

"I think that would be most appropriate, My Lady."

They continued selecting items for the balls for the next thirty minutes before Amaleah turned to face him. She had been thinking about what he had said to her about her father's threat. If this were true, then her father's madness had spread well past just his abhorrent desire to have her as his wife. Perhaps there was room in her plan to use the pastry chef, and others like him, to aid her in her escape from the palace. But she needed to be sure of him.

"Mr. Sweets, I have a special request of you."

"Yes, My Lady?"

"For the masquerade ball, I am planning on dressing as a butterfly. Well, as a butterfly for part of the evening anyway. I'll be transforming part way through. I was wondering… is there a pie that I could be added to? The way the doves were? I want to make a grand entrance."

"A butterfly, Princess?"

"Yes. For the first part of the ball, I will be dressed all in green, like a caterpillar. Midway through the night, I'll change into a dress full of bright colors and a set of wings. I think it's quite fitting for the circumstances. What do you think?"

Mr. Sweets clasped his hands tightly together and his face turned a deep shade of red. Stammering, he responded, "I think that would be quite beautiful and is such a creative idea, Princess."

Touching his arm lightly, Amaleah leaned in close, "Come now, Mr. Sweets, that not what I meant at all. I know the butterfly costume is a grand idea. But what about the transformation and the flitting out of a pie?"

"I believe, My Lady, that whatever you do will be just splendid. And I am quite sure that I can create a cake fitting of your grand entrance." Amaleah wasn't sure why he had seemed so nervous before, but she continued.

"Mr. Sweets, how exactly would I get into the cake without ruining my dress?"

"Well, there's really only one way to add you to the cake. After I have baked it, I will need to cut a piece of it away. It'll be like a trap door. One entrance will lead into the cake and the top entrance will pop open the top of the cake. To make it perfect, I'll need time to decorate the back of the cake once you're inside. That way, no one will know you're there when it's wheeled out."

"I see. And would it be possible to add a third door to the cake?"

"A third door, My Lady? Whatever for?"

Amaleah paused briefly as she contemplated what she was about to do. Could she trust him? Namadus may have bribed him to say the things he had said in order to gain her trust. Pushing the thoughts aside, she plunged forward. She didn't have enough time to second guess herself.

"I have a grand idea, Mr. Sweets, that I think will send everyone into awe over your creations."

Mr. Sweets leaned towards her expectantly.

"I don't want anyone to know about this plan," she paused, "even if Namadus asks you about what I have in store for the balls and parties, you must promise not to tell him about this one small detail. I think that it will be the most exciting thing that has happened in Lunameed for some time."

She clasped his hands in her own, "What if you added a third opening on the bottom of the cake that I could come in and out of? That way, people could see me enter the cake from the back and, while you're decorating the cake, I can sneak out and change into the butterfly costume." Amaleah clapped her hands excitedly, "I think that would be perfect, don't you?"

Mr. Sweets nodded enthusiastically. "Splendid, My Lady, just splendid."

"As I said before, it's very important that no one know of this plan. Not even High Councilor Namadus or the king."

At this, Mr. Sweets stopped nodding. "But... My Lady... I have been made to promise that I will tell the high councilor everything that we discuss."

He gulped loudly and looked down at their clasped hands, "Otherwise he may harm my family. I can't-"

Amaleah cut him off. "But what a thrill it will be! Think about my grand entrance into the masquerade as a butterfly and the delight that everyone in attendance will have. I'm sure the king will be so delighted that Namadus will excuse you for keeping this one little secret."

Mr. Sweets stared down at his feet and twisted his hands. "I'm not sure, Your Majesty."

Amaleah sighed wistfully. "This is my first masquerade ball, Mr. Sweets. And I do so dearly want to keep this as a surprise for my father. I have had so little opportunity to surprise him of late."

She squeezed his hands gently and looked down at him with a sad smile on her face. "All I want is for this to be the best surprise my father has ever received. I'm absolutely positive that if you tell Namadus about this plan that he'll tell my father and ruin it all."

She pouted slightly and looked up at him through her eyelashes.

The puffy man's face turned an even deeper shade of red and purple. He tapped his fingers on his chin. Amaleah knew that he was contemplating her words.

"Oh all right." He finally said. "Heaven knows I can't deny a child, especially one as beautiful as you. Why, even my daughter always gets what she wants." He chuckled to himself. And then, in a nervous lilt asked, "Are you sure that the high councilor will not be upset that he didn't know of this plan ahead of time?"

Amaleah could hear the worry in the man's voice and felt a small stab of guilt seep into her. She hoped she wasn't condemning his family to death with this plan.

"I'm positive." She flashed the most beguiling smile she could muster and watched as the tension left Mr. Sweets's shoulders.

"Oh, alright. I'll begin the preparations." He smiled at her with a fatherly expression. For just an instant, Amaleah felt guilt haunt her. If this plan succeeded and she was able to escape, his family might feel the ramifications.

She couldn't think about that now. The possibility of what *could* happen wasn't as important as what *would* happen if the king succeeded in his quest. Shaking her head beamed at him.

"Thank you so much, Mr. Sweets. I am sure my father will love it. I cannot express my gratitude enough."

They continued on with the preparations.

Eventually, Amaleah called her servants back in to help the pastry chef carry his trays of now nibbled on pastries back to the kitchens. She gave strict instructions for Mr. Sweets to take part of the food home to his family and to give the rest to beggars in the street. Uncomfortably, he accepted her request before swiftly exiting her suite.

As Mr. Sweets was leaving, Sylvia walked over to Amaleah and helped her remove the day dress she had been wearing. It was already time for the evening meal and time for Amaleah to change. Amaleah wasn't even hungry after tasting all of the many desserts Mr. Sweets had prepared. However, her presence at the Great Hall was required almost every night. She sighed.

"I certainly hope you were not dissatisfied with the pastry chef's work, Princess," Sylvia said lightly as she undid Amaleah's corset. It was a short respite from the constriction, but Amaleah appreciated it greatly. She breathed in deeply without the stays pressing into her ribs.

"No. Of course not, Sylvia. He is a great talent. I'm just a little overrun with all of the planning." She glanced around the room, noticing that a few of her ladies' maids were listening. "There's just so much to do to prepare for the balls and the wedding. I enjoy it, of course, but it has a way of draining me."

Amaleah's eyes darted over her maids. Even after six months, she still did not trust them.

Sylvia removed the last of her undergarments that needed to be switched out for the evening and Amaleah sank down into one of the carved wooden chairs covered in ruby red and gold brocade pillows.

"Ladies, I would like a few moments alone with Mistress Sylvia. It's been such a long time since she and I had a moment to ourselves. I miss our conversations."

Amaleah used as much command in her voice as she could muster. The ladies nodded curtly to Sylvia as they left the room. Amaleah had not asked to be alone with any of them and she was sure they would be jealous of the favor she showed towards the old woman. Amaleah didn't care. She spent enough of her days trying to please everyone else that she just wanted a moment to be herself. She had forgotten what it felt like to not have to pretend, to no longer be worried about the reactions her servants had. Her ladies strode out of her room in a slow line. They glared at Sylvia as they went.

"My Lady?" Sylvia said once the younger ladies had left the room.

"How much time do you think we have?" Amaleah asked in a hushed tone.

"Enough time for you to tell me what's going on."

"There's been a new development. One that I think we need to discuss for it could change the entire landscape of our plans."

Amaleah went on to explain her plan. The entire court would see her enter the cake and would assume that she would be in there until the big reveal at the end. But, because of the false bottom, Amaleah would have the chance to sneak out the bottom of the cake and escape. Guards wouldn't be posted around the cake because they would assume that she was stuck inside it. She would have plenty of time to leave the palace.

Sylvia listened without interrupting until the very end of Amaleah's plan.

"It sounds like a solid addition to our plan, Amaleah. However, I caution you to not trust the pastry chef as blindly as you seem to. He is well known for aligning his loyalties to the highest bidder when it suits him."

Amaleah picked at a loose thread in one of the chair's pillows. Sighing, she responded, "I know. I could tell he was trying to gauge how I would react when he told me about the threat against his family."

"That threat may be a real threat, Amaleah. If he is afraid that his family could be in danger, this puts you in even more danger of being betrayed." Sylvia came over to where Amaleah was standing and took her hands. "But I think that if we play this right, we could use this opportunity to save you."

"Do you really think so? How could this save me if he betrays me?"

"Yes, I really believe that we can use this ill-conceived plan to our advantage." Sylvia spoke firmly. "We'll need to come up with some sort of a phrase, a password if you will, so that if guards are posted anywhere near the cake I can call out the word and you'll know to go forward with the surprise for your father."

"You would be assuming quite a bit of risk, Sylvia."

"Yes, but Mr. Sweets would know that you were leaving the cake and I could be in the waiting area with a, let me see, a wheelbarrow of supplies for your room. It would be the perfect cover since your father still trusts me implicitly."

"That may be true, Sylvia, but does Namadus?"

Sylvia frowned. "Not exactly. Namadus and I have had our differences, but he always ends up listening to me in the end."

"So you think you can handle him?"

"Perhaps. It all depends on Mr. Sweets."

Amaleah frowned. She hoped she hadn't acted too rashly. "Perhaps there is more to our Mr. Sweets than we give him credit for. He could turn out to be a genuinely kind man who won't betray the princess of Lunameed, Sylvia."

"He could."

Sylvia's tone of voice was not convincing. Amaleah's shoulders slumped as she realized that her plan was not as foolproof as she had originally thought it would be.

"Perhaps you should rest before the dinner party tonight, My Lady."

"I wish you wouldn't call me that. I tire of the names they call me. Please, Sylvia, just call me Amaleah. It's what I want to be called."

Sylvia nodded once and began picking jewels that coordinated with the gown. Amaleah watched as her nursemaid selected finery that would go with her evening gown. She had such a large collection of dresses now, she wasn't sure how Sylvia knew where everything was and coordinated her outfits so well. Amaleah doubted she would have been able to keep up with the fashions without Sylvia's help.

After several moments, Amaleah whispered, "Do you think that I will be able to escape him?"

Sylvia didn't look at Amaleah as she responded, "I have every reason to believe that you will be able to escape, child."

"But why? Why do you have so much faith in me?"

"Because there is much that is yet to come and I believe you are the key." Sylvia laughed quietly to herself, "Besides, we have done too much preparation for this to fail."

"When I go, will you go with me?" Amaleah's voice came out quietly. As she asked the question she realized just how much she didn't want to be alone when she escaped. She realized how much she still wanted her nursemaid to comfort her. Sylvia must have picked up on Amaleah's distress, because she crossed the room to where Amaleah lay on her bed.

"I cannot go with you, child," she whispered. "This is a challenge you must face on your own. But with the blessings you received from my sisters, the fae, you are well equipped to succeed." She reached across the bed and rubbed Amaleah's back. Amaleah hiccupped several times as she tried to force the sobs down. She felt Sylvia pull her hair off of her shoulders and begin brushing out the knots. Relaxation swept over her body, making her yawn.

Sitting up on the bed, Amaleah asked, "Sylvia, do you think… do you think he'll actually be able to make the gowns and the cloak within the next six months? Half of his time is already gone and as far as I know nothing has been put into production." She turned on the bed to face Sylvia.

"Amaleah, my dear, your father is a very determined man. A very powerful and determined man. Despite the support my sisters and I showed you, the court of the fae changes swiftly with the moods of our queen. And your father has been able to compel the rest of the magical beings to conduct his business for years. I would not be surprised if he was able to complete the dresses and the coat within the year with the help my mother, the fae queen."

Amaleah's face fell as Sylvia spoke. "I am afraid, Sylvia. I don't… I can't marry him. And after everything

I've seen him do since we've been back at court..." Tears welled in her eyes and silently rolled down her cheeks.

Sylvia embraced her wordlessly. They remained like that for several moments.

Pulling back, Amaleah continued, "Do you know what he calls me sometimes?" She didn't wait for Sylvia to respond before continuing, "He calls me by mother's name, Sylvia. It's such a strange thing. His eyes look at me but they don't see me. It's as if he isn't there at all."

Sylvia scowled at Amaleah and stared up at the ceiling. Amaleah knew her nursemaid was thinking about how to respond to the information she had just shared but she wasn't sure what Sylvia would say.

"I have heard rumors, Princess, about your father. There has been talk in the servants' halls that he comes down to the kitchen at night and talks to people who aren't there." She paused and Amaleah felt herself leaning forward, anticipating Sylvia's next words.

"Others have said that they've seen him wandering the gardens. When approached, he raves about finding the queen. A few servants have said that when they ask him if he would like for you to be fetched he goes into a rage and demands to see Lady Orianna."

"No." The word slipped out in a whisper. Amaleah let out a breath of air she hadn't realized she'd been holding. She'd let herself think—hope—that since he had stopped calling her by her mother's name over the past several months that he was getting better.

"No." She said again, more firmly. "Sylvia, if these rumors are true, then my father's madness has progressed even further than I feared. If these rumors are true, then I am in more danger than we had realized."

"Your father is a very intelligent man, Amaleah. This disease, this madness, will push him even harder to succeed in his endeavors to marry you. If these rumors are true, then he is no longer in touch with reality. This also means you have an opportunity to triumph in the end. But we will need to change our plans, I think."

"What do you mean?"

"I know that you just organized things with Mr. Sweets, but I think that waiting until the masquerade ball would be a mistake. The longer you stay in the palace, in Lunameed, the deeper your father's madness will creep into his mind and take control."

"I'm not ready," Amaleah gasped. "I'm not ready."

Her heart pounded in her chest and she had difficulty breathing. She couldn't do it. *Not yet.*

"You'll need to make yourself ready." Sylvia took both of Amaleah's hands in her own. "Amaleah, you are meant for so much more than ruling Lunameed. I wish I could tell you all that is in store for you, but I cannot. Just know that I have watched you grow from a small child into an intelligent, brave, and caring young woman. You will escape this place. You will accomplish more than you can even imagine. You will succeed."

Tears filled Amaleah's eyes. She had never cried so much in her life as she had in the past six months. In a quavering voice she asked, "Do you really think so?"

"Of course, Princess. Your coming has been foretold across the ages. I do not believe that, now that you have arrived, you will be a disappointment."

Amaleah straightened her back and leaned away from Sylvia.

"What do you mean that my coming has been foretold across the ages?"

Sylvia's face reddened. "I am sorry, My Lady. I have said too much." More quickly than Amaleah would have thought possible, Sylvia jumped up from the bed and moved away from her.

Amaleah grasped Sylvia's arm tightly.

"Sylvia, please tell me what you mean. I need to know everything you know if I am to be successful."

"I cannot, My Lady. I am sorry, but there are laws that dictate that which we can proclaim to the world. The prophecies about you are some of the most precious of all. You don't understand—can't understand—what it has been like. We once told the world what had been foretold, and the prophecies became broken." Sylvia's voice broke as she said the last word. Shaking her head, she continued, "If I were to tell you your destiny now, then there is a chance that it, too, may become one of the broken."

Heat flooded Amaleah's face. So much of her life had been decided for her. She did not want prophecies. She did not want expectations. She only wanted freedom.

"Leave the dress Namadus gave you orders to put me in for tonight. I'll have one of my ladies dress me tonight." Her voice was colder than she intended.

Sylvia's face fell slightly, briefly. Determination followed. "As you wish, My Lady."

Chapter Eleven

Miliom, Szarmi

It was a red sunset. Deep shadows filled the valleys surrounding Miliom. As Colin stared out at the city from his personal balcony, he was once again in awe of the beauty that the towers, streets, and buildings held. Bright lights twinkled in an array of colors, filling the air with bursts of pink, blue, and orange light. The dusty hues looked like fae floating in the air—or, at least, what Colin imagined fae would look like if they were allowed to live in Szarmi.

The kingdom's scientists had spent years developing the technology that powered the tiny clusters of light and building the infrastructure of pipelines that ran beneath the city. Natural gases were pumped through the lines and were lit each night to provide light to the people of Miliom. A stone wall stood high around the city, above all but the castle's towers, ensuring its safety. Beyond the wall, Colin saw the windmills twirling from the powerful gusts that were constantly filling the valley where Miliom sat. These windmills pumped water from the Milo River into the city.

Colin's father had dedicated his life to ensuring that continual progress was made towards the enlightenment of the city. When he died, Colin vowed to himself that he would follow in his father's footsteps when it came to pushing the boundaries of science and technology.

Colin breathed in deeply, letting the cold twilight air fill his lungs. Soon, she would join him on the balcony. Even the thought of her made his skin warm and his breathing heavy. It had been almost eight months since the last time he'd seen Vanessa. During that time, she had fostered with his mother at Ducal House. When he began his journey home, he'd sent for her. And now, here he was, waiting for her at their favorite spot. He did not enjoy the waiting.

To distract himself, Colin looked down at the streets. People milled about the stone walkways in the city. They looked like tiny ants from atop Colin's balcony. Curls of smoke created a haze above the city as kitchen fires began blazing in the small houses that filled it. Colin was too far away to smell the food, but he could imagine the customary spicy dishes he knew his people craved.

Somewhere, Colin wasn't sure where, he could hear a flute and a guitar playing a duet. The music was quiet, almost to the point of being imaginary, but Colin knew it was there. The notes were carried on the wind as they whipped through his body, sending shivers down his spine.

In just two months, all of this would, officially, be his. His to command. His to rule. His to care for.

Closing his eyes, Colin listened for the faint notes of the flute. He could see the player dancing around one of the city squares in his mind's eye. Children would play with brightly colored ribbons. Maybe there was a little old woman who would tell dark tales about the magical creatures who lived to the north and east.

"I will be a better king than my father," Colin whispered to himself. His words slipped through the wind, disappearing the way the notes of the flute had. He hoped he would be ready.

"My Lord?"

Colin turned at the soft voice behind him. A shadowy figure stood hidden in the open archway leading to the balcony. The nearly translucent robe revealed the woman's plump breasts beneath its folds. Her golden blonde hair fell in ringlets around her heart-shaped face. Colin felt his body respond to the scent of her vanilla perfume. In the setting sun, her exposed skin shimmered.

"Vanessa," Colin smiled as he said her name.

Her cerulean blue eyes glistened and Colin instinctively knew that they were filled with tears.

He took a step towards her and pulled her close to his chest. Her hair pressed into his face and he could smell the fresh soap on her body. She wrapped her tan arms around him.

They stood like that for several moments as the sun descended behind the hills that surrounded Miliom. Once he was crowned king and his mother was no longer regent, Vanessa would be his to care for as well. He smiled into her hair.

Eventually, she pulled away from him.

"How long have you been back?" She asked.

"Only for a few hours," he responded in a husky murmur. Now that she was outside of his arms, he felt suddenly cold. He wanted nothing more than to take her into his arms and kiss her until he couldn't kiss anymore.

"And you didn't send for me?" her lips pulled into a perfect pink pout as she spoke.

He stroked her cheek with his thumb and peered deep into her eyes. She shivered slightly as the cool breeze blew through them. Tugging her gently into his arms, Colin led Vanessa back through the archway and into his bedchamber.

A warm fire crackled in the hearth, sending dancing sparks into the air. Two large, overstuffed chairs rested before the fire with a soft rug stretching out between them. Colin's travel bag lay beside his bed where he'd thrown it on his way into his room. Shelves filled with books and mechanical toys lined the walls on all sides. Colin had never felt as comfortable in a space as much as he did when he was in his bedchamber.

Once inside the room, Vanessa gently pushed on Colin's chest until his legs pressed up against his bed. He stared down at her, heat rising up within him. Slowly, without breaking eye contact with him, she pulled the sleeves of her robes down her shoulders, revealing silky smooth golden skin beneath. The gentle curve of her breast was visible above the robe's top.

Colin gulped and leaned down to kiss Vanessa on the lips. She turned his face away from her with a tiny slap against his face. This was new, Colin thought as he turned to face her again. He could feel her warm body pressed fully up against the length of his. His entire body quivered.

"Did you miss me when you were on your travels, Colin?"

"Yes," he whispered as he once again leaned in to kiss her. She turned his face away from hers again.

"How much do you desire me now?"

Instead of answering her, Colin grasped the silky cloth of her robe in a fist and pulled it down. Her breasts popped above the cloth. Colin traced the curves of her body with his fingers and felt her tremble beneath his touch.

"How much would you be willing to sacrifice for me?"

Bringing his head up to her ear, Colin whispered, "Everything. I would be willing to sacrifice everything for you."

Her body was hot beneath his touch. Pulling her closer to him, they fell onto his bed. Vanessa instantly straddled him, her robe flapping open as she positioned her body firmly on top of his. Colin pressed into her, desperate to escape the trap of the clothing separating them.

She pinned his arms above his head and leaned down to finally kiss him on the mouth. Colin pulled gently at her grasp. The urge to flip her onto the bed and take her consumed his thoughts.

"I love you," he whispered over and over again.

She didn't respond.

Colin closed his eyes as she trailed kisses from his collar bone down to his navel. This is what he had been missing during his journey. He sucked in a breath of air as her lips grazed the top of his breeches.

Suddenly, Colin felt Vanessa's weight shift atop him. Opening his eyes, he saw a glint of metal as she raised her arms high above her head.

His body instantly went cold as he realized that she was holding a long, thin dagger in her hands.

"What are you doing?" he asked. His voice rose as he spoke and his heart hammered in his chest.

"You said you would sacrifice anything for me, Colin," she paused, "would you be willing to sacrifice your life?"

"What? What are you talking about? Vanessa, this isn't funny."

Bile rose from his stomach as he realized that she wasn't smiling.

"Vanessa?"

Her eyes were as cold as ice as she looked down upon him.

"You are not fit to be king," she said as she brought down her arms at an alarming speed, right towards his heart.

Colin managed to catch her arms in his hands. His muscles strained as he fought to keep the blade from plunging into his chest. Thankful for all the extra training Captain Conrad had given him on the staff, Colin was able to keep her weight and force held in place high enough above him that the blade wasn't even close to his body.

"Why are you doing this, Vanessa?" he asked in a quivering voice. "I was going to marry you. We were going to rule Szarmi together."

She pushed down on him with all of her weight. The blade shifted and Colin dug his fingers deep into the soft tissue of her wrists. She yelped and dropped the blade. Colin jerked his head instinctively as the blade plunged deep into the bed.

"Guards!" Colin yelled as Vanessa pushed herself away from him. He watched as she pulled another blade from a garter around her thigh. *Why didn't I notice those earlier?* Colin thought to himself as she passed the blade from hand to hand.

Vanessa lowered herself into a low crouch and growled in a deep, rough voice. Colin had never heard her make such a sound before.

"I thought we were in love," Colin said plaintively, as he held his hands out in front of him, as if to say 'I don't want to hurt you.'

"You never did have the stomach to hurt another person," Vanessa said in a cold voice. "It's one of the reasons you are such a terrible fighter." She sneered as she spoke. "You are pathetic."

She lunged at him. Colin quickly sidestepped her and dashed out to the balcony. He yelled for his guards as he went but he heard no movement from the other side of his chamber doors. *Where are they?*

His staff leaned against the open archway where he had left it after going through his evening routine. Grasping the hard, smooth wood in his hands, Colin positioned himself in the middle of balcony. The staff felt comfortable in his hands. Once again, Colin was thankful for the extra lessons the captain had given him during the last six months of his training.

Vanessa's form stood in the shadows of the archway. Colin wanted to take a step away from her, but stopped himself. He needed to stop being so afraid of fighting if he was going to be king.

"Just tell me why," he pleaded. "Please, Vanessa. I loved you so much. I still do."

She laughed.

It was a bitter, cold laugh that sent chills down Colin's back. This was not the same woman he had fallen in love with. It couldn't be.

"You are a simpering child, Colin. You think that you are capable of ruling Szarmi, but you're wrong. Everyone knows it. The nobles, the peasants, even the men you have trained with your entire life. You are not fit to be our king."

Pain coursed through Colin at her words. Tears stung his eyes, but he forced them to remain contained. She didn't deserve to see the pain her words caused.

"Even now, as I threaten to kill you—and I will kill you, Colin—you stand there with tears in your eyes. If you can't even kill the woman you love to save yourself, how are you going to protect an entire kingdom? You're weak. You've always been weak. And it's time that our great kingdom was rid of you."

She took a step towards him and Colin swung the staff up into a horizontal line so that it blocked her path.

"Stay where you are, Vanessa. I don't want to hurt you. I just want you to tell me why you're doing this."

"Haven't you been listening at all? I don't love you. I've never loved you. I just wanted to get close to you to see how weak you were with my own eyes. The rumors were nothing compared to how pathetic you really are."

She lunged at him and Colin brought the staff up in a quick, smooth motion. The wood caught Vanessa in the cheek, sending her head flying backwards. She dropped the dagger as she fell to the ground. Colin pulled the staff back to him and held it in position for a moment before creeping over to the woman lying on the hard, stone floor.

Bending down, Colin felt for her pulse. As his fingers met her skin, her brilliant blue eyes opened and she grasped his arm. She twisted around his body until Colin stood behind her. Too late, he realized that she was about to flip him over her shoulder. He had a momentary sensation of flying over her back and then landing—hard—on the ground.

She looked down at him with yet another blade in her hand. Colin wasn't sure where she'd pulled this one from, but he knew he couldn't remain motionless for long. Jumping up from the ground, Colin slammed into her. She tried plunging the blade into his side, but he smashed her hand against the balcony railing as they stumbled backwards.

"You love me," he whispered. "You do."

"No."

He pushed her against the railing again and heard the blade clatter to the stone floor.

"You have to. I've done everything I could for you. For us."

She smiled a sad smile at him, "You've been fooled since the start, Colin."

179

He held her close, their bodies melding together as they each struggled to gain control of the other. Colin knew that she had underestimated him. He still wasn't the best fighter in Szarmi, not even close, but he had gained muscle and skill through his trainings with Captain Conrad.

He flipped her around and pinned her arms behind her back. Her body was locked between him and the balcony railing.

"You can kill me, Colin, but the attempts won't stop." She laughed as she spoke. "Events have already been set in motion. You will never be king."

She flung her head back and hit Colin in the nose. Blood spurted from his broken nose as he shoved her as hard as he could in order to break away from her.

She disappeared over the railing.

Rushing forward, Colin bent over the railing. He arrived just in time to see her body slam into the hard earth below. Her arms and legs were sprawled out in unnatural angles. As Colin watched, he saw Vanessa's body shimmer in the dark light of the night. Her features shifted.

Colin paled.

And then he raced through his bedchamber. Opening the locked door of his room, he saw the slumped, bloody bodies of his guards. Apparently, Vanessa had killed them before entering his rooms. Colin gulped. She had planned this.

Not pausing to see if his guards still lived, Colin rushed to the courtyard beneath his balcony.

A crowd of servants had already begun gathering around the body; their bright torches illuminating the courtyard.

Her body had turned a molten, grey color with purple markings covering her skin. Her hair was no longer blonde but dark, as dark as any raven. Colin pushed past the servants to kneel beside the woman he loved. Her body was still warm.

A thin trail of blood slid from her mouth as Colin turned the body over. Her eyes were still open, still the brilliant blue Colin loved. But in a different body. A different face. It didn't make sense to him.

"No," he whispered as he gathered her in his arms. "No."

He let the tears fall from his eyes and mingle with the blood from her mouth. He shuddered as he cradled her body in his arms. He knew, cognitively, that she had tried to kill him. That she had betrayed him. That she would have killed him the way she had killed his guards. But each time he looked at her blank, dead eyes, all he saw was the woman he loved. Dead. Because of him.

"It's a shapeshifter."

"The prince killed it."

"Look at its body."

"Why is the prince crying?"

The voices of his servants pulled Colin's attention away from the corpse in his arms. He shifted so that he could face them.

"This is the Lady Vanessa Wilhelm. Please, send for the Sisters of Sorrow to prepare her body for burial," Colin didn't speak to any one person. He knew at least one of the servants would eventually follow his command.

"Of course, Your Highness."

"Right away, Sir."

Colin blocked out the rest of the soft murmurs from his people. She was dead. He stroked her grey cheek. It felt so different from the skin he was used to.

By the time the sisters arrived, Colin had set Vanessa's body on the ground. They inspected the body before the Old Sister knelt before Colin, her face a wrinkled mass of kindness.

"Your Highness, this woman was a shapeshifter. A damned creature from Lunameed. According to our laws, she cannot be buried in our hallowed grounds."

Colin nodded. Somehow he had known this would be the sisters' answer.

"Of course," he said. He glanced at the purple and grey creature before him. The sisters had closed her eyes. She no longer looked like the woman he had loved. The woman who had betrayed him.

"Burn the body," he whispered and turned and walked away.

Chapter Twelve

Estrellala, Lunameed

Amaleah stared at herself in the mirror. The gown was more glorious than any she had been given before. It was a violet gown with light embroidery of green and silver stitched into the bodice and hems. The corset overlaid the dress and matched the detailed design that the royal seamstress had sewn into all of Amaleah's gowns since the engagement announcement. Despite the splendor of the gown, Amaleah felt trapped in its folds. Her mother had worn a dress identical to this one on the day her father had proposed.

Namadus was cleverer than Amaleah had given him credit for. Or, at least, he was more confident in his abilities to thrust her father over the edge. Her hair hung in loose curls around her head. A pearl and emerald strand had been woven into her hair so that it glistened as she turned her head. Even her hair was styled to look the way her mother had worn hers in the paintings King Magnus kept in his rooms. Her face was different. Green eyes instead of violet. And she was heavier set that her mother. Despite this, she was still beautiful, according to the word of the people and the nobles. But she was not her mother. And Amaleah was determined to prove that fact in any way that she could.

In just under an hour, Amaleah would make her grand entrance into the royal ballroom. Every courtier had been invited to attend the first of the balls. King Magnus had even invited the prince and princess of Dramadoon to attend. Their arrival to court a mere three hours before the party was to begin had been the first time royalty from Dramadoon had visited the Lunameedian court in one hundred and twelve years. And that had been when the old Dramadoonian king had come to demand a duel with King Swardne of Lunameed over the jilting of his daughter. Tensions had been high between the two countries ever since. Amaleah hadn't had a chance to meet them yet, but she was anxious to see what they had looked like and what they had to say about the engagement.

Smirking, Amaleah remembered the tantrum her father had thrown when Namadus had suggested that they also invite the prince of Szarmi. He had acted like a small child who had been told no for the first time. Despite the tension between the two countries and the impending war if the tension was not resolved, Namadus had tried to convince King Magnus that Prince Colin was not a threat to the kingdom. In the end, Prince Colin had not been invited.

To not be invited to the first ball of the engagement celebration was one of the greatest insults King Magnus could deliver to the Szarmian court.

And he had done just that.

Secretly, Amaleah hoped that the crown prince of Szarmi would risk sneaking into Lunameed in order to attend the ball. She had heard that he was kind to his equals and his servants. This was something she had not yet encountered among the nobility of the Lunameedian court. Despite the fact that Lunameed still honored and accepted all species as central to the order of life, many of the poor were mistreated within the kingdom. Aside from his kindness, Prince Colin was said to be incredibly intelligent and well read. Among the servants within the Lunameedian court, he was also known to accept all people, whether they be magic or not. And, considering the main reason for the tension between their two countries was the presence of magic within Lunameed, his acceptance of magical creatures could be the start of a bridge between the two kingdoms.

Before her father's insanity, Amaleah had imagined what it would be like to be betrothed to the Szarmian prince as a way to bind their kingdoms together. She had believed that a union between them could end the brutality and mistrust created by the Wars of Darkness.

Still, at least to her, it made sense that her father wouldn't invite him. He had always been a jealous man. In the moments of his lucidity, Amaleah was certain that her father didn't want the competition, or the talk among his people about the match that might have been between her and the prince of Szarmi.

However, despite the displeasure the suggestion of inviting the royalty from Szarmi had been to the king, Namadus had continued to champion the idea of bringing the Szarmian court to Lunameed. Amaleah couldn't fathom why Namadus would risk the king's favor in this particular pursuit, but she doubted he had the best interests of the king at heart.

She stared at herself in the mirror. *Would I look so much like my mother if I changed my hair?* She doubted that it would matter. What Amaleah couldn't figure out was why Namadus would want to push her father over the edge. At least, she understood that the more the king's madness took hold of him, the greater the danger of him creating chaos and destruction within the kingdom was. As the high councilor, Namadus was supposed to care for the state of the land and its people. Yet, from Amaleah's perspective, he appeared to care little for the results his actions had on anyone but himself.

Her ladies patiently waited around the room as Amaleah continued to peer at herself in the mirror. Any moment Namadus would send one of his cronies to escort her to the ball. A mixture of excitement and dread filled her as she contemplated how the nobility would react to her attire. As she heard the knock on the door, Amaleah motioned for her ladies to wait for her command before opening the door. Steeling herself for the first ball, Amaleah motioned for her youngest lady to welcome in Namadus's man.

Chapter Thirteen

Sylvia waited patiently in the servants' hall. Everyone around her was chattering about the prince and princess of Dramadoon. They were twins, and they looked alike. Princess Saphria was reportedly quite a bit more personable than her brother, Prince Fredrerik, who was, apparently, quite shy. The coming of the royal twins had been a surprise to Sylvia. She had known that they had been invited, of course, yet she had not anticipated that they would accept the king's offer. The Dramadoonian people were known for their old-fashioned ways and staunch belief in the Light. In Lunameed, belief in the Light had begun to wane after the end of the Wars of Darkness. Under the belief in the Light, all creatures were given life through the life-water of creation. The Light's rivers run deep within the lands of Mitier and provide glory to all who know it. All who chose to hone their abilities and pursue the Light could harness the magic contained within themselves. Everyone had potential. Everyone had a purpose. Everyone who believed in themselves had the ability to tap into their abilities. If they were lucky, they would be blessed by the Light and be gifted with strange and amazing abilities.

The religion did not explain why some magic seemed to be hereditary. It was true that the fae and other magical creatures believed in the Light. It was part of the reason the Keepers had been formed. But it did not explain how even the nonbelievers of her kind, tiefs, possessed magic while others, like herself, had been unable to tap into their full potential.

To believe in the Light in Dramadoon was to believe that all magical beings were enlightened and that everyone else was doomed to live a life lacking in purpose. Sylvia had heard reports that the Dramadoonian nobility would leave any children who did not exhibit magical potential to die in the elements at ages as young as three. Rumor had it that this practice sometimes had the ability to 'bring out' a child's magic. The risk didn't make sense to her. She could not imagine raising a child for that long just to doom it to a terrible death.

But it wasn't just their religious practices that made Sylvia uneasy with their presence in the kingdom. She had made an excuse to be in the guest rooms while the servants were unpacking the twins' luggage. One of the prince's personal attendants had let slip that the prince was planning on making an offer to the young Lunameedian princess to run away with him to safety. The attendant had believed, when Sylvia cornered him later and asked grueling questions, that the prince intended to abandon Princess Amaleah to her own demise. Even if that wasn't the prince's plan and he truly did intend to save her, Dramadoon was not the place Sylvia wanted Amaleah to go.

She did not like that the twins were in the palace. They could thwart all that she had worked so hard to achieve since the king had decreed that Amaleah would be his bride. Yet she could do nothing about their presence now except prepare Amaleah for interacting with them.

Steeling herself for a conversation with her young charge, Sylvia slipped out of the servants' quarters and into the hidden hallways leading to the royal suites. Timidly, she rapped on the door. And waited.

There was no response.

Knocking again, Sylvia felt a wave of anxiety wash over her. If Amaleah met the Dramadoonian twins before she had a chance to speak with her, to warn her, then the princess's carefully crafted plans might all be for naught. Sylvia knocked one last time, as loudly as her feeble hand would allow.

Suddenly the door flew open. The youngest of Amaleah's ladies, Claudette, stood before the old woman. Sylvia groaned inwardly. Claudette was one of Namadus's many nieces. He had hand-picked this one to serve as one of Amaleah's ladies right after the king had made the announcement that he was going to wed his daughter. Despite the fact that Amaleah didn't trust the twelve-year-old, Claudette had been allowed to attend many of Amaleah's meetings and planning sessions. The girl was unassuming and, in Sylvia's opinion, quite senseless. She was constantly talking about how attractive the palace guards were and who was who in the court nobility. She was an annoying little bird as far as Sylvia was concerned.

However, Sylvia suspected that, despite her age, Claudette was being used by Namadus to spy on Amaleah. She was a sweet child, as far as children go, but Sylvia had caught her watching Amaleah's every move since she'd arrived at court.

Claudette smiled widely at Sylvia, her eyes brightening.

"Miss Sylvia!" she exclaimed, "It's so good that you are here." She ushered Sylvia into the rooms. Pointing emphatically towards Amaleah, Claudette nearly shouted, "Look how beautiful she is."

Sylvia's heart beat rapidly when her eyes met Amaleah's in the mirror across the room. She was the spitting image of her mother.

"My Lady, you look... lovely." Her voice was stilted. Amaleah broke eye contact as Sylvia spoke. Claudette, on the other hand, barely seemed to register the note of disapproval in Sylvia's voice.

"She looks so amazing!" Claudette filled the room with chatter as she continued to exclaim about how beautiful Amaleah was. Sylvia hobbled over to her charge. *When did my bones get so stiff and old?* She thought to herself as she felt her knees shake beneath the weight of her aged body.

Amaleah turned away from the mirror and faced Sylvia directly. Sylvia could see in her princess's eyes the distress she felt at the dress and hair, but it was too late to change anything about the outfit. If only Amaleah hadn't sent her away, Sylvia could have saved her young charge from the torture of wearing a dress identical to the one that her mother had worn when King Magnus had proposed to her.

Sighing, Sylvia spoke in a deliberate, clear voice. "My Lady, is there anything that you would like for me to do for you?"

Before Amaleah could respond Claudette answered for her. "Why, Mistress Sylvia, we have already done everything for our lady. Can't you see how beautiful she looks?"

Sylvia resisted the urge to roll her eyes. *Can this child describe Amaleah in any other way other than beautiful?*

"My dear child," she started, "your enthusiasm is a tribute to your loyalty to Princess Amaleah, but please, let her speak for herself." She tried to contain the contempt in her voice as she spoke but she found it difficult to control.

Claudette's lower lip trembled slightly and she looked as if the chastisement would make her cry. Amaleah laid a gentle hand on the younger girl's shoulder as she shifted past her and Claudette's frown shifted to a small smile. She looked at Amaleah expectantly as the princess began to speak.

"Thank you, Sylvia. I appreciate the support."

Sylvia slipped her arm through Amaleah's and looked at the young lady's maid through her eyelashes. She tried to gauge the young girl's response to Amaleah's dismissal. Claudette shot daggers at Amaleah through her eyes and Sylvia knew that Amaleah would pay for her dismissal of the young girl once Namadus heard of this conversation. She shook her head dejectedly. All of the social intrigue was beginning to wear on her.

She only hoped she could maintain her strength until Amaleah was able to escape from the palace. Sylvia was sure Amaleah would be able to find help within the Faer Forest if she was only able to get away. However, the forest was not the ultimate destination Sylvia had in mind for her young charge. Although she had not yet spoken to Amaleah about her desire for her young mistress to take passage through the wilderness to the kingdom of Szarmi, Sylvia desperately wanted for Amaleah to do just that. She had hoped that King Magnus would have seen past the tension between Lunameed and Szarmi to invite Prince Colin to the first engagement ball, but he had not been swayed by High Councilor Namadus. Getting Amaleah to Szarmi would have been so much simpler if she could have been smuggled out of Estrellala by the Szarmian entourage.

Sylvia, unlike many of the other members of the Keepers, believed that the Foretold Prophecy was intricately linked to the kingdom of Szarmi. However, like the rest of the Council, Sylvia believed that Amaleah's destiny was to fulfil the Foretold's call. Unfortunately, the Council strictly forbade Sylvia, or anyone else from the Council, to reveal what they knew about any of Mitier's prophecies.

Ever since the Wars of Darkness had ended over three hundred years ago, the magic had been dying, leaving the land of Mitier. As the Light left, entire species of magical creatures began dying out. Fewer and fewer humans had been gifted with the Light. No one knew for certain why this was the case; however, many believed that the magic had been broken by the public foretelling of prophecies that had failed to come to pass. This was why the Keepers had been founded: to protect the prophecies, to ensure that none outside of the Keepers heard of them, and to protect the Harbinger. Sylvia, along with the other Keepers, believed that Amaleah was the Harbinger, the savior spoken of throughout the ages who would bring peace back to Mitier.

The Keepers feared that Amaleah would not be ready in time. Indeed, some had even begun to naysay her because she had yet to demonstrate any magical ability. Their fear that she may not exhibit her abilities in time, if she ever did, was well founded. Sylvia head heard tales of the disappearance of the magic in Szarmi. The Szarmian nobility both feared and hated magical beings and so they had waged war on all magical creatures since the end of the Second Darkness. Entire species residing within Szarmian boundaries had been wiped out completely. Recently, Szarmian guards had been seen murdering magical creatures along the Lunameedian and Szarmian border.

Sylvia could not abide of the creatures of the Light to be eliminated within Lunameed.

Too much was at stake if she failed to save the princess from her father's marriage proposal. Even if Sylvia risked her spot among the members of the Keepers, her mission to ensure the successful completion of the Foretold Prophecy was of the greatest importance to her. Even if that meant breaking her vow of silence about the prophecy, it would be worth it to see Amaleah achieve her destiny. Besides, her old bones were ready for a rest.

Yet, she also knew that if King Magnus succeeded in his promise to procure a coat made of all the furs of the kingdom and three gowns made to reflect the elements of the heavens and the seas that he could find a way to trap Amaleah within the city of Estrellala. This is what Sylvia feared the most. Nevertheless, she believed that if enough magic still existed in the land to help a man as broken as the king, then there would be enough to save the Harbinger: to save Amaleah.

Sylvia recited the lines of her sisters' blessing on Amaleah silently within her mind as she and Amaleah strode out of Amaleah's chambers. Glancing down, she noticed with approval that the princess was wearing shimmering tights in order to hide the silvery tattoo the blessing had left upon her skin. She would have their protection; Sylvia was sure of it. However, she could not shake the feeling that something dreadful was about to befall Amaleah. She worried that the dreadful thing she was feeling ominous about would occur before Amaleah would have the ability to properly plan for her escape. The trouble with Amaleah was that she had meticulously planned out an escape, but only if events occurred in just the right sequence. The princess had not yet developed contingency or emergency escape plans and Sylvia was concerned that she might need to deploy an escape sooner rather than later.

Sylvia glanced up and down the hallway. There was a small chambermaid turning the corner ahead of them, but that was all. Gripping Amaleah's arm tightly, Sylvia ushered the princess into the room nearest them. Thankfully, it was empty. No fires were lit and the room was dark. Sylvia quickly shut the door and locked it. Pressing her ear against the door, she listened for spies on the other side of the door. Footsteps echoed in the hallway but there was no sign that someone knew they were in the room.

"What is it? What's wrong?" She heard Amaleah ask in the tiniest of whispers.

"My Lady, we need to discuss your plan if tonight does not go as intended," Sylvia responded in her own whisper, still grasping Amaleah's arm.

Amaleah squirmed under Sylvia's touch and tried to wrench free from her, but the older woman dug her nails into Amaleah's flesh. "Listen to me, Amaleah. I don't know how to explain it to you, but I believe that tonight will go poorly. You need to be prepared."

Amaleah laughed softly. "Sylvia, trust me. I've been involved with every aspect of tonight's events. Nothing will go wrong."

"But, My Lady, you haven't-"

"Enough." Amaleah interrupted briskly. "I am tired of your constant worrying, Sylvia. One can only plan so much before the planning becomes a hindrance to progress. We will just have to trust that the plans I have put into place will work."

She smiled at Sylvia comfortingly, but her usual charm did not work on her nursemaid. Sylvia stood dumbfounded at the girl's naivety and boldness. *Reckless girl,* she thought as she released Amaleah's arm from her grip.

"Listen, Amaleah, you may choose to be rash and impetuous; however, it is my sole role in life right now to protect you and to set you on the correct path. I'll be blighted if I let you enter the lion's den without a firm grasp of the situation. The servants have been talking, My Lady. And it hasn't been good."

The king is mad.

Surely it would be better to say it. Confirm it. Make Amaleah know it beyond a shadow of a doubt. His madness made him unpredictable and Sylvia needed Amaleah to take action no matter what her father said or did.

"Your father, the king, has forsaken his senses, My Lady. I am sorry to say it, but the timeline you've created may not be sufficient. It would be better to act now and be rushed than to wait and have your plans thwarted, I think."

Sylvia held her breath as she waited for Amaleah to respond. The young woman stood in silence. Sylvia could tell that Amaleah was breathing hard because she could hear the puffs of air each time Amaleah took a breath. It was heartbreaking.

Slowly, deliberately, Amaleah looked Sylvia straight in the eyes. "What would you have me do?"

Sighing in relief, Sylvia regarded Amaleah with a penetrating look. "I would have you court the men in attendance tonight. Make your father jealous. Show him that you are not afraid of him."

Amaleah stepped away from Sylvia with a stunned expression on her. Or was it awe? In the darkness of the room it was difficult for Sylvia to tell. Amaleah shook her head emphatically, but still Sylvia continued.

"Amaleah, listen to me. If you can win the favor of the Lunameedian nobility, really all of the Mitierian nobility, then you may be able to barter passage out of the castle. Make the men believe that they have a shot with you and you can escape."

"And chain myself to another situation where a man has domain over my life? Do you honestly believe that this is the course of action I would choose, Sylvia?"

"Honestly, no. But, we have to be practical. There is too much at stake, Amaleah. You don't know—you can't know—what your escape from Estrellala would mean for the magical world. Nothing else matters."

Once again Sylvia watched as Amaleah processed the older woman's words.

"Sylvia, you know how I was raised. I know nothing about the ways to seduce men." She blushed in the dim light of the room. Sylvia sensed rather than saw Amaleah's discomfort. "Truly, Sylvia... I can't. I can't do this. Not just because it would just be another form of imprisonment, but because I just don't know how." She trailed off.

"Then you must learn."

Amaleah snorted at this. "Sylvia, if I haven't had a chance to learn how to seduce men in seventeen years of life, especially during the past six months, I highly doubt that I can learn in enough time for it to be useful. Furthermore, I'm not sure I want to be rescued by a man. If I am to rule Lunameed once my father dies, then I need to be able to make decisions on my own."

Sylvia regarded Amaleah thoughtfully. In many ways, she was correct. She would have to make decisions on her own. She would have to be a strong leader in times of need. But she would also be expected to marry, to leave an heir, and to share her power with her consort.

"Child, you will be a strong leader one day. But this will only come to pass if we can successfully help you escape from Estrellala. Please, Amaleah, let us at least try my approach. I fear that you will not have enough time to make your plan come to pass."

A myriad of emotions passed over Amaleah's face as Sylvia waited for her to respond. She knew her princess would be questioning whether or not she would be able to succeed in securing the desire of the men at court. And, although Sylvia didn't want to admit it, the possibility that Amaleah would fail was high; however, Sylvia was willing to assume this risk if it meant Amaleah would be able to survive.

Amaleah began picking at a bead on the sleeve of her dress. Sylvia smiled faintly at this. Ever since Amaleah had been a small child she had always picked at things when she was in deep thought. Sylvia knew this meant that Amaleah was, at the very least, considering her options.

"Fine. We will try your plan," Amaleah finally said.

Sylvia smiled and nodded. "Now. The thing that you must first understand about men, My Lady, is that you have all the natural beauty in the world. This means that men will flock to you like bees to honey. But the real key is to use your court skills to make a man feel comfortable, secure, and cared for. If you are able to do this, you will know how to bring a man to his knees and beg for more."

Amaleah visibly, even in the dimness of the room, pulled back at this statement. Sylvia continued, "There may be those who need more than just a pretty face and a sweet temperament to capture their hearts and their attentions. Your father... is not one of these men. He has always been beguiled by beautiful women. Although many people believe that it was your mother who cursed him into this madness, I do not believe that to be the case. I just know that the only thing he keeps coming to is her beauty. Not her mind. Or her heart. Or her spirit. Just her beauty."

"I do not believe that you could be happy with a man who does not inspire you to be more than just beautiful. In order to achieve this feat, you must be able to show your brilliance and challenge him to demonstrate his own mind. This is the most difficult task of all. It will require you to be subtle. To ask questions at just the right moment. To challenge his way of thinking. In times such as these, finding a man who cherishes your mind as well as your heart and beauty will be dangerous. Your father will have servants—spies—watching your every move. You'll need to be quick in your judgments about what kind of man you have met. Once you have found the right one, you'll need to convince him of your father's madness. You'll need to convince him to help you escape."

Sylvia took a long, deep breath after she finished speaking. Her throat felt scratchy and she wished she had some water.

"I think... I hope... I can do this." Amaleah sounded nervous but determined.

"You can." Sylvia paused, "You must."

Bells began to ring. Amaleah gripped Sylvia's hand at their tolling. It was time.

Pressing her ear once more to the door, Sylvia tried to determine if there was anyone on the other side. She couldn't hear anything. In one swift motion she unlocked the door and pulled Amaleah out into the hall.

In the natural light streaming in from the high windows all down the hall, Amaleah looked more like the dead queen, Orianna, than Sylvia had originally realized. In fact, if she hadn't known that the woman before her was Amaleah, she might have thought the dead queen had risen from her grave.

Looking away from Amaleah, Sylvia led the young princess down the hall. Amaleah shook slightly as they neared the ballroom.

"Sylvia, what if they don't fall for it? What if they don't want me?"

"Is this pride speaking or fear of failure?" Sylvia didn't mean to sound as harsh as she knew her words were.

"I suppose a mixture of both," Amaleah said resolutely. "I will not become one of those girls I've seen in court who flaunt themselves for the pleasure of men. I am not one of those women. I fear that my true thoughts and feelings on this matter will shine through and that no man within the Mitierian courts will pursue me, especially since they would know that their actions would mean war. Perhaps I should-"

"You should stick to this plan, at least for tonight, and see where it takes you," Sylvia cut her off. "Do not be foolish, My Lady. There are only so many nights between now and when your father will present the three dresses and the coat of many furs to you. Do not let your fear and your pride stop you from achieving your goal to escape from this fate."

"But I want... I want to be free from the governance of men."

"Child, we live in a world whose very core is governed by men. But do not forget that men are governed by the whims and desires of their consorts. You must become such a central person in his life that he will risk everything for you."

"I certainly hope not all men are governed by the whims of their consorts. I want someone who views me as an equal partner in life, in the ruling of our kingdoms. My father is not this type of man. He is a villain, a coward who would force a girl to love him, even if she did not do so willingly. Look at me, Sylvia, and you will have your proof. If I do what you're asking, won't I just be lying to the men I seduce to get what I want? Won't I essentially be forcing them down a dangerous path when I know that I will abandon them in the end? I don't want to be like my father, Sylvia, yet I know that if I do this... if I beguile and seduce them into helping me... I will be no better than he."

Sylvia's dark brown eyes bore into Amaleah's as they stood in the hallway. Sylvia could hear voices and music wafting the short distance it would take them to enter the ballroom. There was so much left that she needed to say to Amaleah—so much that she needed the princess to understand. They were at a precipice with neither one making the move to the other side. Once they entered the ballroom, there would be no turning back. Amaleah would need to become the princess who was not afraid to do what was necessary to survive and Sylvia would need to accept her place in the background of Amaleah's life. Either way, the end of Amaleah's childhood had begun. Tears sprung unbidden to Sylvia's eyes. She had never been able to express how much she loved the little girl and now the young woman before her. *Is it too late?*

She felt Amaleah's smooth hands clasp her rough old ones. The princess's skin was warm to the touch. As they stood in the hallway, Sylvia took the moment to breathe in Amaleah's familiar scent. It was like rainwater and lilies and freshly scrubbed skin all rolled into one. She smiled and squeezed Amaleah's hands.

Quietly, Amaleah whispered, "I don't want to go tonight."

Amaleah's voice sounded so much like the little girl she used to be in that moment that Sylvia nearly let the cry she was holding back escape her lips. Instead, she placed her other hand on top of their clasped hands and said, "I know, child, I know. But you must."

Amaleah's face crumpled at Sylvia's words. Sylvia wrapped her free arm around Amaleah and drew her in close. She cast furtive glances down the hallways, but still she didn't see anyone wandering the halls. She sighed in relief as she stroked Amaleah's back and whispered soothing words into her ear.

Sylvia knew that Amaleah would face much greater challenges than just escaping her father. She only hoped that because of her care and guidance that Amaleah would be able to keep her head held high and her heart full of hope, even in the darkest of hours. Her sisters' blessing would help in Amaleah's endeavors, yet Sylvia did not know if it would be enough to keep Amaleah from forsaking all hope. Tears gathered in her eyes as she silently pushed Amaleah away from her. It was time.

Chapter Fourteen

Amaleah's heart thumped in her chest rapidly. She wasn't having difficulty breathing, exactly, but the pounding in her chest distracted her. She tried breathing in deeply to calm her nerves, but couldn't make the pounding stop. It slowly spread to a dizziness in her head that made her weak. *What am I doing?* She thought as she made her way through the hallways.

Sylvia stood beside her. She had never noticed before how much the older woman wobbled as she walked. Although their relationship was a strained one, Amaleah had grown to trust the woman. To rely upon her. She would never admit this to Sylvia, of course. But, it was good to know that someone in Lunameed was on her side.

They were just turning the last corner in the hallway before they would arrive at the ballroom doors when Amaleah almost ran straight into one of the palace guards. He caught himself before he slammed into her and fell backwards onto the marble floor. Amaleah knelt to help him up but he waved her away. His face was flushed and Amaleah could tell that he had been in a hurry.

Coughing, he spoke in a rushed voice, "His Majesty the King requests the presence of Amaleah Nazdrina Madregala Bluefischer, Princess of Lunameed and betrothed of the King in the ballroom at once."

He mumbled the last few words, obviously uncomfortable commanding the princess to do anything. Amaleah smiled at him brightly. Perhaps he could be won to her side. Lightly touching the small conch shell hung around her neck, Amaleah replied, "Well, now that you've found me I suppose that you should lead the way."

His cheeks turned an even deeper shade of red than they already had. Amaleah wasn't sure why he had blushed at her request, but she liked the fact that she had the ability to affect him in such a strong way. Looping her arm through his, she tugged on him to move forward. When he didn't, she turned her face up to his.

His expression made Amaleah want to laugh. His eyes were so wide they looked like they were size of saucers and his face was now so red that it was almost purple. She patted his arm and his lips trembled.

Suddenly, as if just now realizing that the princess of Lunameed was holding his arm, he said, "My Lady... I did not intend... I'm sorry... but... should you really..." he continued to stammer incoherently until Amaleah finally cut him off.

"If you are to escort me to the ballroom then I think you should truly escort me." She tapped his arm with her hand. "After all, this is my first ball and it would be simply dreadful walking into the room alone."

She glanced back at Sylvia to see how she was doing. Sylvia only smirked at her. She was, apparently, laying it on a little too thick for her nursemaid's taste. The guard stood stiffly in the hallway. He did not remove her arm from his, but neither did he start moving towards the ballroom doors.

"You're sure, My Lady, that entering the ballroom on the arm of a guard won't... make you uncomfortable?" He sounded more confident than he had before.

She smiled at him again and looked up at him through her lashes. "Yes. I think, given the scenario, that entering the ballroom with anyone else—aside from my father, of course—would be an insult. But walking in with a guard will show that my father is protective of me."

"Besides," she continued, "you look so strong and capable that I'm sure my father will reward you for helping me to the ballroom." She rubbed her hand up and down his arm as she spoke. She certainly hoped that her father would reward him. The alternative made her cringe.

Slowly, he nodded his head as if deciding to believe her. They began walking down the hall arm-in-arm.

Midway down the hall, the guard said, "Princess Amaleah, I am Aaron Blackwater, at your service. I'm sorry I didn't introduce myself earlier. It's just that- I just didn't..." he blew out a long stream of air and flexed his fingers, "Meeting you is just such an honor that I quite forgot myself."

Amaleah laughed softly. "It's nothing to worry about. Now that you've met me, is it really so bad?"

Aaron took several steps without responding. "No, Your Highness."

His tone was low and soft. Amaleah stole a quick glance at his face, but it was slack of emotion. *Well then, if he doesn't want to carry on a conversation with me, we will just have to walk in silence.*

Guards saluted her by slanting their swords as she walked by them. They lined the hallway leading to the double doors at the end of the hall. The few knights who still resided in the palace pounded their shields when they saw her. Their salute made her cheeks flare red, but she kept moving. The first of twenty balls was about to begin. Nerves coursed through Amaleah with each step she took. It was her first ball. Ever.

She took a deep breath as the herald opened the doors to introduce her. *This is it.*

The sparkle of all the jewels overwhelmed her. Light reflected off of their facets, creating shards of colored light across the room. They looked like rainbows dancing to the music. Crystal chandeliers hung from the balcony-level railings. They glistened in the flickering candlelight and cast shadows into the hidden crevices of the ballroom. Massive staircases rose from both sides of the room. The banisters were covered in pink roses and vines. Everything was how she had planned it. Of course she had known what the ballroom was supposed to look like, but Amaleah's breath still caught in her chest as she looked around the room.

Every man and woman wore gems of every hue, price, and cut. Amaleah's simple gown, though beautiful, paled in comparison to the gowns the women of court wore. Amaleah had never seen so many people covered in such an assortment of colors and designs. Everyone was powdered and primped. Blinking rapidly, Amaleah tried to force her eyes to adjust to the splendor of the room.

Music engulfed her. An orchestra of musicians sat on a dais at the back of the room. They held small guitars, flutes, and clarinets. As Amaleah looked closer she realized that they weren't playing. Standing in front of the band was a group of six elves who sang a strange, sorrowful song. Their long, lean bodies were covered in the palest white clothes Amaleah had ever seen. All of them had long, flowing blonde hair. They were the most beautiful creatures Amaleah had ever seen.

Their voices were low and melodious but each note carried a hint of loss with it. Their voices penetrated the very core of Amaleah's body. She shivered as she walked closer to where they stood. No one else in the room seemed to notice the elves' song as much as she did. Groups of nobles stood about the room talking cheerfully to one another. Everyone was smiling. Thousands of pink rose petals adorned the tables, chairs, and throne. Her father sat on the gilded chair, his face stern and his back straight. He wore a black suit with brass medals hanging across his chest. Amaleah tried to discern if his expression revealed what he thought of the ball, but she was too far away to tell. Mr. Sweets had outdone himself with the tower of pastries stacked on many of the curved tables that were placed throughout the room. The entire room smelled of roasting meat, flowers, and rich perfumes.

She was in awe of it all. And she had planned each and every detail of it. Everything seemed more wonderful than the last. It was difficult for Amaleah to focus on any one thing as she made her way through the room. She kept finding herself tugging on the young guard's arm and pulling him towards the pastry display or one of the tables laden with paintings of the realm. Or the sparkling cider the dwarves had prepared just for Amaleah on the first ball of the betrothal. He followed along beside her. Each time she stopped, he stood with his back straight and his arms at his sides. It wasn't until they were halfway to her father's table when she noticed that the soldier was sweating profusely. Great big drops of his sweat dropped on her arm whenever he turned his head.

"Are you quite alright?" Amaleah whispered to the guard.

He glanced around the room before leaning down towards her. His eyebrows were knitted together and his eyes darted around the room, even as he whispered back, "Just a bit nervous is all, My Lady."

If Amaleah had known that the guard was going to act like a guilty person, she would not have asked him to escort her. Sighing heavily, Amaleah squeezed his arm and said, "We're not doing anything wrong, Aaron."

He flinched when she used his given name.

Amaleah's shoulders slumped as she realized that she had asked this man to risk her father's ire without considering the effect it would have on him. If she was going to be a fair and just ruler, she needed to stop only thinking about her own wants and desires.

Sliding her arm out from his, Amaleah turned towards him, "I think you've successfully delivered me to the ballroom, Aaron Blackwater. Thank you so much for your service."

He stared at her, dumbfounded.

She cocked her head towards the guards standing in groups around the room. "You should go rejoin your peers. I'll go to my father alone."

Relief washed over his face and a wave of guilt settled on Amaleah's stomach. "Thank you," the guard whispered before rushing away.

Amaleah watched him go, her face hard as ice. The realization that to be a princess in her father's court was to be alone. She only gave herself a moment to feel the loneliness that followed before turning towards her father's throne.

As Amaleah walked through the crowds of people she noticed a man and woman standing together in the shadow of one of the enormous staircases that led to the balcony level of the ballroom. Amaleah didn't recognize them but assumed that they were one of the visiting noble families from the southern region of Lunameed. Their clothing was not as ornate as the other guests. Instead of jewels, they wore furs. Instead of long coats and dresses, they both wore tunics that were belted at the waist. They had long black hair and pale faces. When Amaleah looked at them, they maintained blank faces and penetrating stares.

They were austere. Warriors. Amaleah kept thinking about the couple as she greeted other Lunameedian nobles on her way to her father's table. The muscles in her cheeks felt sore as she plastered a court smile on her face. The constant chatter of the people around her was exhausting, but Amaleah kept moving forward.

Finally, Amaleah made it to the table at the front of the room where her father sat on his throne. He smirked at her as she slid behind him to get to her seat.

"It's good to see you." His eyes were dull, almost lifeless.

"And you, Father."

He made no response. Amaleah sat and looked down upon the rest of the tables. Nobles began sitting and the dinners were delivered to the tables. Her father sipped his wine but continued to say nothing to her. He rose and greeted the guests when the last plate had been placed. Amaleah ate her meal of roasted duck and vegetables in silence. No one else had been seated at her father's table and, since he was refusing to talk to her, she was left with nothing else to do but stare out at the groups of people vying for her attention. She smiled at the nobles whenever they caught her eye, but otherwise tried to ignore them. No one approached the royal table.

Amaleah scanned the room searching for the odd couple she'd seen standing beneath the staircase, but couldn't find them in the crowded room. She finished her meal quickly, barely taking breaths in between bites. She had planned the menu to match her tastes, but she couldn't enjoy the food. Not with her father sitting silently by her side and the attendants watching her every move upon the dais. She tapped her fingers absentmindedly on the table. If this was how all of the balls were going to be she would have to bring a book next time.

The greasy liquids of the meal had dribbled down her father's chin; they left dark stains on the white tablecloth as he dabbed at them. He winked at Amaleah as he stood before the congregation of nobles, knights, and visiting royalty. The room became entirely silent. Amaleah could hear his legs groaning under the weight of him. She looked down at her hands, afraid her face would bely her disgust of him. He cleared his throat and spoke to the crowd of seated attendants in a booming voice.

"Come. Let us celebrate the impending nuptials between me and my beautiful bride-to-be. As you well know, I am a man of few words. But I cannot wait to take this next step in life with the woman I love and cherish above all others." He grinned at her boyishly. "Let us toast to the Lady Orianna."

A gasp swept through the room. Amaleah looked up at her father with a stricken look on her face. *Did he really call me by my mother's name in front of all of these people?* Surely he wouldn't have.

He looked out over the crowd, clearly expecting applause that never came.

There was only silence.

Amaleah dared to glance out over the seated crowd as well. They didn't move. *He must have.*

Her heart beat wildly in her chest, drowning out all other sounds.

Her eyes met those of Namadus as she continued to scan the tables. He slowly rose from his seat and sipped from his wine glass. Amaleah cringed as all the other nobles and knights of the realm followed suit. In one gesture, Namadus had normalized her father's desire to marry her.

Chapter Fifteen

Amaleah sat in shock at the table as the servants cleared away the plates and silverware. A dance floor had been assembled in the middle of the floor with all of the dinner tables encircling it. Amaleah contemplated leaving the table to roam about the room, but something in her father's posture stopped her. She was afraid that he would throw another one of his tantrums if she were to leave his side. She wasn't sure what to do. She'd been too young to attend balls before her father had exiled her. Now, she felt completely unprepared for the world her father wanted her to be a part of.

As she tried to entertain herself by watching the slew of dancers twirl about the room, a swift movement from the corner of the room caught her eye. Turning to see what was happening, she saw the strange young woman in the fur and tunic walking towards her. Her steps were graceful and delicate. Amaleah had never seen someone move with as much ease as the stranger did now.

The stranger stopped short of the table and peered at King Magnus. Her eyes hardened as she examined him. Amaleah glanced at her father, but there didn't appear to be anything different about him. When Amaleah looked back at the stranger, her face was mere inches from Amaleah's. Amaleah gasped slightly. *How did she move so quickly?* She could smell the remnants of the meal on the stranger's breath and wondered if she could smell the things Amaleah had eaten as well.

A tattoo ran down the woman's face in the shape of a tiger. Its fur had been colored an even paler white than the stranger's skin. The tiger bared its teeth in a loud roar that Amaleah swore she could hear as she stared the woman in the eyes. The woman smiled, revealing pearly white teeth that stretched across her face.

As the woman stepped away from her, Amaleah noticed the intricate patterns woven into her tunic and the way the white fur on her cloak smelled like wood fire and oranges. It was a strange combination.

The woman was so tall that Amaleah barely came to the woman's torso, even though she was seated on a raised dais. Amaleah doubted that, even if she stood on the dais, she would be as tall as this woman.

The stranger quickly collapsed into a curtsy. "Princess Amaleah, it is a pleasure to meet you, I'm sure." Her mountain accent was thick and she pronounced some of her words differently. Amaleah wondered if she was a noble from their south-eastern border with Dramadoon. The stranger rose from her curtsy and looked into Amaleah's eyes. She had wide-set deep brown eyes that reflected Amaleah's face within them.

"I am Princess Saphria Michelle de Vain of Dramadoon." She bent her knees slightly again so that she bobbed before Amaleah. "It would give me great joy to take a turn about the room with you and discuss the future of our countries."

Amaleah glanced at her father, but he still sat sternly in his seat. He hadn't even turned towards Saphria's voice. Amaleah desperately tried to remember exactly what it was that she was supposed to do when addressing visiting royalty. *First ball. First time meeting foreign royals. What else will I face tonight?*

Clutching at the conch shell tucked beneath her bodice, Amaleah nodded primly at Saphria and got up from her seat. She smiled at the other princess and stepped down from the dais. Her father still did not look at her.

"It is a pleasure to meet you as well, Princess Saphria. I believe I would enjoy a turn about the room."

Saphria took Amaleah's arm as they began to walk about the room. They moved in silence for several moments. Amaleah's heart beat rapidly in her chest and several questions began tumbling through her mind. She wondered if Princess Saphria would be able to help save her.

"Amaleah," Saphria paused, "may I call you Amaleah?" Her question startled Amaleah out of her thoughts.

"I'm sorry, what did you say?"

Saphria laughed. Her voice tinkled like a ringing bell. "I asked if it would be alright if I called you by your given name instead of your title. I know we just met, but-"

"No. That's perfectly fine." Amaleah smiled at the other woman, the warmth reaching her eyes. "I would like that."

Saphria returned the smile and continued.

"Amaleah, as you know, my brother and I were only invited to remain in the city of Estrellala for two days after the conclusion of this ball." She looked at Amaleah to ensure that she was listening. "I would like for us to have a chance to spend some time together during those days. Perhaps we could even invite my brother."

She motioned towards the young man standing in the shadows of the stairwell. Even from the other side of the dance floor Amaleah could tell that he was just as tall—if not taller—than his sister. And muscular. Amaleah could discern even from their distance that he was handsome. He and his sister looked much alike. His hair a tad shorter than Saphria's and, instead of a tattoo stretching down his neck, he had a piercing through his eyebrow. As they moved closer to him, Amaleah realized that his smile met his eyes. His body appeared relaxed and supple. His outfit didn't fit as neatly as Saphria's did and he slouched a little as he leaned against the wooden railing.

"I think that can be arranged," Amaleah whispered. She wasn't sure why she had spoken so quietly, she just felt that she needed to keep her intentions as hidden as possible from the rest of court. Nobles were already looking at her curiously as she and Saphria continued to walk around the room.

"Excellent!" Saphria exclaimed as she suddenly gripped Amaleah's arm tightly and pulled her to a stop. "You have to promise that we can meet in private though. No outside influences. Only us," her voice came out in a rushed murmur.

"Of course, Saphria."

Amaleah's thoughts turned to Sylvia. As much as she didn't particularly care for her nursemaid at the moment, she trusted and needed her. Sylvia was older and wiser than many of the tutors Namadus had provided since Amaleah's return to Lunameed.

"But," she bit her bottom lip, uncertainly, "would it be alright if I brought one chaperone with me? It's just that I don't think my father would approve of my being with a member of a rival kingdom without having at least my nursemaid, Sylvia, in attendance."

Amaleah wore her court face or, at least, the court face she had practiced so many times in the mirror. She hoped it came off as free of emotion as she had planned.

Saphria looked at Amaleah for several moments before nodding her head. She stuck out her hand for Amaleah to shake. Tentatively, Amaleah took the other woman's hand and shook it. Saphria smiled, and Amaleah, for the first since Nicolette Blodruth had left the palace, felt as if she had a friend. Amaleah smiled back.

Amaleah led Saphria over to one of the tall, stained glass windows on the far side of the ballroom. Releasing Saphria's arm, she turned to face her.

"I know we shouldn't talk in the ballroom, but I was hoping that we could determine our meeting time and place."

Excitement and something Amaleah knew was fear bubbled inside her. She tried to maintain her court face, but she could feel the corners of her mouth twitch into a smile as she waited for Saphria to respond.

"Let's meet in the Sun Garden," Saphria said in her thickly accented voice. "I hear that the garden was a favorite of your mother's."

Amaleah's hands went cold at the mention of her mother. Why did everyone always refer to her mother? She watched Saphria's face to see if the other princess would reveal anything about her plans, but Saphria's court face was, apparently, well-practiced. She didn't reveal even the tiniest tendril of what she was thinking.

"It was," Amaleah conceded, "but the gardeners have let the plants run wild and the vines cut off the life of the flowers. It's still a beautiful garden, it's just gone wild."

Saphria nodded, "This would be perfect, no?"

"I suppose," Amaleah said uncertainly. In truth, the Sun Garden was not her favorite place. It reminded her too much of the other things in her life that had gone awry after her mother passed.

"We will meet you there after morning tea then."

Amaleah was about to respond when she caught a flash of her father scanning the room. Her heart pounded in her chest so hard that she felt like her breast bone would break from the rhythm. Without meeting Saphria's eyes, Amaleah nodded once and turned away from the foreign princess.

The beating in Amaleah's chest subsided as she left Saphria behind. Her thoughts still frantically clamored for attention, but Amaleah forced herself to ignore them. Following Sylvia's suggestions, she began mingling with Lunameedian noblemen as she made her way across the ballroom. It was better for her father to see her flirting with men than flirting with potential enemies. Or, at least, she hoped it was. She wasn't as sure of her father's expectations as she had been after witnessing how the guard, Aaron Blackwater, had responded to escorting her into the ballroom.

Amaleah was pondering what Saphria wished to discuss with her near one of the tables laden with sweet and sparkling ciders when she heard a slithering, low voice whisper in her ear. She cringed as she felt his slimy breath gently caress her neck.

"Your Highness," he said, "you need to circulate more. Meet and greet as I always say."

Putting on her court face, Amaleah turned around to face him.

Namadus's black billowing robes hung from his lean body, evoking images of the wraiths Sylvia had told her about as a I child. Amaleah shivered.

"I saw you," he sneered as he looked down his nose at her.

Amaleah's thoughts immediately went to Sylvia. And then to Mr. Sweets. The cavern. All of it. *Which one is he referring to? What had he seen?* Her mind kept jumping from one answer to the next but then discarding the solutions as impossible. She had been so careful to protect her plans, her secrets. He couldn't know about them.

Gripping her arm, he led Amaleah towards the ambassadors from Macai and Borganda, "You need to be more careful of who you make friends with, Your Majesty."

He spat her title at her and his grip tightened on her arm, "I know that we invited the royal members of Dramadoon to attend several of the upcoming balls, but it is necessary for you to remember your place as the heir to the Lunameedian throne and betrothed to the king."

He yanked her, hard, so that she faced him. "In the future, you will come to me should you wish to meet any of our royal guests and I will introduce you in a controlled environment. You are young, naïve, and, to be quite candid with you, stupid. You need me. You need the protection of your father's council to protect you from those who would seek to destroy our kingdom."

His voice rose as he spoke and several members of the Lunameedian nobility glanced sideways at the two of them. Tiny droplets of spittle hit Amaleah's face as Namadus finished his speech in fervor. She flinched as the droplets slid down her cheeks, but did not wipe them away. Amaleah shrank within herself as she listened to him talk. *Did I make an error in speaking with Saphria alone? What of my promise to meet with the her in private tomorrow?* She blinked away the tears that sprang unbidden into her eyes.

Namadus scowled at her as he saw the tears glisten on her cheeks. "You dare cry during your first ball?" He nearly shouted at her. And then his voice dropped so low that she could barely hear his words at all. "If you ruin everything that we have worked so hard for, girl, you will regret ever coming back from exile."

He emphasized 'girl' in such a way as to imply that she was nothing more than an insignificant child. Anger billowed within her. Straightening her back and wiping away the tears, Amaleah looked him square in the eyes. She was no girl. Not anymore.

"You may be the high councilor, you may have the power to make decisions that concern my life, you may even be able to control my father, but, Namadus, you will *never* speak to me in that way again. You're right. I am the heir to the throne. And I am betrothed to the king. If you ever embarrass me in this way—in front of the other councilors, my father, our guests, or our people—YOU will be the one to regret it."

She tried to keep her voice quiet as she spoke, but her words echoed in the small area surrounding them. Several guests glanced at them, obviously curious about why the princess was arguing with the high councilor. Amaleah ignored them.

He blinked.

Wordlessly, Namadus pulled her the remaining distance to the ambassadors. His fingers pressed so firmly into her skin that she knew would have bruises in the morning. Every time she caught his eye, she could see that fury was only just contained beneath his high councilor façade. She would pay for her words in the days to come. She could feel it.

As they approached the two ambassadors from the Island Nations, Namadus suddenly looked down at her.

In a voice so quiet, Amaleah could barely hear it, Namadus said, "You will be cordial to our guests, Amaleah. These are the type of people you should be forming bonds with. Not the barbarian you seemed so fond of during your little stroll around the ballroom."

Turning to face the two ambassadors, Namadus began the introductions. The ambassador from Macai was rotund, greying, and full of gaseous odors. Amaleah could smell the stench of rotting flesh, a wound he'd received while hunting one year that had never healed. It made her want to vomit. Namadus called him Count Vicroy. Amaleah allowed him to kiss the top her hand. His lips lingered too long upon her skin and she could feel the sticky drops of his drool slip onto her fingers. She wanted to pull away from him, but she caught Namadus's glare from her side vision and couldn't dare herself to upset him further.

The ambassador from Borganda was little better, in Amaleah's opinion. He was tall and thin with dark skin, hair, and eyes. His muscles bulged beneath his skintight clothing when he bowed to kiss Amaleah's hand. Many of the young women at court considered him handsome, charming, and, unfortunately for them, a scoundrel. Amaleah had heard her ladies talking about the rumors of his many conquests. As she looked at him, Amaleah didn't see the appeal. She could admit that he was quite handsome, but, lurking beneath his courtly airs, Amaleah could sense a deep desire from him to destroy. She wasn't exactly sure what he wanted to destroy. She just knew that he wanted to.

He held her gaze without a hint of embarrassment, testing her nerve and strength. Amaleah placed him in the same category as all the other nobles who desired her, not because of who she was but because of what she was: a princess, heir to the throne, soon to be queen to a dying king. They wanted her for her influence, her title, her kingdom. This man before her, this Ambassador Sienkle from Borganda, was no different. She instantly detested him.

Both men avoided any discussion Amaleah brought up about their home nations. Since the Island Nations' Civil War and their formation into the United Island Nations, the kingdoms of Borganda and Macai had faced many challenges. At points, their people had starved from a famine that swept across their lands. Their civil war had meant reduced gold, magical items, and other rare and valuable goods. Although the islands still produced some of the most valued crafts in the lands, their reduced holdings meant they had less bargaining power than the Mitierian kingdoms. In preparation for the ambassadors' arrival to Lunameed, Amaleah had read her father's annual reports on the Island Nations. In them, she had discovered that her father had been exploiting the islands for years without their apparent knowledge.

She hoped that neither of the men knew of her father's abysmal approach towards their homes.

Instead of discussing the political matters Amaleah was so rapt to learn more of, they exalted her beauty and party-planning skills. They discussed the magnificence of the castle's gardens. They even discussed other dignitaries who had arrived safely from the surrounding kingdoms in mocking tones that made Amaleah feel like an involuntary conspirator. Ambassador Sienkle lamented the fact that the Smielian king, Chucarlo, hadn't been able to make it, but he did so in a way that made Amaleah's skin crawl.

"You know as well as I do, Ambassador Sienkle, that the Smielians have not left their borders since the Third Darkness ended. After Szarmi rerouted their river—their connection to the heart of our world, Lake Amadoon—they were left with nothing to sustain them. They were once one of the lushest, most extravagant kingdoms in all of Mitier.

Now, they have only dry land and heat," Amaleah's voice quivered as she spoke.

"You are mistaken, Your Highness, they have not left their borders because they are cowards. Real rulers fight for what is due to them. If it were the fault of the Szarmian's that their river changed course, they should fight for what is rightfully theirs."

His eyes gleamed as he spoke and Amaleah had the distinct impression that he was not talking about the Szarmians at all.

"How can you say these things, Ambassador Sienkle? Surely you cannot believe because they are trying to rebuild their kingdom after a catastrophic event that they are cowards. Come now, where is your empathy?"

"You assume that they have been rebuilding their society, Highness. We have no proof that this is the case. We know nothing of Smielian society as it is today. I say this not to be harsh, but to be realistic. They are dying. They have been dying. And they will continue to die in their heat and their suffocated lands until they make the decision to fight back."

Amaleah's cheeks flared as she listened to the Borgandian Ambassador speak. As she was opening her mouth to respond, Namadus suddenly took hold of her shoulder and bit into her skin with his nails.

"Your wisdom is great, Ambassador Sienkle. I am sure that our young princess has learned much from your discussion. Unfortunately, I see that the king is waiting for us. Please do excuse us."

He bowed to the ambassadors. Namadus's hand pushed down firmly on Amaleah's shoulders, forcing her to squat into an awkward curtsey.

"Yes, our conversations have been most insightful," Amaleah said as she came back to her full height.

They turned to leave, but Ambassador Sienkle grasped Amaleah's hand. His grasp was like a clamp pressing down on all sides of her flesh. When his lips met the bare skin on her hand for the second time that night Amaleah felt the sting of his hot breath and the slime of his spit as he held his lips against her. Pulling her hand away as quickly as possible, Amaleah followed after Namadus at a quick pace.

When they were a fair distance away from the two ambassadors, Namadus whispered in her ear, "You need to learn your place, Princess. Elsewise, you might end up in a most unfortunate situation."

I'm already in an unfortunate situation, is what Amaleah wanted to say, but she stopped herself from sharing this thought.

"It would be a whole lot easier to remember my place if I knew where my place was," Amaleah hissed into his ear.

"Your place is with your father, here in Lunameed." Namadus paused before continuing in a tentative voice,

"Your Highness, you must do better at controlling your temper. Although I think our dear friend, Ambassador Sienkle, enjoyed sparring with you, not all of our foreign dignitaries will feel the same." He paused and then continued. "Speaking of this, it would be better if you were more careful about which of our visitors you showed favoritism towards."

"Then why did you make me converse with the ambassadors of our enemies from the sea? Tell me, Namadus, why were they invited to our country, to our ball, to our home, when they have done nothing to repair the damaged relationship between our countries? At least we're trying to rebuild the broken bonds with Dramadoon." Amaleah spoke in such a rush that she wasn't sure Namadus had fully understood what she'd said.

He regarded her sternly before saying, "It would be better for you to remember that your place is not to govern our foreign affairs. This is what you have councilors for. This is what you have me for." He laughed softly to himself. "No, Princess, I think your place is with your people and for your people: as a figurehead. They will come to love you because you choose to listen to your elders instead of following your whims. As for the Dramadoonian whore I saw you with," he sneered as he spoke the word 'Dramadoonian,' before continuing, "please, Princess, don't degrade yourself by associating with that riffraff."

"That 'riffraff,' as you call her, is the crown princess of Dramadoon. And she is our ally, however strained the current relationship may be. My talking to her will only strengthen that bond, not break it. As the high councilor, I would expect you to understand this."

He snorted in an undignified manner. "Princess, you clearly have no understanding of royal politics. They are only our allies, as you call them, because their country borders ours. What you need to understand is that they are barbarians. They have always been barbarians. They will always be such." He raised one eyebrow as he continued, "Now, besides our ambassadors from the seas, I have several other people I would greatly desire for you to meet."

He smirked at her and she could feel the coldness wash over her. More people to meet. More smiles and good graces to give to people she didn't believe would be true allies in the future. She didn't understand what Namadus's game was, but she wanted nothing to do with it.

She danced with several stuffy, middle-aged, and balding men who wore powdered wigs to hind their balding heads. She could feel her father's gaze on her as she twirled leapt to the fast-paced music. The men Namadus chose as her dance partners always held her a little too tightly or were so intoxicated from the wine that they stepped on her feet. With each dance, Amaleah groaned inwardly. Her father, on the other hand, appeared to be enjoying himself. He laughed joyfully as he watched her struggle with the men of his country. Amaleah knew that her father felt no jealousy as he watched the men drool over her. She was his. Secured by her promise. And there was no escape.

Chapter Sixteen

She was his. The knowledge that no other man would ever possess her made his heart throb with joy. His beauty. His love. His Orianna.

He watched her dance across the room. *How long has it been since I've seen her dance like this?* He craved her. She was his first and only love.

Every time he looked upon her face, he saw only his Orianna. Every time he held her in his arms, he felt only the woman who had haunted his dreams for seventeen years. Every time he heard her talk, he heard only her voice. He was in love all over again.

He stood and clapped his hands as she finished yet another reel with one of his dukes. Catching Namadus's eye, Magnus motioned for him to move Orianna to the middle of the room. That way, she would be the center of attention. All would see what a beautiful and talented bride he had chosen.

The trumpets resounded in the great hall. Magnus left the great dais onto which his throne had been placed and bowed before his betrothed. He took her into his arms and pulled her in tight against him. Everyone else left the expansive open space in the middle of the hall. They formed a tight circle around the royal couple. He pressed his hands into the small of her back, feeling her quiver beneath his touch. He delighted in her movement.

"Orianna, my love, how long has it been since first we danced? How I've missed the feel of your body between my hands. Promise to never leave me again."

He laughed softly to himself as if he were sharing a joke with someone only he could see and hear. His love remained silent, a frown creeping across her face. *Why is she sad?* He couldn't stand to watch her cry. Not again. Not ever.

Again he whispered close into her ear, "You look beautiful tonight, my dearest, but why do you look so somber? You must smile! Be merry and mirthful! For we are to be wed within the next six months."

He smiled broadly, allowing his face to be seen among the people. Clapping echoed through the acoustic room. The musicians ceased their playing.

King Magnus stared at her face. She was exactly how he remembered her. Except for her eyes. They were all wrong. Too light. Too green. This wasn't right. *She* wasn't right. He scowled.

Chapter Seventeen

Taking his hand in her own, Amaleah bowed with her father to the crowd of courtiers who filled the ballroom floor. As they rose from their bow, Amaleah noticed a deep frown on her father's face. Fearing that she had done something to upset him, she looked at her feet in a sign of reverence as she thanked him for the dance. He did not respond to her as he handed her off to Namadus.

Her stomach turned to ice.

The madness, she thought as she let Namadus lead her away. *He is consumed by the madness.*

She let Namadus guide her towards another group of courtiers. They were the delegates from the provinces that comprised Lunameed. Many of them were old families who had deep ties to the royal line. Although Amaleah had seen them as a child, she didn't remember who any of them were. She hoped she wouldn't embarrass herself by calling one of them the wrong name. She breathed heavily, as if she were running a long race. Anxiety filled her as she contemplated talking with these courtiers while her father fumed about whatever it was that she had done. Glancing around the room, she caught sight of her father. He was staring right at her. His eyes were as sharp as a blade as he glared at her from across the room. *What did I do to flare his anger like this?*

Namadus's voice droned on like a buzzing bee in Amaleah's head. She barely paid attention to his words. Instead, her sole focus was on her father's expression. His glowering face peered about the room but did not appear to actually see anything at all. Amaleah's stomach tighten each time she saw his face.

"Amaleah?"

Sighing, Amaleah turned to look at Namadus.

"Yes," she said in a confused tone, "I'm so sorry. What were you saying?"

Namadus's voice was cold as he responded, "We were just discussing the idea of going for a picnic tomorrow."

His eyes bore into her as he spoke.

"That would be lovely."

The rest of the group of nobles began talking at once as they vied for Amaleah's attention. The clamor made her head pound. Draining what remained of her wine, Amaleah excused herself to find new refreshments. Namadus's face took a dark, stony countenance that made Amaleah swallow hard as she regarded him. *Too late now*, she thought to herself as she picked up her skirts and fled from the group as regally as she could.

She breathed out a long, slow breath. *How am I supposed to win the favor of the nobles if I can barely stand to talk to them?*

She headed purposefully towards the back of the room. Slipping into the shadows, Amaleah pressed her hand against the wood paneling of one of the ornately carved reliefs. The wall shuddered as it slid back from the entrance. Taking a quick glance around her to make sure no one was watching, Amaleah slipped into the secret chamber.

Spider webs covered every corner of the room and dust piled itself high on the tables and floor. Amaleah had never seen anyone venture into this room other than herself the entire time she had been in Estrellala. She doubted anyone even knew about it. Amaleah had been quite surprised when she'd discovered that the wall moved when she put pressure on the relief. She had been tracing the carving with her fingers when she'd tripped over her own feet and almost fallen. Her hand had pressed into the wall, triggering the mechanism for the door to slide open. She had been escaping to the room ever since.

Striking a bit of flint against steel, Amaleah quickly lit the stub of a candle close to the doorway. Its dim, flickering light provided Amaleah with just enough light to make her way towards the large fireplace. Bending down, Amaleah again struck flint against steel once more. Smoke curled up from the logs as the flames grew.

Books, falling apart at the seams and bindings, filled every space of the room. Tiny bits of leather fell from their covers whenever Amaleah brushed against them with her skirts. Old scrolls, speckled by countless water droplets, could be seen in niches lining the walls. Moldy tapestries covered what little space remained.

Amaleah breathed in a sigh of relief.

Sinking into one of the two overstuffed chairs that were crowded around the fireplace, Amaleah let her mind mull over the details from the evening. Despite the feeling of dampness in the room, Amaleah felt warm and comfortable by the fire. Much more comfortable than she had in the presence of the nobles with whom Namadus wanted her to form connections. Her eyes began to droop the longer she sat in the chair. Soft notes of music from the ballroom began lulling her to sleep.

Just as Amaleah's head fell to her chest, a loud noise startled to her. It sounded like a loud, mechanical puff of air. Amaleah jolted upright from the chair and spun around the room. *Did someone follow me into the chamber?* Fear spread its tendrils around her heart like the icy fingers of winter.

"Hello?" Amaleah asked.

No one answered.

Shivering, Amaleah cautiously treaded towards the door. Pressing her ear against the musty, cold wood, Amaleah tried to hear what was happening on the other side.

Women were laughing loudly; she could hear their bellowing cries of joy distinctly through the door. She could hear men talking, but their voices were distant and indistinct. She waited for several moments, but did not hear the loud sound again. Drawing in a breath and counting to three, Amaleah tried to stop her heart from pounding in her chest. She released the breath in one long, steady stream.

She counted as she exhaled, feeling the tension release itself from her shoulders. *I'm going to be fine*, she told herself as she continued to breath and count. *It was nothing. I'm going to be fine.* Eventually, her heart stopped hammering in her chest and her breathing became steady.

Slumping to her knees, Amaleah clasped one of the books residing on the floor. The cover was falling off, only held on by a tiny thread of silk. It contained an inlay of a drawing that felt familiar to Amaleah, although she didn't know why. Opening the book to the first page, Amaleah marveled at the small script of the manuscript. Someone had spent hours poring over these pages, ensuring that each word was precise, elegant, and eternal. It was a collection of short stories and poems about the rebirth of Lunameed after the Third Darkness.

Each story was told in first person. Fantastical creatures Amaleah had never heard of fell and died at the hands of the Island Nations and their allies, the Szarmians. The stories told of the creatures' bravery and talent, of their unwavering devotion to the protection of the Light. Each story contained the life and death of the creatures. Amaleah couldn't take her eyes from the pages. With every new story, she understood a little bit more about the history of the creatures of the Light who resided in her kingdom. None of them were familiar. *Why have I never been given this book before? Why have I never heard these stories before?*

Some of the stories were familiar in nature, but different in perspective. Her eyes roamed over one of the tales she had almost forgotten. During the Wars of Darkness, the Szarmian government had built trenches to reroute the rivers of Moorica and Borad so that they no longer flowed near the country of Smiel. Although the Smielian people had been allies to Szarmi during the wars, their relationship was full of jealousy and distrust. As the war came to a close, Szarmi finished constructing a dam on the Szarmian and Smielian border near Lake Pur. The dam blocked Smiel from Lake Amadoon's waters.

Smiel turned into a desert and lost all connection with the other kingdoms of Mitier. Amaleah had never once heard from their rulers or met a Smielian in person. She'd heard rumors, or course, that the Smielian people were little more than desert pirates who stole and murdered anyone who entered their land.

Of course, she had never truly believed these tales because *someone* would have been able to escape the murder part in order for there to be rumors. Regardless, Smiel was now a place of mystery. Someday, she would like to visit there for herself, even if it was just to see if she'd be murdered by desert pirates.

Her eyes began to water as she continued reading. Words melded together into incoherent messages that she couldn't quite understand. Exhaustion overwhelmed her, yet she still did not wish to put the book down. She read for at least another fifteen minutes—it was hard to tell the time—when she yawned so big that her ears popped. Closing the cover of the book as gently as she could, Amaleah was appalled to see that pieces of leather fell into her hands as her fingers lightly ran along its cover. Sighing, Amaleah tucked the book gently into a well-protected spot on the bookshelf.

The music stopped. Amaleah's heart skipped a beat as she tried to calculate how long she'd been absent from the ballroom: too long. She would have been missed by now. Namadus was sure to have noticed her absence and Amaleah didn't feel like risking the loss of her hideaway.

Placing her ear against the wall, Amaleah listened for voices, music, and movement on the other side. Nothing. She knocked the small panel at the bottom of the floor to prop open the hidden door. Peeping one small eye beyond the borders of the door to ensure that no one was looking, Amaleah sprinted out of the room and quietly pushed back against the door with her body. Breathing heavily, Amaleah joined the ball once more.

Many of the courtiers had already disappeared. Countless others were groggily waltzing and chatting about the room. Her father snored from his throne on the dais. Not wanting to create a disturbance, Amaleah feigned fatigue and yawned before slumping into her own throne. It was smaller and lower than that of her father's, but still as ornately carved.

She watched her subjects socialize. Namadus was in a small group containing other councilors of her father's court: Zaphiniro, Miccilous, and Matheus. They appeared to be having an argument but Amaleah could not imagine what it could be about. The four of them always seemed to be in accordance with one another. She'd never seen them disagree on anything during the past seven months she'd been at court. Miccilous began yelling, quietly at first then loud enough for the group of courtiers around them to move away with bewildered expressions upon their faces.

Amaleah didn't stir, but strained her ears, trying to hear what they were saying, what they were arguing about. Although the music had stopped several minutes ago, countless voices echoed through the hall, drowning out even the raised voice of Miccilous. None of the other councilors seemed to be yelling, although their faces were red with distress and their eyes showed anger as well as contempt. *What does this mean?* Amaleah thought as she carefully slid out of her chair and began to walk in the councilors' general direction.

"Princess Amaleah, a pleasure I'm sure." The voice startled Amaleah. She flushed and spun quickly around to face her companion. As she met his gaze she felt her breath catch in her throat. The prince in the fur coat stood before her. She did the only thing she could think to do.

She curtsied.

He reached for her hand and kissed her knuckle. His hot breath tickled her skin before he let her fingers drop from his own. "I was beginning to believe that I would never have the opportunity to catch you alone. You did disappear from the ball, after all." His voice held a hint of conspiratory notes in it. He raised his eyebrows at her as he continued, "But then, just as I was beginning to give up hope, there you appeared." He motioned towards the secret door Amaleah had come through moments before.

"I'm sure I don't know what you're talking about," Amaleah said.

"Are you sure? I could show you exactly where I saw you enter the ballroom."

Startled, Amaleah leaned towards him. He was so forthright, not like the other men she'd met at court. They were so close that she could smell the deep aroma of his soap. It was a combination of cedar and pine needles. He was intoxicating.

"No," Amaleah said shakily, "That won't be necessary."

The man grasped her hand and led her towards a more secluded area of the ballroom. When they were hidden away in the shadows, the man said, "You must be wondering who I am."

"Not exactly."

He chuckled, "No?"

"No, you're Prince Fredrerik Fonshan Marclous de Vain," she paused. "And your sister is Saphria. She already warned me about you," she said this last part jokingly. He blushed.

"You can call me Freddy. Everyone else does."

"And you may call me Amaleah."

They fell silent for a moment. Amaleah peered out at the ballroom. Couples still waltzed around the room in grand circles. Amaleah sighed. *Do they not realize what they're celebrating? Do they even care?*

Finally, in an attempt to break the silence, Amaleah said, "Your sister has a very pretty name."

"Yes, well, she was named after our great-great grandmother, Princess Melody Saphria de Vain. She's actually quite famous, that one. She fought against the outliers in Szarmi as well as the privateers from the coastal nations of Macai and Borganda. Have you heard of her?"

"I have read of her, yes. It's said that she was one of the few members of the royal family that survived not just the Wars of Darkness but also the aftermath. She used her magic to survive until the ripe old age of one-hundred and fifty, if I remember my facts correctly. Nothing was recorded about her death, though."

"Her death? Our grandmother still lives." He looked at her bewildered.

"But, that would mean that she's well over three hundred and eighty years old. How is that possible?"

Freddy looked away from her, his eyes clouding. He trembled and fidgeted before falling still. Coughing, he turned back to face her as if nothing had happened.

"May I have the pleasure of accompanying you to the garden for a walk?" His voice was soft and light, like the gentle caress of a breeze, yet Amaleah shivered. *Why does no one answer my questions?* she thought.

Freddy continued, "The air in here is so stifling, I do believe a walk would do me well."

What about your dead grandmother who is actually alive? Amaleah almost asked him about his supposedly living grandmother again but stopped short when she realized that he might not be allowed to discuss the circumstances surrounding his grandmother. She, more than anyone, understood what it meant to have a secret she didn't want to discuss.

Taking his hand, she responded, "Yes, I would be delighted to take a walk with you. Though, I must warn you, even our winters are warmer than your summers. Or at least this is what my tutors have always told me," Amaleah paused and then asked, "Are our lands so very different?"

"Certainly so, Princess, which is why my sister and I have not the attire for your warmer climate. I know it is still winter here, but the air feels like our spring."

"Is that so? Well then, you must be pleased that I am a Lunameedian rather than a Szarmian. For if you had need to travel to *that* neighboring kingdom, I'm sure you would have been excruciatingly hot," she paused and then said, "If you like, I can have my tailor make you and your sister clothing better suited to our climate."

"I'm sure he would be able to accomplish this task. But I am afraid we will not be here long enough to enjoy them. Please, don't trouble yourself or your tailor."

They continued chatting as Amaleah led Freddy out into one of the many gardens enclosed within the walls of the Palace of Veri. Amaleah felt comforted by his presence; she didn't understand why his company had that effect on her. She just felt a sense of safety that had been missing since her return to Estrellala.

As they strolled through the gardens, Freddy told her of his country. He described how the winter fae and dwarves lived with them in their castle, Yeron, throughout the duration of the year. He and his sister took classes with them to learn about the art of mining, nature, and spell casting. He told her how snow fell in such abundance each winter that his world was turned into a glittering snow globe. Dramadoon was a mountainous country, and her peaks rose above the tallest spires of Yeron. The few elves who lived within their court used their magic to create light shows on special occasions, changing the clouds into an array of color and striking lighting across the sky. Sorceresses lived in hidden towers with their consorts. Magic was not something only some possessed. It was in the air; it could be seen, felt, tasted, and even smelt. It was everywhere in Dramadoon.

"I would love to see that someday." Amaleah whispered in rapture as he finished talking. His kingdom seemed to represent everything that Lunameed had been in the past but had lost during the years following the Wars of Darkness.

"Perhaps you will one day, Amaleah. Perhaps you will," Freddy whispered back. He squeezed her hand gently and they fell into a comfortable silence.

As they rounded a bend in the path, a fountain tinkled lightly in a small alcove. Amaleah smiled at the sound, only the fae's magic kept the water from freezing and the flowers from frosting over. Even in winter their gardens were kept in bloom. Queen Orianna's roses sparkled in the moon. Their fragrance circled around Freddy and Amaleah as they continued on their walk. A cold breeze tickled the air, sending a shiver down Amaleah's spine.

"Are you cold, Amaleah?"

"No, I'm alright, thank you."

He wrapped his arm around her as they sat down upon a bench in the middle of the garden. No candles or torches were lit this far into the greenery. Only the light from the moons lit their surroundings. Sculptures and fountains surrounded them. Amaleah could see their outlines as she stared into the darkness.

"Amaleah, may I talk with you about something that I think may cause you some discomfort?"

Oh no, Amaleah thought, *I hope I haven't done something to upset him.*

"Please do," she said, despite the feelings of disquiet that settled upon her.

He clasped her hands in his own. Started, sputtered, and stopped several times before finally exclaiming in the softest of tones, "I believe that you should leave this place, Your Majesty."

"Why, what do you mean?" She already knew that she should leave, but she wanted to know why members of another kingdom's royal family believed that she should.

"Stories of your father's sickness have spread, My Lady. Even the humblest of the Dramadoonian people have spoken about his desire to marry you, his own daughter. Their worries have spread to the nobility. And it is not just within Dramadoon. We have heard reports that the tension between Lunameed and the rest of Mitier has continued to grow. You cannot stay here. You cannot be a part of this insanity."

Amaleah remained silent for several moments, processing this information. She had not been aware that so many people outside of Lunameed knew of her father's madness.

"Every nation will rise against you," Freddy whispered. His voice was so soft; it was almost like a lover's caress. However, his words had nothing to do with love. Amaleah leaned away from him.

Is this what Saphria wanted to speak with me about tomorrow? If so, why is Freddy telling me all of this now?

Amaleah's heart beat rapidly in her chest and her breathing caught. She couldn't let him know that she didn't have a plan, that she wasn't capable of ruling herself.

"Freddy… please. Do you think I do not already know this, think about this, and abhor the condition in which I am placed?" She looked into his eyes, trying to decide if she could trust him. The sense of safety she'd felt earlier was still there, hidden beneath her anxiety. *What do I have to lose?* "Please believe when I say that I am trying to fabricate a plan of escape, even as we speak now."

He sighed in relief, "So you do not desire to marry him?"

"No! of course not! He's my father, for goodness sake. He exiled me for five years, and when I returned his insanity had consumed him. Ever since he made the announcement that we would be betrothed I have been plotting my escape. But, I do worry about him, about Lunameed. He is so unwell." Amaleah blinked up at him, trying to keep the tears from spilling out.

"Amaleah, I can offer you relief," Freddy said as he leaned into her. He cupped her cheek in his hand, and stroked his thumb across her skin. It would have been comforting, had Amaleah's heart not been hammering so hard in her chest, "Come back to Dramadoon with my sister and me. Please, Amaleah, we can hide you in our mountains. You can meet with the fae, dwarves, and other creatures of the Light who reside in our kingdom. We can protect you."

He leaned his forehead against hers as he finished speaking. Amaleah breathed him in: the cedar, the pine, even the sweat.

She wanted to say yes. With every part of her, she wanted to agree to leave with him. Yet as she sat on the bench with him and contemplated his offer, she somehow knew that going to Dramadoon would be a mistake. The tattoo the fae had given her burned coldly on her ankle with a feeling so ominous it made Amaleah shiver. The wind picked up and the moon became shrouded by the clouds.

"Be wary, Amaleah. This is not your destiny. Don't go."

The words passed through her mind so quickly and so softly, that Amaleah thought she had imagined them. As soon as the words stopped, the moon shone again, but the feeling the words left behind remained. She knew she had to refuse. "I cannot leave yet," she whispered, "I am bound by a promise to remain here until I have received the gowns and coat my father has promised to make."

"But Amaleah," he exclaimed as he pulled away from her, "can you not see the danger that puts you in? He could-"

"He can do nothing that he has not already done. By the time that he intends for us to be married, I will be far gone from this place."

They sat in silence for several moments. Amaleah felt the remnants of the warning the fae's blessing press upon her. The words left a sour taste in her mouth. *How I wish I could ignore these blessings!*

"How do you plan to escape?" Freddy finally asked.

"I have a plan." It was only a partial lie, "My nursemaid and I have set a plan to smuggle me out of the country. I am to go to Szarmi."

"To Szarmi? But they are enemies to the magical world! You can't go there."

"Yes, they are, which is why my father would never to think to look for me there. I will be safer behind the borders of our enemies than in the confines of both our nations." Amaleah reached out and took his hand. His warmth gave her strength. She continued, "I've already solicited the help of the creatures of the Light in Lunameed to help me in my endeavors. I do not believe I will fail."

Amaleah could feel the frustration building in him. In a husky voice, Freddy exclaimed, "You can't be seriously considering trying to escape on your own." His voice caught as he continued, "What about the tension building between the nations? What about the talk of a new war that has been spreading across the land?"

He didn't give her a chance to continue before asking, "Have you heard the rumors about the savior?"

Why is he asking me about that?

"I know these rumors, Amaleah. My people have kept a careful ear on the magical world since the end of the

Wars of Darkness. Even though the prophesies are said to be broken, we seek out the few remaining ones. I know that they have been locked away in secret by the remnants of the Keepers, but surely you must have heard something."

He looked at her full in the face then, his eyes boring into her own. Amaleah gulped. Cordelia and the fae had mentioned something about a savior. Only the person they had been talking about had been her.

"I have only heard what my father's high councilor, Namadus, tells me," Amaleah lied. "None of it is good. I fear the same as you, that we shall enter into another war if we are not cautious. But if you remember, Szarmi did apologize for her actions during the Wars of Darkness. I am of the opinion that the nation misses the magical influence and prestige she used to enjoy before the wars."

Freddy slapped his hands down on his knees, his face changing to a purplish-red color, "Then you are a fool! They slaughter all who pass their borders. You should know this, Princess." He reached over and squeezed her hand tightly, "You shouldn't put yourself in such danger."

"And why are you so concerned for my safety?" her voice was cold as she spoke. She was tired of people telling her what to do and how to do it in the name of her safety.

"Amaleah, can you not see how we are intricately joined by destiny?"

She opened her mouth to respond but quickly shut it as she heard footsteps coming closer to their hiding spot, a lot of footsteps. Amaleah released her hand from his and stood, putting some distance between the two of them. Torchlight blinded her before the shadowy figures of several guards entered the small clearing in the garden where Amaleah and Freddy stood.

The guards immediately latched onto Amaleah's arm and pulled her towards the palace. She tried to resist them, but they only gripped her more tightly. Freddy followed at a distance, but not close enough for them to talk. The party was over.

Chapter Eighteen

Miliom, Szarmi

Colin slumped into the chair beside his desk, letting the letter from his mother fall to the ground. He had been summoned. After so many years of being the pariah of the family, the unfortunate crown prince, his mother had finally decided to call him to Ducal House. He hadn't seen his mother for more than a year; she had not been present for his graduation from the military academy at Fort Pelid. Nor had she returned to Miliom to honor the death of Vanessa Wilhelm.

His mind tormented him with thoughts of Vanessa. The once-sweet memories he had of his love for her had been warped into what were little more than scenes from a nightmare. She had betrayed him. She had attempted to assassinate him. Somehow it didn't matter. There was nothing he could do to change how much he had loved her. And it was tearing him apart.

Shoving the memories of Vanessa aside, Colin picked up the letter and reread his mother's words to him,

"My dearest boy, you cannot begin to understand how much I have missed you. Now that your twenty-first name day is upon us, it is time to finalize the plans for your coronation. For this purpose, I require your attentions at my estate..."

Crumbling the paper, Colin threw the letter to the floor once more. *Does she really think I believe her?* All his life, his mother had never regarded him with more than contempt. He knew she saw him as a weak, simpering little boy who had never turned into a man. Colin didn't view himself this way. He had changed too much since his father had died. It wasn't his fault that his mother couldn't recognize the man he had become. All she saw was the failure.

His sister, Coraleen, on the other hand, was everything that his mother thought a ruler of Szarmi should be. His sister was beautiful, intelligent, and strong. It was no secret that Queen Vista had wanted to usurp Colin as the rightful heir to the throne. Thankfully, his father had seen past Colin's lack of physical power and declared him the heir.

Despite the barriers Queen Vista had laid between Colin and his sister, Colin had come to adore Coraleen. She was four years his junior and meant everything to him. Since their father's death three years ago, Colin and Coraleen had developed a bond that he had seldom witnessed in other relationships. Every time he saw her, his heart was filled with joy.

At least one of us is loved, he thought as he imagined his return to his mother's estate. Seeing his sister was the one highlight Colin anticipated for his return to Ducal House. That, and removing himself from the city of Miliom. No matter where he went in the city, memories of Vanessa haunted him. He hoped this would not be the case once he arrived at his mother's estate.

He knew he was a disappointment to the queen. Colin leaned back in his chair and imagined what his homecoming would be like. She would, of course, greet him in person, as was expected, but she wouldn't kiss or hug him. It would be as it always had been. She would turn her icy eyes upon him and beckon him forward. She would appraise him and find him wanting. Throughout his life, Colin had wanted nothing more than to earn his mother's approval. Despite his many accomplishments, she had never told him that she was proud of him. Pain seared his heart as he thought of his mother's contempt for him. *One day,* he promised himself, *I will stop seeking her approval.*

Her letter had informed him that she had important news to share with him that would greatly increase their chances of winning a war, should that be the direction that they take. His mother had sent him countless letters hinting at a desire for him to wage war on Lunameed and Dramadoon with the aid of the Island Nations. Colin secretly wondered if she was pushing for war so that she could watch him die. She had never said this outright, of course, but he did wonder.

A king must know the facts of life, whether they are cold and distressing or not. This was how she had raised him to be: concise, controlling, cruel, and calculating. But he hadn't become all that his mother had wished for him. No, he had become quite the opposite, which was why he was such a disappointment to her.

Although Colin's father, King Henry, had loved Queen Vista greatly, he had recognized in her a desire for power and domination over the lives of their children, especially Colin. On multiple occasions, Colin had discussed his mother's coldness and apparent hatred of him with his father. Despite their agreement that Queen Vista did not care for Colin, neither of them had been able to determine why.

Even before King Henry's death, Colin had made changes that greatly benefited the kingdom. Through their combined interest in science and technology, King Henry and Colin had been able to increase production and exportation of their crops by twenty percent. With more money being designated towards the schools and new recruitment strategy employed to find the best scholars in all of Mitier, their schools had risen in renown. Although Colin was not a great warrior the way his father had hoped that he would be, the Szarmian military had become more innovative and productive. This achievement, above all others, had made his father proud; it had solidified the Szarmian armies as the greatest force within all of Mitier.

Colin believed that his father had loved him, despite his shortcomings. Although Colin was the oldest child, Szarmian law declared that the ruling king had the right to declare any of his children the future heir. Colin knew his mother had pleaded with his father to place Coraleen on the throne instead of him. Thankfully, his father had denied her and declared Colin the crown prince of Szarmi. Within a month of the inheritance decision, his father had died from a sudden illness. Coraleen and Colin had been separated by their mother ever since. Now, in just two months, Colin would be crowned king of Szarmi and would have the power to change his mother's opinion of him once and for all.

A gnawing pit in Colin's stomach told him it wouldn't be possible. Colin couldn't seem to rid himself of the words Vanessa had spoken during her attempt to assassinate him. She had called him pathetic, unfit to rule Szarmi. He knew his mother felt the same. *Why is it that every woman I love turns against me?* Colin sighed heavily to himself. He didn't know if he would ever be able to free himself from the doubt crowding his mind. *Am I unfit to rule?* His thoughts drifted to the only woman in his life who hadn't betrayed him: his sister.

His sister was beautiful: dark with gold-flecked eyes and curly, black hair; she was lively and vivacious, charming and good natured. She had a way of making the world seem so much brighter than it actually was. As children, Colin had adored his sister and doted on her more than even their father and mother had. Once he was crowned king, he intended to give Coraleen a prominent place within the Szarmian court. She could rule beside him until she married into her own kingdom.

Yes, Colin thought to himself as he rang for his servants and began to prepare a trunk for his travels, *I will treat her with the respect she deserves and give her the power that she has always been denied. She deserves to be important.*

Jameston, his most trusted and oldest servant, as well as his close friend, entered the room.

"You rang, Your Highness?"

"Jameston, how many times must I tell you to call me Colin and be done with all this formality, at least while we're in private?"

"At least once more, Your Majesty."

Colin raised an eyebrow at his friend, but said nothing, "I am to leave to for Ducal House on the morrow, my good man. You are to come with me, if your wife will spare you."

Jameston bent to pick the letter up from the ground. Now crumpled from where Colin had scrunched the delicate parchment, the letter appeared to be nothing more than a scrap, a piece of trash. "You know, Colin, she does love you in her own way."

"You say that, Jameston, because you must, not because it is the truth. I will attend to her. I will be her dutiful son. I will even allow myself to be made the fool while I am at her house. But I will not let her get the better of me. In just two months, I will be crowned king of Szarmi, and when that happens, Jameston, she will regret ever pushing me away."

"And what of your sister, Coraleen, Your Majesty. What will become of her?"

"She is my beloved sister. She will be given everything she wants. She will be married into a noble family, if not a royal one. She will be happy."

"And for yourself?" Jameston asked hesitantly.

Colin immediately thought of the vision he and Vanessa had created for their future together. His stomach turned as the images turned to dark shadows.

"I'm not sure yet, Jameston. I'm not sure," he said, his voice thick with emotion.

"Your father always said that your life's work would be to find the woman who is the second half of your soul." Jameston paused before continuing, "I know what happened with Vanessa still haunts you, Colin, but I believe you will find the right person. I know she's out there somewhere."

Colin didn't respond to his friend's comments, but rather stared at himself in the mirror. He did not like the hallowed look of the man staring back at him. *Is that really how I look?* Since Vanessa's death, he had carried his despair with him. Although his advisors still brought up the idea of marriage to him, he hated this line of discussion. He no longer desired a wife, much less the burden of children. He wanted to be happy and loved, but he did not want to rush into another romance until he was sure he could trust the woman with his life. *I thought I had that in Vanessa.* The thought nagged at him.

"How long will we reside at your mother's estate?" Jameston asked, pulling Colin out of his thoughts.

"As long as she needs me or until I return to Miliom for the coronation," Colin replied. He remembered her message about important news, "I believe she has some plan for me. Perhaps a princess from the outlands," he said with distaste, "Perhaps even the princess of Dramadoon or Lunameed to meet. That would be something now wouldn't it? The daughters of our kingdom's enemies to meet the future king of ours. I'm sure that is just the type of thing my mother would love: to have me hated by my own people even before I'm crowned king."

"I'm sure it's not as bad as that, Colin. You must give her some credit."

Colin didn't reply. His mind was already at work, his imagination flying. He packed a trunk as he thought. For that was what Colin was, a dreamer. Everyone who knew him said the same. It was the reason he was quiet and reserved, why he never spoke until he'd watched people beforehand. Most of the time, he lived in a completely different world than the one everyone else did. Szarmi hadn't had magic in its kingdom for almost three hundred years. After the Wars of Darkness, every magical creature had died, been killed off, or left. Every sorceress, magic speaker, and wizard had vanished. Now the tales of old had become myths—a world that no longer existed, if they ever had.

Colin lived in a world where such things were in abundance, where everyone was free. He dreamed of changing Szarmi back to her former glory. It didn't matter to him that their military, education, and industry were prized possessions and coveted by most of Mitier. It didn't matter that Szarmi was the richest kingdom of the land and sea. It didn't matter to him that Szarmi had more power than any other nation, including the ones with magic. No. He wanted the magic and the mystery that comes with what the common people called "the Light." He wanted to see the wonders of the world, hear the music of the fae, smell the flowers of the elves. He wanted so much for his kingdom than just technology and science. He wanted to see what would happen if the two worlds worked together.

Within hours of receiving the letter from his mother, Colin's entourage had departed Miliom.

Chapter Nineteen

The Battle of Alnora, the Third Darkness

The door flew open as Kilian pushed inward. The initiates' bodies—the ones who had attempted to kill him—lay broken about the room. At least, Kilian assumed the bodies belonged to the initiates. There wasn't much left except cracked bones, blood, and scattered flesh. Kilian stared at the scene in disgust. This was not the way of the Light.

"You came for us," a cold, piercing voice said into the dim light of the room. It was her voice, but not her voice at the same time. Kilian paused in the doorway, uncertain of what to do. Sticky blood dripped on his shoulder. Kilian's eyes roamed over what was left of the corpses, trying to determine where she was.

"Did you kill these sorcerers?" he asked. His voice shook as he spoke, and he hoped she wouldn't be able to detect the fear in his voice over his heavy breathing.

"They were a threat," she responded in the same cold voice.

Kilian stopped breathing. One of the initiate's severed heads looked up at him with unseeing eyes. He almost shivered.

"That's what you created me for," he paused as he felt his stomach squirm as he saw the remains of an initiate who couldn't have been older than thirteen. "I was to fight your battles for you."

"Yes," she said. "And you have performed quite nicely. Until today." Her voice was cutting.

"What do you mean until today? I'm here aren't I?"

"You're too late."

No, Kilian thought, *it can't be true.* He took a step into the room and immediately heard the crunch of bones as his foot pressed down on what remained of a hand. Shuddering, he looked about the room, but couldn't see her or any of the other members of the Light Council. *Where are they?*

"You failed us, Kilian. You failed me," she said in such a low voice that Kilian almost thought that he had imagined it.

"No," he whispered. "It cannot be."

He took another step forward into the room. "Tell me it isn't true. Tell me-"

"Silence!" Her voice came as a sharp command and Kilian snapped his mouth shut. "These deaths are on your hands, Kilian Clearwater," she paused. The next time she spoke, she sounded incredibly forlorn, "I loved you once. I fear that I shall never again love someone as much as I loved you."

"Loved? What are you saying?"

"For your failure," she continued, ignoring his interjection, "you shall be cursed."

Kilian took a step away from the center of the room. He noticed, for the first time, the carvings that covered the walls. Each of the designs was so realistic that Kilian almost mistook them for creatures they represented: the members of the Light Council. As he peered closer at the carvings, he realized that she was featured in many of them, that her likeness was everywhere throughout the room. His stomach dropped.

Even though the initiates had sacrificed their lives in the process, they had been successful. The binding was complete.

Kilian gasped.

"Let it be known that until the broken prophecies are made right and the first is made complete, you, Kilian Clearwater, are doomed to roam this world as a stranger. None who know you as the Light's Hero will see you for who you really are. Until the day comes when the prophecies have been made whole, you shall remain lost."

"What does that mean?" Kilian asked as he felt an intense heat wash over him. He stumbled in the stairwell and almost fell down the long flight of stairs. The heat was so excruciatingly hot.

"We all have a part to play, Kilian," she said, with only a minor hint of condemnation. "We all have a destiny. Trust in the Light; it shall not lead you astray." Her voice was different when she said the last part. It was softer, more gentle. It was the voice he remembered.

And then the fragileness of her voice was gone and replaced by the harshness he had heard earlier.

"You, Kilian Clearwater, are doomed to spend all eternity seeking for a way to rescue us from our imprisonment. Only then shall you have peace." It wasn't her voice. He wasn't even sure it belonged to any member of the Light Council.

He shook his head. *This isn't right*, Kilian thought as he felt a darkness enter his body. It sent shivers down his spine and left a tingling feeling in his toes and fingertips. It was unlike anything he'd ever experienced before. He felt powerful and mighty. He could take on the world and live to tell the tale. His eyes glowed with the power and he began to laugh maniacally.

Suddenly, his entire body shook violently.

The darkness left his body almost as quickly as it had entered. A cold emptiness spread throughout Kilian's body at its loss. *She's gone*, he realized in agony, *I've failed her.* Crouching, he let himself lose control of his breathing. Let the sobs wrack his body. He called her name. Wailed for her to come back to him. She didn't respond.

Looking wildly about the room, Kilian saw a carving of her from her younger days. He barely noticed the blood, flesh, and bones of the initiates as he crossed the room to where the carving was inlaid in the wall. Reaching up, Kilian traced her face with his thumb. He had never loved anyone the way he had loved her. For one long moment, he cupped her cheek in his hand and imagined that the wooden structure was actually her.

"Leave. Now. Go. This isn't the place for you anymore, Kilian. Please," her whispered voice spoke urgently. As if breaking free from a trance, Kilian looked all around him.

All he saw were the atrocities the Light Council had committed. He looked at the broken bodies, barely recognizable. He saw the blank stares of the few faces that had remained intact. *The Light Council is supposed to be good. They are supposed to bring life, joy, and peace to the world.*

They alone had been granted the gifts of inspiration. They alone could create new magic. And they had betrayed all of the Light's creatures. They—she—had betrayed him. Despite all of the death Kilian had seen during his military career, the sight of the massacred bodies made him retch.

When he was done, Kilian wiped his mouth clean with the sleeve of his shirt and peered around the room. Kilian now knew why the Wars of Darkness had started. Why hadn't he been able to see it before? *Why didn't I realize that she—the woman I love—had been corrupted?*

Now the Light's Council had been bound. They were gone. He was alone.

No, he told himself, *I can't let this be the end.*

Chapter Twenty

Szarmi, Three hundred years later

Colin looked up from his book as the carriage bounced on a rutted curve. They'd been traveling for two days now. One day to cross the Borad River and another to travel by coach to Ducal House. Jameston sat across from him, snoring with a pastry sitting precariously atop his rotund body. Jameston had always been a large man, but he had been made even larger after he married a chef from the southern shores of Borganda. Claire was her name. Although Colin had only met her twice, he felt as if he knew her quite well. Mainly because whenever Jameston discussed anything—love, food, politics, games—he always mentioned his wife. Colin was both happy and jealous of his friend's happiness. *But I did find love, didn't I? She made me happy...* Colin pushed the thought away.

She tried to assassinate me, Colin told himself. Since Colin's father had died, there had been multiple attempts on his life. Many of them were rumored to be at the request of his mother, Queen Vista. He had heard countless accounts of plots to put Coraleen on the throne instead of him. *Could Vanessa be connected to my mother?* The thought did nothing to quell Colin's anger or discomfort. Either way, he had been fooled.

Pounding his fist into his palm, Colin thought about all the other attempts on his life throughout the years. He had been shot at, poisoned, and, once, almost hung. None of the attempts had been successful. *They never would be,* he told himself.

Coraleen had no desire to rule. She had no desire to have the pressure of a nation and its people placed upon her. Colin had had multiple conversations with her about the throne and she had said this to him on every occasion. Besides, the people of Szarmi loved him for creating more jobs, money, and prosperity for them all. He worked fairly for all his citizens, not just the nobility and the middle class. He supported people's ingenuity and hard work, rather than their purses. It was for this reason they forgave him his quiet ways and lack of physical strength.

Colin could not understand why his mother hated him so. Even as a child, she had despised him. He looked like her in all regards. His dark, golden skin was different from the dark browns and blacks of his people—just like his mother's Borgandian skin was different. He had rich black hair and hazel eyes that seemed to change between green and brown. All these traits belonged to his mother. Coraleen, on the other hand, resembled their father. *Perhaps this is why she hates me. Maybe she just wants to forget her Borgandian heritage.* Colin didn't really believe that.

He could hear the horses' hooves clip-clopping on the hard, cobblestone roadways. Transitioning the roadways from packed dirt to stone had been his most recent project. Coraleen had begged him to do it in order to make traveling easier from Ducal House to Miliom. And so he had. In doing so, he had created more jobs than had ever been necessary in Szarmi before. And his people had prospered.

Still, traveling across the final stretch of land between Miliom and Ducal House was slow. At each town, the carriages were slowed by people throwing gold and silver-veined starlight flowers at him in the streets. The rare flowers only bloomed one hour out of the entire year, but if you cut them during their blooming period they would last the entire year. They were the last of the magical emblems of the kingdom, a novelty among the people of Szarmi. The flowers had always fascinated him, just like most things from the magical world. The petals formed a star shaped design that curled slightly inward at the tips. The golden petals veined in silver were like silk to the touch. They were fire, water, and star all at the same time. He loved them.

And so his people stayed up late in the night, when the moon was brightest, and would wait for the flowers to blossom. When they did, they cut the delicate blooms from the stems and laid them out to dry and retain their beauty. The tossing of the flowers was a small gesture—a small sacrifice—but it made Colin love his people even more.

As they were passing through the town closest to Ducal House, their carriage suddenly jerked to a stop. The people were cheering for him and music was playing in the distance. Despite his guards' warning, Colin stepped down from the carriage and tossed silver coins from his purse. Delighted children screamed in surprise as they collected their bounty. Colin smiled at them and spoke with their elders. *Just two months,* Colin thought, *in just two months I will be able to help these people even more.*

As Colin climbed back into the carriage to continue their journey, he noticed how low the sun was in the sky. He waited until they had passed through the bulk of the town and the river came into view again before ordering his men to stop for the evening meal.

Jameston gulped air and fluttered out of his sleep, spouting saliva and pastry crumbs as he did so, "Have we arrived, My Lord? Are we there?"

"No, we have not arrived yet, but I thought it best we take a meal before we continue on. We won't reach my mother's house until dark as it is."

"You're quite right... quite right indeed."

They left their coach and walked around the grassy embankment of the Borad River. Jameston bemoaned his lack of meals and his desire to see Claire while Colin watched the birds soar through the skies in an arch. It was getting colder. The harvest season was upon them, yet there was little to harvest. The public schools across the country would begin their lessons soon. The University of Szarmitec had already begun their classes. Scholars from all over Mitier came to the university to study the sciences, the arts, and the mechanical mathematics. Colin had ensured the university's success by upping the amount of funds spent on the school, changing some of the professors around, and publicizing the university throughout Mitier. Many of the professors had made tours around the continent encouraging scholars to come to Szarmi and learn the newest and most innovative techniques. They'd been published. They'd been praised. They'd been prominent in all things scholastic.

His men let Colin know that the meal had been prepared by the inn's barmaid. Jameston immediately walked towards the inn, leaving Colin behind.

Colin remained by the river for a few moments of solitude. The air was cool and smelled of fish, but he found the solitude peaceful. He skipped stones across the calm water of the river. How he wished he could be one of those stones, solid, unyielding except to water. He imagined that he wouldn't mind existing without thought or feeling. He would be able to finally forget Vanessa. He would just exist. Although Colin smiled at the thought, it did nothing to ease his pain. He stood in silence, listening to the sounds of nature by the river.

A strange sound a short distance away caught his attention. Turning towards the sound, Colin realized that someone was loading an automatic crossbow. And aiming it right at him.

Before he could move, before he could yell, before he could do anything, the assailant launched a spray of bolts straight at him. Colin watched them fly through the air but couldn't seem to make his body move. He just stood there, locked in what felt like an eternity of watching the bolts arch towards him.

The first bolt struck the stone in his hand and fell flat to the ground. The second bolt flew past his face, nipping his ear as it continued into the night. Colin felt hot blood stream down his neck where his skin had been broken. The third bolt missed him entirely.

But the fourth one pierced his arm. He howled in pain as the bolt lodged itself inside him.

The pain was enough to break him out of his stupor. Colin could hear the assailant reloading the crossbow with its four bolts. It would take a few more seconds for the assassin to launch an attack again. Thankfully, Colin had studied the mechanics of fighting with automatic crossbows and understood their limitations. He knew an expert crossbowman would need at least thirty seconds to load the four bolts and crank the internal gears into the proper position. Calculating that the assailant had started reloading immediately after the fourth bolt had been fired, Colin estimated that he only had fifteen seconds before the next spray.

Dropping to his knees, Colin half-crawled, half-pulled himself to a large tree a few feet away. The cold, damp mud seeped between his fingers as he pulled himself forward with his uninjured arm. The feeling disgusted him, but he kept moving forward. He needed cover. And time.

Once he was behind the tree he calculated how far away his men were. *Will they be able to hear me if I shout as loud as I can?* He wasn't sure.

Five seconds left. That's how much time Colin calculated he had. Leaning out from behind the safety of the tree, Colin peered at his assailant. The crossbow fired.

Colin jerked his head back as three of the bolts slammed into the tree right where his head had just been. The fourth bolt flew past him, entirely missing.

He tried shouting, but he wasn't sure his men could hear him. His voice caught on the wind and disappeared quickly into the dusk.

Ripping off a section of his undershirt, Colin prepared himself to staunch the bleeding from his arm. First he would need to break the bolt and pull it out. Gritting his teeth, Colin pulled one of his knives from his belt and leaned against the tree.

Fifteen seconds again. More bolts would come.

His arm was slick with blood.

He used the tree to hold him in place and pressed his knife against the bolt. The bark seemed oddly soft again his skin; Colin couldn't make sense of it. Swiftly, he swung the blade through the thick shaft and watched as the fletching fell to the ground.

Gripping the shaft, Colin pulled.

Pain shot through his entire body and blood flowed, unobstructed, from him arm. His mind went fuzzy and he found it difficult to think.

With a trembling hand, he quickly tied the length of cloth around his arm to stop the bleeding. The knot was clumsy and didn't work as well as he had hoped. He could already see the stain of blood seeping through the white linen.

More bolts hit the tree and the dirt near where his legs were. The would-be assassin had changed positions.

Groaning, Colin laid flat against the earth and tried crawling towards his people. He had lost count of how long it had been since the last assault. *How long do I have?*

He didn't want to shout again. He didn't want the attacker to know his position. All he could do was crawl. His blood, seeping through the now red-linen cloth, mixed with the ground. He smelled the musty scent of the earth and heard the wind rushing above him. *Is this how I am going to die?*

Every time he moved more pain shot through his body. The pain in his arm felt like every bruise he had ever had combined into one. He could barely see in the darkness, through his pain. He pulled himself forward and felt his body go slack as another bolt struck him in his leg.

Everything went black.

Chapter Twenty-One

Estrellala, Lunameed

King Magnus stared at his daughter. She looked so much like her mother. There was something he needed to remember. Something he did remember. No, wait. He didn't. But he should. It was difficult to think. His mind felt so foggy. So clouded.

There was defiance in her eyes and in her posture. Magnus couldn't remember the last time someone had looked at him like that. What had he done to her to deserve that glare.

Oh, wait.

He had required her to marry him. It hadn't happened yet. He knew that much. But still, it was in the works. *What had I been thinking? She is my own daughter. I can't marry her. I can't—*

A spasm ran up King Magnus's back as he opened his mouth to speak to his daughter. The words fell away. He couldn't speak. He couldn't think.

But she was there. Oh, how he had waited for her to return to him. Her beautiful auburn hair. Her graceful, plump body. She was the love of his life, and he knew that he could never forsake her. Not now that she had returned to him.

Orianna.

But there was something. Something not quite right about the way she looked. Her eyes. They weren't the violet he remembered. His daughter. It was Amaleah, not Orianna.

Magnus shivered. And once again opened his mouth to speak. This time, though, his entire body went erect and he couldn't move a muscle.

Orianna, he thought as his body began to shake.

Chapter Twenty-Two

Amaleah watched as her father's body shook violently. She wanted to help him, but the guards still clung to her arm. She tried to pull away from them, but one of them gripped her around the middle and held her close to his body.

"Father?" she asked plaintively. "Father, are you alright?"

He didn't answer.

None of the servants moved to help him. *Why aren't they helping him?* She glared at the one closest to her father, but he looked away from her.

Her father stopped shaking.

He looked at her through clouded eyes.

"You have betrayed me," he said in the coldest voice Amaleah had ever heard.

"No, Father. You misunderstand—" she started to say.

"I misunderstand nothing. You were found in the garden with that... boy. Why? Why do you do these things to me? You know—you should know—how much I care for you."

"Yes, Father, I do, but, you can't keep doing this. I need to have a life. I need to be able to be friends with whomever I choose."

"Let me stop you there. You are my bride-to-be. You are the woman I have chosen to rule beside me. You are the woman I love above all others. And yet you betray me. I will not abide this."

Amaleah's heart beat quickly in her chest. "What do you intend to do?"

He didn't answer her. Instead, he motioned towards the guards. Wordlessly, they pulled her away from her father and through the corridors of the palace.

"Where are you taking me?" she shouted as they pulled her past her chambers. "What are you doing?"

They didn't say anything, but Amaleah felt her stomach sink as she realized the direction they were heading: the dungeons. *Is my father really sending me there?*

She dug her nails into one of the men clutching her arm. He squirmed a little in pain, but continued holding onto her. She tried twisting out of his grasp. The other one slapped her across the face.

Pain seared its way through her body. She could feel heat rising from her cheek where the guard had struck her. And then wetness. Tears poured unbidden from her eyes. The guards looked away from her but did not try to comfort her.

When they finally arrived at the dungeons, the guards shoved her into the small room with rough hands. She fell, scraping her knee on the hard stone floor.

"I'm sorry," the one who hadn't struck her whispered as they left her alone in the darkness.

The cell smelled of urine and despair. Amaleah shivered as she listened for the guard's footsteps to fade before resolutely wiping away the tears. Crying was not going to solve anything for her. Now that the light from the guard's torches was gone, she could barely see anything around her.

Lifting her dress, Amaleah tried to examine the cut on her knee. She couldn't see the scrape, but when she touched her knee with her hand, it came away wet. Her bottom lip quivered as she realized she was bleeding. Like a child, all she wanted was to be comforted. *I need to be strong,* she told herself. Ripping a section of her slip off, she bound the wound as tightly as she could. She felt around the bars to see if any of them were loose but they were all firmly held in place. Defeated, Amaleah sunk back onto the cold, damp stones of the dungeon floor.

She needed to think, to plan. Her father couldn't keep her in the dungeon until the wedding, could he? She felt panic rise within her. *Of course he could.* He had all the power in their relationship. Not even the servants were truly willing to stand against him. Shivering, Amaleah realized how cold the dungeon actually was. The walls were slick with… Amaleah couldn't tell what, and the air was quite cool and carried the scent of decay. Her ball gown, though full at the bottom, was lightweight for a winter gown. The rest of the palace was well heated with numerous fires blazing. The dungeon offered no such comfort.

As Amaleah's eyes adjusted to the darkness, she looked around the small cell. There was what appeared to be a small rag lying on the floor. Besides the rag, the only other item in the chamber was a pot for her excrement on the opposite side of the room. Picking up the rag, Amaleah sniffed at it. It smelled like body odor and rot, but there was nothing else for her to do. Huddling beneath the makeshift blanket, Amaleah leaned against the wall furthest away from the door. Her cheek ached dully from where she'd been hit and she was afraid of what would happen in the morning, but she somehow found a way to drift to sleep.

Chapter Twenty-Three

The sound of boots against stone woke Amaleah from a troubled sleep. Weak sunlight filtered through a small high window at the top of the stone wall opposite her cell. Through the haze of half-sleep, Amaleah realized that guards stood outside of her cell. *So many guards*, Amaleah noted. More than was necessary. Pushing the rag away from her, Amaleah stood up. She tried looking into their eyes as they remained standing, but all of them avoided eye contact with her. She smiled at this. *At least they feel guilty*, she thought as she continued to stare them down.

Suddenly, the guards parted and Namadus walked through the center of them. He wore a cloak so ornate and heavy looking that Amaleah wondered if the advisor would be crushed beneath its folds. *That would be a sight to be seen*, she was sure. He peered at her through the bars. Despite knowing that she was dirty and that there was probably a terrible bruise on her cheek, Amaleah held her head high.

Unlike the guards, Namadus looked upon her unabashedly. His eyes were like two lumps of coal smoldering in the dim light. His gaze was so penetrating that Amaleah felt like he could see straight through her.

Amaleah blushed.

Namadus clapped his hands loudly and Amaleah watched as the guards funneled out of the relatively large hallway outside of her cell. Within moments, they were left in solitude.

"So, I see that you still have not learned the art of humbleness," Namadus spat out the words making Amaleah cringe. *Maybe defiance isn't the right tactic in this situation.*

"I'm just not sure why I'm here, High Councilor." She tried to keep her voice firm, but even she could hear how it shook as she spoke.

"I see."

"I don't wish to bring my father pain. Nor do I wish to betray him," she paused. "I have not betrayed him; despite what he thinks."

The air around them felt thick and the hair on Amaleah's neck stood straight up in the air. The tattoo on her ankle hummed with energy. *A warning.* Amaleah looked down at the cell's floor, feigning shame.

"I love my father, truly, Namadus. Please, help me."

The silence hung in the air like a damp sheet on a clothesline. The absence of sound was oppressive.

Finally, Namadus cleared his throat and responded, "Be that as it may, your father believes that you were colluding with Prince Fredrerik." He paced several times in front of the cell, his hands clasped behind his back. "But I believe that we can turn this around. That is, as long as you make certain promises to me."

He smiled at her, but the warmth did not meet his eyes.

"What kind of promises?" Amaleah asked.

"The kind that must be kept," he said vaguely as he tapped his fingers against the bars. "Princess, if you are to escape this place, you will need my help."

Amaleah sighed, "Namadus, if I am to make a deal with you then I must know the terms of the agreement. I will not barter myself out of this prison just to end up in a new one."

"Let's just call it a favor, for now." He peered through the cell bars at her, "When the time comes, I want you to listen to me, to follow me, to ensure that whatever I ask for is done."

"How can I make that kind of promise, Namadus? I am to rule all of Lunameed. I must have our kingdom's best interests at heart. I can't do that if I am bound to a single person's desire." As she spoke, Amaleah realized that she may very well be throwing away her last chance of escape. Still, she thought it was better to hold firm to her beliefs than to let them slip away.

"Then you are a fool." The anger in his voice made Amaleah flinch.

Who does he think he is? I may be locked away now and I may never free myself, but I am still the princess of Lunameed. She took a step toward the bars. The fae's tattoo grew hot on her skin.

"Be wary," a voice whispered in her mind. Amaleah ignored it.

"You are the fool, Namadus. My father will let me out of this cell eventually. Remember that it is I who *will* rule Lunameed, and you can be sure that I will not forget this conversation."

She stared at him as she finished speaking, defiance in her eyes. He stared at her with a calculating expression on his face as if he were determining what the best course of action should be.

Namadus did not respond to her. Instead, he turned on his heel and left her in the cold, damp darkness of the dungeon.

Chapter Twenty-Four

An inn near Ducal House, Szarmi

Colin woke to a searing pain in his leg and arm. He groaned loudly. At least he was still alive. At least, he thought he was. The room was so dark that he wasn't quite sure.

A soft rustling beside him made him jump, at least as much as he could. His arms, he realized, were strapped to the bed by thick, course ropes. The skin beneath the ropes was bruised and bleeding. *Where is my assassin?* He thought as he tugged at his hands. The rope bit into his skin. Pain shot through his arm so strongly that he slumped back against the bed. Sweat slid down his face and his sight went blurry.

Just breathe, he told himself as the pain subsided. *Just breathe.*

A flickering candle blossomed into life as he stared at the place he heard the rustling. His eyes darted in the direction of the light, momentarily blinding him. In the aftermath of the brilliance, Jameston's face came into focus. Colin breathed a sigh of relief. He was safe.

"There now, old fellow, there now. It's just me. You're alright," Jameston cooed.

Colin tried to speak, but his throat was too dry to get the words out. Jameston, apparently recognizing that Colin needed a drink, brought a ladle of cool water to Colin's lips.

The water was sweet and soothing. Colin gulped at the steady flow as much as he could. The more Colin drank, the more Jameston tipped the ladle towards him. Too quickly, the water filled Colin's lungs, causing him to cough. He sputtered a little as Jameston withdrew the ladle.

After his coughing had subsided, Colin asked, "W-where are we? What happened?" His throat ached as he spoke.

"Well, you see, sir, you were attacked when you were all by your lonesome out by the river. We heard you yell, but by the time our men got to you, you were passed out with one bolt through your leg and a hole in your arm. Your ear was bleeding badly as well. But of course, we picked you up and carried you back to our camp. We've been at the inn ever since." Jameston's brow crinkled and Colin could tell that he was thinking.

"What is it? What's wrong?" Colin managed to croak.

Jameston's fumbled with his hands. "We found a ripped section of your mother's sigil as we were searching the area around where we believe the assassin was." He paused before saying in such a soft voice that Colin could barely understand him, "We decided, in your condition, that we ought not risk the journey to your mother's estate. It was safer, here, Your Highness."

Colin lay in the bed for several moments without speaking. *Is this somehow connected to Vanessa?* His heart sank. He didn't want to believe it. He knew he had problems with his mother, but he couldn't—wouldn't—believe that she wanted him dead.

"How long have we been here?" he asked.

"You have been unconscious for three days now."

"Three days!" Colin coughed again. "But we were expected. We need to finish…" Colin trailed off as the small amount of energy he had saved up vanished.

Jameston, for his part, looked incredibly uncomfortable at having to tell Colin that he had been immobile for over three days.

"Did you, at least, catch the assassin?" Colin tried to contain his frustration, but he wasn't sure how good of a job he was doing.

"Unfortunately no, Your Highness. He had already disappeared before our men arrived. It is lucky that we heard you, otherwise, you would have bled to death."

Colin sat for several moments. Dumbfounded, he finally asked, "Did someone send word to my mother?"

Jameston stuttered as he responded, "No, Your Majesty. We thought it was best… to wait for you. Especially since the sigil…" Jameston's voice trailed off.

"I see," Colin said. *Another attempt on my life. When will these stop?* The idea that his mother had lured him out into the open just to kill him made his skin crawl. Still, if word hadn't been sent to her that he was dead, she would have expected notice that he had been injured. Colin didn't want to give his mother any reason to believe that he suspected her. He wanted to be able to catch her in one of her attempts. Only then would he truly be able to rid himself of her.

Sighing, Colin yanked tenderly at the ropes that bound him. He looked over at Jameston, expectantly, "So. Are you going to undo these restraints or not?"

Jameston flushed as he quickly undid the knots holding Colin in place. Each time his friend touched one of the spots where he'd been shot through with a bolt Colin groaned in pain.

"Are you sure you want to get up?" Jameston asked in a plaintive tone, "The doctor said that it would be best to restrain you until the wounds have completely healed."

"And did the doctor mention that he would contact my mother about my condition?" Colin raised one eyebrow expectantly.

Once again Jameston looked uncomfortable as he helped Colin sit up. "Well, no-"

"Then you should trust me when I say that we need to send a rider ahead of us with a message for my mother about what happened to me and then be on our way to her manor as soon as possible." Colin grimaced as he slid a pair pants over the wounded leg. "If my mother really was behind this attack, it is important that she believes that we are not onto her. Do you understand me, Jameston?"

Colin's entire body ached as he stood. Jameston turned as if to leave the room. Colin stopped him with a single touch of the arm. "Listen, Jameston, I need you to gather a group of our most trusted soldiers. Even if it wasn't my mother, someone attempted to assassinate me and we need to find out why. Can you have them gathered by the time we arrive at my mother's house?" *She won't attempt to assassinate me once I'm within her walls. She can't. It would be political suicide.*

Jameston nodded once before walking ahead of Colin out of the room.

Chapter Twenty-Five

Estrellala, Lunameed

Sylvia walked into the throne room as quietly as she could. The proceedings had already begun and she didn't want to draw attention. King Magnus was droning on about irrigation concerns and how to divert the kingdom's rivers to other regions of the kingdom. Many people in the crowd were fanning themselves and hiding yawns behind gloved hands. This, apparently, was not what they were waiting for.

Sylvia settled onto a small chair at the back of the room. She couldn't see the king while she was sitting down, but she didn't need to. She just needed to be able to hear the fate of Amaleah. Nervously, she squeezed the flesh between her thumb and index finger on her left hand. Her hands were dry, too dry. *How old I've gotten.*

She needed to know what the king intended to do to his daughter. She assumed that was why everyone else was here as well. Most days only a handful of people were in the throne room at any given time. Now, there were at least three hundred. The room was so crowded that even though it was in the dead of winter the space was stifling. Amaleah had been in the dungeon for over three days now. Every day, Sylvia had waited for news about what would become of the young princess. Now her wait would finally be over.

A loud thumping sound came from the front of the chamber followed by a booming voice.

"Let it be known. Princess Amaleah of the Bluefischer line is hereby betrothed to King Magnus Bluefischer, lord over the Lunameedian waters, ruler of the magical realm, and father of the Light. Come and bear witness. The king has produced the three gowns required by the princess and the coat of many furs. Let us celebrate the future."

The room erupted in excited discussions. Sylvia caught a few snippets of the conversations as she prodded her way to the front of the room. This was not what she had been expecting. Shoving past an old man with a cane and a wispy beard, Sylvia finally made it to the front of the room.

And there they were: a dress made in tribute to the sun, a dress in tribute to the stars, and a dress made in tribute to the ocean's depths. A long fur coat made out of an assortment of pelts was hung from a tall rod positioned in the middle of the room. Sylvia gasped as she realized that the unachievable task Amaleah had given her father had been completed.

"Forthwith, the king decrees that instead of waiting the customary six months before he and his bride are wed, they shall be wed within the fortnight," the herald continued.

Many of the women in the room covered their mouths at this. Several of the men left the room is such a hurry that Sylvia almost didn't notice them leave. She, herself, was having trouble breathing. How was Amaleah going to escape now?

"As part of the celebrations, the prince of Szarmi, the nobility of the Island Nations, and the prince and princess from Dramadoon will all be invited to a ball one week from today. They will be invited to remain in the castle until the king and princess are wed."

Sylvia glanced at the king. He sneered as he listened to the herald speak about the betrothal. Sylvia's stomach dropped as she saw the anger mixed with the lust in his eyes. She couldn't let Amaleah marry him. She couldn't let her charge be placed in the hands of this man.

The king clapped his hands, drawing the attention of all the lords and ladies who remained in the room. A hush fell over the crowd.

"I hope you will join me in celebrating the glorious nuptials of my beautiful bride-to-be and I. From this day to the day we are wed, there will be parties and fairs for you and all who you invite."

Is that a note of fragility in his voice? Sylvia could have sworn she heard him struggle to speak. She needed to speak to the Council about her suspicions. She needed help. She glanced around the room. None of the nobles rose in defense of Amaleah. They nodded to the king as if he had made some great declaration or the kingdom, instead of the declaration of a madman.

She left the room as quickly as her old body would allow her. By the time she reached her rooms, she was breathing hard and her legs shook from the exertion. She ignored all of this as she slammed the door behind her.

With trembling hands, Sylvia lit the last remnants of her fae dust. She spoke the words that allowed her sisters to speak with her. The light of her candle flickered in a wind that wasn't there and hope rose within Sylvia's heart.

She waited.

No one came.

She repeated the ritual with the dregs of her supply. She emptied the bag of incense into the flames. She wept. She begged other members of the Council to aid her in her attempt to save the young princess. Still, she did not receive a reply.

Only silence.

Slowly, Sylvia blew out the candles and sat in the darkness of her room. *What am I going to do?*

Chapter Twenty-Six

Ducal House, Szarmi

Queen Vista welcomed her son as he rode into the center courtyard of her estate, Ducal House. He appeared forlorn, weather beaten, and exhausted. One of his arms was in a sling and she could tell that it pained him to be in a saddle. She smiled to herself as she watched him approach.

"Oh, my dear boy. I am so glad that you weren't more seriously injured. I was so worried when you didn't arrive and we didn't hear from you." She added a tiny tremble to her voice and one of her guards stepped closer to her in case she fainted. *Men are so easy to manipulate when you understand them.* She batted her eyes up at the guard and almost smiled to herself when she saw him tremble.

She understood Colin. He was young and still brooding over that failure of a girl, Vanessa. She could only hope that he would believe the Lunameedians had attempted to assassinate him. *It was wise to use a Lunameedian skin-changer,* she thought, *no one will suspect me.* She knew Colin missed his father and that he was nervous about being crowned king. He had surprised her, though, when he'd been able to survive the multiple assassination attempts on his life. *What was it he said to me in his letter informing me of Vanessa Wilhelm's death? 'You know how much I loved her and to be betrayed in this way breaks my heart.'* Vista's lips curled into a sly smile as she remembered the pain she knew he had felt. It was a pity the young woman had had to die. But sacrifices needed to be made.

Now, as he stood before her with his most recent wounds, she was surprised at how tall he looked and how strong. This was not the Colin she remembered. *He's not strong enough to be king,* she reminded herself as she tried to pull him into an embrace. He pulled away from her. *This changes nothing,* she told herself, blocking out the sinking feeling in her stomach. She didn't love him. She couldn't. Every time she looked at him all she saw was-

She shook her head. *I can't think about that right now. Not when there is so little time left before his coronation. Plans need to be solidified.*

"Well then," she said as she patted his arm. "You must be tired from your journeys. Come. Let's get you settled in, shall we."

His eye twitched when he looked at her. Vista wondered what he was thinking but said nothing. She gently laid a hand on his uninjured arm.

"Where is my sister? Where is Coraleen, Mother?" he asked as he turned away from her.

Vista thought she noticed a hint of annoyance in his voice. Gleefully, she responded, "Your sister was too busy with her studies to meet you. You'll see her when the time is right."

Just at that moment, a young woman with dark hair and a blue dress burst out of one of the adjacent rooms and leapt into Colin's arms. Vista watched as her two children hugged each other tightly. *How little they understand each other.* She smirked at them, careful not to scowl.

"Coraleen, where is your tutor? You are supposed to be learning the history of the Wars of Darkness for your demonstration later this week. Colin will still be here when you're done," she said sternly.

Coraleen nodded and timidly slunk back into the room she had come from without argument. *Good girl,* the queen thought.

"You don't need to be so harsh on her, Mother."

Vista stiffened. "Until you have children of your own, Colin, please refrain from telling me how to raise my own. I raised you, didn't I? And look at you now. The heir to the throne." She attempted to keep the contempt out of her voice. *He is not fit to rule, never had been. Why hadn't Vanessa been able to dispatch him when she had the chance?*

Even as she bemoaned the fact that Colin was still alive, he was still her son. She had just never wanted him. He was a burden that had been forced upon her against her will. For that, she could never forgive him.

She led him to the rooms she had set aside for his stay. "When you are ready, I expect for you to tell me all about the assassination attempt you survived on your journey here. I was so worried about you when you didn't arrive on time." The lie came so easily that Vista almost believed it herself. "Thank goodness your men heard you crying out for help. Otherwise, we wouldn't be having this conversation."

His body language told her everything. His back remained stiff and he barely looked in her direction. *Maybe I've pushed him away too much.* She hoped Colin took this statement as a sign of concern for his well-being. She patted his arm in a mechanical motion.

"Yes, Mother," he said as he opened the door to his quarters, "Thank you."

"I'll leave you now. Dinner will be served promptly at the evening hour. Do not be late."

Vista walked away from her son's rooms as quickly as her short, slender legs would take her. Her footsteps echoed on the polished marble floors as she left her son to contemplate his next moves. *He will never be able to outsmart me,* she laughed at the thought. *Never.*

Chapter Twenty-Seven

His mother had ordered one of Colin's favorite meals for the evening. A succulent pig rested on the large serving tray in the middle of the long table. Apples and pears had been baked with cinnamon and were decorated with flowers and spun sugar. Roasted corn and peppers were spread across the table. Colin's mouth watered the moment he entered the dining room.

Coraleen was her normal, talkative self throughout the meal. Although Colin barely spoke through the first and second servings, he enjoyed listening to her talk. Her stories made him smile and he found the tension that had been building in his shoulders slip away. For the first time since Vanessa had attempted to kill him, he felt safe.

Until his mother leaned over and grasped his arm.

Her sharp nails clenched his shirt and dug into his skin; she smiled vindictively. Colin was reminded of a snake before it strikes its prey with the final death blow.

"Colin, my dear boy, I have some news."

"And what would that be, Mother?"

She tapped her nail on his skin, making him flinch. Her lips, impossibly, stretched into an even wider smile.

"You are to attend the balls and wedding of Amaleah Bluefischer, princess of Lunameed." Her voice sounded excited, but Colin wasn't sure he believed it, "To her father."

Colin stared his mother, dumbfounded. When she didn't look away from him, he began laughing.

"You cannot seriously believe that I would leave Szarmi so close to my coronation. Come now, Mother, that would be a major risk to assume, especially since it was my understanding that we were at a standstill with Lunameed." The longer he spoke, the more nauseous he became. His mother was not responding the way he had expected her to. She was just staring at him, blankly.

Clearing his throat nervously, Colin continued, "I am not sure that attending the princess's wedding to her own father would sit well with our people, Mother. We are clearly not barbarians."

Besides, Colin thought to himself, *I'm not sure I trust your intentions, Mother.*

"Who cares how the people perceive this opportunity?!" Queen Vista exclaimed, "You must go, Colin. Your father was never invited to cross the Szarmian-Lunameedian border, and you need to take this chance to learn more about their court." She slammed her hand down on the table as she spoke, making Colin fidget uncomfortably.

Yes, but Vanessa came from Lunameed. She must have, otherwise she wouldn't have been a skin-changer. Colin almost said the words he was thinking but was able to stop himself.

Instead, he said, "Be that as it may, Mother, we don't know who attempted to assassinate me." He looked at her pointedly as he spoke, "What if it was a Lunameedian assassin and this is their way of tricking me into crossing the border?"

Or maybe it was you and you're trying to throw me off your trail. "No. I don't believe I will be going to this ball of theirs. Besides, I do not agree with their nuptials."

Vista screamed as she scooted away from the table.

"Do you not see what you are doing, Colin? Can you not tell that you are ruining the future of our kingdom? This could be our chance to make peace with Lunameed once and for all. This could be our chance to find out more about their country, their people, their court, and discover a weakness that would allow us to squash them like the bugs they are. Don't you see? You must go."

Her voice trembled at the end of her speech and Colin knew that she had meant every word of it.

"Would you send Coraleen to the homeland of our enemies?" Colin's voice was cold.

"If it meant a chance to learn their weaknesses? Yes. Yes, I would."

Colin glanced at his sister. Her face remained blank and unreadable. He couldn't tell if his argument with their mother was affecting her or not, but he was ready to depart the dining room, Ducal House, all his responsibilities behind. *Perhaps I should go to Lunameed, if for nothing else than to bring back stories for my sister.* He knew Coraleen had always dreamed of going to Lunameed, just like he had.

Until he'd met Vanessa. She had ruined his desire to love.

They had bred magic out of their kingdom over the three hundred years since the last Darkness War. Theirs was a land of machinery and innovation. Lunameed was known for its magic and adherence to the old ways.

"Fine. Send us both."

Coraleen squealed with joy at this. His mother just stared at him with a blank expression.

Chapter Twenty-Eight

Coraleen watched the interaction between her mother and brother with bated breath. She desperately wanted to travel to Lunameed with her brother and see the magical world of myth. Everyone said magic still existed there. Everyone said it abounded throughout the land, that you could actually feel the pressure of the "light," as the common people called it, coursing through the very air. She'd had dreams about it. Dreams about visiting the fae and the elves. Dreams about meeting all the half-breed creatures said to live in the wilderness. Dreams about exploring the enchanted forests and haunted buildings.

"Mother," she quietly said, "I would like to go with him." The words tumbled out before she could stop them.

Vista stared blankly at her daughter. The air felt so thick that it was stifling. Coraleen forced herself to not break eye contact with her mother, even when her mother's lips curled into a thin smile. She knew that this was not part of their plan, that they were supposed to send her brother to Lunameed on his own, but she couldn't stop herself.

Queen Vista tapped her nails on the hard, wooden table before finally saying, "I do not believe that would be prudent, Coraleen." The way her mother said her name made Coraleen cringe. Without seeming to notice, her mother continued, "What if something were to happen to you? Both heirs should not go into enemy territory." Queen Vista patted her hand over her chest as if the thought of losing her children were just too much.

Coraleen was unperturbed by her mother's words; however, anger bubbled inside her as she realized that her dream of visiting Lunameed were slipping through her grasp. *I didn't even know I wanted to go until now,* she thought as she said, "Something were to happen to me? Really, Mother, do you honestly believe anything could happen to me, so long as I am with Colin?"

Coraleen smiled slyly at her mother. She knew that if her mother denied Coraleen's request to travel to Lunameed that she would be openly admitting that Colin was weak. *Is she willing to openly humiliate him?*

Vista stood from the table without answering. Anger blazed in her eyes.

Coraleen whimpered slightly, not used to disappointing her mother. Still, she held her head high and regarded her mother with a defiant expression.

Colin stood and wrapped his arm protectively around Coraleen's shoulders, "Perhaps I spoke too hastily. You are right, Mother. Until we have a stronger bond with the Lunameedian government, we shouldn't risk both of the heirs in a single trip." He squeezed her shoulders in what was meant to be a comforting touch. Coraleen choked down the bile that rose up her throat. She remained stiff-backed and stone-faced as Colin continued, "Coraleen, I think you should remain here."

She sighed heavily. *I was so close.* Biting her bottom lip until it was painful, Coraleen forced herself to smile up at her brother.

"But of course, you are right, dearest Brother. It was silly of me."

Colin leaned down to hug her. It took everything in Coraleen's willpower to stop herself from pulling away from him. *Even his hugs are weak,* she thought as he awkwardly wrapped his arms around her from a standing position. She regarded her mother over Colin's shoulder; she only shrugged her shoulders at Coraleen's discomfort. If there was one thing her mother had taught her, it was how to manipulate other people.

Pulling away from Colin in one, brisk motion, Coraleen turned her face away from him and feigned tears, "I just so wanted to go!" she nearly yelled. "I understand it's dangerous. I know the risks. I just wish… I just wish you and Mother stopped seeing me as a child and truly saw me for the woman that I have become."

Coraleen breathed heavily, her nostrils flaring. Colin took a step away from her in surprise. "I trusted you, Colin," she whispered.

Her words had their desired effect. Colin flushed and began stammering incoherently in an attempt to fix the damage he believed he had done. Standing up from her seat, Coraleen advanced towards him in a smooth motion. She seemed to glide the short distance between them.

"I stood up for you all those times Mother spoke ill of you. Even now I support you." She flailed her arms at him, "And how do you repay me? Huh? How do you do it?" She slapped him, leaving a red mark across his face. "You betray me! I want to go with you, Colin. Please allow me this one moment of freedom. Do not take it away from me!" She allowed her pent up anger to course through her body as she slapped him again. *He is such a weakling,* she thought as she fell into his open arms to conceal the smile that spread across her face at his pain.

He hugged her tightly to his chest. His arms, though strong in a way Coraleen didn't remember, were still weak compared to her own strength. *Why should he get to be king when I am left to follow in his shadow? Why should he get to achieve his dreams and leave me behind? I have just as much right to rule as he does... if Father—*

The memory of her father's bedside declaration that Colin would be king of Szarmi had permanently branded itself in Coraleen's mind. King Henry's face had been wan—paler than she had ever seen it before. He had been a large man with a thick stomach that hung over his legs and down to the middle of his thighs. In his early years, he had been a great warrior. Her mother told her how he had swung his sword, Lightning, so quickly that it was just a blur to all who saw it. As he had aged, his muscles had grown weak. On the day of his death, the illness that took him came quickly. He had spasmed at the dinner table, clutching at his heart as if an arrow were lodged inside him, but nothing was there. His guards carried him to his bedchamber and rushed to find the royal physician. It all went so quickly, too quickly. They had all been there: her mother, Colin, and Coraleen. Even King Henry's most trusted knight remained in the room with his lord.

Coraleen had known that her father would pick her to rule. They had discussed it on multiple occasions. She was the stronger of his two children, the more skilled at combat. She was the one who played the games of political intrigue with ease. She was the one whom he claimed was his favorite. In the end, he had turned against her and chosen his first born: Colin. Her father had been a weak king and he had created a weak son.

Coraleen was determined to claim the throne for herself, using any means possible.

"Coraleen, dearest, I only do this for your safety. I would not want—" her brother was saying when she interrupted him.

"You would not want?" her voice rose as she spoke, "My safety? You cannot be serious! I am a princess of Szarmi, and I can take care of myself. Haven't I proved that yet?" she shrieked. Then in a quieter tone, she said, "I am stronger than you, Brother."

Her brother's face flushed and there was sheen of sweat on his brow. Coraleen had the urge to thrust her dagger into his belly right now, but she knew no one would believe that an assassin had made it into her mother's estate without the queen's awareness. Ducal House was the most fortified location in all of Szarmi, including the military forts.

"But there are more dangers for a woman than there are for men when traveling," he stuttered over his words.

Coraleen continued to stare at him blankly. "There are worse things than death, Coraleen."

What a coward. She knew he was right. There are worse things in life than death. *Like being the spare,* she thought bitterly.

"I still want to go," she said, forcing a single tear to roll down her cheek. Colin took the bait. Cupping her cheek in his hand, he wiped away her tear before pulling her into a tight embrace again.

"Will you give me time to think it over?" he asked. He held her away from him, gently, "I do not want you to fall into the hands of our enemies. I only want for you to be safe. Promise me, Coraleen, that you will wait for my decision, if I promise to weigh the options. Perhaps we can strike a deal."

"And if you choose to not let me go with you?"

"Coraleen, you are a grown woman and despite what our mother says, you have the right to make your own decisions. You can still go; it just won't be with me. I would only hope that you consider my worries and my love for you."

She took his hand and kissed it, smiling, "I will."

They left together, talking about the wondrous myths they grew up with about the country to the north, the kingdom of Lunameed. Colin was more silent than he normally was, and she wished she could read his mind. *Does he suspect?* It didn't appear like he did. *That was good.* Coraleen had made mistakes the first time, but if she was patient and bided her time, she wouldn't make the same mistakes twice.

Chapter Twenty-Nine

Estrellala, Lunameed

Amaleah woke to three guards roughly yanking her to her feet. The cell was so cold this morning that she could see her breath in the air. She stumbled on the icy stone floor as they pulled her out of the cell and up the stairs.

"Where are you taking me?" she demanded.

They didn't respond.

She didn't struggle at they led her through the castle. Any place that wasn't the dungeon was a better place to be. They wore the green and silver livery of her father's guard. *Maybe my father finally wants to meet with me.* She had lost count of how many days she'd been in the dungeon since Namadus had visited her. All she had done was walk through the garden with the prince from Dramadoon. She had thought of him and his sister often since she'd been imprisoned. She hoped they had escaped Lunameed safely.

The guard led her to a room Amaleah had never been in before. They shoved her to the floor and then promptly left. Once again, Amaleah was alone.

She shivered as she realized how cold the room was. It was barely better than the dungeons. No fire was lit in the hearth; however, sunlight streamed into the room, casting sunbeams on the hardwood floor. Wrapping her arms around her legs, Amaleah huddled in the middle of the room and waited.

She did not have to wait long. Within minutes of the guards leaving, a door at the back of room opened up and revealed a figure in a black cloak. As the figure strode into the room, Amaleah noticed a sword gleaming from a sheath on the figure's back. *Perhaps the dungeons aren't the worst place to be*, she thought as she let out a yelp of surprise.

She scrambled away from the figure, but it continued advancing towards her. She couldn't see its face, but she could smell the scent of death on it. It didn't speak. It didn't even seem to walk but rather glide across the room. Amaleah continued stumbling backwards, away from the figure, until her back pressed against the wall behind her. She didn't know if there were any other ways out besides the door to her right and the door at the back of the room where the figure had come from.

She took a quick glance at the door that was only a few feet away. The figure followed her gaze and drew his sword in one, swift motion. Squeezing her eyes shut, Amaleah waited for the pain of metal slicing through her flesh.

She heard the footsteps stop right in front of her. She breathed in and waited.

Nothing happened.

Timidly, she cracked one of her eyes and saw a pair of black boots standing before her. Sweeping her gaze upwards, Amaleah peered straight into the darkened hood. Still, she couldn't see the figure's face.

"Amaleah Bluefischer, princess of Lunameed. Harbinger of the Light. Your presence is needed," the figure said in a gruff, deep voice.

"What do you mean by the Harbinger of the Light?" her voice trembled as she spoke. *Don't tell him anything,* she told herself. *He's probably working for my father.*

"Your presence is needed," the figure repeated.

The figure bent down to grasp her arm. As he did, the hood slid from her head, revealing the horror within. It had deep pits for eyes and scaly skin the color of maggots. Its teeth had been filed into points so sharp that Amaleah knew they could bite into flesh as easily as she bit into an apple. Bile rose up the back of her throat. She tried to scream, but the sound never came. She stood immobilized as its icy-cold hands pressed against her arms.

They stood like that for a single breath before the monster picked her up in a single sweep of its arms and carried her across the room.

Amaleah fell limply into its grasp. *Is this how I am going to die?* she thought as she suffocated under the monster's decay-scented body odor. She could feel the creature's bones beneath its thin cloak. Their hard, pointy structures dug into her skin uncomfortably. She opened her mouth so scream, but the creature clamped his massive hand across her mouth and squeezed. She inhaled deeply and the pungent scent of narco flower overwhelmed her. Her mind became fuzzy and her muscles relaxed as the drug coursed its way through her body. The monster continued weaving his way throughout the castle. Not once did they encounter a single person who could help her.

It didn't stop moving until they were in the cavern she'd made into her own personal sanctuary. She hadn't been able to visit as often as she would have liked since meeting Cordelia, but the pillows, books, and candles were still spread across the cavern floor. *How does he know about my cavern?*

The monster set her gently down upon the pillows. She lay crumbled on them for several moments as the narco flower's effects left her body. Slowly, sensation came back into her joints. The smell of oil and fire caught her attention and for the first time she realized where the light that filled the cavern was coming from. Sylvia and several ladies from court stood at the edge of the pool. Each one held a torch that cast shadows on their resolute faces.

"Don't be afraid, My Lady." Sylvia's voice came out clear and firm but it did nothing to quell the fear Amaleah felt.

"Your father hasn't told you yet, but he's decided to marry you sooner than expected. It has been scheduled for two weeks from now. We want to make sure you're out of the castle before that happens," one of the ladies said in a smooth, high voice.

Amaleah blinked. *The wedding has been scheduled for two weeks from now. But how?*

"I know this must come as a shock to you, Princess. But while you were locked away, your father completed the three dresses and the fur coat. He plans to present them to you in three days' time at the first ball in the two-week period."

"No," Amaleah said the word so quickly that she didn't have time to consider her response. "No. This cannot be. This cannot-"

"Amaleah, you have to come to terms with this," another of the ladies said. "Either you use our help to escape or you marry your father. You have the right to decide, but I would highly suggest using our help."

Amaleah turned to face Sylvia, "Please," she whispered. Her voice echoed throughout the cavern walls.

Sylvia moved forward and took Amaleah into her arms. The older woman's plump body sent warmth straight to Amaleah's bones. She nestled in tightly against her nursemaid's bosom and let the familiar scent of Sylvia's perfume ease her tension.

"Explain this to me," Amaleah whispered. "Tell me what's going on."

"Amaleah, you've been held captive in the dungeons for eight days now. I don't know if you realize that or not. But it's true. During that time your father revealed the dresses and the coat to the nobles. He moved up the wedding without your consent. He's invited all of the nobility and our neighboring royalty to stay within the castle walls until the wedding occurs," Sylvia's breath tickled the back of Amaleah's neck. *Eight days.* Amaleah could hardly believe that she had been in the dungeon for eight days.

"We believe we have a chance to help you escape," Sylvia was saying. "You just have to be willing to trust us, to trust our plan."

Amaleah's mind was too muddled from the narco flower and shock to truly comprehend what Sylvia was saying to her. She glanced at the hooded creature and realized it was staring at her. She wasn't sure how she knew the empty holes in its face were looking at her, she just did. She shivered.

"What is that thing?" she asked as she pointed at the monster.

"*His name* is Yosef and he is a tief. His mother was a mermaid but his father was a reaper. Don't worry. Despite how he may look, he is actually quite friendly."

"Friendly?" Amaleah spoke the word as if it were foreign to her. It—he—certainly didn't look friendly to her.

"Never mind that," Sylvia grasped Amaleah's face, forcing her to look at the older woman. "Listen to me, child, we need to know your answer now. Your father intends to release you for your prison cell this evening and we need to return you before he sends his guards. It cost me a fortune to secure your passage this far."

Sylvia pulled Amaleah even closer to her body, "Listen, Child, we have a plan. In three days' time, you will attend the first of the balls planned over the course of the next two weeks. Although your father will have multiple spies following you, you need to pack a bag with your traveling attire and as many jewels as you can pack that won't be missed by your ladies-in-waiting. During the ball, Yosef will come for you. You must be ready."

"How can I trust," she began, but Sylvia shushed her.

"I cannot tell you of the deals I have made to ensure your safety, Amaleah," Sylvia whispered as she pressed her lips into Amaleah's dirty hair and kissed her. "You just have to promise me that you will do this."

Amaleah thought she heard the woman's voice catch as she spoke. She had never seen the older woman cry. She forced herself to focus. Her father had made the gowns and the cloak. *I don't have time*, she realized. *If I'm going to escape, I have to do it now.* Shaking her head, she thought about the proposition Sylvia and the ladies had laid out for her. They would help her escape in three days' time if she were willing to trust them. It was her best chance.

"Fine," she said resolutely as she pulled away from Sylvia's comforting arms.

The older woman smiled and turned towards the ladies. "She has agreed," she said loudly, as if the women hadn't been able to hear Amaleah's echoing voice. The women smiled in response.

Sylvia motioned towards the monster—Yosef—and he came and picked Amaleah up.

"I'm sorry to scare you, Princess," he said in a gravelly voice. "But Lady Sylvia needed a way to ghost you out of the dungeon and I was her only option. Please forgive us both."

He smiled. Or at least Amaleah chose to believe that the gruesome upturn of the creature's mouth was a smile.

"There is nothing to forgive."

He didn't respond as he wrapped his arms around once more. This time Amaleah didn't struggle as they moved forward so quickly that she had to close her eyes in order not to get sick. By the time she felt her feet hit the ground she was so dizzy that she couldn't stand, and she sat down heavily on the cold, stone floor of her dungeon cell.

"Good," Yosef said. "Stay here until the guards come for you this evening. And remember, tell no one of the plan we discussed today."

"But we didn't discuss a plan," Amaleah responded. *Not really, anyway.* She glanced up at the place Yosef had been standing but realized he had already disappeared into the darkness of the dungeons.

As she waited for the guards to arrive, Amaleah thought about what she needed to do in order to prepare for her escape from the castle. She would need food. And money. She couldn't remember what Sylvia had told her to pack. Her mind was still muddled from the narco flower

Yosef had used on her. Settling into the now-familiar corner of her dungeon cell, Amaleah curled into a small ball and pulled the smelly, ripped rag over the top of her body. *I'll ask Sylvia in the morning,* she thought as she yawned. Sinking deeper into the corner, Amaleah allowed her eyes to droop and sleep to take over.

Chapter Thirty

Ducal House, Szarmi

Colin folded his tunics and shirts around his armor. He was leaving for Lunameed the next day. Coraleen would not be going with him. Their mother had seen to that. Queen Vista had decided that, instead of traveling to the north, Coraleen would greet the ambassadors from Borganda at Port Aceliso to the south. She would travel with the Borgandian ambassador to Miliom for Colin's coronation. He knew that their mother had planned the visits as a way to trap Coraleen into staying within the boundaries of Szarmi. She couldn't risk losing her favorite, even if she could risk losing the heir. He snorted in disgust, but kept packing.

A messenger had arrived the day before proclaiming that the wedding between the king and princess of Lunameed was set for less than two weeks from the day. He wasn't sure how his mother had known that the king was planning to marry his daughter *before* the messenger arrived, but he assumed she must have heard from one of her spies. *I'll have to keep an eye on that,* he thought as he moved to pack his armor.

It clanked as he placed his sword in the same bag. He had not packed his decorative armor but rather his mechanically reinforced armor that the scholars at University of Szarmitec had crafted for him. It had weapons crafted into the metal such that when he moved in a certain motion or pulled a particular lever, they would come popping out of the suit. He'd only worn in it during lab tests at the university but he was sure he'd be able to defend himself in it.

There was a thump on the door. At first he thought it was only one his mother's dogs pawing at the wood, but the knocking grew louder and more consistent. Cracking the door slightly, Colin peeked around the corner. His sister's face startled him. Tears were in her eyes, but not falling. She fell into him, a heavy weight, as her entire body sagged. Colin held her. No words escaped her mouth, but Colin felt that she was trying to tell him something important. She heaved, then fainted.

Frantically, Colin placed her on his bed. She seemed so fragile, like a porcelain doll. She was so creamy white with perfectly red lips. *No wonder all the men at court have fallen for her*, he thought to himself as he covered her up in his quilt and left to get a tall glass of water. She was breathing, gently, shallowly. Colin didn't want to stir her, but curiosity consumed him. He needed to know what had happened.

Tapping her lightly on the forehead, Colin woke Coraleen from her stupor. He stroked her hair as he waited for her to explain her sudden appearance to his room and her fainting spell. She wrapped her arms around his neck. Her faint, flowery perfume made Colin's eyes water—as it always did—but he resisted the urge to pull away from her. Her entire body shook from the force of her tears as she stuttered and stopped. Words caught themselves in her mouth before they could escape. With every failure to explain herself, she hugged him tighter.

"Hush now, darling. There's no reason for all these tears," Colin cooed. He could feel her tears soaking through his shirt.

"Oh Colin... you don't know. You don't know." The room seemed to close in around them as Colin continued to hold his bereft sister in his arms and coo to her.

"What don't I know, dearest?" he asked as he released himself from her grasp so that he could peer into her eyes.

She bit her bottom lip, leaving a trail of white marks along her cherry red lips. The powdered minerals Coraleen's personal maids used to make her eyes shine brighter than natural slid down her face in great big globs of color. Her hair tangled itself around her ears and head band. Colin had never seen his sister so disheveled before.

"I am to be married." No tremble entered her voice as she spoke. She seemed resolute in the fact that their mother had finally chosen a suitable husband for her. Colin knew it was his mother's way of getting revenge on Coraleen for defying her. Although Coraleen had, ultimately, decided to follow her mother's wishes, Queen Vista was a vengeful woman who forgot nothing.

"To whom?" He held her tighter as he spoke.

"To the second son of Borganda's king."

Colin peered into her eyes. She seemed lost, unfocused. He didn't know exactly what to say to her to make things better. He knew their mother had the power to force Coraleen to marry anyone she liked; however, he had never believed that she could sink as low as to marry off her favorite child to the second son of a lowly kingdom. *What power did Borganda bring his mother or Szarmi?* His mother was Borgandian, he remembered. She never discussed her family ties to the kingdom and Colin had always assumed his mother despised the island kingdom. *Apparently not.*

Cursing, Colin broke eye contact with his sister. *I'll be crowned king in just over a month now,* he thought, the idea bringing him hope.

Excitement coursed through him.

"When?" he asked, "when are you supposed to marry the king's son?"

Coraleen shook her head. "No dates have been set yet..." her voice trailed off when Colin rose from the bed.

He spoke quietly to her, "Then there's still time! I promise, as long as I am crowned king before your wedding, you will not have to marry the Borgandian prince unless you want to."

His sister's face flushed, "But our mother—"

"Will understand," Colin finished her sentence for her, although he knew it was not what she had been about to say. He paused, "Listen, Coraleen, I know we haven't spent much time together since father's passing, but you must know that I wouldn't let anything happen that would hurt you. I will protect you. Do you trust me?"

She nodded and Colin heaved a sigh of relief.

Chapter Thirty-One

Estrellala, Lunameed

The guards that came for Amaleah in the morning did not take her back to her chambers immediately. Instead, they brought her to the Sun Garden—the one her mother had planted all those years ago. It was the same garden she had promised to meet Princess Saphria in all those days ago. *I hope she's safe,* Amaleah let the thought slip through her mind and then locked it away. She couldn't think of that now. She needed to focus.

As she walked through the entrance of the garden, she caught glimpses of herself in the shiny metal her mother had insisted be placed throughout the garden. The mirrors were designed to catch the sun's light and provide warmth to the plants and all who entered, even in the dead of winter. Each time she saw her face, she grimaced. Her clothes were tattered and dirty and her hair was a giant knot. *I certainly do not look like my mother now,* she thought.

Her father sat on a dais in front of her. He wore an oversized fur coat that closed tightly around his thick neck. His eyes were cloudy, but he was not trembling. Amaleah searched his face for any sign of forgiveness. He frowned at her.

"Come closer, my dear."

His voice was calm, too calm. Still, Amaleah had no choice but to continue walking towards him.

"It has been too long since last we met, my love. How are you feeling?" His eyes roamed over her body as he spoke and Amaleah felt the urge to wrap her arms over her body. She remained still until he smiled at her.

She tried to smile back, but found that she couldn't. Her eyes moved past her father and took in the scene before her. She noticed what she had not noticed before. She opened her mouth to scream but it caught in her mouth.

There were heads.

She took a step back. Surrounding her father were a dozen heads on wooden spikes. Their faces showed agony, as if they had been still alive when they were decapitated. Dried blood stained their otherwise clean skin. Their eyes were the worst. They stared accusingly at her. She recognized some of them as the ladies from the cavern— the ones who had concocted a plan to save her.

Frantically, she looked for Sylvia's face among them but didn't find it. Feeling a sense of relief, Amaleah turned to face her father.

"Who are these women, Father?" she asked as calmly as she could. Her voice came out high-pitched and trembling.

He laughed. "Don't you know them, my love? Did you not meet with them yesterday to map out a plan of escape? Don't lie to me, Orianna."

So the madness still hadn't left him.

"Father, my name isn't Orianna. It's Amaleah. I'm your daughter."

She watched as he looked her up and down. And then his body shook violently for a moment before he returned to his normal state.

"Orianna, I tire of your games. Look, I have completed your wish." He clapped his hands and servants walked forward, carrying four different parcels. One of the servants carried a heavily padded chair and set it behind Amaleah. None of them spoke or looked at her.

"Go ahead, my darling, open your presents," he sneered.

Amaleah did as she was told. Slipping her fingers through the ribbon tied around the parcel, she opened the first parcel. Silky, golden fabric slid from the paper and into Amaleah's lap. The cloth shone with the brilliance of the sun. Amaleah gasped. It was more beautiful that even she could have imagined. She looked up at her father.

"Keep going," he commanded.

Amaleah's fingers shook as she opened up the second and third packages. They each contained one of the remaining dresses. The moon dress was made from the finest lace she had ever seen. It shimmered in the light so brilliantly that she was sure it would blind anyone who looked upon it. Amaleah almost would have thought that the dress made to honor the ocean was black, but when she looked closely at the fabric, she realized it was a deep blue.

"You will pick one of these to wear tonight at the ball. Do you understand me?"

"Yes, Father."

"Stop calling me that. I am no father to anyone. I expect you to call me 'my love,' or 'my darling' from here on out. Is that clear?

"Yes, F- my darling."

Her father smiled down at her.

"Excellent," he whispered, almost to himself. "Now, open your fourth parcel."

Amaleah knew something was wrong the minute she began to untie the strings of the paper wrapping the fur cloak. It was wet.

No, she thought to herself as she pulled back the paper, *No.*

The fur was folded over. Shutting her eyes, Amaleah whipped the outer edge back and revealed a head dripping with blood.

She screamed.

Chapter Thirty-Two

The lands of Szarmi

The borderlands between Szarmi and Lunameed were crowded with soldiers. Of course, Colin had visited the various forts and towns on the border during his yearly tour of the kingdom, but the men stationed at the outposts pressed against him as his entourage crossed the border. It was the first time the crown prince had left the boundaries of Szarmi.

Colin's heart thumped rapidly in his chest as he anticipated the transition from Szarmi to Lunameed. Vanessa had been a skin-changer, which meant that she had been a Lunameedian. His heart ached at the thought of her and his excitement dimmed. *How many other Lunameedians wish me dead?* Colin hoped it wasn't many. Although Jameston had been successful in gathering their most trusted soldiers, his mother had insisted that he travel with a troupe hand-selected by General Doami.

Although Colin had met the general on multiple occasions, he had not formed a strong relationship with him and feared alienating his armies before he was even crowned as king. There hadn't been enough time to contact Captain Conrad to determine if the men the general had selected were trust worthy. In the absence of the captain's opinion, Colin had approved the soldiers for travel. Only two of his current guards, excluding Jameston, were men he trusted. *Hopefully nothing happens that will allow my mother to claim that I died here,* Colin thought as rode hard towards the border.

He had dreamed of visiting Lunameed since he was a young child. He had loved a Lunameedian woman. But, she had also tried to kill him and Colin had the uncanny feeling that he would be in danger the entire time he remained in Lunameed. Still, he hoped the magic of the land would be as glorious as he had always imagined.

His horse's hooves clomped on the wooden and steel bridge as they crossed the Arcadi River. Colin had studied Lunameed's landscape—or at least what they knew of her landscape—before departing his mother's estate. He knew that it would only take them four days to travel from the border to Lunameed's capitol: Estrellala. They would pass through the Arcadi Forest and follow the Estrell river to the city's center.

The moment his horse touched Lunameedian soil, Colin felt a wave of heat pass through him. It wasn't the searing, harmful heat of a fire, but more like the gentle warmth of a woman's caress. Although his shoulders had been tense and sore only moments before, the pain dissipated as the warmth left him. He felt completely at ease. Colin peered into his men's faces. None of them demonstrated the same ease he felt when passing the border. In fact, each of them passed furtive glances at one another as they entered the close-knit trees of the Arcadi Forest.

The trees were so dense that no sunlight filtered through their boughs. Owls hooted and Colin could hear small creatures scrambling through the trees above them. His men drew their swords as they followed the path through the woods. Of the ten men who accompanied Colin on this journey, only three of them carried lanterns with them. Even with the high quality oil he had insisted that they pack for the journey, the lanterns barely gave off enough light to see beyond the heads of their horses.

They rode in three lines with Colin in the middle. The path was so narrow and the horses so close that Colin could smell the sweat of his soldiers and hear their horses' breathing. The air was oppressive, pressing down upon them with a warning, *"Leave. Leave. Leave,"* the trees seemed to say as they rustled in the wind. Still, Colin was not afraid.

Colin ignored their warning. Instead, he pressed his heels deep into his horse's belly and leaned down tight to her back.

"Run," he whispered.

His horse's ears twitched at the sound of his voice before she shot through a small gap between the soldiers ahead of him.

Branches struck Colin's face, leaving lines of red, hot blood streaming down his cheeks. Colin ignored the stinging pain. He was in Lunameed. He could feel the magic. It pulsed in the air. He knew it. It was in the very earth they walked on.

"Leave. Leave. Leave," the trees continued saying as Colin pressed on. Eventually, his men followed him in the magical wilderness.

*** *

Colin and his entourage passed through the Arcadi Forest and into the Faer Forest without fanfare. The whispers in the trees had spooked his men enough that they had barely stopped to eat and sleep until they reached the boundary of Estrellala. Colin's legs had saddle sores on them from the hard ride and he had tender calluses on his fingers from holding the hard leather of the reins.

By the time they entered the outskirts of Estrellala, Colin was tired, hungry, and ready for a hot bath. As the crown prince of Szarmi, he had expected to be greeted by a member of the Lunameedian nobility. Even with the tension between their two nations, he *was* royalty. But, there was nothing. *Fine*, he thought to himself, *if the king and princess of this kingdom can't welcome me properly, then I'm not sure I want to form a truce with them.*

The landscape was colorful; flowers with rich scents and in vibrant shades of pinks and purples climbed their way up the river's bank. The trees' leaves seemed to glow at night. Colin wasn't sure if it was because the fae were following them or if the leaves naturally glowed in the dark. Either way, the forest was beautiful.

For all the magic that Lunameed contained, the kingdom certainly smelled rancid. Ever since they'd reached the outskirts of Estrellala, Colin had caught wafts of rotting flesh in the wind. His men hadn't seemed to notice. They were too preoccupied with ensuring that none of their enemies popped up from within the River Estrell or from behind one of the many trees of the Faer Forest.

As he rounded a bend in the road, Colin noticed a cluster of crows pecking at something impaled on a spike ahead of him. At first, he had thought that the mass of black birds was one of the magical creatures described in his history books, but as they had gotten closer, Colin realized that that the birds were swooping in and out of the murder. He reined in his horse a few feet away from the pole.

Covering his nose with his hand, Colin leaned over and retched on the side of the road. The smell of decay was so strong now, it nearly made him pass out.

A decapitated body with the pole impaled all the way through the torso hung from the spike. Colin coughed as he realized the body was wearing a dress: a woman. The king had murdered a woman in this way and then left her body here for all his incoming guests to see. *What madness is this?* Colin thought as he quickly dismounted.

His guards formed a tight circle around him as he walked towards the impaled body. Colin ignored them.

He wouldn't leave the body there to be eaten by the crows. Calling for his men to help him, Colin attempted to knock the pole over so that he could pull the body off. He could see holes in the corpse's flesh where the birds' beaks had already torn away her muscle and fat. Flies swarmed the body; Colin could hear their buzzing as he pushed his body against the pole. A drop of cold blood splattered across his face as Colin shook the pole. He gagged, but kept pushing. The pole shook but didn't budge.

Eventually, his soldiers pulled their battle axes from their belts and began hacking at the pole. Chips of maggoty wood flew into the air as his men swung their axes. Slowly, the pole fell to the ground. The body made a sickening crunch as it slammed into the hard earth. Colin's face paled, but forced himself to stare at the body. He could feel the pressure of tears pressing into his eyes as he looked upon the dead woman.

Suddenly, Colin felt a warm arm stretch across his shoulders. It was Jameston. Never in all his life had he been so grateful that his friend was with him.

"Please, Colin. Consider what you're doing. You don't know why this body was left here or what she had done. This is the first time royals from Szarmi have been invited to Lunameed since the end of the Third Darkness. We can't risk ruining this opportunity before we've even been introduced to them."

Colin looked from his friend to the body. *How can he say that?* Colin asked himself as his entire body shuddered from the sight of the dead woman.

"Enough," Colin ordered firmly. "I will not let this woman's body, whoever she is and whatever she has done, be humiliated in this way. No person, whatever their crime, should be left to be pecked clean by the birds."

With that, Colin knelt down and tugged on the woman's body. She pulled off of the pole easily, leaving pieces of her entrails behind. Maggots squirmed from her rotting flesh and once again Colin retched.

"See. It wasn't even difficult," Colin grimaced as the smell of his vomit and the corpse hit him once more. He coughed. "Let's bury it here before we continue on. I don't want to bring the body back to the castle."

It took his men about an hour to dig a hole deep enough into the hard, frozen ground to bury the body. Colin felt he had done the right thing, but he was also concerned. If the king was leaving bodies like this out in the elements for the birds to eat, what else was he doing in his kingdom? *Perhaps the Szarmian government has ignored Lunameed for too long.*

Spurring his horse forward, Colin gritted his teeth through the pain that occasionally twanged his arm and leg. The village's doctor on the banks of the River Borad had done a great job healing him during his time in their care. By the time Colin had awaken, he had decided not to use the healing device the physicians at the University of Szarmitec had given him during their brief visit to Miliom. Colin hadn't tested its powers yet, but the physicians had told him that the medicine the medallion contained healed even the direst of wounds. He hoped he would never have to use it.

As they rounded a second bend in the road that turned into a straight stretch directly towards the castle,

Colin once again reined in his horse. Both sides of the road were lined with poles and bodies—all decapitated.

Colin turned in his saddle and vomited once more. *Lunameedians are barbarians. Where are these people's heads?*

Chapter Thirty-Three

Estrellala, Lunameed

Mr. Sweet's head rolled out of the folds of the fur coat in a bloody mass. Amaleah let the head drop to the frozen ground. As it hit the earth, the skull squished inward and greyish-purple matter oozed from his head. Her father laughed as Amaleah frantically tried to scoot away from the head.

Her father laughed.

"Put the coat on, dearest. Surely, you must be cold out here." His voice was harsh and biting.

Amaleah's hands had turned blue from the cold and she was shivering, but she couldn't bring herself to touch the bloody coat.

"No. Please no, Father," she plead. Tears streamed down her face and her hands trembled.

"Put the coat on or you will regret it."

She did as she was told. She could feel the blood on the coat staining her body red. *How did he know about Mr. Sweets and his plans to help her?* Mr. Sweets hadn't even been in the cavern with the rest of the women yesterday. She had only ever had the one discussion with him. He had been an innocent man.

Her father motioned for her to step forward.

She did as she was told. She stopped when she was at the bottom of the dais.

"Do you know why this is happening, my dear?"

"No," she lied.

He sighed and gave her a knowing look, "This is happening because of you. You wanted to escape me, to desert me. The man who has given you everything, including the coat and dresses you asked for. It was you. All of it."

He spat as he spoke and his saliva hit Amaleah in the face. It was hot in contrast to the cold air. She had a strong urge to wipe his spit away, but resisted it. Even as her father's face turned red and his eyes bulged, she did not back away.

"You are a disgrace to this household. You have broken your promise," he spoke so quietly, that Amaleah had to lean in to hear him, "Well, you shall see. You are mine, Orianna. You will always be mine."

He motioned towards his guards and they brought out a slumped figure.

Sylvia. Amaleah's heart stopped beating.

Blood dripped from her fingertips and her head lolled in front of her. Amaleah desperately wanted to run to her nursemaid but knew that showing affection for the older woman now would only cause more trouble for both of them.

The guards dropped Sylvia to the ground with a nauseating crunch. *She is such an old woman,* Amaleah thought, as if for the first time. *So frail.* Amaleah felt anger growing inside of her. *How could he?* He had trusted Sylvia to raise her, to love her, and this was how he was repaying her: by torturing her.

"Father, what is the meaning of this?"

Her father stared down at her.

"What did I tell you to call me?" he barked.

The guards picked up one of Sylvia's hands and, using the sharp side of his blade, sliced off Sylvia's pinky. Blood spurted from the wound in a bright red spray. Amaleah's stomach dropped as she watched the old woman squirm.

"I'm sorry, my love. Please forgive me," she dropped to her knees as she spoke and bowed before him. "Please."

The king nodded and waved his hand in front of her. Amaleah rose and took a small step towards him.

"Now, where were we? Ah yes. Tell me, my darling, why do you test me so?" He motioned towards the guards once more and one of them kicked Sylvia in the gut. The older woman coughed blood.

"Stop it!" Amaleah screamed. "Please, my love, stop it. You're killing her."

The king laughed.

"I'll do anything. Please. Just make it stop," Amaleah's voice shook as she spoke.

"You'll do anything?" the king said in a menacing tone.

"Yes," she whispered.

"You will stop trying to escape. You will stop defying me. You will no longer seek the counsel of anyone other than me. You will do all of these things?" His voice was eager, like that of a small child.

Amaleah looked her father square in the eyes. "Yes, if that is what it will take for you to stop hurting her."

"Done."

Amaleah heaved a sigh of relief and stepped up to give her father a kiss on the cheek. As she did, she noticed that he was once again shaking in his chair. She laid a hand on his to try to still him but quickly withdrew it. He was burning hot.

"Father?" she asked as she took a step closer to him, "What's wrong?"

"Kill her," he said simply as his body relaxed. "Kill her!" he shouted.

Immediately the guards yanked Sylvia's body up from the ground. The older woman met Amaleah's eyes for a brief moment. They were sad, defiant eyes. *Why didn't I take more time to know her better?* Amaleah tried to look away, but she was too late. As if in slow motion, one of other guards thrust his sword through Sylvia's neck. The older woman's head hung on the sword for several seconds before the guard wrenched the sword back.

Blood spurted out, spraying Amaleah and her father in a splattering of red. King Magnus laughed as the liquid streamed down his body.

Amaleah sank to her knees and began to sob.

Chapter Thirty-Four

Colin stood in the center of the throne room. He had pieces of his mechanical armor on in case he needed to defend himself against the Lunameedian court. Despite his desire to remove all of the bodies on their ride to the Palace of Veri, Jameston had convinced him that removing the bodies this close to the castle could cause a war. And so, they had left the corpses hanging from the poles, rotting and being eaten by the birds. Colin felt sick just thinking about it.

"Jameston, where do you think the king is?" he whispered as they continued to stand. The throne room was by no means empty. Several courtiers stood in a ring around the Szarmian entourage, but Colin could not stifle the feeling that something was amiss. Aside from the decapitated bodies, of course.

"I have no idea, Your Majesty," Jameston spoke louder than Colin had intended and his friend's voice echoed throughout the hall. Several courtiers glared at them both from the outskirts of the room.

"Be careful, man," Colin said quietly through gritted teeth. He was afraid to move his mouth too much for fear that the courtiers would turn upon them.

Jameston didn't respond, which was just as well since he had trouble controlling the volume of his voice.

They waited several more moments before King Magnus stormed into the throne room. His face was splattered with a red liquid that Colin swore was blood. He stood firm in the middle of the throne room as the Lunameedian king took his place on the gilded chair.

A servant immediately came up with a steaming rag and wiped the red spots from the king's brow. *It must be nice to be washed clean of any atrocities one committed*, Colin thought as he stared the king down. King Magnus didn't even have to ask for it.

Men, whom Colin assumed were his councilors, formed a half circle around the throne. Their faces were taut as they stared straight ahead. Colin wondered what made them stare in such a concentrated matter. He was tempted to make a funny face at them, but resisted the urge. If any of the nobles saw him making faces in the king's general direction, he would never be able to keep an audience with the king.

After several moments of the king being waited on, a herald finally stepped forward and announced Colin and his men. King Magnus looked very pleased that they had arrived. He smiled and laughed as he rose from the throne and walked towards Colin's party. He trailed the red liquid behind him.

"I see you received my invitation in time," King Magnus slapped Colin on the back. It stung, but not enough to make Colin stumble.

"I did."

"And, how was the ride here? No trouble crossing the border, I guess." The king stared at Colin with unblinking eyes.

"No. No trouble at all. The Lunameedian border guards were actually quite pleasant."

"That is how it should be, boy," King Magnus spat. "While your people murder the magic folk who pass your borders, our own kingdom welcomes all who will enter."

Colin, for his part, flushed at King Magnus's frankness. He knew he had been baited into this course of discussion, but he couldn't help feeling like he needed to defend his kingdom.

"You are correct, King Magnus, on many accounts. My men do kill any Lunameedian civilians who cross the border without proper paperwork. This is to protect our land from the terrors of war. You forget that it was Szarmi that used to be the most magical kingdom in the realm. It is only because we gave up on the Light during the Wars of Darkness that Lunameed rose in power."

Jameston poked Colin in the ribs causing Colin to grimace slightly. His face burned with anger. It was not Jameston's place to reprimand him for defending Szarmi to this barbarian king. Still, it wouldn't do him any good to offend the king on his very first night in Estrellala.

"I'm sorry if I have offended you, Your Grace," Colin said quickly in an attempt to assuage any issues he had created with his words.

King Magnus just laughed.

"You are a spritely one, aren't you?" he said as he slapped Colin on the back. "Come on then, let me show you around the palace." King Magnus smiled warmly at him, "Besides, I want to hear more about your impressions of my great kingdom."

Is this the same man who murdered all those men and women impaled on the road? Colin wasn't sure, but he found it hard to believe that the man before him was capable of such behavior.

Colin followed King Magnus through the throne room and out into a large garden. Pieces of glass reflected the sun's light, creating a slightly warm haze. Still all of the bushes were covered in frost. The frozen ice sparkled in the light, causing Colin to smile for the first time since he'd been in Lunameed.

"My Orianna planted all these bushes herself. And the flowers. You should visit us during the summer months. This whole place is fluttering with life." The older man smiled warmly.

"I may do just that, Your Highness," Colin responded. He wasn't sure why, but he felt as if he were currently seeing something that not many were privy to.

"My wife and I used to love coming out here. We'd sit in the sun and laugh until our sides hurt." The king's voice was soft and carried a note of sadness on it. "I miss laughing with her more than anything."

Colin glanced at the king. His eyes were clouded over and his voice trembled as he spoke.

"This is Amaleah's garden now. I gave it to her this morning as part of her wedding gift."

Again, the older king smiled. Although, this time, there was a little less warmth in his smile.

"She is such a good girl. My Amaleah. Always looking after me. I love her dearly..." his voice trailed off.

"Where is she now?" Colin asked. He had been surprised that the princess hadn't been there to greet him.

"Who?" the king's voice sounded confused.

"Princess Amaleah?"

Colin watched as the king's head shook for a brief moment. It moved so quickly that Colin almost believed that he had imagined it. And, just as suddenly, the king's head stopped moving.

"Orianna is in her rooms. She's so beautiful," King Magnus said wistfully, "and she's all mine."

As if realizing that Colin might have an ulterior motive for asking about the princess, King Magnus's face flushed a deep purplish-red. He shouted, "No! You can't have her. She's mine. Do you hear? Mine."

The king's mouth seemed to froth as he spoke and Colin took a hesitant step away from the older man. *Where are my guards?* he thought.

"What are you talking about, Your Grace?"

"You can't. She's mine. No. NO!"

King Magnus's eyes glazed over and he began flailing his arms wildly.

"I don't want her. Please, Your Highness, calm down. It's alright," Colin said as he tried to soothe the old king, to no avail.

King Magnus continued to rant about Orianna being his and that none of the courtiers could do anything about it. He deserved his bride, his one true love. He had made her part of his plan. He had kept her safe.

Does he actually believe that the princess is his dead wife? Colin cringed at the thought. Before coming to Lunameed, Colin had believed that he would hate King Magnus. Now all he felt was pity.

That is, until they came upon the dais.

The severed heads from, Colin assumed, the bodies he'd seen on his ride into Estrellala, were heaped in a mound in the center of the platform. Their faces stared blankly at him, accusingly. Colin swallowed hard. *The king is mad.*

King Magnus motioned towards the heads, "These are just the heads of the men and women who betrayed me. They attempted to take Orianna from me. They needed to be punished."

King Magnus stated this so matter-of-factly that
Colin shivered slightly.

"I see," was all he could say.

"Don't worry, my boy. You wouldn't dare try to
steal my bride-to-be away from me, would you?" The king
eyed Colin but kept talking, "No. I don't think so. You're a
good boy. I can tell." King Magnus winked at Colin.

"No… no, I would never betray the trust I hope to
build between our two kingdoms." Colin's voice was
hoarse and he was having difficulty focusing on anything
other than the severed heads.

"It'll never work," King Magnus mumbled quietly.
So quietly, in fact, that Colin nearly didn't hear him.

"Forgive me, but, what did you say?"

King Magnus turned to face Colin, his face
unreadable, "Nothing, nothing." He patted Colin on the
back, "Now, let's see about getting you settled into your
rooms so that you can prepare for tonight's ball. There will
be lots of beautiful ladies here tonight." Once again the
king winked at Colin.

He let the king lead him out of the garden and back
into the throne room. The more he observed the king's
behaviors and words, the more he believed the rumors
about the Lunameedian king were true: he had gone mad.

Chapter Thirty-Five

Amaleah paced around her chamber. Sylvia: dead. Mr. Sweets: dead. The women who had pledged to help her escape: dead. All of them, every single one: dead.

She felt like weeping again, but knew that no tears would come. She'd already used them all up.

She wanted to scream in frustration, fear, anger, depression, all the other emotions rolling through her, but knew that too many servants, courtiers and guards had been told to keep watch over her that she wouldn't be able to grieve in peace. Even the smallest sound of her voice would bring them rushing to her side. She didn't want any of them.

All she wanted to do was feel Sylvia's comforting arms around her.

She shook her head. She couldn't think like that. Sylvia was gone. Amaleah had spent too much of her life hating the older woman for spying on her, keeping her away from the Lunameedian court, and being cruel to her. Now she understood what the older woman had known all along: it was to save her, to keep her safe, to protect her from her father's madness.

Amaleah's face remained blank as she looked at the three dresses. She had never seen anything as ornate and magnificent as these dresses were. The fabric was so fine that she wasn't sure how it had been spun, much less sewed.

Which should she wear? She knew her father would expect one of them. He would want as many people as possible to see the wondrous gifts he had given her. He had fulfilled their bargain and she was honor bound to uphold her end of the deal.

Her entire body shuddered. *Is my life to be completely destroyed by him?* No. She couldn't think like that either. She'd lost count of the things she couldn't think about today. She needed to focus. If she was going to escape, then it needed to be tonight, before the rest of the balls, before the wedding. The longer she stayed, the more likely it was that her father would become completely unhinged. She couldn't be in the palace when that happened.

She could hear courtiers talking in the hallway outside of her chambers. They whispered about the dresses the king had revealed and their excitement over the balls. For one, brief moment, Amaleah allowed herself to believe that she was one of them. She imagined that she was just an ordinary girl, excited for a fancy ball with handsome young men and a night full of dancing.

The fantasy passed quickly as the ladies' shrill voices became a clamor of excitement.

"Did you see him?"

"He's so handsome."

"I wonder if he noticed me."

Who are they talking about? Amaleah wondered as she glanced at herself in the mirror. Reluctantly, Amaleah pulled off the simple, cotton dress Sylvia had made for her. She could almost believe that Sylvia was still with her. Faint traces of the older woman's perfume still clung to the fabric. Amaleah breathed in deeply as the fabric slipped over her shoulders.

She stared at her nearly naked body in the ornate mirror of her bedchamber. Her light, golden skin appeared almost white as she held up the dark blue, sparkling dress. She set it aside as she picked up the dress that was as golden as the sun.

Holding it to her body, Amaleah smiled at herself in the mirror. This was the one, she decided. Without calling for help, Amaleah finished dressing herself for the ball. The gown, despite its length and intricate jeweled designs, was the lightest dress Amaleah had ever worn. She twirled in a circle in front of the mirror and almost smiled at the way the fabric clung to her body in just the right places while flowing over her curves without hiding them. The dress would have been perfect, except for the fact that its creation had meant the death of her nursemaid. Sighing, Amaleah stared herself in the eyes. Putting on her court face, she turned from the mirror without looking back.

She left her rooms with her head held high. She did not acknowledge the courtiers as she walked down the hallway towards the ballroom. She knew she had stunned them because they immediately fell silent as she continued to leave them behind. She heard the sound of their heeled shoes tapping on the floor as they trailed behind her. *Good,* Amaleah thought, *stay away from me.*

A few moments later one of the braver courtiers came up to Amaleah and strode next to her. Amaleah chanced a glance at the young woman beside her. She couldn't have been more than thirteen years of age. Her bosom had barely come in and her hair was pulled back into a tight bun, as was the style for younger girls. Her face was all hard lines and narrow bones. She wasn't exactly comely, but Amaleah knew she would never pass as beautiful in the Lunameedian court. Even as young as the girl appeared to be, she wore the customary ribbon around her waist and the bright colors of a woman accepting marriage proposals.

The girl looked at Amaleah confidently and smiled. When Amaleah didn't return the smile, the girl nervously picked at the blue ribbon tied around her tiny waist. Amaleah grinned as she watched the girl. She could tell the younger girl wanted nothing more than to disappear after what she perceived to be a huge slight. However, she kept walking next to Amaleah while the others remained behind.

This girl could be dangerous.

"How are you doing this evening?"

The young girl jumped a few centimeters off the ground when she heard Amaleah speak. She didn't say anything for several moments before finally saying, "It is quite beautiful, My Lady. I went on a walk through your mother's garden and wished that I never had to leave."

Amaleah smiled at that. Namadus had trained this girl well. He knew how much she loved her mother's garden.

That is, until today.

Memories of what her father had done earlier in the day flooded her mind and she shivered. The girl didn't seem to notice Amaleah's discomfort. The girl swung her arms as they walked, imitating dance moves. *At least she is graceful.*

"Do you know what I'm most excited about for tonight, My Lady?" The girl continued without giving Amaleah a chance to respond, "The prince of Szarmi will be here. My sister told me that she saw him arrive earlier today and that he is the most handsome boy she's ever seen. She's seventeen just like you. Do you know her: Viola McGellian?"

The girl prattled on as Amaleah tried to place her sister's name. They were the same age so she should recognize it. And then it struck her: these girls were more of Namadus's nieces. He'd sent for them right before she'd been imprisoned. Viola and Starla McGellian.

A pit grew in Amaleah's stomach as the girl continued to walk beside her. Sylvia had warned her about Claudette, one of Namadus's other young nieces who had been added to Amaleah's list of ladies. Starla touched Amaleah's arm to guide her. Amaleah cringed and the girl dropped her hand quickly, as if she'd been burned. Starla's eyes shone with something akin to anger, but Amaleah couldn't quite place the emotion.

She slowed her gait and then stopped, suddenly, in the middle of the hall. It took Starla a few paces before she realized that the princess was no longer walking beside her. "I'm sorry, Starla, but I seem to have forgotten my dance card in my room. You go ahead, I'll catch up," she spoke as calmly as she could and she thought she did a good job at masking her panic.

"Oh, I don't mind going back with you, My Lady. I am here to be your lady-in-waiting after all." She made as if to come back to where Amaleah was standing.

"No, that's quite alright, dear," Amaleah held up her hand. "It'll only take me a moment. I must insist. Please go ahead. You never know, Prince Colin of Szarmi may already be in there waiting for a beautiful girl to dance with."

Starla looked to be considering Amaleah's words. She had a confounded look on her face that Amaleah found amusing. *She is only a child after all*, Amaleah thought. Guilt rushed through her as she realized how judgmental she had been towards the young girl. Starla tapped her hands against the length of her dress and smiled broadly.

"Do you think the Szarmian prince would really dance with me?"

Amaleah smiled in spite of herself. "I know he will," she said.

Starla looked between Amaleah and the ballroom doors where music could be heard playing.

"Well, if you're sure that you don't need my services," she said cautiously.

"I'm sure," Amaleah said in a rush.

Nodding, Starla turned around and skipped—Amaleah wasn't imagining this—*skipped* down the hallway to the ballroom. Amaleah sighed in relief as she watched the young girl disappear. *It is time.*

Chapter Thirty-Six

Colin hummed to himself as he walked down the hallway. He had insisted that his guards and Jameston let him explore the castle alone before the ball. Not surprisingly, the guards his mother had handpicked to protect him put up less of a fight to accompany him than Jameston or his select personal guard. However, after several hours, all his guards had finally conceded to his request as long as he wore one of the safety medallions the professors at the University of Szarmitec had created. Directly following his father's death, Colin had enlisted a team of engineers and medical doctors to create a wearable healing device that could cure even the deadliest of wounds. According to the professors, with just one press of the medallion's button, a healing medicine would be released that could reconstruct bone and knit muscle back together within a matter of minutes. They had given Colin the device during their visit to Miliom—after Vanessa attempted to kill him but before he left for his mother's estate. During the assassination attempt at the river, Colin had forgotten that he had the device.

After seeing how the king treated people he distrusted, Colin swore to himself that he would never forget about the device again. He patted his pocket to ensure the device was still safely tucked away. It was.

Colin hadn't used the medallion, but he had witnessed the professors' giving a demonstration of its power. One of the professors had sliced his hand open right in front Colin. Warm, coppery blood streamed from the man's hand, but the man pressed the small button on the device. The mending process had made Colin feel nauseous, but the demonstration had done its work. Colin believed that the professors had finally found a cure for any illness. Never again would someone lose a loved one simply because of an illness.

The professors had gone into a long explanation of how the medallions worked, but all Colin could remember was that the healing medicine contained inside the device could be accessed by pressing the button. Colin assumed that the medicine was made from the various herbs found within Szarmi's borders since the professors rarely traveled outside of the University of Szarmitec, but he wasn't sure. Supposedly, the medallions could be used up to five times before running out of the medicine. Although the medallion was still in the testing phase, the professors had given Colin one of the devices to carry with him to his mother's estate. Colin wasn't sure, but he sensed that they trusted her as much as they trusted a healer from Lunameed, and that wasn't very much.

Colin was certain that once the medallions had been tested, that they would become not only a source of healing for any number of his citizens, but would also become a staple of the Szarmian armed forces. His ultimate goal was for the professors to develop a variety of medallions that could be used in times of warfare. So far, they hadn't been able to create anything as powerful as the healing medallions, but Colin was hopeful that they would, eventually, come up with medallions that would increase strength, hearing, sight, and courage. He wasn't sure how the last one could be added to a medallion without the use of magic, but he had instructed them to try. *Maybe I'll find answers for my quest here, in Lunameed,* Colin thought as he strode through the palace.

Colin rubbed his thumb across the healing medallion as he walked down the hallway. He hoped he wouldn't need it. The king of this land had demonstrated that he had been taken by a madness unlike any Colin had ever witnessed. How had he killed his own people like that? Killed women like that? Colin shuddered at the memory of the women's corpses hanging from the poles as they rode into town. Except for the first one, they had not given any of them a proper burial. The image of the impaled bodies haunted him as he continued to walk.

Colin was so distracted by his thoughts that, as he rounded a corner, he walked straight into a girl.

She gasped as their bodies collided and Colin stretched out an arm to keep her from falling. He, of course, missed her entirely and she went crashing to the ground. He stumbled a bit and accidently stomped on her hand. Colin blushed deeply and mumbled an apology as he reached down to help her up. She had on the most beautiful gown he had ever seen. It was as brilliant as the sun and seemed to cast a warm glow upon him.

When she looked up at him, Colin realized that it wasn't just her dress that was beautiful. Her auburn hair perfectly framed her golden, freckled face in ringlets and her green eyes shone when she looked him in the eyes. He gasped and nearly dropped her again.

Thankfully, he didn't.

Colin noticed how small and dainty her hands were. They fit so neatly into his own. Unfortunately, his own hands had begun sweating as soon as their skin touched. He gulped, loudly. She dropped her gaze from his, but allowed him to continue holding her hands. Her cheeks were flushed a light peach color and Colin realized that she was blushing as well. He found himself wondering what it was she was thinking about as she continued to stare at her feet. He hoped that it wasn't about what a clumsy dolt her was.

"I'm so sorry, My Lady," his voice cracked when he spoke and Colin abruptly stopped talking.

"It is nothing," she said. She spoke in barely a whisper and Colin had difficulty hearing her as she continued, "Please don't mind me. I was just on my way back to my rooms-"

"Then let me accompany you. It is the least I can do to apologize for knocking into you." *Vanessa.* An image of Vanessa's cold, dead eyes came unbidden to his mind. He dropped the woman's hands as if they were burning.

What am I doing? Colin thought when he saw the look on the woman's face. She looked as if she were about to cry.

"I'm afraid I must apologize again. I hope my request wasn't too forward. Please forgive me. It's just that

I don't meet beautiful women every day." That was a lie, but he didn't want to tell her that. He blushed.

"Really, it's no trouble. I'm almost there and-"

"Nonsense. What kind of a prince would I be if I let you walk back to your rooms by yourself?"

"Prince?" she asked in a startled voice. She met his gaze once more and Colin once again found himself wondering what she was thinking.

"Oh dear. And now I've broken the first rule of etiquette between a beautiful young woman and a man. We must be introduced if we are to speak privately. Or is this not the custom in Lunameed?"

"It is," she said with a small smile.

"Gears and levers!" Colin exclaimed as he slapped himself on the forehead. "Then let me introduce myself. My name is Colin Sammial Stormbearer, prince of Szarmi and the Forgotten Isles. And you are?"

The young woman before him turned a deep shade of puce. Colin wondered what he'd said to make her look as if she were going to vomit. *Are the Szarmian people so hated in this country?* He certainly hoped not.

"I shouldn't be talking to you. I'm sorry," she said in a rushed voice. She didn't give him a chance to respond. Instead, she dashed away from him.

Colin tried to follow, but once she turned around a corner, she was just... gone. There was no trace of her as far as Colin could tell. He stood for several moments in the hallway, stroking his thumb over the healing medallion before finally turning around and walking towards the sound of the music coming from the ballroom.

Chapter Thirty-Seven

Amaleah stumbled down the hall as she fled from Starla. As she zipped around a corner, she slammed right into another human being so forcibly that she nearly fell backwards. Thankfully, the person caught her hand and before her head slammed into the ground. She blushed profusely as she tried to figure out how to talk her way out of this one. She was positive that Namadus's spies were lurking throughout the castle. *What if this person is one of them?* Paranoia strangled her.

Chancing a glance upward, Amaleah saw a tall, almost looming, man with dark, golden skin and a well-made shirt and trousers standing above her. He did not look like a Lunameedian. *Perhaps he's not one.* He tried to help her up, but nearly dropped her when he saw her face. She cringed as she realized that he probably hadn't realized he had knocked over the princess.

He stammered a bit as he spoke and Amaleah could tell that he was struggling to find the right words to say to her. His discomfort made her smile, but did not make her trust him.

But then, he surprised her. He told her that he was the prince of Szarmi.

This was worse than if he had been one of Namadus's spies. If one of those very spies ever saw her standing in a hallway, alone with this prince, then her father would have him expelled from Lunameed. Or worse: killed. She couldn't be responsible for that. She had already put

Freddy and Saphria in too much danger. And had gotten her would-be saviors killed. She couldn't be responsible for any more pain.

"I shouldn't be talking to you. I'm sorry," she said resolutely, and then she fled.

She could hear him following her so she did the only thing she could think to do. She rounded the corner and quickly pulled the lever that opened up her secret passage to the cavern. She slipped in and closed the door silently and instantly behind her. Pressing her ear against the door, Amaleah waited with baited breath as she heard the prince pace in front of the doorway several times before turning and walking back in the direction he'd come from. Sighing Amaleah counted to ten before slowly descending the stairs. She hadn't returned to the cavern since she'd been taken out of the dungeon by Yosef to meet with Sylvia and the others. She sent a silent prayer to any of the gods who listened that the cavern had not been discovered by her father.

Taking one of the torches that lined the wall leading into the cavern, Amaleah flicked the bottom on the handle to spark the flame at the top. It flickered to life, illuminating the entirety of the cavern.

It was completely ransacked. The pillows she'd left in the room were slit with the fluff strewn across the cavern floor. The blankets had been ripped. The entire cavern looked like whoever had been here last had been searching for something. Amaleah's whole body shook as she looked around. Everything she had left here had been destroyed.

Pressure filled her head and Amaleah knew the onslaught of tears was about to erupt. She couldn't allow herself to cry. Her tears wouldn't change anything now. Straightening her back, Amaleah set her jaw and left the cavern. She vowed that she would never return there again.

By the time she finally made it back to her rooms, her breathing had steadied. *I need to leave tonight.* There was no other option. Everyone who had tried to help her had been murdered by her father. *Or by Namadus*, a nagging voice inside her head whispered to her.

At least everything in her room had been left untouched. Amaleah sighed in relief as she lifted the loose board in her bedroom floor and pulled out the large satchel she had prepared earlier that day. It contained a small amount of food, several pieces of jewelry, the other two dresses, and the fur coat. She remembered the words of the fae: that when she escaped she must take the dresses and coat with her.

She'd been able to wash the blood off of the coat before packing it. The memory of Mr. Sweet's head rolling out of it made her cringe every time she looked at it, but she knew it had been made for a reason, even if she wasn't sure what that reason was. She had promised him he would be safe, that she could protect him. And she had failed.

Tears swam in her eyes as she looked around her room to see if there was anything else she should pack. She still had one stop left to make before she would attempt her escape. She prayed she'd be able to get there without anyone noticing.

Carefully, she dropped the satchel back into its slot in the floor. Resolutely, she exited the room and made her way to the ballroom.

Chapter Thirty-Eight

King Magnus strolled around the room, watching as the Lunameedian nobles and foreign royalty filed into the room. He smiled when he noticed the dark-skinned prince from Szarmi walked into the room alone. *So, the princeling has left his men and is fending for himself. Excellent,* he thought as he changed direction so that he was headed towards the young prince. This was the man who was to take over the southern kingdom in just a few short weeks. *What a pitiful thing he is.* Magnus doubted the boy would be able to lift a sword much less defend his kingdom from an attack by Lunameedian forces.

True, the Szarmian Armed Forces were the most well-funded and well-trained of all the Mitierian armies. And they had invested in mechanical weapons that could defend them against all odds; however, the Szarmian military lacked what Lunameed had: magic. And it would be with magic that Lunameed wreaked its revenge on the kingdom to the south, the place where so many Lunameedian subjects had been brutally murdered by the magic-hating people who defended the border.

"It is such a pleasure to see you again, Prince Colin," King Magus smiled, but he could feel his anger boiling inside of him. "Come, let me introduce you to the most eligible young ladies from our realm."

But not his Orianna. He would never let this snip of a boy meet his beloved, his future queen. King Magnus was pleased to note that the young prince did not resist him as he led the boy around the ballroom. Several ladies fawned over the prince, as they had been instructed to do. His plan was going exactly how he had envisioned it.

He noticed the Lady Orianna enter the ballroom from the corner of his eye. She had chosen the golden dress. The one he had had made first. Good. It suited her, with her long auburn hair. Her skin almost looked pale in comparison to the golden splendor of the dress. *She is so beautiful.*

He left Colin to continue talking with the ladies from court and made his way towards his bride-to-be. She didn't seem to notice him. Instead, she closed her eyes and pressed against one of the walls nearest his dais. And then she disappeared.

Magnus stopped dead in his tracks as he watched Orianna's body disappear into the wall. *How did she do that?* He began to think quickly, almost too quickly for him to really understand all of this thoughts. She was gone. But where? His body began to shake. He couldn't lose her again. His Orianna. His precious, precious Orianna.

He strode towards the wall he had seen her disappear into. Several nobles, including Namadus's nieces, Starla and Viola, approached him as if to speak with him. He ignored them all in his pursuit of his lady. He was so preoccupied by his desperation to find Orianna that he didn't notice the prince and princess of Dramadoon walk into the ballroom. They wore their customary fur-lined attire. He didn't notice as they looked at each other and nodded. He also didn't notice as one of them, the Princess Saphria, reached into her cloak and withdrew a vial of vibrantly colored liquid.

All he saw was the wall and no way for him to go through it.

Chapter Thirty-Nine

Amaleah sighed in relief as she entered the small library at the back of the ballroom. The musty smell of the books made the tight, almost-painful tension in her shoulders momentarily leave her.

Everything was where she had left it. Running her fingers over the covers of the books she'd cherished since finding the room, she began to search through them, looking for the old manuscript. The one that contained a history of Lunameed and the Wars of Darkness. The one that contained the beginnings of her story. Amaleah quickly found the book she had been looking for in the hidden library. She clasped it to her chest, cherishing the feel of the frail leather binding beneath her fingertips. She once again felt tears sliding down her cheeks as she realized this would be another goodbye. Because of her father. Because of his madness.

She didn't care if her father found out about her secret library anymore. If she was successful, it wouldn't matter. She'd be gone and her father would be left to pick up the pieces. He deserved whatever he got. For the women. For Mr. Sweets. For Sylvia.

Tucking the book of tales about the Wars of Darkness deep into the folds of her dress, Amaleah readied herself to exit the hidden library. She hadn't been careful when entering her hideaway. She'd been brazen, and anyone could have seen her enter through the secret door. As she prepared herself to leave the room, Amaleah pulled a thin blade she'd hidden in her stocking garter out from beneath the length of her dress. She trembled slightly as she held the blade in her hand. She hoped she wouldn't have to use it. She wasn't even sure she knew how.

Pressing her ear against the hidden door, Amaleah tried to hear if there were people on the other side. She could hear the faint sounds of the orchestra her father had hired for the occasion, but nothing beyond that. Quickly, she pressed against the door and pushed through to the other side.

Her father stood directly in front of her and Amaleah gasped.

He appeared to be looking directly at her, but his eyes were glazed over, unseeing. Amaleah stepped towards him and still he didn't blink, didn't move. She sighed a little in relief and moved more confidently towards him, past him.

Just as she was beginning to slide by him, his hand shot out and grasped her arm, hard. She could feel his fingers forming tight manacles around her wrists. She swallowed a scream.

"There you are, my beautiful Orianna." His voice seemed hollow, as if he didn't realize what he was saying. "I have been looking for you everywhere. Tell me, where have you been?"

Amaleah tried to wrench her arm free, but his grip was too tight. "Nowhere, Father. I just arrived." This was partly true. She hadn't been there for very long.

"I saw you." His eyes still didn't seem to focus. "I saw you walk through the door."

Panic started to rise up in Amaleah as she listened to her father speak. There was something seriously wrong with him, she just couldn't pin down what it was.

"No, Father. I was just standing here." She motioned to the far side of the doorway. "You must have seen me come around the corner."

"I couldn't find you." His voice sounded so lost now. It made Amaleah want to comfort him, want to lessen his pain.

"I'm right here, Father." She patted his arm with her other hand. "Please, Father, don't be sad. You'll always have me." The lie stung her mouth like a thousand bees, but she forced it out anyway.

He still hadn't let go of her.

She was about to say something else when she heard a loud crash come from behind her. Whipping her head around, Amaleah had just enough time to see the percussionist fall from where he was sitting and slam into his drums. His large, rotund body rolled slightly on the floor. There was a visible stab wound directly in his heart.

Amaleah's heart wrenched as she saw the blood and images of Sylvia's murder flooded her mind. *No. No. No.* The word echoed in her mind. *Not again. Please not again.*

There were a few moments of absolute silence as the partygoers processed the dead man's body. No one moved. No one spoke. Amaleah stared at the dead man in shock. *Who would do such a thing at a ball?* Amaleah finally let the breath she had been holding out in one long, steady exhale.

And then there was chaos. Women began shrieking and clawing at their partners for protection. Men began running about the room, trying to find all the members of their parties. Amaleah just stood there with her father's hand around her wrist thinking about Sylvia's murder. That is, until her father yanked her, hard, on the arm and pulled her towards the dais.

He shoved her against the raised platform until she fell to her knees behind the gilded throne.

"Stay here," he whispered. His voice didn't sound as lost as it had just moments before. "I'll find us help."

The palace guards were nowhere to be seen. Amaleah's heart hammered in her chest. *This is the distraction I need to escape*, she thought as she nodded to her father absently.

She watched him walk away from her. Now could be my chance, she thought as she realized that her father was no longer watching her. She peered around the room.

Several more bodies lay on the floor with stab wounds to their hearts. Amaleah cringed as she looked at them. Blood seeped from their bodies, staining the normally white floor a deep shade of red.

Lifting her small blade Amaleah began wading through the throng of panicking people. They barely noticed her as she passed them, they were so afraid of being the next victim. Amaleah wasn't afraid, despite the randomness of the deaths, despite the danger. She only felt calm.

Suddenly, a firm hand grasped her shoulder. Amaleah instantly stopped moving. She knew that if her father was the one who had found her, she'd receive a much harsher punishment than just being thrown in the dungeons for nine days and being forced to watch her nursemaid be murdered.

Making the decision to fight rather than surrender, Amaleah momentarily struggled against the tall figure who wore a long, black cloak. She almost screamed, until she realized that it was just Princess Saphria. The woman was smiling at her, but Amaleah wasn't sure why.

"Come with me, Princess," Saphria said as she pulled on Amaleah's arm. The princess's body twisted and Amaleah saw a long, thin sword covered in blood grasped in the woman's hand. Amaleah's skin turned to ice.

She yanked her arm away from Saphria. "No," she said. "I cannot come with you. I'm sorry, Saphria." Knowing that princess and her brother were most likely behind the killings, Amaleah continued, "I owe you a great debt for what you have done tonight, but I have to leave. I can't stay here." The words made her want to retch, but she forced herself to say them. She couldn't condone the violence that they had used to save her, but she also couldn't leave without thanking them for all they had done.

Saphria caught Amaleah's arm as she made a move to leave. The Dramadoonian princess held up an empty vial and said in a very matter-of-fact tone, "I've poisoned the wine with this. It won't kill anyone, but it will put them all into a deep sleep. Tell me, did your father drink any of the wine tonight?"

"I don't know," she responded. "I had only just arrived when you…" she paused, "when the killings began."

Saphria shrugged her shoulders. "We wanted to give you a chance, My Lady, even if you choose to not come with us."

Amaleah wished they had found a more peaceful way of helping her, but she was grateful. "Thank you," she whispered.

As Amaleah turned away, she saw a flash of color as a body slammed into Saphria. Making a quick decision, Amaleah began running towards her rooms. She did not turn to see what had become of the Dramadoonian princess.

Chapter Forty

When the killing began, Colin had been chatting with a young girl named Starla. She saw the percussionist fall to the ground and her jaw dropped open, but she didn't scream. Colin thought that the young girl had gone into shock, but he quickly realized that wasn't the case as she drew a dagger from the sash tied around her waist.

"Prince Colin of Szarmi," she said, "you have been cleansed."

She'd thrust the dagger into his side and then into his neck.

Blood sprayed from the wounds, drenching the girl in red. Colin felt himself collapse to the ground but could do nothing to stop the pain. There was so much pain. Even when he'd been beaten up by the other soldiers during his training, day after day, layering bruises upon bruises, he had never felt as much pain as he did now.

He reached towards her, unable to speak because of the wound in his throat, but she slapped his hand away. She watched him. He was sure she was waiting for him to die. Wanted to be sure she had completed her job thoroughly. So he stilled his hand from using the healing medallion that was clutched tightly within it. Closing his eyes and breathing as shallowly as possible, Colin pretended to be dead. It wasn't that far from the truth.

He lay there for several moments but didn't feel or hear anything other than the screams. There were so many people screaming now. How many people had met their fates tonight? He hoped that Jameston and the rest of his men were safe and secure in his rooms. He was glad that he'd left them behind on this night, for if the goal was to kill him, then his guards would not have been able to save him in this chaos.

He could feel his strength slipping away from him as he lay there in a pool of his own blood. His mind became fuzzy as he tried to remember what he was supposed to do. He couldn't quite seem to hold onto anything other than the girl's name: Starla. He wasn't sure why he remembered her name, but it was the only thing that kept running through his mind. His limbs felt numb. Could he still move them? He wasn't sure.

He felt cold metal in his hand: the medallion. Remembering what he was supposed to do, Colin cracked one eye open to see if the girl was still there. She no longer loomed above him. *I am safe*, he thought weakly.

Clutching the medallion tighter in his palm, Colin activated its power by pressing a small button submerged within the metal. Immediately, he felt his mind clear and his breathing stabilize. The hole in his throat mended first. He could feel the skin stretch across the hole, forming a patch. And then, the wound in his side healed itself as well. He continued to lay on the floor for several moments as his body finished healing itself. He felt stronger. More alive than he had even before he'd been stabbed twice.

This was the way the healing medallion worked. He wasn't sure if he had four or three charges left, since he'd been stabbed twice. This worried him slightly, and he resolved to keep himself out of danger so that he wouldn't have to find out.

Putting the healing medallion around his neck so that he didn't lose it, Colin pulled out a small dagger from the inside of his boot. He had also worn the under-pieces of his special armor. They weren't as robust as the exterior elements of his armor, but they still contained hidden compartments that would fling throwing blades out and protect him from any wounds across his chest.

Colin leapt up from the floor and quickly began moving towards the doorway. Several other men and women were doing the same. There were still people falling to the ground with wounds to the heart but Colin couldn't identify who was causing them. There were too many people. *Gears and levers!* he thought as he tried to maneuver himself to the front of the pack of nobles.

Out of the corner of his eye he saw the girl he'd met earlier. Her hair had fallen out of its pins, and she was clutching a short, thin sword closely to her chest and backing away from a tall, thin figure in a dark cloak holding a bloodied sword. The person appeared to be trying to coax the girl to come closer to them, but she just kept moving closer to the wall.

Colin looked ahead of him. He was only a few paces away from the door. The way out from the madness. He could get his men.

He looked back at the girl. The figure in the black cloak was waiving something small in front of Amaleah's face. He saw the girl's face turn into a scowl. *Is she alright?* he wondered. She didn't look to be in harm's way and yet, he wavered. *I could be her savior,* he told himself as an image of the yellow-clad girl leaping into his arms filled his mind.

Changing direction, Colin burst from the crowd and plunged into the figure with the long blade. The person crumpled beneath him as if they were old and frail. Colin reached out to grab the person by the collar of their cloak but realized that there was no one there. The person had completely disappeared and all that remained was the cloak and the blade. Colin looked back to where the girl had been standing but she had once again disappeared.

Panicked, Colin looked around the room, searching for her. He caught a glimpse of a yellow skirt fluttering around the corner of the room in the opposite direction of where he'd been heading. *Where is she going?* Picking himself up, and grabbing the sword left behind by the cloaked assailant, Colin trailed after her.

Chapter Forty-One

Amaleah ran down the hallway as quickly as she could in the golden dress. The screaming from the ballroom followed her as she passed through several sets of rooms before finally ending up in her chambers. She was breathing heavily from the run but didn't let herself stop as she collected her satchel from the floorboards.

She looked around her rooms one last time. This place had never felt like home to her, but it had been where she'd learned of the first prophecy, met members of the fae, and started to forgive Sylvia for all the heartache she'd experienced growing up. She closed her eyes and whispered goodbye as she opened her door and left.

The corridor was chaos. People congregated at various places in the hallway, talking frantically about everyone who had been killed in the ballroom. They looked at her and then quickly averted their eyes. She noticed that they would huddle down after she passed and would speak in hushed tones. None of them tried to stop her or speak with her. For this, Amaleah was grateful. If her plan was going to work, she needed to move as quickly as possible.

As she was threading her way through the corridors, Amaleah tripped on something solid lying in the middle of the hallway. She stopped and looked down. A dead nobleman lay on the floor, an arrow lodged in his throat. *That is new. All of the others had been killed with a knife to the heart, or possible by Saphria's poison,* she reminded herself. Amaleah shivered as she looked down at the man.

He was so far away from the ballroom. Where had he been going? Or a much better question was, where had he come from? Amaleah began to back away from the body when she heard a voice in the shadows.

"Where are you going, My Lady?"

The voice was feminine and sweet, yet somehow sinister. A pit formed in the middle of Amaleah's stomach. *What is happening here tonight?*

"You should not be in the hallways alone right now, My Lady." The voice carried a hint of sarcasm on it as it continued, "You could get hurt."

Amaleah tried to place the voice as she took another step backwards. The voice had an edge to it that Amaleah didn't like.

"Your father will be wondering where you are."

Her father. The hair on Amaleah's arms stood on end as she tried to figure out where the voice was coming from. The tattoo the fae had given her seared her skin with a burning hot flash.

"Run, Amaleah. Get away from her," a voice inside her seemed to be saying. Her hands became clammy as she glanced around the shadowy hallway. It was only then that she realized there were no other nobles visible in the darkened hall.

"You should come with me. I will take you to safety," the voice was saying in its sickly sweet tones. It was distinctly feminine.

Amaleah still had not said anything, but she feared that the woman, whoever she was, was a danger to her.

"I don't think you will take me to safety," she finally said, her voice trembling.

"You have nothing to fear from me, Amaleah. I have been trained to protect you."

This statement did nothing to quell Amaleah's fears. She took several steps back, away from the woman. In one quick motion, she turned around and began to run away. She heard footsteps behind her. They were moving more quickly than Amaleah was.

Something whizzed by Amaleah's ear and embedded itself in a doorway at the end of the hall. Amaleah whipped her head around to see who was behind her but saw no one.

"Next time, Princess, I won't miss."

The voice was close to Amaleah. She shivered.

"Who are you?"

"Who I am doesn't matter, Princess. All that matters is that you are safely returned to your father. He has been asking for you, looking for you. He just wants you to be safe in this time of danger."

"Then where is he? Shouldn't he be facing me himself?"

"Oh, Princess, you have no idea about these things, do you?" the woman said in a condescending tone. "You don't understand your role in what is to come."

"I'm not sure I know what you mean."

The voice laughed, not a jovial laugh that was full of joy, but a maniacal laugh, one that sent a shiver down Amaleah's back and made gooseflesh cover her arms.

"I know more than you think," Amaleah said defiantly.

Amaleah finally recognized the voice. It belonged to Namadus's niece: Starla.

"You know nothing," Starla responded in a tone that was hard and cutting.

Amaleah reached over and took one of the torches down from the wall. She began to twist the bottom of the handle to spark the flames, but the woman shot another arrow past her. It stuck to the wall, in between two stones.

"Drop the torch, Amaleah."

Amaleah thought about her interactions with the young girl. She had already admitted that she needed to take her back to her father without injury. She had no reason to be afraid of her. Starla had already revealed her hand.

Amaleah twisted the handle and light flooded the hallway.

Starla stood in the middle of the hallway, a bow stretched back in her hands and an arrow notched. She was aiming straight for Amaleah's heart.

"You are more foolish than my uncle led me to believe," Starla said. "Did you really think that you would be safe here?"

Amaleah stared at the young girl. She had killed that man. How many of the others had she killed?

"Why are you doing this, Starla?"

"Why? Are you seriously asking me this? My uncle is the most powerful man in the realm, aside from the king, of course. But he has demonstrated an ability to control him. The king is weak. You're weak. The royal lineage is weak, and you no longer deserve to rule." She paused to chuckle to herself as she took a step towards Amaleah. "My uncle told me about you: your simpering, your inability to stand up to your father. He had hoped that since you'd been raised away from your father that you'd be different. But he was wrong."

"I'm nothing like my father," Amaleah said firmly.

"You're exactly like your father."

"You don't know anything about me. Your uncle doesn't know anything about me. Starla, you're so young. Why are you throwing your life away like this? You *killed* that man." Amaleah's voice was accusatory, but she wanted the younger girl to know that what she was doing was inexcusable.

"And I would kill you if my uncle had given me permission," Starla snarled. "For some reason he wants you alive, although I am not sure why."

So it was Namadus who didn't want her dead. Why? What purpose did she serve for him?

"And does your uncle control everything you do?"

"No," she spat in distaste.

"He does, doesn't he?"

Maybe if I can distract the young girl for long enough I will be able to think of a way to escape. Maybe I can reach the door at the end of the hallway. Maybe I can be free. Amaleah's thoughts jumbled as she tried to come up with a solid plan for escape.

Starla let out a shriek of fury. "You insolent, senseless girl! Who do you think I am? Just another courtier? Since birth, my sister and I have been raised to be court assassins. We were trained in the art of destruction. What were you trained for? To rule? To be benevolent to your people? You are nothing but a spoiled, petty, little girl who won't ever receive the Lunameedian crown."

The girl's words cut through Amaleah. There were elements of truth to them. She was spoiled. And she had been trained to rule a kingdom benevolently. But she was so much more than the crown. Hadn't Sylvia, the fae, and Cordelia proven this to her?

"You might be right in some ways, Starla. But you should remember that I was raised in exile for five years. That was not a period of pampering. In fact, my father essentially forgot me. There were times that he wouldn't send me the basic necessities of life. And now," Amaleah laughed, "now, he has lost his mind and is forcing me to marry him. Do you honestly think I *want* to marry him? You're still just a little girl, Starla. And you clearly know nothing of court. Or of me."

Starla pulled the bowstring back even further as her lips curled into a cruel smile.

"Amaleah Bluefischer, you have been-"

She didn't get the chance to finish whatever it was she was about to say. A dark figure bolted out of the darkness and slammed straight into Starla's body. Amaleah looked on in surprise as the figure smashed one of the sculptures lining the hallway into Starla's head. The girl immediately began bleeding.

Strangely, Starla didn't appear to feel the pain. She simply rolled away from the dark figure and reached for another arrow, notched it, and released it. Amaleah's heart thumped rapidly in her chest as she watched the arrow zoom through the air. It grazed the figure's cheek in a gush of blood. The figure, Amaleah guessed it was a man, shook his head before dashing towards Starla in a burst of speed. His sword whipped through the air. Starla withdrew a sword of her own from a sheath at her waist and parried his attack.

Starla struck back and scraped the man's side with her sword. It came back with a gleam of blood on its blade. Amaleah stood in silence, watching the two fight. Starla clearly had the upper hand. She seemed to be able to sense where the figure was going to move next. Amaleah wanted to pull away, to make her escape, but she couldn't force herself to leave the dark figure to his fate. He continued to lose ground as they engaged in hand-to-hand combat.

"Aren't you supposed to be dead?" she heard Starla ask the figure as they continued to parry blows.

"Not if I can help it," he retorted. His voice was familiar to Amaleah.

"I thought I watched you die. I won't make the same mistake again." Starla swung her sword at the man's head. He barely had time to duck. The blade cut through the top of his hair but didn't do any permanent damage. Amaleah looked on in horror. She had to do something.

Making her decision, Amaleah leapt towards the two battling figures and waved her thin dagger at Starla. In a move that Amaleah hadn't even been sure she'd be able to accomplish, she kicked with both feet towards the girl's chest. The young girl gasped in surprise as Amaleah's kick landed squarely in her chest, sending her backwards. Amaleah dropped to the ground in time to see Starla's head snap against the stone wall and slump to the floor. Starla didn't move again.

The man turned towards Amaleah and she realized for the first time that it was the prince of Szarmi.

"What are you doing here?" Her voice was high pitched and cracked as she spoke. He didn't even know who she was.

"Well, you left me wondering who you were the last time we met and I couldn't resist the chance to meet up with you again. Thankfully, I did." He nodded towards the slumped figure on the ground.

"Yes... well... thank you." Amaleah wasn't exactly sure what to say to the prince. *Does he truly not recognize me?* Surely he would have been sent paintings of the royals from other kingdoms within Mitier. Then again, Amaleah hadn't recognized the prince, even after Sylvia had forced her to study his painting for hours. He looked scrawnier than he had in his paintings, but his eyes were kinder.

"So, are you finally going to introduce yourself or are you going to disappear again?"

His voice was gentle, but grim. Amaleah's tension eased slightly, but she still felt wary of him.

"I think it is better if you do not know who I am," she said firmly.

"Please, just tell me who you are," he said in a pleading voice.

Amaleah almost told him then. He had saved her after all. But something made her pause. She needed to escape this place and she wasn't certain the young prince would help her escape if he realized who she was.

"I guess you'll have to find out another day," she said as she stepped closer to him. "Goodbye, Colin of Szarmi." Using the hilt of her dagger, Amaleah knocked the prince in the head with as much force as she could muster. Then she ran.

Chapter Forty-Two

King Magnus paced. He couldn't stop pacing, or thinking. He ended up in the courtyard between the stables and the castle. What was he doing here? He couldn't quite remember. He just knew that he needed to be there. Wandering through the castle grounds. He needed to be here.

But for what?

He tried to grasp the thought. Tried to remember what he was looking for, what he was waiting for. He didn't quite know.

He thought he was waiting for a girl.

In a yellow dress? Or was it a blue one? King Magnus began muttering to himself as he tried to recall why he had come out to the courtyard in the first place.

He saw a girl in a yellow dress dash out from the castle. Her long auburn hair flowed behind her. *It is her*, he said to himself. *It has to be her.*

He ambled towards her.

She stopped dead in her tracks, but didn't say anything.

He looked at her. Her golden skin, freckled by the sun. Her yellow dress flowing over an ample body. Her auburn hair. Her violet eyes.

No.

Not violet. Green.

This was wrong. All wrong.

She didn't have green eyes. She had violet eyes. He remembered those eyes. The ones that had first captivated him. The ones that had made him feel safe, loved. Loved for the first time in his life. They hadn't been green.

This girl was wrong.

He began to tell her that she was the wrong girl. That he hadn't been waiting for her. That she didn't belong to him. The words were on the tip of his tongue.

But then his body began to shake.

Chapter Forty-Three

Amaleah stared at her father. *He isn't supposed to be here.* She stood as far away from him as possible. He hadn't said anything to her, but she could tell that he was thinking. At least his presence here confirmed that Starla hadn't been working for her father, just Namadus.

It had always been Namadus.

Amaleah cursed herself for being so daft. She should have recognized the High Councilor's power within the Lunameedian court. It was Namadus who was controlling the nobility. It was Namadus who would take control of everything once she left. Her father, despite being king, was simply to mad to maintain the support of the people.

The realization didn't change anything.

Her father stood before her, breathing heavily, with his eyes glazed over. She wondered what he thought about in his times of silence. She wasn't even sure he knew.

Suddenly, her father began to shake violently. She took a step closer, wary of how he would respond when he came out of the seizure. He just kept shaking. He frothed at the mouth and his arms flailed. He looked like a grotesque animal being tortured.

His pain couldn't matter to her anymore. She couldn't waste the time trying to help him. He'd committed too many atrocities, hurt too many people, killed too many people. *Sylvia.*

His body stopped shaking and Amaleah stopped walking towards him. He still didn't move towards her or give any sign that he recognized her. It was difficult to tell in the darkness, but she had the strange sense that he was staring right at her without really seeing her at all.

"Father?" she said, her voice plaintive. "Father, can you hear me?"

He didn't respond. *If I could just see his face.*

Warily, she reached towards the torch hanging from the castle wall. Her father didn't move or speak. She lit the torch and her father's face became illuminated.

It was completely slack. She had never seen a face reflect so little emotion before. He barely blinked in the blinding light cast by the torch.

"Father?" she said again. Still, he didn't respond, didn't move.

I have to keep going.

Inching her way past him, Amaleah prayed that the flowy material of her dress wouldn't touch him. The space between him and the walls of the stable and the palace were so narrow that she barely had room to fit. She could smell the putrid scent of his sweat and cologne as she made her way past him.

His head followed her movements and she nearly froze. Her heart hammering in her chest, Amaleah convinced herself to keep going. She was almost to the other side of him when he reached out in a sudden motion, grabbing her arm in the process.

"Amaleah," he whispered once before his body convulsed in a supremely violent way. His shaking shook Amaleah as he continued to hold onto her arm. She could already feel the bruises forming beneath his fingertips. Her teeth chattered and she just barely managed to keep a hold of the torch as he jolted her about.

Finally, the shaking stopped.

"You are mine." His voice held no emotion. *Oh Father,* she thought, *do you even realize what you're doing?*

His hand was still clutching her arm. She tried, gently, to extricate herself from him but couldn't wriggle her way out of his grasp.

"You will always be mine."

She took a step back, extending her arm to its furthest reach away from him.

"Father, please," she said plaintively. "Don't do this. Just let me go."

He sneered. "Let you go?" he said quietly and then, "Let you go!?" He shouted the words forcefully. "I let you go once. I could never survive that again."

His eyes seemed sad, lost in memories that Amaleah couldn't share. Her heart ached for him, but she couldn't concede to his desires. She wouldn't give up.

In a split decision, Amaleah thrust the torch she was still holding at her father's feet. The cloak he was wearing immediately began to burn as she twisted her body around and kicked him in the leg. He grunted but didn't let go of her arm. He didn't seem to notice the flames creeping up the side of his body. Amaleah could smell the melting fabric and another, underlying scent that made her stomach turn.

"Don't you remember how much you loved me, Orianna?" his voice trembled as he spoke.

"I'm not Orianna!" Amaleah enunciated each of the words with force. She felt a warmth growing in her belly as she thought about how enraged she was at the pathetic man standing before her. Fathers were supposed to protect their children, to love their children without thought of themselves. They were supposed to help their children succeed. He hadn't done any of these things. He'd exiled her, forced her to enter into a betrothal she didn't want, and killed her oldest companion. He had destroyed her happiness.

The warmth bubbled up through her uncontrollably. Both the conch shell and the fae tattoo blazed on her skin and began to glow a silvery-white color. They seemed to whisper encouragement to her as she slowly raised her free hand.

The tattoo pulsed on her skin. Suddenly, she knew what she needed to do. Amaleah pushed her hand towards her father's body in one, powerful thrust.

The world around her exploded.

Amaleah quickly dropped her hand, dazed from the brilliance of the light and the force of the blast. She watched in awe as her father, releasing her arm, shot through the air like a rag doll being tossed into the sky. The fire at their feet extinguished as the gust of wind caused by the blast passed through it. The blast shook the castle walls. Stones crumbled and fell. A chasm formed between where her father had just stood and where Amaleah currently stood. The hum of power slowly dissipated and the vibrations from the blessings disappeared. Her thoughts jumbled as she tried to connect the pieces of what had just happened.

After several moments, Amaleah realized that she could run, her father was nowhere to be seen. For the first time, she was free.

Chapter Forty-Four

Colin jolted awake from a cold blast of wind that passed over his body. He heard stone cracking all around him. Glancing around, he realized that he was alone. Both Starla and the girl in the yellow dress were gone. *How am I still alive? Where is Starla? And the girl in the yellow dress?* His head pounded. He couldn't quite remember what had happened. *How did I end up on the floor?*

His men, he needed to get back to his men.

Jumping to his feet in a state of dizziness, Colin walked as quickly as he could down the corridor in the direction he hoped his men would be in. He didn't remember which way they were.

Lunameedian nobles huddled in groups in the hallway. Their nervous chatter made Colin's head pound even more than it already was. He paused. *Why are they still here? Should I be afraid of them?* They didn't seem like they would be a threat, but then again Starla had seemed like an innocent little girl. He still had four—or was it three? —charges left in his healing medallion. He remembered that he'd hung it around his neck. Silently he reached up and ensured the medallion was still there. The cold metal of the device slid into his grasp.

He sighed in relief.

He began walking through the throng of people. They turned away from him as he passed. They shielded their faces with their hands. Colin wondered about this but kept going. He tried to remember military strategy. *What does someone do if they have an enemy behind their walls?* They'd fake an attack and kill as many of that enemy's men as possible. They'd kill that enemy if they got the chance.

What had Starla said as she'd stabbed him? 'You have been cleansed.' Colin wasn't sure what he needed to be cleansed of, but he was certain that whatever punishment Starla believed Colin deserved, there was still more to come. *For that matter*, he thought, *why didn't she kill me when she had the chance?* His memories came back to him in a rush. He had tried to save the girl in the yellow dress. Starla had been there, but they'd knocked her out. The girl in the yellow dress had betrayed him. *Why did women always betray him?* She'd hit him on the head and left him for dead. *How am I still alive?* His head continued to ache.

Colin refused to let thoughts of Vanessa cloud his mind. It was hard to keep them at bay. She had been the first woman to betray him. He was certain, now, that she would not be the last. Tears stung his eyes as the pain of her betrayal swelled within him, as if for the first time. He yelped in a muffled voice as he tried to contain himself.

A nobleman in a fur-lined cloak came up to him. "You are Colin of Szarmi, yes?" the man said in a heavily accented voice. Colin found it difficult to understand the man's words through the haze in his mind, but understood what he was asking him through the hand gestures the man had used. He tried to recognize the accent, but he didn't believe he had ever heard it before. *Who is this man?*

"Yes," Colin responded, but he couldn't think of a better way to respond.

"You will come with me, Colin of Szarmi. There is much for us to discuss." The man began to walk away, clearly expecting Colin to follow. Colin hesitated, but only for a short second. He followed the man down the hallway.

They went quite a way before the man turned and waved his hand over a door. It unlocked with an audible click. Colin's stomach flipped. The man had just performed magic. A mixture of excitement and fear churned within him, making it even more difficult to think or breathe.

Colin had seen magic only once in his life. During one of his father's multiple attempts to bridge the divide between Szarmi and Lunameed, he had allowed King Magnus to send a caravan of magicians to Szarmi for a world bazaar. The royal family had attended, despite Vista's concerns. The magicians had eaten fire, created animals out of thin air, and flown. How Colin had wished that he'd been gifted with magical abilities the way the magicians had been. He loved watching them soar through the air, creating trails of glowing dust in their wake.

Every single one of the magicians had been murdered on the road back to Lunameed. His father had never been able to identify the culprit. There were still too many people in Szarmi who feared magic. It was the first time in Colin's life that he could remember feeling separate from his people. How could they hate something so much when he had been awed by it? How could a thing that seemed so good, be bad?

This one incident had ruined all the strides forward his father had been taking to resolve the remaining conflict between the two kingdoms. After a few skirmishes on the border that resulted in Szarmian deaths, the king had allowed the most anti-magic of his people to set up patrols along the border. Only Lunameedians who could prove that they possessed no magic were allowed to pass.

And now, here Colin was, with a real-life magician.

A woman in a fur coat and long dress stood by a small fireplace at the corner of the room. The man standing beside Colin waved his hand over the lock once more and Colin heard the pin latch into place.

"This is the man, the prince of Szarmi?" she asked in the same heavily accented voice as the man standing beside him.

Before the man could answer, Colin strode forward and stuck out his hand. "I am Colin Sammial Stormbearer, prince of Szarmi and the Forgotten Isles. I am quite pleased to make your acquaintance."

She did not take his proffered hand.

"We are in need of your services," she said firmly.

"Alright," Colin felt sweat bead on his forehead. *What do they want?* "I may be willing to help you, but first

I need to know who you are and what, exactly; it is that you think you need."

"We are the prince and princess of Dramadoon," the man said. He stepped around Colin to stand next to his sister.

"I've read about you!" Colin blurted out before he could stop himself. "You are quite famous in Szarmi. Tales of your magical prowess scare little children in their beds."

"You must be joking. We are not old enough and have not accomplished enough in our young lives for there to be tales about us," the man's voice was stern.

"You may look young, but, if the rumors are true, you are not young at all. You've been alive since the Golden Days right after the Third Darkness. I've read about the pair of you. You're older than you look." Colin's thoughts seemed to clear the more he spoke to the siblings.

The brother and sister laughed in unison.

"It has been a long time since anyone outside of Dramadoon pieced together that we are the same Saphria and Freddy from the bygone days as we are today. Most assume that we are descendants of the first Saphria and Freddy, but we are not. We have lived through the ages in the hopes that one day a time would come that would heal the rift in the magical world."

They stared at him with blank eyes.

"And you think that time is now?"

They laughed again and Colin had the distinct sensation that they were mocking him. He opened his mouth to speak, but the woman began speaking.

"Of course that time is now. The world is in a state of destruction. Did you not see what happened here tonight?" the woman asked. "My brother and I were responsible for part of the bloodshed, but not all of it."

Colin nodded. He had first-hand experience with at least one of the other murderers. He'd nearly died at her hand.

"We fear that this is only the beginning. We have heard rumors that the Island Nations intend to war against the rest of Mitier if we are not able to stabilize our kingdoms. We have been at a stalemate for too long, Prince Colin. It is time for us to act, I think," the man, Freddy, continued.

"And you think I should play a role in this fate as well?"

"It has been written that you will play a role," the woman, Saphria, stated mysteriously.

Colin paused at this. Superstitious beliefs about fate and prophecy were as much a part of magical lore and culture as practical thought and trial and error were part of the Szarmian way of life. He couldn't fault them for their beliefs.

"What role do you believe I will play?"

Saphria turned to look Colin in the eyes. He could tell that she was not accustomed to people challenging her ideas and thoughts. Her eyes narrowed as she peered into him.

"Your role will be great, Prince Colin. The path has already been set in motion. You will just need to choose to follow it."

"I don't know what you're talking about."

"You will understand one day. Until then, we believe that it is prudent for our two nations to discuss what our next steps will be."

"What?" Colin asked, shocked. "You want to discuss this now? Here, in a deserted room in our enemy's castle?" Colin infused his next words with as much sarcasm as he could muster, "I don't know if you realize this or not, but the entire castle is in chaos."

The brother and sister laughed in unison. "We know. We did help to create the chaos happening outside of this room, Prince Colin. This chaos provides the perfect opportunity for the three of us to discuss what will come next for our kingdoms, I think," Freddy responded.

"I see," Colin said. And what would you propose our kingdoms do to help each other? My people fear your magic."

"We know this."

"And yet you still believe that there is hope for our nations?"

"We do."

"But why? Why do you believe that we can mend the rift between our kingdoms now, after all this time? If anything, I think my people's hatred of magic has risen since the end of the Wars of Darkness."

"We know this, as well, Prince Colin."

They didn't exactly sound annoyed at Colin's speech, but they didn't sound enthralled by it either.

"And what do you propose we do?"

"We suggest that we come to terms with the feelings of our people and find a way to join forces. There is a force, a darkness, growing that I cannot explain," Saphria said. She trembled slightly as she spoke and her brother wrapped his arms around her. "I have been given the gift of foresight, Colin of Szarmi, and if what I have foreseen comes to pass, then none of us shall survive. Not Szarmi. Not Lunameed. Nor Dramadoon or even Smiel. The whole of Mitier shall be consumed."

Colin stood in silence for several moments. He felt numb as he contemplated Saphria's words. The whole of Mitier shall be consumed. It sounded to ominous to be true.

"Who is this great enemy that we will face?" Colin asked. He wasn't sure he believed the princess's prophecy.

"It is not who but what." She paused as he considered her words. "Have you ever considered where life comes from? Where magic comes from? Have you ever questioned what happens to us after death?"

Colin opened his mouth to respond to her questions, but she held up a hand and he stopped before he had begun.

"Our world is made up of two halves. Each with its unique abilities and powers. The Pool of Life and the River of Death. The Light and the Dark. Since the start of the Wars of Darkness, there has been an... imbalance between them. We used our magic to destroy one another and it has come back to destroy us. We were never meant to use our gifts to cause harm. Only to heal."

"But-" Colin began. This time, she just kept talking.

"But power corrupts and the hearts of men were turned to dark shadows of what they once had been. We are the children of the broken, Colin of Szarmi, and we must mend what has been broken."

"But if you can see the future, don't you already know if we will fail or succeed in this endeavor?" Colin finally asked.

"That's not how my gift works. I... catch glimpses of the future. I have feelings of what is to come. But they're not definite. They change as we change. Some glimpses may not happen for several years, while another may happen only moments after I see it. It is impossible to tell when the destruction of our world will occur. But I can promise you one thing: if we do not change what we are doing now, the world will end. And we will be the cause."

Colin reached for the healing medallion hidden beneath his shirt. He clasped the cold metal in his palm as he considered Saphria's words. He had never dreamed that he would be alive for the end of the world, but now that there was a possibility he would be, Colin felt only emptiness. He only had one person in his life that he wanted to be with at the end of days: Coraleen. The thought triggered him into action. All he wanted was to return home and see his sister.

"I will need time to consider."

His words hung in the air like an apple waiting to fall from its tree. The siblings looked at each other, and Colin got the sense that they were conversing without the use of words. Despite the warm fire burning in the hearth, Colin shivered. He had grown up being told magic was akin to devil worshiping, to murdering your own blood. And here he was, talking with two of the most renowned sorcerers in all of Mitier.

"Of course," Freddy finally said as he clapped his hands together. "Come. We will survive this night and live to speak of this another day."

Colin nodded in agreement but couldn't shake the feeling in the pit of his stomach that something was still wrong. His head still throbbed from where he'd been hit in the head. He hoped he would have enough clarity of mind to lead his people out of Lunameed and back to Szarmi.

Absently, Colin paced about the room. "I need to leave," he muttered to himself, "I need to find my men." He kept repeating these phrases over and over again.

"Prince Colin," Freddy said in this thick accent. "If you wish to leave, all you must do is ask."

Colin froze at Freddy's words. He hadn't even realized that he had been pacing or repeating the mantra inside his head out loud. He blushed, but nodded his head to indicate that he was ready to leave.

Without speaking, the other man waved his hand over the door's lock and Colin heard the distinctive sound of the lock popping out of place.

"Thank you," Colin whispered as he left room. "I'll be in contact with Dramadoon soon about my answer."

"Be sure that you do," the prince and princess of Dramadoon said reflexively.

Colin wandered down the hallway wondering at the things that had transpired throughout the night. He could barely believe that just moments before he had been in the same room as the prince and princess of Dramadoon. Hours before that he had been nearly murdered by a girl assassin. And he had met the girl in the yellow dress. Despite all of these things, he knew one thing for certain: Lunameed was no longer safe.

He quickened his pace as his fears from earlier resurfaced. His men, if they were still alive, would be waiting for him. Or searching for him. He didn't know which was worst. By the time he reached the set of doors leading into his and his men's rooms, Colin was sprinting. He didn't care that the few remaining Lunameedian courtiers stared at him as he passed. Sweat dripped from his brow as he reached out for the door.

He paused as his hand came to rest on the cold metal of the handle. *What if I find my men slaughtered on the other side?* Concentrating on the door itself, Colin forced himself to breath in and out. In and out. He needed to be calm.

Slowly, Colin pushed the door open. It seemed heavier than it had before, the solid wood pressed into his hand with its weight.

No candles had been lit, despite the late hour of the night, the room was only lit by the dim light filtering through the doorway. Colin's belongings were spread out over the floor. The sitting room couch had been overturned. Colin's mouth went dry as he looked through the door. For one fleeting moment, he thought he was too late.

And then he heard someone cough from within the room.

"Hello?" he called into the darkness.

"My Lord, is that you?" one of the guards, he thought it was Markus asked.

Colin let out a sigh of relief as he stepped into the room. His guards began lighting candles when they realized that their prince had returned to them. Colin counted the guards, three of them were missing—including Jameston.

"Tell me, where are the rest of the men?" Colin exclaimed.

"We were so worried, My Lord," one of the other soldiers said in a low voice, raw with emotion. "We've been sending out parties of men to search for you in rounds. So far only one party has gone missing."

The soldiers voice trailed off as he spoke.

Colin tapped his chin as he waited for the soldier to continue. When he didn't, Colin asked, "Who has gone missing?" Colin kept his voice steady, but knew that it would only do so much to conceal his fear. He waited for the soldier to confirm what he already knew.

"Lucas, Tyler, and... Jameston, My Lord," he said the last name with a catch in his voice. It was no secret how Colin felt about Jameston.

"I see," was all Colin could say as he sank onto the floor. He heaved in a heavy sigh. Either the group of men were lost to them or they had been delayed. Either way, they didn't have time to go searching for them. Not now, anyway.

Realizing that he was showing weakness in front of his remaining men, Colin leapt to his feet and began barking orders. They were to leave the castle as soon as possible. Colin explained what he had witnessed in the ballroom. He left out the parts about being stabbed by a girl and then being knocked out by another one. Instead, he just reminded them of the bodies they had seen when entering the capitol.

"We leave within the hour, with or without the remaining men." Colin said a silent prayer that Jameston would return to the room before the hour was up.

Chapter Forty-Five

Faer Forest, Lunameed

Amaleah fled through the trees. Branches scratched her face and clawed at her hair as she forced her way through the dense forestry. The fae tattoo vibrated on her leg. Somehow, she could feel him following closely behind her. She wanted to scream out, call for help, but she knew that any noise she made would just make it easier for King Magnus to find her. Fear enveloped her like an iron cage. It made her vision blur as she kept looking behind her to see if she could see him. She stumbled over rocks and tree roots as she continued to run. She ignored the pain they caused in her feet and legs.

She could already hear the hounds chasing behind her, following her scent. She dreaded their finding her. The torch she carried flickered in the darkest night she had ever seen. No stars shone. No moonlight lingered upon her face. Tears streamed down her cheeks as she thought of everything she was leaving behind. *I'm not ready,* she found herself thinking.

Suddenly, Amaleah's foot caught on an upturned root and she fell to the muddy ground. Pain shot through her knee as it landed on the hard, rough bark of root that had tripped her. She whimpered slightly as she half crawled, half pulled herself to a tall tree just a few feet away. Using the tree as a support, she staggered to her feet. She could feel the hot blood on her knee seeping down her leg from where she had fallen. Now that she had stopped moving, she could hear the thumping of her heart in her chest and the sounds of forest animals running through the treetops. Somewhere, an owl hooted in the night. Amaleah shivered as she realized how cold it was outside of the palace. It was even colder in the forest than it had been in the dungeons.

"You'll never escape me!" The voice rang in her head like a bell clanking and reverberating through the mountains: echoes that never stopped. Using what little strength she had remaining, she ran as fast as she could, chasing the relative silence of the forest.

"You promised me! You promised you'd always be mine. You can never escape. I will find you, Orianna, I will find you!"

The voice no longer echoed as much as it had earlier. *Surely, he can't be catching up with me.* Panic swelled within her as she forced her tired and aching legs to move even faster than they already were. She tried to remember the route that she and Sylvia had discussed. Thinking of Sylvia pained her greatly, but she needed to. She needed to remember what the wiser, older woman—tief—had told her. If she could just make it to the Serpiet River, and cross it, Amaleah was certain that her father wouldn't be able to find her.

This thought was the only thing that gave her hope as she continued to push forward. The blood running down her leg made her yellow dress cling to her body. She nearly stumbled again, but was able to maintain her balance this time.

She could hear him, breathing hard and struggling to push through the trees. But he was so close, closer than she had originally thought. She heard branches snap right beside her.

And then there was a bright flash of light followed by an intense, suffocating heat. The wood smoke stung Amaleah's eyes and made her cough as she came to an abrupt halt.

Fire.

Blue flames shot into the air all around her, but didn't seem to burn the forest. The fire blazed before her, cutting off her path. Cursing, Amaleah attempted to change course, but more fire sprang up all around her. The only place the flames didn't seem to be burning was the place she knew her father was standing. She could see him. Standing in the shadows, watching her struggle to find a way beyond the flames. The heat was sweltering. As she moved about, she could feel the flames licking her skin, leaving tiny blisters in their wake. The hair on her arms was completely singed off, and the smell of burning hair penetrated the air.

"You'll never escape me. You promised me, Orianna. You promised that you would never leave me. You promised that I wouldn't be alone," his voice cracked as he continued speaking, "I can't be alone again. Please, Orianna. You can't leave me. Not again."

His voice was pleading, like a child begging for a toy from one of the local shops his parents couldn't afford. He sounded so broken that Amaleah felt an urge to give in, to take away his pain.

But she couldn't take away his pain. Not while he continued to believe that she wasn't his daughter but rather his dead wife.

She watched in horror as the shadowy figure she knew to be her father began walking towards her. He completely disregarded the flames. He seemed to not feel their heat at all.

"Do you continue to defy me?" He didn't wait for her to answer. "I am more powerful than you can imagine. I alone control the magical world, even without magic of my own. And you, Orianna, will be at my side when we conquer the world. Together."

His face became illuminated by the flames during the last few words of his speech. It was twisted into a horrible scowl that made Amaleah cringe as she tried to step as far away from her father as possible without getting burned by the flames behind her.

"Do you know how I control these flames, Orianna?"

When she didn't answer, he continued, "I have friends within the fae, and they created these specifically for me." He gestured around them, as if she couldn't see the flames for herself.

Amaleah took another step back. She could feel the pressure of the heat pressing in on her. She would rather be consumed by the flames than concede to her father.

"You're mad," she whispered.

He laughed at her, a cruel, daunting laugh.

Then, in a voice Amaleah didn't recognize, her father said, "If you do not uphold your end of the bargain, Princess, you will be destroyed. We will destroy you."

We? Amaleah examined her father's face more closely. His eyes were glazed over like they were when he was having one of his seizures, but his body was not shaking.

He continued speaking in the strange voice, "You, who have not yet discovered your own power. You, who have attempted to thwart us at every opportunity. We sought to use you. To provide you with the gifts that only we can give-"

"You can give me nothing that I want," she said firmly, cutting her father off.

He blinked at her in surprise.

Amaleah thought about all the people her father had killed. She remembered the screams and the smell of burning flesh, and the tears she'd shed when the Baron and Nicolette Blodruth had been sent away. She remembered how isolated she'd felt during her exile and the look on Sylvia's face as she had been murdered. She remembered the pain in her own heart as she had seen her father destroy everything she had ever loved. Tears streamed down Amaleah's face as she stared at her father. He had been the harbinger of so much pain. *He won't stop. He will never stop.* Amaleah took a long, shuddering breath.

Making up her mind, Amaleah strode towards her father until her face was inches away from his. "You're weak, Father. And your weakness has only brought you— and everyone around you—misery. I can't be a part of this anymore. I can't be who you think I am."

With that, she slammed the small knife she'd strapped to her forearm into her father's gut. She felt the hot blood spill onto her hand and seep down her arm. His eyes bulged and he attempted to speak but gurgled on his own blood.

Wrenching her blade free Amaleah stepped away from her father. He fell to his knees, clutching at his wound.

"Goodbye," she cried out as tears once again streamed down her face. "I'm so sorry."

She turned and ran into the flames.

Chapter Forty-Six

The borderlands between Szarmi and Lunameed,
Two weeks after the massacre at the ball

Colin and what remained of his men trekked through the forest. They had been traveling for two weeks now but they didn't feel as if they had gotten any closer to reaching their destination: The Szarmian border. For the first three days, they had ridden their horses nonstop through the Encartia Forest until their horses were past the point of exhaustion. As the horses began dying, Colin had ordered that his men continue the journey home on foot. They piled their gear on the few remaining horses and tied them together as they passed through the trees.

The Lunameedian countryside was vastly different than the Szarmian one. Large rivers coursed through the landscape, cutting it into sections but also providing life. The land was lush, vibrant, and full of color. Szarmi, too, had rivers, but they were narrower. The plants were less colorful and vibrant. There were more hills and valleys in Lunameed. Colin and his men had only been walking for a few hours after dismounting from their horses before his men began to complain about being tired from walking through the hills.

But still, they carried on.

They needed to. They needed to escape this kingdom, this land where so many people had died.

Colin couldn't stop remembering that night. The screams. The blood on the floor. His own wounds, which had healed. The girl in the yellow dress. The royal siblings from Dramadoon. *Will I be able to convince my people to form an alliance with that magical kingdom?* Colin had his doubts. His people were less open minded to the world of magic than he would have liked. It had always troubled him that they were so comfortable killing innocent men, women, and even children if they suspected that they had magic in them.

Colin made a vow to himself that, once he was crowned king, he would stop the killings.

Colin's boots had begun pulling apart at the seams. His traveling clothes had been lost in the chaos of escaping the palace. None of his remaining shoes were designed to withstand as much walking as he and his men had been doing over the past week and a half. By the time they crested a hill and saw the tiny dots of light across a winding river, Colin had so many blisters on his feet that he could barely stand. He sighed in relief as they began their descent down the hill.

The guard post on the Lunameedian side of the border was dark and lifeless. Colin and his men could see the Szarmian outposts on the other side of the river. The red and black sigil of the Szarmian court was raised at half-mast. Colin found that odd. The last time he had seen the sigil at half-mast had been the day his father died. Men carrying power-loaded bows and crossbows milled about the small town. His men began talking excitedly among themselves as they prepared to cross the main bridge connecting Szarmi to Lunameed. They had been in this strange kingdom with its magical forces for too long and they were ready to return to their families.

The first thing Colin noticed as they approached the bridge that crossed the Arcadi River was that the Lunameedian blockhouse was in shambles. The wooden planks that served as the walls of the structure were so rotted that he could see through them in several places. It leaned to one side precariously. The second thing Colin noticed was how dark the Lunameedian side of the border was and how bright the Szarmian side was. He found it strange that Lunameed didn't have guards posted on their side of the river when Szarmi had an entire outpost on theirs. The third thing Colin noticed was how wide the bridge was. It had long, sturdy-looking wooden planks and iron-enforced pillars holding the bridge up.

Just before Colin set foot on the bridge, he peered back into the wilderness of the Lunameedian forest. His eyes settled on the path that he and his men had just taken and he prayed that Jameston and the other missing men would be able to follow their lead, that they would be able to make it home.

He also thought of Vanessa. This was the land she had come from. *No wonder she had been raised as an assassin,* Colin thought, *Lunameed is a brutal, barbaric place.* He touched his fingers to his lips and waved them out at the forests and hills of Lunameed.

"Goodbye," he whispered beneath his breath.

Sighing heavily, Colin took a step onto the bridge to lead his men home.

An arrow lodged itself into the wooden plank in front of Colin's feet.

"Who goes there?" a booming voice called out from within the Szarmian camp.

"Colin Sammial Stormbearer, prince of Szarmi and future ruler of the realm," Colin responded in as steady a voice as he could muster.

There was a long pause before the men on the other side of the bridge, the Szarmian side, began laughing loudly.

"You expect *me* to believe that *you* are the crown prince?" the booming voice asked.

Colin stared ahead of him silently fuming. His men looked at him with slightly bulging eyes. They were ready to be home, Colin knew, but how could he convince the captain of the border guard to let them pass? He wasn't sure.

"I am, the prince, sir. My men can attest to it."

His men shouted their agreement in rushed voices. The captain didn't say anything for a long moment, but then, just as Colin was beginning to lose hope, he responded, "It is too dark for us to determine who you lads are." His voice had lost its robustness. Colin thought that perhaps the captain had become fearful that he was mocking the true heir to the throne. He would be right, of course.

"Ya see, we can't risk letting magical folk into our kingdom. It wouldn't be right. So, how about you and your men stay at the Lunameedian inn just down the river about a quarter-mile distant? The innkeep there is a mighty fine fellow," he drawled, "and I'm sure he would take care of you."

Colin heaved a sigh of relief. They would have baths and pillows tonight. He could feel the tension leaving his men's bodies. Tomorrow they would be home.

"Fine," he rumbled, hoping that the captain would be able to sense his relief and frustration all at the same time. "Lead us to this inn."

The captain waved his torch and began leading Colin and his men to the inn from the other side of the river.

At the inn, Colin found the missing men from the Lunameedian border patrol. All twenty of them were sprawled about the various chairs and couches within the large, square front room. Their green and silver uniforms with a giant tree insignia on them were enough to stop Colin in his tracks as he approached the open door to the inn. He thrust his arm out to stop his men from going in and looked across the river reproachfully at the Szarmian captain. *When we are safely at home on the morrow,* Colin thought to himself, *that captain will learn a thing or two about ignoring an order from his future king.* Still, Colin trusted the man enough that, when he gave his signal that everything would be alright, Colin led his men into the smoky room.

Colin immediately began coughing as the pungent smoke from the soldiers' pipes filled his lungs. None of his soldiers seemed to even notice the smoke clouding the room. Colin supposed they had more practice with smoke than he did. He wouldn't be surprised if some of them even smoked, although it was strictly forbidden in Szarmi. Buxom women sat on the Lunameedian soldiers' laps. If the border patrol noticed that a group of Szarmian soldiers had entered the inn, they gave no indication. They just continued drinking their pints, kissing their women, and smoking their pipes.

Colin made his way to the wooden bar that stood at the far end of the room. He tried to keep himself from coughing as he walked as quickly as he could towards what he hoped would be an ally.

Colin stopped only a few feet away from the bar. His jaw dropped several inches before snapping back into place. The man behind the counter was the largest person that Colin had ever seen. He had big, broad shoulders that stretched the full length of three wooden barrels. He had a mop of dark hair on his head, but his bushy beard was a shade of red that Colin had never seen on a human's face before. His large, rotund belly hung over his legs like a boulder getting ready to fall from a mountain. The man's arm muscles bulged as he lifted a large keg from the floor and set it atop the bar. Colin was certain the man would be able to squash him into mush if he had the inclination. He was certain he didn't want to test this theory.

Walking a bit more timidly now, Colin approached the bar and set a small bronze coin onto the wooden table.

"What can I do you for?" the man asked in a surprisingly smooth voice.

"I need rooms for my men and me for the night. We need to be kept together. And, if possible, we need several baths drawn. We have been traveling on foot for the past week and a half and need to wash the grime of our travels away."

"So, you're an adventurer then?"

The question caught Colin off-guard. He had never thought of himself as an adventurer before. Sure, he enjoyed reading about the great adventurers of the past. His father had allowed him to read about the Lunameedian hero, Sir Kilian Clearwater, as a way to teach him about the merits of bravery and strength. Kilian's stories quickly became some of Colin's favorites. The legends say that he still lived, despite having rescued magical beings during the Second and Third Darkness over three hundred year ago.

Do the plights that my men and I faced while at the Lunameedian court make us adventurers? "Something like that," he said.

The innkeep nodded solemnly, "I used to be an adventurer like you, until I took an arrow to the knee." He paused. "Now all I do all day is run this inn."

He smiled broadly, revealing shiny white teeth.

Colin's men joined him at the bar as Colin asked, "What brought you to the borderlands?"

The innkeep filled several mugs of brown liquid and passed them out to Colin's men before responding, "I was born here. Originally I came back to take care of me mum before she passed. Now, The Red Heron is all I have left."

"So you're Lunameedian?"

"Born and raised. My family has lived on this side of the river for dozens of generations."

"I see." Colin contemplated the man's words.

"What brings you to the borderlands?" the jovial innkeep asked.

The question caught Colin off-guard. Should he tell the innkeep the truth? Making a split decision, Colin responded, "We're traveling home."

"So, you're Szarmian then?"

The innkeep's voice held no hatred in it, which surprised Colin. He had expected the Lunameedian people this close to the border to despise all things Szarmian.

"Yes, we are."

The innkeep nodded and gave Colin a look that made him feel as if the bigger man could see right through him.

"I hope your experiences in Lunameed have changed your people's perception of my country."

Colin thought about everything that he and his men had seen since coming to Lunameed. "Unfortunately, I doubt that our experiences have helped change my men's minds about this place."

The innkeep set down the mug he had been wiping clean and stared Colin straight in the eyes, "Then it will be up to you to change their minds."

Colin sipped at his beer quietly for several moments. He knew the huge man was right, but he wasn't sure what path he could follow that would change the beliefs of his kingdom without turning his people against him. The fear that held his people captive had been passed down for generations. The hatred of magic was so ingrained in them that many of them were unwilling to even listen to alternative ways of thinking.

"I'm Colin, by the way."

"It is nice to meet you. My name is Jeor Ansel."

"Jeor Ansel?" Colin said out loud before bursting out in a fit of laughter. "Your parents must have really disliked you!" He slapped his hand down on the counter of the bar.

"Or they knew that everyone would ask my name for the rest of my life," the innkeep laughed along with Colin. "No, mostly people call me Redbeard on account of my beard."

"That's a much better name than Jeor Ansel."

Redbeard nodded in agreement.

"So, tell me, if you had the ability to change the relationship between Szarmi and Lunameed, what would you do?"

"Well, assuming that I wanted to change the relationship between our two countries, the very first thing I would do is outlaw all the killing. Sure, people would be angry at this, and mighty fearful too, but once such a law is in place, our people will become more open to differences."

"And how would you enforce that? Would you kill anyone who broke the law?"

"No. Doing that would only generate more hatred and anger. No, I'd send them to a place where they can see that, despite our differences, we're really not that different at all."

Colin thought about his own ideas and plans he'd been working on to end the killings, at least on the Szarmian side of the border. After the events leading up to and at the ball, he wasn't sure any of them would work now.

The two men continued talking late into the night. Colin didn't leave the bar's counter until after all of his men and the majority of the Lunameedian border patrol had gone to their rooms for the evening. Colin wasn't for certain, but he felt like a spark of change had been planted in him during his conversation with the man named Jeor Ansel—Redbeard. He hoped he would be able to remember everything they'd discussed. He'd drunk enough to knock out a horse.

Chapter Forty-Seven

Faer Forest, Lunameed,

The night of the massacre at the ball

Amaleah's clothes were on fire as she dashed through the trees. The fire spread as her clothes touched their branches. She didn't stop running. Not even when the fire blazed so hot that she could smell her own hair burning.

She ran until she bent over, coughing. Her side ached as she tried to control her breathing. She couldn't stop, not now.

As she stood panting in the middle of the forest, she felt a single drop of water fall onto her nose. And then another one. And then there was a torrent of rain the likes of which Amaleah had never encountered before. Realizing that the rain might put the forest fire out, Amaleah began running again. She ignored the pain in her chest and sides.

She had been running for what felt like an eternity when the leg cramps started.

Slowing her pace to a crawl, Amaleah knelt to the ground as the muscles in her legs spasmed uncontrollably. It was only then that she realized that her clothes had stopped burning. There were holes in various places of her dress, but, other than a few blisters, her body had been left unmarred by the flames. She sighed heavily before slumping to the ground. She needed a plan, and quickly.

As she lay in the mud and leaves of the forest bed, Amaleah inspected the burn holes on her dress. The delicate material was charred a dark, black color. Any other time, she would have been devastated to have had such a beautiful dress damaged in this way. Now, all she felt was numb. She put her finger through one of the burn holes and wiggled her finger. The fabric, once smooth, was now rough. Sighing, she dropped the fabric and stared up into the treetops.

She wasn't sure if her father had survived the fire or not, but she didn't want to be waiting for him if he had. She tried to forget how his blood and covered her hands in hot, coppery liquid as she'd plunged her knife into him. She didn't know how he could have survived that, even if he had been able to survive the fire. Tears stung Amaleah's eyes. Everything she'd planned for—everything Sylvia had helped her with—had been for nothing.

Thoughts of Sylvia brought burning tears to Amaleah's eyes. She punched the ground as hard as she could so that she would have a different type of pain to focus on. Her knuckles were scratched from the rocks and tree branches cluttering the ground, but that was all. She couldn't even hurt herself properly. How was she supposed to escape her father, rescue her kingdom, and rule happily ever after?

The leg cramps passed.

As Amaleah stood to begin traveling again, she noticed that the holes in her yellow dress had become completely mended. Tentatively, she traced her fingers over the area of the dress where the charring had occurred. Only smooth, golden silk remained.

The fae, she thought. Scrambling, Amaleah pulled the coat of many furs out of her sack and wrapped it around her shoulders. It smelled of the smoke and fire but didn't have any other marks on it. *I may as well wear this. Its very existence is one of the reasons I'm in this predicament.* Sighing, Amaleah began to wander through the forest. She was cold. And hungry. And alone.

Amaleah had never been alone before. Even in her sleep, a servant had been just outside the door, in case she needed something. Even at Maravra's Tower had been full of people bustling around to ensure her comfort. Whenever she had ever needed someone to converse with, there was always someone there. The rain stopped so suddenly, Amaleah didn't realize how much noise it was making until there was only silence.

And now the silence was deafening. She tried paying attention to the sound of the trees as their leaves rattled in the wind and the animals scurrying around in the brush. But it all sounded so unfamiliar to her. She was used to the patter of feet on marble floors and the whispers of servants as they chatted amongst themselves when they thought no one else was around.

Amaleah contemplated her situation. All she had was a small knapsack in which she'd packed a loaf of bread, some nuts and berries, and a skein of water. She knew that before long, she would run completely out of her supplies. She had a small amount of jewelry packed with her, but it wouldn't be enough to barter for longer than a few months.

She would need to find work, and quickly.

That's when she remembered his name: Prince Colin of Szarmi. Soon to be crowned king over the land to the south. His father had been dead for three years and he was about to turn twenty-one, the age of adulthood in Szarmian culture. He was said to be very kind and generous. He had taken care of Szarmian's beggars by providing a means for them to become employed within the government. Amaleah had read that he had brought clean water to the desert regions to the eastern region through his irrigation system. Perhaps she should travel south, to Szarmi. *It was what Sylvia wanted*, she reminded herself.

Swinging her bag over her shoulder, Amaleah changed directions. She had never traveled south before and was unsure how to get there, but she trusted her memory of the maps she had studied during her sessions with her tutor. She was so busy looking up, trying to catch glimpses of the sky between the treetops, that she didn't pay attention to the ground she was walking on.

Her foot caught on an upraised tree root, spraining her ankle as it twisted in the wrong direction. Amaleah crashed onto the soft ground beneath her. Mud squished into her mouth and nose as she tried to breathe. Dead leaves clung to her now-damp dress. The coat of furs remained dry and clean. *The fae, the fae must have made the coat as well.* Just like everything else that her father had enlisted them to make in the past, the coat was enchanted so that it didn't have any scorch marks from the fire or any dampness from the rain. She looked down at her dress. The scorch marks and holes had repaired themselves. Her dress made to represent the sun was now whole again.

Sylvia had tried to warn her, tried to tell her that the court of the fae was tumultuous and changed on a whim. They had blessed her, and then they had ruined her, all within a year. Or maybe the fae had been unaware of her father's true intentions. After all, they had been friends of her mother's family. She had been raised by one of their own. *Hadn't she?* Yet, they betrayed her. *Or had they?* At this point, Amaleah wasn't sure what she believed.

She continued to lay in the mud. What she wouldn't do to be with the fae now. At least then she would be someplace warm and dry where she could ease her mind and remove her coat without fear. She wanted to be safe again. *I doubt I will ever truly be safe again.*

Tears rolled down her face as Amaleah pushed herself against a tree and huddled closer to herself. Wrapping the fur coat tighter around herself to block out the damp and rainy world, Amaleah let herself cry in a way that she had refused to while she had been in Estrellala. She couldn't stop the tears from coming as they mixed with the rain. Her eyelids began to droop and her head lolled, but still she tried to remain awake. The thought of wild animals didn't scare her, but the idea that her father would find her did. She couldn't afford to let her guard down, not even to rest.

She tried to stand and couldn't. Her ankle was so swollen that she could feel it pressing against her boot. Settling closer to the tree, Amaleah tried to keep her eyes open as she contemplated what she was going to do next.

A light twinkled in the distance and began growing closer as Amaleah watched it, a fire in the night. As it drew closer, Amaleah could tell that it was swinging in the wind, or with the gait of the being who carried it. She thought about trying to hide behind a group of ferns nearby, but didn't think that she would be able to make it without further injuring herself.

Praying that it wasn't her father's men, Amaleah made a decision.

"Help me," she called out in a voice so small she wasn't sure the person holding the lamp would be able to hear her.

The light came to a stop and started moving towards her at an unnatural pace. Amaleah's senses heightened as she saw a cloaked figure stop a few paces away from her. It was only one person, not an army, not her father's men. Relief washed over her as she waited for the person to come closer.

The person pushed the hood back away from her head, revealing a small, hunched woman beneath its folds. As the woman came closer, Amaleah realized how short she actually was. Barely the height of the bushes her father had planted in the gardens back in Estrellala, Amaleah estimated her to only be about three and a half feet tall. At first, Amaleah thought that perhaps the woman was really a child, but, as she stepped closer Amaleah could see that the woman had pure white hair that was frizzled on top.

As the woman peered into her face, Amaleah noticed how wrinkled the woman's face was. Her wide eyes held wisdom in them that Amaleah only hoped to gain by old age. She instantly trusted the old woman, although she couldn't quite pinpoint why.

"You are not what I was expecting." The old woman's voice was raspy and deep, not what Amaleah had been expecting either.

"I am sorry to disappoint you." She wanted to stop there, but continued, "My name is Amaleah, and I am seeking refuge within the forest. I… was… trying to find my way to Szarmi. But I think I took a wrong turn or… I don't know. And I was trying to remember which star cluster to follow when I fell. I think I've twisted my ankle. I don't think I can walk."

Amaleah's stomach lurched as she spoke. She was helpless, alone, and injured. And now that she had spoken, she had given this old woman all the means she needed to turn Amaleah back over to her father. What a fool she had been.

The old woman regarded her tentatively. She began mumbling to herself as she set the lamp down and began rummaging through a small pack she carried on her back. Finding what she was looking for, the old woman flipped her wrist absentmindedly and Amaleah shot into the air. Amaleah yelped in surprise, anticipating a fall that never came. She hovered a few inches above the ground.

"How did you-" she began but then stopped as the old woman turned away from her and began walking. Amaleah's floating body followed the lamp into the foggy darkness of the forest.

"That's an interesting coat you have on. Are you trying to steal the souls of the animals that you had killed to create such a monstrosity? You know this is what many people do when they slaughter the innocent. Or are you simply so in awe of our wildlife that you wish to be one of them?" There was no hint of sarcasm in the woman's voice, only anger.

"No. It's not like that at all. You see, my father he... well, he..." Amaleah trailed off as she tried to find the right words to express how she was feeling and what she was thinking. "He gave me no other choice than to challenge him to make something that I didn't think could be made. This coat was the result." Amaleah flushed even though the old woman wasn't looking at her. She didn't understand why she couldn't keep from telling this woman everything that she was thinking.

"What could he have possibly done or asked for that would have made you want to murder the innocent?"

Amaleah's heart began thumping wildly in her chest. "I didn't. I... didn't know. I didn't understand what my request would entail." Amaleah felt tears pooling in her eyes, "I just wanted to escape."

The little old woman didn't ask any more questions of her, for which Amaleah was incredibly grateful. She didn't know if she would be able to continue holding back her tears if she had to think about the past and the actions she had taken in order to be free from her father. Thankfully, the woman appeared to be content walking in silence.

Amaleah had no idea where they were within the woods. Her ankle was throbbing and she was having difficulty paying attention to anything else other than the pain. She knew she was cold, and damp. Despite the coat's magical properties to repel water, the dampness had soaked in through her hair and the bits of clothing left unprotected by the coat.

They reached a small clearing in the woods where a rather large tree stood. Over the sound of the rainfall, Amaleah could hear a river rushing nearby, engorged by the heavy rains. The old woman let Amaleah gently fall to the ground as she bent over to tap five times in different locations upon the trunk of the tree. A door appeared and swung open, revealing a short corridor with many closed doors within.

Reaching down, the old woman brushed her fingertips over Amaleah's ankle. The pain receded almost immediately. Amaleah gasped as coldness seeped into her. She hadn't realized just how cold she actually was.

"Watch your head," the woman said as she motioned for Amaleah to follow her.

She tucked her head deep into her chest as they entered the small hallway.

"I'll set you up in one of the guest quarters. Someone will be in shortly to examine your ankle."

They walked down the hallway. There were so many closed doors; Amaleah wondered what lay behind them. The pain in her ankle was dull, but still present. Amaleah found herself wondering who the old woman was and how she made the pain dissipate so quickly. Just like before, Amaleah couldn't control herself.

"May I ask you a few questions?"

"You have already started. I don't see any reason to stop you from continuing." The woman's voice held no humor in it, but neither did it sound irritated. Amaleah found it quite difficult to determine what exactly the older woman was feeling.

"Alright. I have told you my name, but you have yet to tell me yours. And… forgive me if you find this rude, but you're so short. Are you a tief?"

Chuckling, the woman responded. "Those are all questions that will be answered in time. But for now, you need to rest."

Frustration flashed through Amaleah. *Didn't she just say that she would answer my questions? Why is it that everyone I encounter wants to be so helpful but they never tell me anything that might actually be helpful?* she fumed. First Cordelia, then the fae, and now this little old woman, none of them had been very helpful.

Opening one of the doors near the end of the hallway, the little woman led Amaleah into a well-lit room. A full-size bed ran lengthwise next to a tall window. Several plush chairs were scattered about the room, each with their own side table and lamp. Overflowing bookshelves were lined against the walls. There was a single picture hung on the wall, but it was shrouded in black fabric. Amaleah couldn't tell who was in the picture. A roaring fire glowed in the ornate fireplace in the center of the room. It was the most decorative piece of the entire space.

Amaleah felt at peace.

"Someone will be in shortly. Rest now," the woman said as she began to leave the room.

Amaleah dropped her knapsack on the floor and let the fur coat fall from her shoulders. The last thing she remembered was drifting over to the bed and lying upon the soft covers of the bed.

Chapter Forty-Eight

Amaleah opened her eyes. Droplets of water cascaded onto her face from the banisters above her head. She could smell rain and hear the pattering of the drops onto the ceiling above her. Tossing the covers to the floor, she looked up at the picture with the black covering more closely. If she squinted a little, she thought she could see through the fabric that the picture was of a woman. Gently, Amaleah tugged at the black shroud. It slid away from the painting as easy as melting butter.

She gasped.

It was her mother.

The picture was stunning. Her mother was even more stunning. Her glossy, luscious, mahogany hair fell in curls down her back. People who had known her mother had talked about the gold flecks subtly imbued in her mother's hair, just as in her own hair. The artist had captured the gleam the gold had given to the dark, auburn locks. The deep violet of her eyes looked supernatural as they peered out of the portrait with a penetrating look. They made Amaleah feel as if her mother were right there staring her down. It made Amaleah shiver.

She had inherited her mother's beauty.

And it was her curse.

Amaleah contemplated why the little woman in the woods had a picture of her mother. Little was known about her mother's past and there were multiple, conflicting stories about who her mother was and how she came to be queen. That didn't explain why her mother's portrait was hung in a magical tree in the middle of the woods. The portrait depicted her mother as a young woman, younger than any of the portraits Amaleah remembered seeing in the palace. Yet, she was featured in a royal purple dress with opals and diamonds studding the bodice. Those were not the clothes of a poor servant. *What is this?* Amaleah thought as she stared up at the portrait.

A creaking noise from the opposite side of the room startled her. She jumped slightly as she turned towards the bedroom's door. As she shifted her body a pain shot through her ankle. She inhaled sharply and held her breath to stop herself from crying out.

"Good. You're awake," a crackly voice said in the dark.

The same squat woman that had rescued Amaleah the night before came over to her bed. She smiled wanly and placed a cold, rough hand on Amaleah's forehead.

"Did you sleep well? Armos didn't wake you as he changed the bandages, did he?"

Confused, Amaleah asked, "Who's Armos?"

"He is one of our brethren."

The old woman motioned for Amaleah to sit atop the bed. She complied and the woman pulled up the bottom of Amaleah's skirts to inspect her ankle. She clucked her tongue as she looked at Amaleah's wound. "This bandage needs changed again." She mumbled under her breath as Amaleah looked on.

Finally, the woman responded to Amaleah's question, "He's the one who bandaged this ankle. I'm not sure how you were able to pop it out of place, but it was in total ruins when Armos put a healing hand on it."

Amaleah nodded but remained silent. She stared blankly at the strange little woman until her guest sat down on her bed and took her hand.

"My dear, you are an odd creature, aren't you?" She clucked her tongue again. Amaleah had the distinct impression that the older woman was trying to annoy her. She was certainly doing a great job.

Ignoring the woman's question, Amaleah pointed at the picture of her mother and asked, "Why do you have this?" Her voice was firm, but only just. She could feel her body tremor slightly as she spoke.

The woman eyed her curiously without looking at the portrait. She chuckled slightly to herself, but Amaleah didn't understand what the old woman found so humorous.

"What's so funny?" She yanked her hand away from the woman, "Why won't you tell me why you have a portrait of my mother? Who are you?"

Her voice rose in anger as she spoke, but the older woman appeared not to notice.

Speaking calmly, the woman responded, "All of your questions will be answered in time. For now, you simply need to trust that you are safe, Amaleah."

"Safe?" Amaleah scoffed. "You have me trapped here. How do I know that you haven't alerted my father to my whereabouts?"

"Your father?"

"You must know who I am since you have a portrait of the dead queen, the person I am meant to replace: my mother."

"You simply need to trust that we do not intend to harm you."

"But you're not willing to tell me anything!"

"You will know what you are meant to know in due time, Amaleah."

"Well, I don't trust you, and I don't think that you're keeping me safe." Amaleah wasn't sure that she actually meant the words she said, but she couldn't stop herself from saying them. Between her father's insanity, the intrigues she'd faced at court, and the danger she'd faced in escaping the palace, she didn't think she could truly trust anyone anymore.

Clucking her tongue yet again, the old woman continued. "You must decide to have faith, my dear."

Reaching into her dress, the woman rummaged through a sundry assortment of items before finally pulling out a tiny black box covered in delicate silver writing.

Amaleah peered closely to try to make out the miniscule script. The writing was cramped and written in an ancient form of the fae language. As Amaleah continued looking at the box, she realized that the lines of writing were moving across the box. The letters shimmered slightly as they changed position.

The woman spoke to the box in a quiet, hoarse voice. Her lips barely moved and Amaleah was unable to hear her words. Amaleah wasn't sure what to expect. The box was one of the most ornate objects she had ever seen, and it was also the strangest. Surely the moving letters indicated that the box was protected by magic. She was certain that whatever was inside of it would be spectacular. Slowly, the older woman undid the small clasp and she opened the box.

Amaleah exhaled a breath she didn't know she'd been holding. Inside the box was a small, dusty silver locket. Heart shaped, the locket was inscribed with the same style of writing that had been on the box. The old woman delicately picked up the locket and cradled it in her weathered hands.

"You must complete the task that has been given to you as your destiny, my child."

Her voice was somber and Amaleah detected a note of reservation, but she wasn't sure why. She didn't have a destiny. She had herself.

"I don't know what you mean."

The woman didn't answer. Instead, she opened the tiny heart, revealing a miniature vial of sparkling purple liquid and a picture of Amaleah's mother. The woman stared lovingly at the picture of the late queen. Amaleah barely noticed the woman as she gently stroked her mother's picture, instead focusing her attention on the vial of liquid. She had never seen anything that was such a vibrant shade of purple. The liquid sparkled every time the woman moved her hand.

"You must take this with you." The old woman snapped the locket shut, hiding the picture and vial again, and thrust the cold metal into Amaleah's hands. "Go to Szarmi. Deliver it to the Lonely Soul. Restore peace to the land." The older woman's voice shook, making it more difficult for Amaleah to understand her already-gravelly tone. "You must make him drink from the vial. He must do so voluntarily. Only then will the Light return to our world."

The woman shuddered slightly as her words faded into silence. Amaleah sat, stunned. The words made no sense to her. *Who is the Lonely Soul and why does he need to drink from the vial?* she thought as she regarded the woman in front of her.

The older woman was breathing raggedly and Amaleah once again found herself wondering who the woman was and how she knew so much about Amaleah's mother and, apparently, Amaleah's future.

"I'm sorry, but I simply don't understand. What is in the vial? Who is the Lonely Soul? How will I know him?" She looked at the older woman, her voice trembling. "And how am I supposed to get to Szarmi? I have very few resources, and what resources I do have left have the potential to reveal me."

The woman just smiled at Amaleah as the young princess spoke. Amaleah found the woman's demeanor incredibly agitating.

She was about to say as much when the woman patted her on her arm and said in a slow, steady voice, "Amaleah, I have known you since before you were born. I have watched you grow up in the absence of your mother. I have seen you struggle. And, unfortunate as it is, your struggle is not yet over. The fate of your kingdom, indeed, the fate of all of Mitier rests on you. The very heart of the magic that binds us all is in danger of collapsing. We need-"

The woman suddenly stiffened. Amaleah watched in horror as the woman's hands flung up to her chest and she began shaking wildly.

Reaching out, Amaleah tried to stop the woman from hurting herself. She wasn't sure she was succeeding. Her heart beat rapidly as she tried to think of something to do to help the woman. Fear consumed her, making her body sweat and her hands feel numb. Dumbfounded, she watched the awful scene unfold before her.

The tremors subsided as quickly as they had begun.

The old woman continued talking as if nothing had occurred. "You. We need you to be the savior, the Harbinger."

Amaleah stared at the woman in confusion. *Did I just imagine the violent shaking and tremors?* She wasn't sure. Her mind was too muddled by what the woman was saying to comprehend the things happening all around her.

Timidly, Amaleah asked, "Why me?"

"Because of who you are."

"And who am I?"

The woman half-smiled, "Not even I can tell you that. You must discover that for yourself."

Nothing the woman said made sense to Amaleah. If she was needed for something because of who she was but she didn't know who she was supposed to be, then how was she supposed to accomplish whatever it was she supposed to do? Her head began to ache.

"But you knew my mother?"

The woman sighed heavily but answered, "Yes. I was one of the five who raised her."

Amaleah's heart skipped a beat. The woman before her looked so ancient that Amaleah wasn't sure that the woman was remembering things properly.

"I had heard that my mother grew up in the streets of Estrellala," Amaleah said.

The woman chuckled at that. "Your mother was a very clever woman and knew that if the common folks of Estrellala believed that she was one of them that they would be more accepting of her marriage to your father."

Amaleah paused, considering the woman's words. "But then, where did she grow up?"

"Why here, of course." She said as if it was the most obvious thing in the world. "With five of the Elite." The woman dropped her head, "We are all that is left of our order."

Amaleah didn't know what to think, or feel. She only felt numb. She hadn't known anything about the woman who had died giving birth to her.

Pinching herself hard, Amaleah continued the conversation, "How did she come to be in the palace? Why not tell the truth? Who are the Elite?" Questions poured out of her more quickly than Amaleah thought imaginable. The woman did not seem perturbed.

"I believe that is enough storytelling for the day. There will be plenty of time for that later." She rubbed her hands together, "Come, child, it is time to get dressed."

Her words were not said unkindly, yet Amaleah couldn't shake the feeling that the old woman was hiding something incredibly important from her. This was too much. How could she expect Amaleah to discover herself, to fulfill her supposed destiny, if she refused to answer even basic questions? This old woman was just as cryptic as Cordelia and Sylvia's sisters. At least Sylvia had given her some guidance on how to do what she was expected, but that was more than this old woman had done. *And she won't even tell me her own name.*

"You know, if you tell me your name, I can stop calling you 'the old woman' in my head." Amaleah's smirk was half sarcastic, half sincere.

"Of course," the woman tutted as she regarded Amaleah, "You may call me Helena."

With that, Helena went to one of the many bookshelves lining the room and retrieved a cloth-bound book. She stroked the cover gently before extending it towards Amaleah.

"This book, this diary, was written by your mother before she left the Elite. As she was leaving, she told me that her greatest wish was that one day one of her children would come to this place and learn about the ones who had raised her." Helena paused, her eyes damp. "And here you are." She wiped at her eyes, "Come now. The others will be gathering, and they wish to meet you."

Helena's squat legs trembled as she made her way towards the door in order to give Amaleah a measure of privacy as she changed. Amaleah fingered her mother's diary and the small locket.

"Helena?" Amaleah's voice came out squeaky.

"Yes, my child."

"What does the vial do?"

"That, my child, will be revealed when you have found the Lonely Soul." With that, Helena opened the small door and exited the room. Amaleah sat on the bed, clutching her mother's belongings.

After several moments of sitting in silence, Amaleah gingerly opened her mother's diary. Tiny drawings lined the margins. The miniscule pictures of fae and flowers made Amaleah smile. *She must have been whimsical.* Silver writing was scrawled across the page. The letters were a mix of Lunameedian and Fae. Amaleah tried to understand what her mother said, but the mixture of her native language and that of the fae was too perplexing.

Skimming through the pages, Amaleah found one that was written entirely in Lunameedian.

I fear that I will never escape this curse. Not that I do not enjoy living with Helena and the others. I do. It's just that they are always telling me that I have some greater purpose in life. That I have much to give back to Mitier. I am supposed to believe them, to believe that I am the Chosen One, the Mother. But the truth is that I am just like everyone else: ordinary. It's as if they see the prophecy and not me, as if they see the child I will one day bring into the world but not me.

I am more than the prophecy. I have my own story to share with the world. I just hope that if I ever do fulfill my prophecy to bring a baby into this world that she will realize that she is so much more. She will be the Harbinger of the Light. But she will also be my daughter. She will be so much more than a prophecy. I just pray that she's strong enough to see it.

Amaleah let the book fall from her hands in shock. *What destiny... what prophecy was my mother speaking about? What curse?* Amaleah's mind clouded with questions. She needed to know what her mother meant. She needed to talk to Helena. To try to find out more.

A light tapping on the bedroom door interrupted her thoughts.

"Come in," Amaleah said.

A wizened and stooped old man entered the room. He was so tall that, even hunched as he was, his head grazed the ceiling.

"Ahh, good. I see my patient is awake." He smiled broadly. "How are you feeling?"

Amaleah stared at the man, dumbfounded.

"My name is Armos," he said as he counted her heartrate. "Good, good," he mumbled as he transitioned to pressing in on the wound on her ankle. "Well now. Everything appears to be normal. But, no one can tell with these things when it comes to those who are strictly humans."

Amaleah looked at him incredulously, "Strictly humans?" she asked.

"Yes, well..."

"You're not human?"

"Well, no, not exactly. I am, as you may be able to tell of the half-human and half-giant variety of tief. Of course, you've already met my half-sister, Helena." He clucked his tongue, similar to the way that Helena had earlier. "Our father was quite the promiscuous one in his old age."

He sat down on the bed beside Amaleah and peered down at the open diary in her lap. His eyes were sad as he peered at her.

"It has been many years since we had a human living with us here in the Treehouse. Your mother was the last. She completed our little troupe here." He patted her hand, "Helena, Leah, Aristo, Castinil, your mother, and I made each other whole. Well, it was mainly your mother. She was the light that led us out of the darkness."

Amaleah counted the names Armos had recited. Six of them lived in this little house, including her mother. *What can they tell me about the late queen?*

"But, as it always is with magic, she was ripped away from us by her prophecy," Armos continued. "We miss her. We loved her. We kept in contact with her until the day she died giving birth... to you." He paused to let that settle in Amaleah's mind. "Even today, she occupies our thoughts. You will be the same."

"What do you mean?"

"You will be taken from us," Armos said this in such a matter-of-fact way that it made Amaleah shiver. "Before you are taken, we must prepare you, the best that we can, for the future, for your prophecy."

Her mother's words rang through Amaleah's head as she regarded Armos. Her mother had wanted more than the destiny that had been laid out for her. Clearing her throat, Amaleah asked, "And what if I believe that we can make our own destiny?"

Armos smiled at her words.

"You are your mother's daughter. It is my greatest hope that this will not be your fatal flaw, as it was hers."

Amaleah wasn't sure what to say in response to this, so she said nothing. Armos continued to pat her hand in a grandfatherly way that Amaleah wasn't quite sure she appreciated since she had only met the man a few moments before.

In an attempt to break the silence, Amaleah asked, "When will I get to meet the others? The ones you mentioned?"

"When the Gathering has been completed."

"What does that mean?"

"Soon."

Sighing in frustration, Amaleah leaned back on the bed. She hadn't changed yet, but she was in no rush to do so if she didn't know when she would need to leave. She would much rather have seen Armos leave so that she could continue reading from her mother's diary.

"Do you know where your name comes from?" Armos asked suddenly.

Amaleah peered at him. She had never been told the history of her name.

"Your name represented an entire generation... no, it's more than that... an entire history of Mitierian magic before the Wars of Darkness."

"Then why have I always been told that I am the first of my name?"

"Ah, that. Humans have a strange way of remembering the past. Amaleah—the first Amaleah—was a sorceress three hundred years before the First Darkness. She was a good one. The best, actually. She saved Lunameed, Szarmi, and Dramadoon from the Corzecos during a time of political unrest. After her reign, all of Mitier lived in peace. She was a hero above all others."

He peered into her eyes. "This name is your birthright. Didn't your tutors teach you anything?"

"My tutors did not speak of many things that had transpired before the Wars of Darkness. Of course, I've read the fae tales, but those are just children's stories told to help young ones sleep at night and encourage good behavior."

"How much you still do not see..."

Once again frustrated, Amaleah responded in a short, tense tone, "You should teach me if I do not understand."

"There is much you need to learn, child. And not enough time to provide you with the tools you'll need, I fear. We must prioritize that which is necessary."

"Understanding my birthright is necessary. Understanding the madness that has taken hold of my father is necessary. There are many things that are necessary, Armos."

"To you, perhaps. But to the survival of an entire population of beings? I think not."

His words struck a chord in Amaleah's chest. *What is it that they know and I do not?*

"Can you at least tell me more about the prophecy Helena spoke of?"

Armos's cheeks flushed, and he puffed out his cheeks, "She said what to you?"

Amaleah blushed. She wasn't sure what she had just done, but she knew that it was bad. Under Armos's direct gaze, Amaleah found it difficult to remember what she had heard from Helena and what she had heard from Sylvia and the rest. Gulping, Amaleah stuttered, "S-she told m-me that I had been mentioned in a prophecy." Amaleah paused. Then more confidently, she said, "I am the Harbinger of-"

"She should not have told you these things," Armos cut her off. "It was not her place. We have been forbidden."

"You sound like my nursemaid, Sylvia. Forbidden by whom?"

Sighing, Armos responded, "That I cannot answer, for it has been writ in the sacred vows we took upon entering the Elite. However, you will hear for yourself when the time comes. For all are called, few are chosen, and even fewer accept the challenge. The prophecies of which we speak do not always hold a flame. Everyone has a destiny, yet we are also given free will to choose our own course." He stared straight into her eyes, "I only hope that you will be ready to accept the challenge when the time comes for you to be tested."

"If I am to be told the prophecy about me in the future, then why can't you just tell me now?"

"I wish I could, Amaleah. But, every chosen path is something we must hear and choose alone. Your mother understood this. She weighed the options. She chose the correct path. In choosing to bear you, she chose to save the Light."

"What do you mean she chose to save the Light? The Light is everywhere. It is the lifeblood of all living things. It is in everything."

"No, Princess, it is not everywhere or in everything. Have you not noticed the changes? Have you not felt the breaking? The magic you speak of is dying every day. There are not many who are left who possess the power. Szarmi was the first of the kingdoms to forsake the Light and their persistent destruction of our world is destroying all that we know. It was the Szarmians who changed the course of the Borad River and turned Smiel into a desert. It was Szarmi who started the Wars of Darkness."

Armos tapped his finger on his cheek, thoughtfully. He sat silent for only a heartbeat before saying, "Others are following. Too many have been lost. The Light cannot shine when it has been snuffed out and I fear that this is the direction we are heading."

Armos stood up and went to stand by the fireplace, "You are our last hope."

He spoke so quietly that Amaleah wasn't sure she had heard him properly. *I can't be the last hope. Can I?*

She sank back into the pillows of the bed, pondering. She had always known that she would someday rule a kingdom—either her own land of Lunameed or her husband's. But as she thought about the words Armos had spoken and realized that the fate of all of Mitier could rest on her shoulders, Amaleah wasn't sure she wanted the prophecy to be about her.

Armos cleared his throat, "I will leave you now, Amaleah." Without looking back, he left the room, giving Amaleah time alone to contemplate his words.

Chapter Forty-Nine

The borderlands between Szarmi and Lunameed

Morning light poured into the room that Colin shared with two of his guards. They were snoring loudly, and Colin decided he didn't want to wake them. Once again, the men his mother had supplied him with hadn't performed their personal guard duties very well. Not a single one of them had been able to stay awake and take watch. He would be sure to reassign them to a different post once they were safely back in Szarmi.

Silently, he pulled on his linen undershirt and made his way down the stairs to the tavern of the inn. The room seemed completely empty. Colin peered around the room before walking behind the bar's counter and pulling out a glass and a large jug of water. Dropping a few mint leaves into his drink, Colin made towards the door of the inn.

"I wasn't expecting you to be up this early, Your Highness."

Startled, Colin spun around but didn't see anyone. Colin's head ached from the movement, and he felt his stomach lurch. How much had he had to drink last night? Stepping towards where he thought he heard the voice, he squinted against the bright light streaming in from the windows encasing the whole eastern side of the room.

"You had so much to drink last night that I would have figured you'd sleep through midmorning. Elsewise, I would have made breakfast for you already."

A shadow moved from one of the tables. Its lumbering form pulled away from the bench that Colin had thought it had been a part of.

"There's no need for that," he said amiably.

"'Course there is. You're the heir to the Szarmian throne."

Gears and levers! When had he told Redbeard that he was the prince of Szarmi? He couldn't recall the conversation ever coming up. He stopped dead in his tracks and backed away from the innkeep. The man had treated him with nothing but respect, but Colin still remembered the contempt he'd heard in the man's voice as he'd discussed his anger at the Szarmian border patrol's continued slaughtering of innocent Lunameedians. Colin knew all too well what anger could make people do.

"Why do you think I'm the prince of Szarmi?" It was a poor excuse at planting a seed of doubt in Redbeard's mind, but Colin felt he needed to try something.

"Oh, come off it, Your Highness. I have my ways of knowing who it is coming into my inn late at night. I knew it was you before you even walked through my doors. Though, I must admit that I was mighty surprised that you did once you saw the Lunameedian border patrol enjoying pints and women."

Colin couldn't detect any anger in the man's voice, but he still felt wary.

Redbeard continued, "Look, Your Highness, I know you just came from the Palace of Veri. I need to know what you know. I saw the flames. I've heard the rumors. They've started trickling in from the travelers and merchants that pass through these walls, but none of them were there in person."

Colin relaxed slightly but, as he walked towards the man, he placed his hand on his sword's hilt. Redbeard was so much larger and stronger than he was that Colin was sure, should it come to it, that he would be defeated by the innkeep if they were to fight. Redbeard smiled at him as Colin sat down on the chair across the table from him.

"What do you want to know?" he asked in a resigned voice.

"Everything."

Colin began telling Redbeard about the bodies they'd found on the road leading into Estrellala, the madness of the king, the murders that had taken place during the ball. Somewhere in the middle of Colin's tale, Redbeard wandered over to a large fire Colin had only just then noticed. He cracked eggs and fried bacon as he listened to Colin go into detail about the things he'd witnessed while a visitor at the Lunameedian court.

"The girl in the yellow dress was trying to get away. I didn't get her name or where she was from. I just... felt like I needed to help her. And then the girl who stabbed me, Starla, was about to attack her so I intervened. I'm not exactly sure how I survived fighting her twice."

Colin had made sure to leave out certain details, like the fact that the scientists in his kingdom had developed a healing medallion. He had also decided not to reveal what he knew of the Dramadoonian plan to overthrow the Lunameedian government, the plan he'd been asked to be a part of.

"Honestly, Redbeard, I think this all came about because of King Magnus. I had never met the man before, and, of course, I'd heard the growing rumors, but the reality of what he's done is far worse than any of the tales I'd heard."

Redbeard had listened in silence to Colin talk, which the young prince appreciated. He'd placed a plate of bacon, eggs, and toasted bread on the table with a tall glass of a deep-orange colored beverage that Colin had never seen before.

"Natorium juice. It's good. You'll like it," Redbeard said when Colin gave him a quizzical look.

Colin took a timid sip of the extraordinarily orange liquid. It was sweet with a slight twang at the end. Colin took a long draught from the cup. Redbeard was right. It was delicious.

They sat in silence for several moments as they ate the breakfast Redbeard had prepared. Colin tried to listen for noise of his men or the Lunameedian guards but heard nothing.

"Colin, may I give you a word of caution?" Redbeard's words were heavy and Colin looked up at him. The man's face appeared troubled, but Colin wasn't exactly sure why.

"Of course, I would be happy to hear anything you have to say."

"You and your men have seen quite a few atrocities committed by my king. The things you've seen, that your men have seen, can change a person. And not for the better." Redbeard paused. He seemed to be searching for the right words to say, but was struggling to determine exactly what would be best. "You're going home today, but the memories of what you've seen will haunt you. Don't let these memories fuel your anger towards all of Lunameed. I know how easily fear turns to hate, and then that hate is applied to everyone associated with the initial fear."

The older innkeep suddenly clasped Colin's hand, "You must promise me that you'll do everything in your power to stop your men's fear in its tracks."

Colin opened his mouth to respond but then shut it. Were his men afraid? If they were, then he hadn't sensed it during their long trek from Estrellala to the borderlands. Then again, he wasn't sure he would have recognized it. All he had seen was anger.

That anger was a result of their experiences in this forsaken land: having to abandon the castle, leave their brethren behind, and their difficult journey to safety. Images of Jameston filled Colin's mind. His best friend had been one of those men left behind. Colin felt the anger too. Bitterly, Colin looked unblinkingly into Redbeard's eyes.

"I can't make that promise. I don't have the power to control how my men will feel or how my people will react when they find out that some of our men were left behind in the bloodshed of the murders at the castle."

Redbeard, to his credit, let Colin speak without interrupting him. His face remained blank as Colin continued, "But I can promise that I'll try. I want the killing to stop just as much as you do."

They remained staring at each other for a single long moment before Redbeard finally said, "I believe that you do."

With that, the lumbering man rose from his seat and picked up the now-empty plates. "Your men will be up soon. I suggest that you prepare yourself for the march back to your home." Redbeard smiled then, "Your sister is here. They rode overnight to bring her here to verify that it's you."

Chapter Fifty

It was several hours before Colin's men were all assembled and they were prepared to cross the bridge to Szarmi. Colin's spirits rose when he saw that Redbeard had been correct. Coraleen stood at the end of the bridge, her face solemn. She wouldn't meet Colin's eyes as he drew closer to where she stood. He willed her to look at him, to let him know that he was finally safe. She looked everywhere but at him.

"Your Highness, can you verify that this man is your brother, Prince Colin Sammial Stormbearer, heir to the Szarmian throne?" the captain asked when Colin and his men were three quarters of the way across the bridge.

It was only then that Coraleen looked Colin straight in the eyes. *Is that hatred I see in her eyes?* Colin asked himself. Her clear eyes were hard and penetrating. Colin gulped loudly.

"It is not," she whispered, her voice was just loud enough for Colin to hear.

No, Colin thought, *this cannot be. Not again.* Colin stopped walking and drew his sword. His men did the same. Thoughts zipped through his mind. Surely she recognized him, even from this distance. They had been raised together. She should recognize him; she had to.

In a commanding voice Colin called across the remaining divide, "Sister, can you not see who I am? I'm here. We've made it home."

Tears stained her face as her gaze never left his. "My brother is dead," she said, "this man—this thing—is an imposter." Coraleen's voice was filled with disgust.

Colin tightened his grip on his sword. His palms were sweaty and the hilt threatened to slip from his grasp. What was his sister talking about?

His sister broke her gaze with him then and turned to look at the captain standing next to her. "We received a letter from King Magnus that my brother was one of the ones murdered during the disastrous ball. He... he sent Colin's manservant's head to prove it to us. We were told that there... wasn't enough left of Colin to send." Coraleen looked back into Colin's eyes, "King Magnus warned us of Lunameed's skin-changers. They can steal a man's face and wear it as their own. He warned us that one of these skin-changers might try to impersonate my brother."

Her face flushed red as she spoke, and Colin could tell that she was barely containing her fury. It was then that he remembered how Vanessa's skin had changed before his eyes. How she had become of these Lunameedian 'skin-changers.' He remembered how a torn sigil from his mother's house had been found near the river where he had almost been assassinated. His thoughts clicked into place, one-by-one. His sister-

"The entire nation of Lunameed is an abomination. My brother must be avenged of his death." She turned to glare at Colin and the remaining soldiers, "The

Lunameedians must pay for their actions. Starting with this imposter and his followers."

Colin barely had time to react as a spray of arrows rained down at them. He jumped off the bridge and let himself sink as far down as possible. Arrows sunk past him, their speed broken by the rushing water. He waited for his men to follow, but they didn't. Not a single one of them made it to the river. He wasn't even sure they'd had a chance to try.

He clung to his sword in a desperate attempt to keep it as the river pulled him deep beneath its surface. He felt himself moving downstream, but he couldn't propel himself to the surface. His lungs burned from a lack of air. He tried pushing his legs downward, but he didn't move upward. Light flashed before his eyes. He could barely feel his limbs anymore they were so weightless. It was a sublime feeling, this sense of barely being there at all.

He shook his head, trying to clear it from the fog that had settled upon him. He couldn't keep his thoughts straight. He just knew he needed to breach the surface of the river, to somehow swim to the top. Kicking his legs violently against the current, he pushed himself forward.

And felt a sudden drop.

Colin had never before experienced the feeling of his stomach climbing to the top of his chest and then sinking back down so suddenly. If he hadn't already been soaked by the river, he was sure that his entire body would have been covered in sweat as he fell. He wanted to scream but he didn't have enough air in his body to do so. Instead, he just wrapped his arms around his sword and let himself plummet through the air.

He crashed into a deep pool of water and was pushed down and out. Finally losing his grasp on his sword, Colin watched wearily as the metal sunk away from him.

And then suddenly he was on top of the water, gasping at the air. His mind slowly began to function again as he gulped in air in great big mouthfuls. His heartrate fell, and he was able to look about him with clear eyes. Using what little strength he had left, Colin swam towards a log he saw floating a few feet away and clung to it as he let it keep his head above water.

If he remembered correctly, the Borad River ran east to west along the Lunameedian-Szarmian border. He assumed the drop was one of the many waterfalls in the Alnora Valley. He and his men must have travelled further east than they intended if they had ended up here.

Exhaustion overwhelmed him as he continued to cling to the log. Slowly, his eyes drooped, and he fell fast asleep to the lull of the river's current.

Chapter Fifty-One

Faer Forest, Lunameed

Amaleah followed Helena down the long hallway. The little woman hummed quietly to herself as they made their way past the entrance and out into the dark woods of Faer Forest. Before they began walking through the forest, Helena turned to look Amaleah in the eyes.

"Once we have begun our journey, you must not speak."

Amaleah started to ask why but then stopped. Helena was holding one bony little finger up to her lips and staring at her. She just nodded.

With that, the little woman spun Amaleah around and they began to weave their way through the trees. Amaleah tried to keep track of the turns they made, but she quickly lost track of the direction they were headed. The trees were so dense that she couldn't see the sky. It felt as if they were walking in circles, but Amaleah didn't know.

When they had been walking for what felt like over half an hour, Helena stopped Amaleah and tied a blindfold over her eyes. Amaleah didn't say anything as the old woman worked, but she wondered what exactly was about to happen. She remembered the warning that Helena had given her and she kept her mouth shut.

Gently, the old woman held Amaleah's hand as she continued to lead her through the woods. Again, Amaleah tried to keep track of the turns, but she couldn't. Suddenly,

Helena dropped her hand. Amaleah felt a cold wind brush past her. She couldn't hear birds anymore, or the rustling of animals in the trees and underbrush. There was only silence. She started fidgeting as she waited for something, anything, to happen. She didn't feel fear, exactly, but her breathing quickened as she anticipated what was going to happen next.

Footsteps.

All around her she heard the sound of loud foot-falls coming closer to her. She began shivering uncontrollably. She tried to stop shaking, but couldn't steady her breathing enough to stop. Wrapping her arms around her body and sinking to the ground, Amaleah tried to stop the convulsions. It didn't work.

The air vibrated with a searing heat. Amaleah huddled down in a tight ball on the ground. Still, she didn't say a single word. Didn't let out the gasp of pain she felt as the hot air burned her skin. She thought about everything she wanted to know about her mother. Everything she had survived for. She couldn't give up now. There was a loud clap of what sounded like thunder followed by a spray of icy cold liquid on Amaleah's forehead.

And then there was nothing.

Amaleah sat huddled in her position for several moments before a man's voice she didn't recognize ordered, "Remove her blindfold."

She was sitting in the middle of a clearing. The brightness of the space blinded her and she had to shut her eyes tightly to block out the light. Cringing, Amaleah stood. Her body ached from where the wind had blasted into her and her legs were cramped from holding them so tightly to her body. Carefully, she cracked one eye so that she could stare out at her surroundings. Armos and Helena were there along with an assortment of all different types of creatures that Amaleah had never seen before.

There was a giant creature that had bark for skin and leaves for hair. It wasn't exactly a tree—it had arms and legs and a face—but it definitely wasn't human. Another being that was so tall Amaleah had to peer up at the sky to see his face stood beside the tree-creature. In between Armos and Helena stood another creature who looked human but who had pointed ears and hair that stretched down past her waist. Her skin was so wrinkled that Amaleah wasn't sure if she had a human's facial features or not.

Turning her head, Amaleah saw other creatures standing behind her. A wolf-like creature that stood on two legs was panting nearby. There was also something that Amaleah wasn't sure how to describe. It had wings and a furry head, but it also had a human mouth. Its eyes glowed yellow, even in the brightness of the clearing. Amaleah almost yelped at its gaze but was able to stop herself.

Lastly, and to Amaleah's surprise, Yosef, the half-reaper and half-mermaid creature who had taken her to see Sylvia, stood within in the circle. So he had survived the massacre of those who had sought to help her, to save her. She nodded in his direction but he ignored the gesture. Instead, he stared blankly ahead. Well, at least Amaleah thought he was looking straight ahead. It was hard to tell since he didn't exactly have eyes. She took a step towards him and bumped into stone.

A small well stood in the middle of the clearing with her. She peered down into its dark depths but couldn't see anything. She tried to hear if anything was sloshing within its water, but there was only silence. Sighing inwardly, Amaleah turned to face Helena. She met the woman's eyes and waited.

And waited.

She stood in silence surrounded by an assortment of strange creatures. She wasn't afraid, but she had a dreadful sense of apprehension about what was about to transpire. Why were they all just standing around her? She didn't like how they were all looking at her with scrutinizing faces. Their eyes were glazed over as they stared at her. She felt like she was completely nude and being examined by a physician. A cold, calculating voice pierced the silence from behind her.

"She cannot be the one for which we have waited so long. Look at her with her weak body and even weaker mind. How could she be the one?"

Amaleah spun around to see who was speaking but couldn't tell who it had been.

"Peace, Gulpin. Thadius has not yet arrived. Hold your counsel until he does."

Amaleah recognized Armos's voice. She wanted to say something, to question why they were all here, but she caught Helena's eye and knew that speaking now would be a mistake. So, she waited for this Thadius to arrive.

They didn't have to wait long. Not a minute had passed after Armos spoke when a bare-chested centaur galloped into the clearing. His muscular, powerful body shook as his breathing calmed. He looked around the circle before saying, "Please excuse my tardiness. I ran into one of the fae princesses on my way here. I didn't want to appear suspicious, so I had to flirt with her until she grew tired of our conversation."

He looked at Amaleah then and winked. His brilliant blue eyes took Amaleah by surprise. She had heard that all centaurs had eyes the color of the earth. She smiled at him.

The cold voice that Armos had called Gulpin spoke again, "That is no excuse for your tardiness, Thadius. If you were taking this council seriously, you would have been here long before the Gathering."

"Yes, well, I can't help that I was given boyishly good looks and you were not, Gulpin. Besides, would you prefer it if I'd have left the fae princess wondering where I was going in such hurry? Would you prefer it if the Fae Council were here now, watching our precious Gathering? No, I think not. And to answer your question about why I didn't leave earlier, I did. She just couldn't get enough of me."

Amaleah looked in the direction that Thadius was and saw the hairy-headed, winged creature turn up his mouth. The creature spoke, revealing sharpened white teeth.

"You know very well that members of the Fae Council are strictly forbidden from attending our Gatherings. They cannot be trusted, or have you forgotten how they forsook our brethren in the Second and Third Darkness?"

"My point exactly, my dear, Gulpin. My point exactly."

"Enough."

All eyes turned toward the creature standing between Helena and Armos: the wrinkled old woman with long hair and pointed ears.

"We have not come here to argue over old wounds or dispute Thadius's lack of judgment when it comes to the court of the fae. What we have come here for is to decide the fate of this girl." She pointed one long, bony finger in Amaleah's direction.

"Thank you, Castinil," Armos said in a clear, steady voice.

Castinil… Amaleah knew that name from somewhere. It came to her. Armos had told her the names of the Elite—the ones who had raised her mother. *Am I about to find out more about my mother during this meeting?*

Castinil continued, in her cold, strong voice, "Now that we have all arrived, I would like to call the Gathering of the Council into session."

Several 'ayes' rang out in the clearing. Amaleah wondered if they were always this formal or if this behavior was on account of her.

"We have gathered here today to determine the fate of this child. Be she the Harbinger of the Light or just the child of our beloved Orianna. We must know the truth," it was the wolf-man that spoke this time. His voice was gravelly and hard to listen to. Amaleah didn't like how his tongue flicked his teeth when he spoke.

"We must take... our... time, Beo," the tree-creature spoke in a deliberate, painfully slow speech that Amaleah found difficult to concentrate on. "There is much at stake."

"We don't have time to deliberate extensively, Gren. The time is fast approaching. We have seen and heard the signs. We cannot wait to see what gifts this child may possess before determining if she is the Harbinger," the wolf-man named Beo responded.

What followed was a long, drawn-out debate about which was more important: deeming Amaleah the Harbinger as quickly as possible so that they could begin her training or taking their time to test her abilities and see what skills she possessed. Regardless of where they stood on the matter, they all agreed that a darkness was once again growing and that the time for the Harbinger had arrived.

Yosef remained silent during the conversation but his sightless face followed the voices as they spoke. It was unnerving watching the face turn one direction and then the next with the empty eye sockets lingering on Amaleah at each pass. She shuddered each time his gaze passed over her.

Amaleah stood in silence through it all, even when they began discussing her merits and her shortcomings. No, she didn't have knowledge of her heritage or the council. No, she hadn't demonstrated any magical abilities that they knew of. No, she didn't have knowledge of her heritage or of the council.

Amaleah thought then about her escape from the palace. About the anger and the blast which had thrown her father across the room. A blast she had caused. But she was drawn back in as they mentioned the Harbinger.

Almost everything the council discussed came back as a shortcoming for her if she was the Harbinger. Amaleah really wanted to ask what, exactly, the Harbinger was supposed to be but didn't feel as if she could say anything. So far in the discussion they hadn't addressed her directly. In fact, Amaleah got the distinct impression that many of them wished that she wasn't present for their deliberations at all.

"Amaleah?"

The sound of her name followed by silence caught her off guard. Coming out of her thoughts, Amaleah realized that the entire council was staring at her. She swallowed. She wasn't sure if she was allowed to speak yet so she just nodded her head.

Helena took a step into the center of the circle. "Amaleah, we would like to hear your thoughts on these deliberations." Helena's voice was soft and comforting, but it did nothing to quell Amaleah's unease at addressing the council.

"I'm sorry, but I've heard a lot about the Harbinger and I still don't know exactly what it is that I'm supposed to do."

The council members erupted into another bout of hurried exclamations on both sides of the debate. Amaleah felt as if they were evenly divided.

"Be calm," Gren's clear, slow voice cut through the chatter. Everyone turned to look at the giant tree. "Child," he addressed Amaleah directly, "it is not your fault that you do not know your birthright. It is ours."

The ones who opposed the idea that Amaleah was the Harbinger started to speak in protest, but Gren once again spoke in his booming voice.

"Quiet. I have been living longer than all others who currently reside on this council," he glared at Gulpin as he spoke. "I believe that Orianna was the Chosen One. I believe that this child, *her* child is the one we have been waiting for."

He turned to face Amaleah once again, "I suggest that we teach Amaleah of the prophecy and what it means to be the Harbinger and let her decide if she accepts her destiny."

"Gren, no," Helena exclaimed. "We can't. It's... forbidden. You know that. You're one of the ones who created the covenant to protect our kind."

Helena continued, "The prophecy has already been shared beyond this council. We are already in danger of our prophecy becoming one of the broken. It is our duty, our calling, to do everything in our power to protect the prophecy and the ones we know to be the foretold."

"And what if she's not the Harbinger?" Gulpin asked.

"Then she will be destroyed along with the rest of us."

The council fell silent for several moments as they contemplated Gren's words. Amaleah wasn't exactly sure what they were so concerned about. Yes, there had been tension among the nations of Mitier, but nothing to the scale that they seemed to be afraid of.

"Can we all agree that this child is the closest we've come to the closing of our most precious prophecy?" Armos's voice was heavy.

Each council member nodded in their turn, even Gulpin.

"Then it is settled," the creature named Castinil said. "She will be taught of her heritage and given the choice. She will be the fulfillment of the prophecy or we shall all perish in the darkness that is coming."

In a flash, Thadius raced forward and shoved Amaleah into the well so forcibly that she barely had time to take a gulp of air before she plummeted into the dark water below.

Chapter Fifty-Two

The borderlands between Szarmi and Lunameed

Colin woke to a roaring fire and a thudding headache. Rough cloth separated him from the straw bed he could smell before he saw it. Peering down at his body, he realized that he'd been changed, but he didn't know by whom. He blushed at the thought of someone he didn't know seeing his naked body. Hopefully whoever had rescued him from the river hadn't been female. That would be a disaster.

As he sat up on the bed, he winced from the pain. His ribs were bruised in multiple places and his entire body ached. No surprise there, he thought to himself. He had been tossed around on the river like a ball being passed between heel-ball players. How long had he been out? He needed to find his sister and explain that he couldn't possibly be an imposter. He was her brother. He was the crown prince of Szarmi. She had to recognize him; had to believe him.

Or, at least, he hoped so.

He tried standing. And immediately sat back down as pain shot up his leg. Looking down, he realized that this foot was tightly wrapped in stiff cloths with a wooden rod stretched up the side of his leg to keep it from moving too much. So much for leaving this place.

He sighed. If his sister hadn't even given him a chance to explain himself to her, he couldn't possibly believe that she would be convinced by a man she now probably thought was dead twice over. Heat rolled over him as he thought about how his sister had looked right at him when she'd condemned him to death. There'd been no hope in her voice, only determination.

Realization dawned on him: she had wanted him dead. She knew that it had been him. That's why she hadn't looked at him. That's why she hadn't even taken the time to verify that it hadn't been him. His stomach did somersaults as these thoughts and more passed through his mind in rapid succession. The only person he had left, the only woman he still loved, had betrayed him.

Tears sprang from his eyes and fell to the floor in slow, tumultuous currents. His body felt warm, too warm. He couldn't breathe. He tried slowing his breath, but all that resulted in was a sense of light-headedness. His entire body shook. Sweat dripped down his face and into his eyes, but he couldn't move. He couldn't think.

He tried to concentrate on his breathing.

Tried to focus on the motion of breathing in and out. In and out. Eyes closed. All he saw was his sister's expression when she had uttered the words, "He is not."

Somehow, he heard the door open and footsteps cross the floor to where he sat shaking on the straw bed. Large, warm hands gently lifted his legs onto the bed and pushed him into a laying down position. A cold cloth was pressed to his forehead.

Fluttering his eyes, Colin noticed a giant face covered by a red beard staring down at him. "Jeor," Colin whispered in disbelief as his head sank back into the pillows of the bed.

"Rest, now, Prince. My men will take care of you, don't you have any worries about that." Redbeard smiled down at him with a toothy grin.

Colin didn't have time to respond as his head hit the pillow and exhaustion washed over him. He closed his eyes and let himself drift away into darkness.

Chapter Fifty-Three

The Battle of Alnora, the Third Darkness

Kilian left the tower without glancing back. The Light Council had been correct about one thing. He had failed them. He'd been blinded by their light—their love—and he had been a part of their collapse. He thought about the murders they had asked him to commit. All the children he had seen taken away from their parents at his hands. He has been made into a monster.

The battle outside had come to a standstill. The Sisters of Sorrow had already begun cleansing the bodies and wrapping them in preparation for the afterlife. Kilian stormed past them, searching for his squire.

Richard was talking with what remained of Knight Patrik's soldiers. They were a weary bunch since their leader had died, but they were resilient.

"Richard, I think it is time that we left this place."

His squire glanced around the battlement. He glanced at Kilian, but his eyes slid right over him without a moment's hesitation.

"Did ya hear me, boy?" Kilian felt his anger rise.

Once again Richard looked around the battlefield. He looked Kilian in the eyes but didn't come towards him. The other knights also looked about the space, but none of them made a sign of recognition towards Kilian.

Haughtily, Kilian marched towards the men and walloped Richard on the back of his head. "I said, it was time that we were leaving, Richard."

The squire immediately whipped his arm up and punched Kilian in the face. Kilian heard bone break and felt hot liquid squirt from his nose.

"What do you think gives you the right to order me around, pig?"

Kilian took a step back in surprise. None of his many squires had ever addressed him thus. He lifted a hand to slap Richard across the face, but one of the knights, Norman he thought, grappled his arms and pulled him to the ground.

The knights spit on him.

"Szarmian scum," one said.

Kilian tried to stand, but another of the knights slammed his face into the ground.

"The little bugger doesn't know when to quit, does he?" the men laughed.

"Richard," Kilian growled, "it's me, Kilian. Tell your new friends what a mistake this has been."

"Did ya hear that?"

"He thinks he can fool us."

"Let's teach him a lesson."

The voices became confused in Kilian's head as one of the knights dropped the hilt of his sword into his temple. His entire head rang and he realized he couldn't hear them talking anymore.

But he could see them. One of them had raised his foot and was coming down to kick him in the gut. Kilian grunted as pain jolted through him. He was used to taking beatings, but this was something so much worse than what he had ever allowed himself to receive.

"Please," he whispered, "Richard, it's me."

He could barely make out Richard's voice as his squire said, "The old fool thinks he knows me. Did he honestly think that he could fool the squire of the Light's hero? I've been with him for over ten years now. If I can't recognize my lord in all his forms, then I'm not a very good squire.

Kilian was apt to agree with Richard's words.

"I wonder what he wants."

"Who cares," Richard said. "Come on, we need to finish scouting the area before making camp. Szarmi and Smiel may have arranged a truce for now, but there is no telling when they will break their word."

The knights murmured agreement as they left Kilian lying alone in the mud. If he had been a normal man, he would have died. Thankfully for Kilian, he was not a normal man.

He lay there, in the mud, for several hours. The Sisters of Sorrow passed over him when they realized that he still breathed. They had no jurisdiction over the injured and could do nothing for him. Of course, Kilian wasn't really injured anymore. His blood had just dried on his body, making him look like he was.

He contemplated Richard's reaction to him. He'd acted—all the knights had acted—as if he didn't recognize him. as if Kilian were a complete stranger. And Kilian thought about his curse.

Chapter Fifty-Four

The borderlands between Szarmi Lunameed, Three hundred years later

The next time that Colin woke, the room was filled with light from a high window and there was a little girl, no older than eight or nine, sitting at the foot of his bed. She was reading a book quietly and jumped when Colin asked for a glass of water. She quickly jumped to her feet and ran from the room, still quiet.

His face quirked into a smile at her timidity. Coraleen had been like that when she was between the ages of four and seven. She'd been so earnest and quiet, always watching the world. Then one day she'd decided that she wanted to be part of the world, not just an observer. Ever since then, she'd been the central guest at every event and party. He sighed. He would probably never get to speak to her again.

Trying to distract himself, Colin examined his body more thoroughly now. His leg was still bandaged, but he was no longer covered in bruises and scrapes. For that, if nothing else, he was thankful. His mind was also less foggy now and he began to think about what his next steps should be. He didn't know how long he'd been asleep but, judging from the way his body had healed, he had been out for at least a week.

There was a timid knock on the door followed by the entrance of not just the little girl, but also an older woman with a stooped back and crooked nose. Her hair was so white that Colin could have sworn it was freshly fallen snow or a spool of perfect cotton. It wasn't, of course, and Colin resisted the urge to touch her hair as she leaned over him to take a look at a few of the remaining bandages on his ribs and chest.

She spoke quietly to herself as she worked in a language that Colin had never heard before. He was about to ask her what language she was speaking when he noticed the pointed ears.

She was an elf.

Colin wanted to pull away from her touch the way he'd been raised to, but somehow he knew that she didn't mean him any harm.

She smiled at him and patted his arm before slowly ambling out of the room. The girl promptly offered Colin a sip of the coldest water he'd ever tasted. Mountain water, he assumed, though he wasn't for certain. Which side of the river were they on? There were tales of the Lunameedian mountain water granting gifts to those who drank it. Colin wasn't so sure of the accuracy of these old tales, but he knew he didn't want to tempt fate and risk being tainted with the magic of the land.

Unfortunately, the little girl didn't stop tipping the glass to his lips until he'd drunk the final drop of liquid held within its mug. Colin coughed as the last of the water ran down his throat. The girl smiled at him and finally spoke.

"Hi! My name's Sasha. What's yours?"

"You can call me Sammy." It wasn't a lie, exactly. One of his middle names was Sammial after all. Colin just didn't feel like he should be telling everyone his real name. At least, not until he'd figured out why his sister had done what'd she done.

"That's a funny name, isn't it?" she scrunched up her face in distaste as she spoke. "I think I'd best call you... Ham."

"Ham?" Colin asked in disbelief.

"Well, you've been laying around doing nothing but sleeping and eating broth for the past four weeks. Seems appropriate."

Four weeks. Colin's stomach dropped as he let the words sink in. He'd been out of it for four whole weeks. His sister would have returned to Ducal House, or worse, his palace by now. They would have announced his death. Held his funeral—without a body of course. What little chance he had at convincing his kingdom that he was who he said he was—that he was the crown prince, the future king of Szarmi—was gone. He was twenty-one now. His coronation had passed.

Sasha didn't appear to miss a beat at Colin's lack of response. She continued chatting away as she tidied up the room. She was talking about her friends who lived in the woods surrounding the village when Redbeard entered the room.

His large frame filled the entire space. He glared at the girl, and she immediately quit talking before quickly vacating the room. She sidled past Redbeard, her face flushed. Colin wondered at her reaction to the man, but didn't say anything as Redbeard came to sit in the rocking chair next to the bed.

The innkeep popped a long, thin pipe into his mouth the moment he had settled into the wooden frame of the chair. The pungent smoke smelled like blueberries and made Colin's stomach grumble. The herbal undertones of the smoke were unfamiliar to Colin, and he wondered what kind of mix Redbeard had used.

Redbeard wordlessly handed the pipe to Colin, who took a long breath on the thin mouthpiece. The flavor of the herb tasted of blueberries too. He had not been expecting that. Unfortunately, he also hadn't been expecting the intense heat that passed down his throat as he breathed in on the pipe. He immediately began coughing.

"First time using the mureechi pipe?" Redbeard asked, a laugh in his voice.

"What was your first clue?"

Redbeard gave him a quizzical look as he accepted back the pipe. "I suppose they don't have mureechi pipes in Szarmi, do they? The plant is a banned substance, though I must say I don't understand why. Once the leaves have been dried it's quite easy to add in a shot of flavor, and the effects of the plant's chemicals on our brains is amazing. Did you know that someone who smokes a single mureechi pipe once a day can reduce stress and prolong life?" He smiled and handed the pipe back to Colin. "You'll get used to its effects after a while. Don't worry."

Colin took the pipe back but didn't take another hit of the substance. He'd heard stories about the effects of mureechi his whole life and knew the dangers of consuming the herbal drug.

"I never took you to be such a prude, Your Highness." Redbeard leaned back in the rocking chair and peered at Colin in a penetrating gaze, "'Sides, you need to regain your strength. The healing powers of the herb will help."

"I've heard that mureechi is only used by vagabonds who idly spend their time and are a drain on society."

"Ridiculous Szarmian propaganda. If you had taken the time to research mureechi, you would have discovered that it is one of the oldest healing substances in Mitier. They used it to staunch blood loss and cure the mind sickness during the First and Second Darknesses. Then, during the Third Darkness, one of your soldiers poisoned a whole barrel of the drug while it was on its way to the Szarmian capital. Hundreds of people died, and Lunameed was blamed for the civilian deaths. It's been banned in Szarmi ever since, although the Lunameedian people still use it recreationally for its ability to cause a sense of euphoria."

"I had always heard that it was Lunameed who had poisoned the mureechi. Since the herb only grows in your kingdom, Szarmi banned it to reduce the risk of something as catastrophic as that massacre ever happening again."

"I can only tell you what I know to be the truth and it is that the poisoner was not of Lunameed."

They sat in silence. Colin felt guilty for blaming Redbeard's kingdom of the massacre on his people, but he knew he was right. Or, at least, he thought he was. It was what he'd been raised to believe. Besides, he couldn't believe that one of the Szarmian soldiers would ever poison his own people.

"Forgive me, Redbeard, but how would you know if it was someone from your country or someone from mine that had poisoned the mureechi? You wouldn't. To be honest, it doesn't matter. The fact is, the mureechi was poisoned. Hundreds of Szarmians died as a result. The hatred of all things Lunameedian grew. That's the end of the story."

Redbeard's smile faded, "You are young and impetuous, still. You haven't yet learned to think critically about what has been taught to you. Not all things that are passed down are true. I think it would be good for you to begin realizing this." The bigger man paused. "I thought you had already begun the questioning process since you seemed willing to stop the killings in the borderlands."

"I want to stop the killings in the borderlands because too many innocents have been killed, not because I believe that magic is good. The Lunameedian government killed my best friend, my men. They turned my sister against me. They-"

"They are reacting to what they have been taught to believe as well," Redbeard cut him off. "Just because there has been historical turmoil between our two nations doesn't mean that it has to continue. The tension, the killings, the hatred between Szarmi and Lunameed doesn't have to continue. We have the ability to create a new way of life."

"And how would you suggest doing that? Even if I wanted to, I don't have power anymore. My sister has seen to that."

"You have more friends in Szarmi and Lunameed than you yet know, Your Highness."

Colin played with a loose thread on the blanket that encased him legs. He had nothing and no one.

"I'm sorry, Redbeard, but I don't think you realize the extent of my situation. I cannot return to my homeland. How am I supposed to cross the border when all of my people think that I'm a Lunameedian imposter—a creature they hate more than anything else?"

"You have to trust that there are those who will follow you no matter what your mother and sister tell them. You are the rightful heir, Colin. There will be those who will believe that you are who you say you are."

"But I've been gone for four weeks. There might have been a chance to convince my people that I'm not an imposter, but too much time has passed," Colin narrowed his eyes and looked at Redbeard, "You don't happen to know why I can't remember those four weeks do you?"

"We drugged you."

"You what?!" Colin shouted, not caring if people could hear his voice outside of the room.

"We drugged you," Redbeard repeated in a calm voice. "It was a necessary part of your recovery. You kept trying to get up and rebreaking your bones. Tonya and I made the decision that it would be better to knock you out completely so that your body could heal uninterrupted."

"You had no right," Colin said in cold voice. "Who do you think you are?"

"I am the one who dragged you out of the river. You don't know what you were like. Your body was broken. You were feverish and delirious. You're just lucky I found you when I did. I could have left you for dead. It would have been less risky for me. You are a wanted criminal now for impersonating a Szarmian royal, or have you forgotten that you're legally dead? Don't blame me for saving your life, Your Highness."

Colin fumed. He knew Redbeard was right, but he couldn't bring himself to apologize for lashing out at the older man, not after he'd been drugged.

"You have just given my mother and sister everything they needed to take my kingdom." His voice was soft and the words trembled slightly as they left him.

He still couldn't believe that his sister had betrayed him in this way.

"Look, Highness, as long as you're alive there is hope. I'm not saying that we don't have an uphill battle or that we'll be successful. It's been a long time since I've led a rebellion, but I have to believe that my efforts to save you won't be for naught."

How old is this man? Colin thought. It had been at least one hundred years since the last rebellion spread through Lunameed. It had been unsuccessful, and Colin had been taught that every single rebel had been destroyed by the Lunameedian government. Even if the man in front of him had been alive for that, he'd be incredibly old. Redbeard didn't look like he was more than forty years of age. Maybe it was the mountain water?

"What do you suggest we do?"

Redbeard smiled again, "First things first. I'm going to have you smoke more mureechi than you ever thought possible, and then, tomorrow, I will call a meeting with my contacts in Szarmi. We have to start building your army."

"And I have to smoke the mureechi because?"

"Because I consider it a sign of good faith that we will be able to work together and that you will begin questioning everything you thought you knew about the tensions between our two nations."

"And if I don't smoke the herb?"

"Then I'll pack a satchel of stale bread and water and send you on your way."

"So you'd go through all that trouble of saving me just to send me to the wolves?"

"Of course. Look, Colin, I like you. I think you'll be a good ally. And I actually believe that you will be a good ruler who will work to resolve the tension between our two nations. But you're only as good to us as you are willing to trust us."

Colin sat for a beat before taking a long drag on the pipe.

Redbeard smiled and clapped Colin on the shoulder, "And so the rebellion begins."

Chapter Fifty-Five

Estrellala, Lunameed

The throne room was shrouded in darkness. The curtains had been drawn against the high windows and there was a sense of somberness that pervaded the room. Namadus stood quietly behind the massive golden throne as King Magnus convulsed in his seat. The convulsions had become more frequent now, since the loss of Princess Amaleah. He picked at his fingernails as he waited for the seizure to pass.

It would pass; this he knew for certain. He just wasn't sure which king would be left. There were too many faces of his ruler for Namadus to keep track of now. He'd learned to adapt to his king's mood as quickly as water can change direction. Eventually, he would understand.

He'd employed all the greatest healers within Lunameed to watch over the king and alert him to any changes they noticed. They still hadn't been able to figure out the cause of the king's seizures, or of his madness.

Namadus scanned the crowd of nobles who had gathered for the day. The catastrophe of the first ball had reduced the number of nobles willing to appear in court. His eyes met those of his niece, Starla. She stood next to her sister. They couldn't be more different. Viola was pleasantly plump and had curves that would help her be married off to a prominent lord somewhere. Despite the current mood at court, Viola had chosen to wear a bright yellow dress with crystals sewn into the bodice and hems.

She had been trained as an assassin, like her sister, but her talents were much subtler than those of Starla.

Starla, on the other hand, was clad all in black. Her skirt was strips of fabric sewn together at the waist. He could tell that she was wearing tight black pants. She did enjoy being able to move freely. He guessed that she had weapons strapped to her body in various places. She'd shown him once all the different places she had access to knives on her person, but there had been so many that he'd lost track.

He had been the one who had taken his nieces when his sister had died at Starla's birth. Their father hadn't wanted them, and so Namadus had offered to take them in. He hadn't wanted children, but he couldn't deny their uses. As soon as they were old enough to send away, he had. And, when he'd learned that he could have them trained as assassins, he'd sent them away again. They were completely loyal to him.

Now, Starla looked him straight in the eyes, and he knew that she wanted to put the king out of his misery. She'd said as much the night before. She was young. She didn't understand how the political games of court worked, but she would learn. It was time for the third part of her training.

He shook his head at her and her eyes dropped. He knew how uncomfortable the king's fits made her, but there was nothing he could do about it. The longer that he had influence over the king's decisions, the more power he gained at court. And, since Princess Amaleah had disappeared, there was a chance for him to gain complete control of the kingdom. Eventually, his niece would understand this.

The king suddenly came out of his seizure and began addressing the court as if nothing had happened.

"I know the attack on our court has placed a great burden on you," the king's voice was steady and Namadus felt himself being pulled into the words. "The kingdoms of Dramadoon and Szarmi have turned against us once more. They mercilessly killed our people. They ruined what should have been a happy occasion. And now they will pay."

Murmurs ran through the crowd. Namadus knew that they were fearful the king would declare war. It had been three hundred years since the Wars of Darkness, but the effects of the devastation still affected the people. They did not want to go to war again.

"The Dramadoonian bastards have stolen your princess. Will you let this stand? Will you allow our great nation to be thus humiliated?"

Namadus leaned away from the king at these words. He was a fool if he believed that the people would willingly follow him into battle. The bodies he'd ordered lined throughout Estrellala had done more than anger their visitors from afar. They had angered the people.

"We must avenge the deaths of our people. We must rescue our princess."

There was a ripple in the crowd and Namadus saw Starla weaving her way out of the throne room. He would have to speak to her later about not being disruptive during the king's addresses.

"There is no other option. Borganda and Macai have signed treaties with us."

The king paused now, and Namadus took a step forward so that he could see Magnus's face. "Today we will prepare. Tomorrow we will go to war."

End Book One...

Acknowledgements

"Allerleirah"

I first began writing the Broken Prophecies series six years ago. At first, it was an opportunity to explore the fairy tales I read as a child. I remember nestling into my mother's arms and listening to her read from the Brothers Grimm. As I got older, there was something about these stories—and their retellings—that captivated me. Thus began the writing of this story. At first, Amaleah was only meant to be the princess written about in "Allerleirah," commonly known as "All-Kinds-of-Fur" or "The Coat of Many Colors." However, as I continued developing my characters, I realized that Amaleah, the prince, and even her father, the mad-king, were so much more than the characters described by the Brothers Grimm. What started off as a retelling of a classic fairy tale turned into so much more. I hope you see the roots of the story and read about the princess who escaped her father's demands.

To my family

Thank you for listening to me read sections of this story for the past four months as I have worked on the editing. Your questions, insights, and criticisms have helped me make this story the best that it can be. A special thanks to my cousin, Ashley, for being willing to edit the book as a second set of eyes.

... Begin Book Two

Destroyers of the Light

Cool air blasted into Amaleah's back as she fell deep into the well. The imprint of Thadius' push burned into her skin. *Did he really shove me to my death?* Time seemed to slow as she fell. She tried to scream but the air caught in her throat the way a mouse is caught in a trap. Her stomach rolled as she continued to plummet through the narrow, stone-lined walls. Her bare shoulders scraped against the cold, hard stone, pulling her skin away from the muscle the way the rind of an orange is peeled from its fruit. Tears streamed from her eyes from the pain, the fear, the air? She wasn't sure and she didn't care.

Suddenly, her body plunged into the dark water at the well's bottom. The impact of the water hitting her body so unexpectedly caused a momentary sense of being paralyzed. The water felt like ice melting against her skin as her body sunk deeper into the depths of the pool. Stretching out her arms, Amaleah could only feel the weightlessness of nothing. No sound traveled through the water, but a dull thudding echoed in her head. Panic lit a fire in her stomach as she realized she couldn't breathe.

Thrusting her arms and legs downward, Amaleah propelled herself upwards. As her legs pushed down, she felt something soft and feathery brush against her foot. She gulped and water flooded her lungs. The water was sweet, almost like a fruit cider, yet it carried an acid taste to it that left her wanting to gag. Kicking rapidly now, she could feel the water create currents around her. She pushed with all her might against the weight of the water, thrusting herself up through its darkness.

She felt the feathery touch slide up her leg.

Screaming into the water, Amaleah kicked out wildly. Looking down, she tried to see through the pitch black well and saw nothing.

Even though she was immersed within the well, she felt the hair on the back of her neck stand up as she tried to listen, to hear if something was close by. She closed her eyes and held her remaining breath. Her entire body went slack as she tried to determine what was in the water with her.

Bubbles burst on her arm, startling her.

Opening her eyes, Amaleah saw two bright yellow lights shining in the darkness mere inches from her face. Their brightness blinded her to anything else except for their light. She blinked. And the light blinked back.

Without warning, the feathery tendril wrapped itself around Amaleah's waist and tightened the way a noose is tightened around a condemned man's neck. She couldn't pull away. She couldn't escape. Amaleah stared straight into the bright yellow lights and noticed that they had lines of dark gold and copper running through them. Along with black slits in the middle. Eyes. Whatever was in front of her had eyes.

The tendril whipped her down through the water and then back up, unraveling as it sent her flinging through the water. Her head broke the surface of the pool and Amaleah sucked in a deep breath of air. The well carried the stench of rotting corpses and Amaleah wondered how many people had been killed within its depths. Pawing at the stone walls, she tried to find a ledge she could cling to. The stone was smooth beneath her touch, worn away by the constant sloshing of the water.

Stones from the top of the well plopped into the water all around her, causing the water to splash against her face. Amaleah looked up through the tunnel of stones and saw light filtering down through its top. It was so high above her—had she really fallen that far?

Her name echoed down the stones. She started to shout up to The Council, but she noticed that the water in front of her was bubbling. Pushing backwards, Amaleah felt the slimy stone press against her skin. She shivered as the two yellow lights popped above the water's surface.

They blinked at her.

Amaleah shivered. The water's surface rippled as the eyes moved closer to her.

"Stop," she whispered.

The eyes blinked again at her voice.

"Please," she whispered again.

The eyes closed again, only this time they dipped beneath the water's edge. Amaleah glanced upwards, towards where she could her name echoing, but she couldn't seem to force herself to speak louder than the quietest of voices.

The slightest of touches from the feathery tendril caressed Amaleah's leg. She looked down, but even with the light seeping to the bottom of the well from the top, she couldn't see beyond the water's surface. She shuddered and moved her leg away from the creature's touch.

The eyes appeared before her once more, this time they were so close that Amaleah could see tiny flecks of gold embedded within them. Amaleah squirmed uncomfortably as she stared into the creature's eyes.

Made in the USA
Lexington, KY
22 March 2017